Acropolis

Veronica Hess

Book Cover by Alexandra Bennett

First edition 2025

To you, the reader.

You are brave, and fierce, and stronger than you realize. Which you will need to be as you step foot into Acropolis.

Welcome, little human.

Acropolis is a thrilling romantic fantasy set in a world ruled by vampires and shifters alike using their human pets as commodities. This story includes elements regarding violence, injury, blood, death, anxiety, graphic language and sexual activities that are shown on page. Readers who are sensitive to these topics please take note as you prepare to enter Acropolis.

Acropolis

Prologue

Humanity came with its risks.
But in the High City,
humanity was a flaw
our owners drained from us
sip by sip.

Chapter One

If it wasn't clear that our only purpose here was for consumption, the sweet smelling oils they massaged into our skin was sure to tip the scales for any more well-intentioned buyers. Though the term well-intentioned didn't suit the vampires and shifters frequenting Acropolis.

I was as good as dead.

My body had been scrubbed, groomed, and polished before they dressed me in a swath of silk that hid absolutely nothing. The dress was probably the most luxurious article of clothing I'd ever worn. It was also, without a doubt, the smallest, leaving my back bare and barely falling to cover the apex of my thighs. I felt naked. Though I think that was the point.

The dirt I had worn like a second skin for weeks was gone. My skin glowed beneath the low lighting of the holding room where I waited with shaking knees. My hair had been cleaned and then coaxed into shimmering curls that they draped strategically over my shoulder to hide the burn marks that were still healing. My curls were soft, tempting to even my own fingers, but I kept my hands firmly at my sides. I'd already made the mistake of running my fingers through the shiny coils and had been met with a sharp bark from a guard with a raven's beak and talons to match.

It was a reminder.

A reminder, that while I felt cleaner then I'd been in weeks, the effort that was being put into my presentation, was for *their* benefit.

Humans were trapped or hunted like feral street cats to be prettied up for our future owners. A rung so low on the food chain, I'd wager most higher beings provided their house cats drastically better lives then those bought and sold here.

Acropolis was nothing but a meat market.

And the humans sold here were not just pets, but prizes.

Trophies.

The pet trade was a danger to humans in both the northern and southern territories, but the southern territories were the most dangerous. Ruled by a group of higher beings still vying for dominance, they used us as a foothold. And what better way to set yourself apart from the lowly humans, than to parade us around by our throats as pets. As things. As whatever they wanted us to be.

Not only were the southern territories more dangerous, they had also rapidly encroached on what little free land was left, forcing humans and our free camps to scuttle farther and farther south. They herded us deeper and deeper into their territory where they could lord over us as they pleased. So for those like myself, taken from a free camp by trappers, it was something akin to luck to be brought to Acropolis.

Here in the High City where the shifter-elite ruled over their southern territories, we fetched a high price. So that's where trappers with the means brought their scores. The beings of the High City, whether they be vampire or shifter, were collectors, dignitaries, and the like.

Their human commodities reflected their status, and Acropolis boasted the best human pets coin could buy. So, the trappers dragged us here hoping for admittance, because if approved, they served to make a year's earnings in just a few hours. Only the finest could be auctioned at Acropolis. The strongest, prettiest, youngest, or even prizes with talents would be bought and sold here.

I had been lucky that my last attempt at fleeing my trappers hadn't resulted in any lasting injury, because I had no talents worth displaying and looked little more than a sewer rat when we arrived.

I'd been with them for eighteen days under constant supervision as we travelled from the outer city where they'd left my family's camp in cinders. My fingers found their way to the delicate silver collar around my throat as the grievous scent of those memories coaxed a chill up my spine.

I swore it was two nights before the smell of burnt canvas and hair faded into just this horrible memory.

They dragged me along as I wretched over and over so thoroughly I thought my stomach would never unknot itself. Night after night, they'd sit around the campfire telling stories of the humans they'd caught and sold and I'd listen, unable to sleep.

I think they knew.

I think they knew each time the fire popped it was like reopening a wound. They'd played right into my fears, knowing I was listening to their stories of raided encampments and the prizes they'd sold before me... and the prizes who hadn't survived long enough to be sold.

It kept me exhausted, afraid, and easily controlled. So, on the fourth night, I slept. I crawled under a tree and latched myself onto it. They left me there laughing, and drinking, and boasting about the human lives they'd destroyed.

I made an effort from that point on to sleep when required, and eat if anything was given to me. It was rarely good, but there was enough to stay full. Apparently they knew better than to starve their only living prize.

On the tenth night I saw my opportunity. I curled around a tree as I had done for nearly a week now, and as they drifted away from their blaze, and drowned themselves in their drink, I waited, keeping my breathing even and deep. I counted to one hundred as slowly as I could after the last trapper sat back against his pack, his bottle limp in his land, before I dared to move.

I think it took me an hour to make it twenty feet to the edge of camp. Then slowly, every step cautious, every step measured, I made my way through the trees until that fire was just a pinprick in the night. It was only then, only when my eyes strained to see that fire, that I dared to move faster. Only then, did I dare to rustle the brush, and ignore the snap of dried twigs and leaves underfoot as I took off, flying through the forest. Little thorns and debris bit into the soles of my bare feet, but I barely felt it. My heart was pounding in my ears as my adrenaline peaked.

I had done it!

Weaving through the trees I didn't dare slow to check my back. I had no way of knowing when they would discover my absence, but I hoped it would be closer to sunrise.

When I was within earshot of the creek, I slowed my pace, but only to keep from slipping on the slick rocks. Easing my way into the water, I traveled along the smooth current as quickly as I could without making too much noise. I was now travelling through the area the trappers had eluded to being occupied. I didn't know how much of what they had said was fable. Scary stories crafted to keep their prizes compliant and scared. But I moved more cautiously down this section of the river, nonetheless.

Not only did the cool waters give my legs a moment to rest, but it helped lower my body temperature, slowing my heart rate, and hopefully, hiding my scent. I dipped my head below the surface reveling in the cool crisp water and the way it tingled against my overheated cheeks. The water filled my ears, and with it the sound of the current rolling over little stones on the river bed below. The slow rhythmic clacks of river rocks and the smooth rush of the current snaking us along was hypnotic.

Begrudgingly, I surfaced and the darkness that greeted me felt calmer than it had moments before.

I dipped back under again.

And again.

Eventually, I could feel the smile pulling at my cheeks, the cool water slipping between my teeth, the river's watery fingers wiping away the tears I finally let fall.

The river was beginning to quicken as it made its way around a bend. I couldn't recall traveling past this section.

Had I missed my mark?

Panic took root as I fought the current, making it to the bank, and quickly scrambling up the incline to the treeline.

I had almost certainly missed my mark, though I couldn't fathom how. I'd only been under the surface a few moments.

We had undoubtedly traveled around this section of river, and I had no intentions of coming face to face with whatever was scary enough to inspire, even those monsters to avoid it.

The ground here was much harder. Harsh thorny bushes clawed at my calves and thighs, as I pushed my way through them. I spun in a small circle taking in details of this area trying desperately to squash the frustration that took up precious space in my sleep deprived brain. If I could just figure out the direction I was facing, I could keep moving. I was off course, but that didn't mean I couldn't keep moving in the right direction.

I could figure this out.

Anxiety had begun to sink her hungry fingers under my skin. I could feel my heart banging against my ribs, sounding in my ears, and pulsing in my fingertips as I curled them tightly against my palms. I had to be cautious not to touch anything, lest I spread my scent as I climbed the steeper terrain.

There.

Just there was faint evidence of the sunrise beginning to crawl across the sky. I smiled, releasing a deep breath and stepped right into a set of arms. A hard body materializing before me.

With a long exhale to match, I blinked myself back to Acropolis just in time to catch a swift thwack from a set of boney fingers.

"Don't touch," the male scolds, adjusting my collar as he shuffled me into the line of other pets facing the heavy curtain.

I shake my head clear, disturbing those shimmering curls.

If I couldn't escape them, then I counted myself lucky to be here. They'd fetch a good price, and be gone. Maybe I'd find myself belonging to a shifter with too many humans to count. One I'd be able to slip away from, or lull into a comfort that would allow me to slit their throat as they slept.

A sharp tug on my collar had my attention returning to the handler, who now stood beside me.

It was time.

The curtains were pulled aside, and we were escorted into the main room, silver leashes draped lazily atop our handlers' palms, as they guided us by our throats to our awaiting owners.

My eyes climbed the vaulted ceilings. The swells of each plaster dome cradled a darkness that may very well have been the night sky itself. Loose flames freckled the air above us as the firelight bobbed and danced overhead.

It was undeniably beautiful, but it didn't stop my pulse from beating an uneven rhythm in my fingertips.

Thankfully, we only paused here long enough for the line of pets to progress into the crowd. When it was our turn, we moved down the steps towards the main hall that held a smattering of small tables topped with gold and silver decorations. Some in the shape of horns or teeth, others, in the likeness of human hands holding candles, or glass globes that throw colors across the bright silk table cloths. It's mesmerizing in the same way a trap must be attractive to its prey. I pulled my lips between my teeth as apprehension pulsed under my skin.

Surely, if the twisted beauty of this awful place didn't have my skin crawling with unease, the patrons would have.

Their pawing and gawking...

Shifters and vampires alike didn't hesitate to pull humans out of line at their whim. Parading us past creatures who would spend ungodly amounts of coin to simply drain us on the street just out front. If we even made it that long.

And why wouldn't they?

Coin is abundant in the High City and we were just ... pets.

"This one's barely sentient, dear," groused a female with blue scales decorating her high cheekbones. She held a thin male from two spaces before me in line by the hair on his chin. Her wide set, jewel-like eyes seemed to take in the whole room as she blustered over her partner's continued perusal of the man. I watch as her partner leans in, running his nose up the column of the man's throat, his fangs making an appearance from behind thin lips as he smiles. The vampire nodded to the handler who passed off the delicate silver leash. Chills slip down my spine as I watch the male wrap that leash tightly around his hand as he runs his tongue over his teeth.

Sold.

The female rolls her eyes as she snarks.

"You think only of your stomach, and never of me."

He takes in his partner with a saccharine smile. "Go ahead and choose one for yourself. Your pool's been looking quite empty."

Her eyes flashed back to the line of humans who had shifted to detour around them and my heart tripped over itself. I glue my eyes to the human in front of me forcing my face to go slack. Resigned. She didn't like how quiet the man her partner had chosen, proved to be, so as long as I made it past her without running screaming, I hoped I'd be in the clear.

I wished that was the trick for everyone; to sabotage my appeal to a potential owner. But, I hoped my buyer would be a lesser evil than the trappers who brought me here. Or the female we brushed past looking to do ... who knows what with humans in her pool.

Did she drown them?

Force them to swim laps until they sank to the bottom?

What if they couldn't swim?

I blew out a quiet breath as I narrowly escaped a clawed hand that latched onto the woman behind me.

"If only their forms would hold, I'd mount them on my wall. At least like that, they cannot chatter." A big bellied man with goat horns and coarse white facial hair snickered as the pet beside him pressed her lips into a flat line.

At least this male was here with a live pet...maybe he was just a collector.

"Or run," the other smiled and I worked to keep my eyes cast downwards, where my glare would die against the polished marble. I couldn't afford to catch the eye of an owner like that. One who delighted in breaking a defiant pet.

Anger pulsed behind my ears loud enough to deafen the sound of the shifter who leaned in to whisper from my left. I had just enough time to lock myself down; to forbid my muscles from jumping, or the gasp from escaping my clenched teeth. He'd gotten far too close without my notice. So close, in fact, that his chuckle coasted across the exposed skin of my shoulder before he responded.

"Although I quite like a chase," he grinned, twisting my leash around his forefinger. What I couldn't fight, however, was the way my heart tried to beat out of my chest. My eyes sharpened painfully as adrenaline pumped through my veins. Even at a molecular level, my body responded to the predator before me, whether I choose to recognize them, or not.

I squared my shoulders and lifted my eyes, if only to level them at the wall, and instead met another's.

But his attention seemed solely focused on the shifter beside me. That was, until he arrived beside us.

He's large. Not only tall, but broad and he used his size to crowd the male forcing him to take a small step back. His eyes, a warm umber, drifted over my form in a bored manner that made me horrifically comfortable in comparison.

"This one's mine," he said, plucking the leash from the shifter's hand. "Yet again, it appears you have been-"

He paused, his grin a sharp thing.

"Too slow."

My lips twitch, enjoying the tempering of these shifter's mountainous egos, but the distraction only lessens my control. A gasp slipped past clenched teeth when the shifter, not ready to accept his loss, reached for me as if he'd simply latch onto the front of my cobweb-thin dress.

I jerk back, the action flattening me against my new owner's side. But as quickly as I registered his hard frame against me, I realized the shifter hadn't so much as touched me, let alone tugged me into his arms as he'd intended. Instead, I found him silent, his throat moving carefully around a clawed hand. The vampire's hand wasn't like the raven shifter who had dressed me backstage. The shifter's had sported real talons. Permanent fixtures. A reminder of the beast he was molded after. But the vampire's hands were ... well, still hands. They had simply transformed. Inky blackness swirled down his fingers wrapping around knuckles that were now tipped with claw-like nails.

He tapped the nail of his pointer finger just under the pulse point of the shifter's ear. Power ebbed from the male as he held the shifter still. Forcing the male to contain his anger, for what may have been the very first time. Anger warred with fear in his eyes as they lifted from me to my new owner. I followed suit, and as I did, I found him watching me. His head cocked in an equally predatory way.

Only then, did I realize the way I had tucked myself against him. Flattened my back to his chest. His coat hung open on either side of me accentuating the heat radiating off of his body, and allowing it to coil around me. His arm, a hard line over my shoulder where he held the shifter at length.

I should've stepped away. I should have removed myself; tucked underneath his arm and hidden behind him, where neither male could reach me without a more obvious movement.

One that would take longer.

One that would leave me time to react.

Or ... not react...

But as I took in his face, really looking at the male positioned like a sentinel behind me, I froze.

I had seen that face before.

I was soaked from the river and hoped to use that to my advantage as I tried to rip myself free of his hold, but his grip was like iron.

Warily, I scraped my gaze up his chest to find him studying me, in turn. I was caught by eyes the color of burnt umber, smoldering with a predatory interest. It was the thin ring of red that rimmed his irises that gave him away for what he was.

A vampire.

His gaze flits across my face and down my neck.

"Let me go," I hissed.

"Why are we whispering?" he asked, cocking his head to the side, a smile pulling at the corner of his lips as his gaze tipped past me to scan the tree line over my shoulder. "Who do you belong to?"

"No one," I snapped, attempting to pry his hands off my arms. Aiming to step around him, or at the very least, use his bulking form to shield myself from view, surprise prickled my scalp when he shifted us both to the right with another quick glance over my shoulder.

He stilled, and I knew he was listening. It was the prospect of what he was hearing, that had that anxiety poisoning the space with my scent. When he dropped those eyes to mine again, they were cooler. More calculated.

"Let me go," I shivered.

His eyes remained on mine, but his hold on my upper arms fell away immediately.

Surprise only lasted a moment before the trappers emerged from the tree line.

"I've got her," and then a gruffer, "You cannot be hunting here on royal lands".

Le stepped around the vampire, cautious but indigent. "We should turn you in, but hand over the girl and we won't have to report you."

"Well, we wouldn't want that," he purred, his gaze sliding over my face and down my frame before returning to the other trappers I could now hear emerging from the tree line. His eyes hardened as they returned to Le, who was stuffing me roughly into Sam's sweaty paws.

His grip was bruising.

"You won't be getting away again girl."

"If you intend to sell her for a decent price," the vampire interrupted Sam, as he leaned in close, teeth bared. "I suggest keeping your hands to yourself. She won't fetch a price worth claiming, if she's broken, or used."

His words - his uncaring tone, had made my blood boil. It wasn't until Sam's grip loosened, and Le's eyes cooled, that I realized he had probably saved my life.

That very same vampire, now coiled my leash around his palm.

But before I could so much as blink in response, his mask slipped back into place. His claws disappeared as he brushed nonexistent lint from the frozen shifters jacket.

"Such a slow creature," he droned, before turning away from us both.

"Come, Pet," he called lowly.

I wasted no time schooling my expression into something as neutral as I could manage and did my best not to fumble along behind him. Shifters and pets parted for him as he led me towards the exit.

But something else trailed me as I made my way out of Acropolis.

A realization.

I was now an owned woman.

And it was going to be damn near impossible to kill this one.

Chapter Two

I could feel the weight of their stares as I stood next to the vampire on the train platform. The impulse to cower was something that had been drilled into me since being taken by the trappers. If I showed weakness, and acknowledged their superiority, it earned me a brief reprieve.

I was again invisible.

A rung so low on the food chain, I faded into nonexistence, until they found themselves bored enough to search me out again.

But shifters like this, I had been raised to understand. Pets, or prizes, had been a recognized trade in both the major cities and free camps across the Mainland. My gran had seen them as little less than the beasts they were modeled after, since it was widely believed shifters had been born of a witches curse far, off on another continent.

But mom had harbored a soft spot for them, and it had gotten us in trouble more than once, ostracized from her family and their home, and chased us out of free camps when we were caught taking in younglings. Mom believed it wasn't a curse, but a blessing. They were strong, and clever, with talents their host creatures granted them. In her eyes, it made them special, but it also made them dangerous. In only a few hundred years, they rose from a cursed few, to a horde of enhanced beings that now vied for near equality with the ruling elite; vampires.

Though my new owner made it very clear this evening, that the gap between species was still quite vast. So I positioned myself behind his left shoulder, with as much space as my leash allowed, without pulling. It was another habit I had picked up from traveling with the trappers.

Keeping just out of sight.

Never wanting to remind them of my existence.

It was for that very reason, that I didn't want to tug on the leash, and draw attention back to myself.

Unfortunately, a passing shifter with tall, pointed ears, pit black eyes, and a skin-like tale felt brave enough to tug on a lock of my hair as he passed, testing my control. I bit down on the gasp as I startled, but caved, and scooted myself closer to the vampire's side.

Frustration had a scowl painting my expression. I swear I had zero survival instincts. But, I was owned now. That had to have the single advantage of protection from others ... right?

The rat shifter tossed his head back on a laugh, his eyes dragging up my legs as he cast a hungry look over his shoulder.

My heart rattled around in my chest, but I narrowed my eyes glaring at the male. What was he going to do? The vampire had kept the shifter at Acropolis from striking me, so best case scenario, he'd step in again. Maybe even start a brawl that would allow me a moment to slip into the crowd...

The thought froze in my mind the moment his head snapped back. His gaze captured mine before whipping to the rat shifter with a low snarl.

Possessive, or protective?

I couldn't be sure yet.

He didn't turn back to me again, but shortened the slack on my leash. The cool rage radiating off of his large frame calmed me a degree. It seemed perverse that his innate power, no matter the threat it could pose to my physical well-being, when aimed at the other shifters around me, made me feel safe.

He'd spent a large sum of coin on me. At the very least, I imagined he'd be willing to protect his investment.

I shivered as the train screeched to a halt, wind whipping around those waiting on the platform. As the doors swung open, his hand pressed to my back, ushering me down the long corridor. His warm hand had another shiver running up my back. This close, I could pick up more of his scent; leather and cedar, something soft and earthly... mildly sweet.

It reminded me of mom's almond cookies.

And the hint of something bright ... familiar.

The interior of the train car was vibrant. Patterned paper lined the walls. Brass hooks and accents were dotted here, and there. I ran my fingertips along the rich crushed red velvet covering the large bench seats positioned by the large window.

They felt decadent even as I perched cautiously on the edge of the bench seat.

Losing the warmth of his touch, had me tucking deeper into the train car chair, hoping to trap it. He closed the door to the private car and settled across from me, pulling a small book from his jacket pocket.

Sprawling would have been a better word for the way he consumed the space around him as he reclined in his seat. A creature completely at ease - because of course he would be. His dark hair curled in an untamed way, that looked as if he'd dragged rough fingers through it once too many times. It was cropped tighter to his ears on either side. I traced his strong nose, and sharp jaw, framed by the hint of facial hair, more visible under the light of the train car.

I dragged my eyes down his frame, emboldened by this quiet moment as he read, to really look at the male before me. His grey coat was well tailored, and even now as he lounged, it draped over him in a way that looked damn near lewd. Thick thighs tested the seams of gunmetal grey dress pants as they stretched wide.

My own legs snapped shut.

The cold air felt like a blessing as I took a small breath to settle myself. Not that the little stockings they had dressed me in were built for warmth. The shier material was dotted with incandescent jewels that sparkled, even now, in the low light. Like everything else at Acropolis, I had to begrudgingly admit they were beautiful.

Distracted as I was, I didn't see him when he reached for me. I stiffened when his knuckles grazed my neck. I made it this far without being fed from, but now that we were alone, I feared my time without a set of canines buried deep in my throat, had nearly expired.

Instead, he undid the latch of my collar, tucked it into his pocket, and sat back against his bench opposite of me.

Uninterested.

I was still breathing hard, watching the male before me when the door to our car pulled open. He placed an order for chicken and roasted vegetables, with a red wine glaze. Just hearing the dish he ordered, had my stomach grumbling loud enough for human ears to hear.

The attendant tucked the little notepad into her apron smiling at the vampire before her. I'd heard about shifters willingly offering themselves to vampires. Feeding, often exchanged for coin or other services.

The way she perused the vampire across from me had me believing those rumors. It was fascinating to watch them interact. Two higher species, not quite on the same level, but close enough that allowed for them to exist in a way that wasn't exclusively fear-driven... but instead, dripping in interest.

Lust.

Unfortunately for her, the vampire only had eyes for the book in his hands.

It must have been the disinterest that spurred her to finally look past the male she'd been mentally undressing. Unfortunately for me, her interest ended there.

Her gaze hardened as she took me in, a delicate scowl souring her pretty face.

"Collars must remain on," she sniffed primly. "It's for their own safety, and the safety of the other passengers." He watched her for a moment, seeming to take in her words as I had been doing. After a beat, he grinned at me, but it held in it an undercurrent of something that made my stomach flip.

"You're not a runner, are you, Pet?" he purred.

With eyes that felt too wide, and my heart slamming in my chest, I shook my head, not trusting my voice with what we both knew was a lie.

Her gaze flickered to my stockings, then the thin silk dress, and I all but watched her draw the very same assumptions I'd been making only moments earlier. Pets were marketed as prizes here for a reason.

Shame heated my cheeks, but it took extra effort to shake off the irritation that, even knowing we were hunted like prey, and sold against our will, each and every one of them found a way to look down on me for something I had no choice in. For a decision that would be made only by my new owner. My gaze flickered to him and I found him waiting. His eyes were trained on my face with an intensity that threatened to expose my worsening attitude. So, instead I leveled my gaze on his hand curling and uncurling just once on the bench beside him.

"Surely she won't outrun me anyway," he assured, his voice bored once again.

"I insist," she fired back without hesitation.

He smiled, flashing a bit too much fang for the motion to be taken as anything other than a threat. The attendant took notice, and while I admired the way she kept her composure, under what I could only see as a physical threat, she just smiled and waited for him to pull my collar from his pocket, wrap it back around my neck, and clip the leash to the little brass hook on the wall. Satisfied that I was stowed away properly, she dipped out of the car. Neither party drew attention to the fact she had paled several shades, or the way her hand shook as it reached for the door handle.

Muttering something under his breath, he settled against the crushed velvet seat. I tried to do the same, but the way my short show collar was attached to the wall, allowed barely enough room for me to perch on the edge, let alone recline against the backrest... or collapse against the seat, curled in a ball, like I wanted.

"Relax" he grumbles, his eyes returning to his book.

"I - I can't."

"I'm not going to hurt you," he assures, that bored tone returning.

"No I -" I hesitate as his eyes lift to meet mine. "I can't."

I reached for the collar, but froze remembering the thwack to my knuckles I had received when I had mindlessly reached for it at the showroom.

I didn't know the rules there.

I didn't know them here.

Instead, I show him, reclining against the backrest, to explain how I'd essentially strangle myself, if I tried.

I'd be lying if I didn't admit that panic gripped me as I realized this moment of sheer stupidity had me showcasing myself as helpless prey before a very real predator. Thankfully, his eyes remained steady as he reached for me. Using one hand to steady me by the upper arm, the other unhooked the leash from the wall. Looping it instead around the armrest beside me.

Food was delivered by a faceless shifter, or at least it may as well have been. The second that food, and it's absolutely mouthwatering aroma, made its way through the door to our car, everything else simply winked out of existence.

As the table is set for him, I stuff my fingers under my legs to keep them from reaching out of their own accord.

"Help yourself," he says, voice gruff.

My eyes snap to his and I fight to keep them calm. Polite. I wanted to accept the offer...but what would it cost me?

"Eat" he insists, sliding the dish across the table, and following it with silverware, and the napkin, set just as it had been before him. "Please." He seemed to put effort into softening the command from his tone.

I shouldn't have caved so quickly. I knew that, but I also needed to know what that chicken tasted like, like I needed air in my lungs. That food hitting my tongue, set off fireworks in my brain, but it also started a frenzy. I ate quickly, finding myself suddenly anxious over the possibility of getting caught. Of some pretty blonde returning to catch me, and insisting I stop eating.

Was food not served to pets here?

Would it be taken away if I didn't finish before they came back?

"Slow down," he warns, setting his fingers to the edge of my plate. The appearance of his hand has me immediately forfeiting the plate with a clatter, but I clutched my fork. Only when he raised his hands in front of him in mock surrender, did I realize I was holding it between us like a dagger.

"I'm sorry," I breathe, letting the fork fall to the table. I shove myself back from the table, sitting firmly against my seat.

"No need." His lips twitched tugging up at the corners. "I understand hunger."

One sharp, unhinged, laugh slid from me then, before I could strangle it.

"Eat your fill, but do it slowly. We have hours still, and there's plenty to eat on the train." He studied me. "When was the last time you ate?"

"Yesterday." I was almost certain that was correct. "But, like this? I can't remember," I said, shaking my head.

He nodded, and from his breast pocket, he retrieved a simple piece of paper. I watched his eyes glide across its face, before he refolded it and tucked it into his book. That seemingly insignificant piece of paper was my whole life.

My worth.

My freedom.

My ownership papers.

Proof I'd been purchased, and who I now legally belonged to.

"You were brought to market by trappers." His eyes met mine. "Did you come from a free camp?"

I swallowed, my mouth suddenly dry, and nodded. It was an effort to tuck away thoughts of my mom and brother. The smell of burning hair, the crackling of fire as it devoured the camp and its residents.

"Children of free folk have names. Real names. Not the ones assigned at market."

Markets like Acropolis assigned their prizes pretty names. Palatable names. The market I came from used flowers. They had named me Dahlia.

"I'd like to call you by the name you prefer. Not this." He tossed the book on the table between us. "So what can I call you?"

Names were a funny thing as a human. Our identities meant so little, that giving up this piece of me, this piece that connected me to my family ... he may have treated me kindly so far, but he hadn't earned this piece.

"Pet is fine" I smiled, but he just nodded. That open expression he'd gifted me, slipping back behind the mask of boredom once again.

I didn't owe him my name. I may owe him my life twice over now, but I didn't owe him this.

My plate was nearly clean, and for that I was thankful, because my appetite waned at the thought.

"My name is Jason," he said, eyes gliding across the pages before him.

The meal sat like a stone in my stomach, leadening my eyes as well. My body felt warm and buzzy as I curled up on my side against the soft velvet seat. He shifted, catching my attention as he slipped his coat down his arms, and stood. I watched him with heavy eyes that I forced wide.

"Easy" he soothed, draping the coat over me. I sighed curling deeper into the seat. Under the warm weight of his coat, I watched him return to his book. Those strong fingers gently turning thin pages until sleep took me.

Chapter Three

A tremor ran through my arm as I propped myself up, another wave of nausea knocking into me. My body was slick with sweat, and shook with the same small tremors that traveled down my arm now.

"I'm going to be sick," I lamented.

His attention snapped to me.

He had unleashed me and was hauling me, quite gently, to my feet before I could process my lack of fear over his speed. It was too much of a relief at this moment.

He deposited me in front of him and swung the door open.

"End of the hall to the right." He ushered me with a hand on my back, but it wasn't needed. "I'm behind you. Go."

I took off as a new layer of sweat beaded on my back and brow. Clapping a hand over my mouth, I shoved through the last door at the end of the hall, and dove for the toilet.

I could barely hear him call to me over the roar in my ears as I forfeited my dinner.

"I'll be right here." The uselessness of that statement would have made me laugh had I not been preoccupied.

After my stomach was empty, I rinsed my cheeks with cool water and patted my face dry. Letting the water soak the small towel, I took a moment holding it to the back of my neck.

The sigh that left my lips quickly transformed into a startled cry as the door unlatched behind me.

I turned to find him swinging the door closed just as silently as it had opened. His speed was something I should be accustomed to after traveling with the trappers, but he moved differently. Maybe it was because they used their speed to scare the humans they collected along the way. To threaten us. To demonstrate to us just how weak we were.

His speed was quiet. Natural. I couldn't tell if he was faster, or if it just seemed so, because he was never trying to *show* me how fast he was. He just moved at the pace that was required.

In the next instant, he had spun us so that my back was pressed to the wall, his hand over my mouth, his forehead pressed to my shoulder just as the door swung open again. I gripped the lapels of his jacket, resisting the urge to bite his hand. The adrenaline pounding in my head made it hard to determine whether I should drag myself against him for protection, or throttle him for manhandling me. Neither seemed like a good idea, and now we weren't alone.

He lifted his head slowly. His eyes blazed as they met mine, then snapped to greet the intruder with a harsh snarl.

"You cannot have pets in here," the new vampire hissed, indignant.

A pause.

"Fine." He surrendered too easily, wiping his already clean mouth with the back of his hand, but didn't release me,

Instead, I watch him as he takes his time lifting the hand from my mouth to brush a curl from my face. His hands ran the length of my neck to my shoulders, gently scraping down my arms before taking a measured step back and adjusting himself as if we'd been truly interrupted. My face flushed from the implication, and the scrape of his hands against my skin.

My next breath lodged in my throat.

"Ah." The vampire grinned. "New prizes are hard to resist," he growled appreciatively. "The lack of control is understandable. They don't stay new for long, do they?"

My vampire - Jason...his name was Jason, moved, then shifted me towards the door. The movement felt harsh, but just as he had held my mouth moments ago, it was with no more force than necessary. If I weren't so dumbfounded and embarrassed, I'd argue he was being gentle with me.

"Now that she's broken in," the vampire said, "we could share."

A shiver ran up my spine that had nothing to do with the temperature, and I watched Jason's muscles tense, before he peered over me to the vampire.

"I don't share," he said with another one of those sharp smiles.

"Pity," the other nodded as I was towed out of the bathroom and ushered back to the train car.

It wasn't until the door closed behind us that I realized I was still holding the soaked towel. I watched the rivulets of water run through my fingers, landing on the plush carpet as my mind caught up with what had just happened.

"Are you alright?" Jason asked, dipping to catch my eyes, effectively breaking my trance.

"I think so." I blinked. "Did I get us in trouble?"

He shook his head, returning to his full height and straightening his shirt. "I'll handle it."

As if my cursed words had summoned them, a knock came at the door.

If I thought I'd felt sick moments ago, it paled in comparison to the acid that churned my stomach now. Fear lanced through me as I lifted my eyes to find Le grinning at me from the train car door.

"Hello girl," he chuckled, brows low, head tilting just so, appraising me in that predatory way that had my blood cooling.

All four of them shoved their way into the train car. Jason snarled as a blade was produced and held between them.

Fear and fury perfumed the space.

"Not only will you give me the girl," he said, flipping the knife in his palm. "You're going to pay me to take her off your hands."

I sucked in a sharp breath. His greed made him astonishingly stupid.

"Oh, I doubt that." Jason smiled.

Le laughed, fingering Jason's lapels, and I stopped breathing. That bored mask I'd watched him don with the blonde attendant, falling effortlessly into place. A dark brow arching in question. With a spark of motion, and a flash of steel, the cold edge of the blade kissed my throat.

Jason's gaze cooled as he shook his head, a dangerous smile quirking those full lips up as he placed two fingers to the edge of the blade against my throat. Hooking those two fingers, he simply guided the blade away from my skin, notching it against his own.

"This is between us," his voice was low, eyes never leaving Le's, as he wiped the blood from his fingers on the front of Le's shirt.

Le growled, anger and tension building. There was a reason this male, a vampire, spent so much time around shifters. And it wasn't how thoroughly he seemed to enjoy tormenting the human population. Because here, standing before another vampire, he was on level footing, and males like Le couldn't lose. His ego wasn't capable of such blows. His gaze snapped to mine as he bared his teeth.

"Ah ah," Jason scolded, his tone mocking, as he recaptured Le's attention. "Don't even look at her."

The smile that lifted Le's lips had dread blossoming in my stomach.

"But she's just so nice to look at. All that skin tempting me all night." His eyes slid over my form and my heart thundered in my chest. "You knew I'd be watching. You-

Had I not been so keenly aware of the males, I would have missed the moment Jason snapped Le's wrist, caught the blade, and buried it in his eye. It all happened in an instant.

He howled as Jason tutted, "I told you not to look at her."

Ren, a shifter I recognized, swung at Jason, but he was too slow. Jason was already latching onto Le and using his body as a shield. Le caught a clawed swipe to the back, a keening scream reverberating through the car. Ren and Le collapsed in a heap in the far corner, just in time for Darin and Grey to jump on Jason from opposite directions.

Using the wet rag in my hand, I whipped it out at Darin, catching his cheek. His head whipped around, pupils thinning, and a vicious hiss erupted from his throat. But before either of us could react, Jason gripped his throat silencing the male. I noted two things in that instant. One, Jason's hand was once again replaced by that onyx claw he seemed to be able to call forward. And two, Darin's brows collapsed just as suddenly as he'd been silenced. Dark veins quickly climbed his throat and face. The shifter began choking, tearing at his own throat as he fell to the ground. Grey took a step back, and Jason tracked his movements with a snarl.

"Fuck this," Ren coughed. "Grab her papers."

Le, having recovered himself, grabs me from behind.

I had enough forethought as his arm wrapped around me, to stuff the wet rag into his mouth as he tried to bring it down on my shoulder. I knew that the book with my papers was still tossed uselessly on the table. Thankfully, it wasn't obvious to the others what that book held, but I needed to reach it.

Le gurgled around the rag as I reared back, landing a punch to his now empty eye socket. It was the most satisfying feeling of my life. The sound he made as he hurled me across the room- like I was a plight, something he wanted as far away from him as possible- would forever live in the back of my mind where I could play it over, and over, and over again, fondly.

I rolled as I was flung across the table, collapsing onto the floor. The hard landing stole my breath, but it was worth it. Because as I lay gasping on my side, curled in my arms was that book. With shaking fingers, I swiped my papers free, folded them twice more, and tucked them into my stocking before rising onto my hands and knees.

Jason shook off both Ren and Grey, before taking two long strides, grabbing Le, and hurling him straight through the train car window.

Wind and glass whipped through the cabin as Ren swiped at Jason's thigh with that blade, only to catch a punch to the jaw, sending him crashing into the cushioned seats before things sped to a level I couldn't follow.

Grunts and snarls sounded as the males threw each other through most of the furniture in the train car. Ren wrenched a sconce from the wall before diving at Jason. But in the next instant, dropped to the ground; his head turned at an impossible angle, finally still.

I crawled towards him, swiping the knife free from where it had been lodged in his shoulder, and clutching it with shaking fingers. Jason shifted his back to me as Grey charged, swinging wildly. Jason feigned to the left, and Grey swung through the space he'd just vacated, leaving his side exposed. Clamoring to my feet, I slammed the knife into Grey's side.

His resulting scream was feral. He pulled the blade free, slicing outwards. He may have taken my arm clean off had Jason not caught him. I truly didn't know if I was being a burden, or an aid, but I couldn't just stand there and shake. This was my first and probably only opportunity to punch a bunch of holes in some shifters, and I was going to take advantage.

I escaped with barely a cut, but Grey flung Jason into the door, which he flew through, landing in the hallway. He turned to me slowly with a bloodied smile that he wiped with the back of his hand.

"You're worthless to me girl, and now I'm pissed."

In a flash, he had me pinned to the wall, my neck craned with a stinging grip on my scalp. His hot breath brushed the base of my throat, a scream breaking across my lips before Jason crashed into us both.

I'd barely had any time to react before he had Grey pinned to the wall, ripping his head clean from his shoulders.

I gasped against the spray of gore, cupping my hand over my mouth when Jason took a stumbling step backwards. His hands clutched at his stomach.

I didn't understand.

I couldn't see what had happened until he leveled his gaze and pulled the blade from his stomach where Grey had buried it.

"Fuck."

I dove for him pressing my hands to his stomach and he grunted, swaying on his feet. This was bad. This was so, so bad. He was the only thing keeping me alive. I was deep into southern territory. I'd never get off this train alone.

I wouldn't be allowed, even with my papers, to walk off this train without an owner.

A living owner.

Jason steadies himself against the wall and sheaths the blade in his boot.

Darin stirred from where he'd collapsed and I couldn't hold back the disbelieving "Fucking how?" that burst form my lips.

Jason had the gall to chuckle before grasping my arm "You trust me?" he swayed.

"No," I exhaled sharply.

And he laughed.

Actually laughed.

"Good," he said, before wrapping me in his arms, and throwing us both through the train car window.

He held me to his chest, his back braced against the broken glass and then the ground as we landed and rolled.

My scalp stung as my hair was snagged on debris or maybe just around, and under Jason, as we rolled. His grip, that had been gentle, was now bruising as he locked me against him.

He used his elbows to support his weight as we rolled, caging me against his hard body. As painful as this tumble was, it was obvious Jason was taking the brunt of it, until a gasp burst from him. His head snapped forward into the back of mine with a crack and his grip went slack. I rag-dolled as I rolled out of his grip, vision going black.

Awareness isn't gentle as it drags me back to my body. I snap awake gasping as I roll from my back onto my side. My ears ring, and my skin stings, as I try to force air back into my lungs. I shove to a sit before I can let the pain catch up. The tree trunk that must have stopped my tumble, supports me as I take in my surroundings.

We were a few yards from the train tracks. The land sloped steeply from the tracks to where I sat now in an alcove of trees. Beyond that, the land was fairly flat. Another treeline a few yards past that.

I half expect to see Jason catching his breath nearby but when I don't... and when the ringing in my ears settles into silence, unease churns in my stomach.

Pushing to my feet, I clamber up the incline to stand next to the train tracks. It's the highest point, and I'm hoping it will give me the vantage I need to find him. He was bleeding and beaten from the fall, and as I dust my hands off on my dress, careful of the glass along the ground, I fervently hope that he's left me here of his own accord. Because the other option is hard to imagine. But there a few yards from the tree line I see his dark figure laid prone in the grass.

I make it to him landing on my knees. He's much heavier than he looks, and I struggle to roll the mountain of a male onto his back. His shirt is stained bloody, as is the soil below him. He's still bleeding heavily, but I sit stubbornly in my refusal to believe this male could be injured so severely. He fought off the trappers to protect me. He caught that knife in the gut pulling that asshole off of me. He could have just handed me over. I ran my hands down his chest, undoing his buttons with shaking fingers.

His chest rose slowly assuring me he was at least alive, but for how much longer he remained that way ... may now be my responsibility. Pulling the knife from his boot I cut open his soft undershirt and gasped at the wound below. My hands flutter over him uselessly until I steady myself.

"I can do this," I breathe, swallowing down the fear. I'm going to stop counting how many times over I owe this male my life. Now, I owe him back. Now, I need to be strong for us both.

"I can do this," I grate as I sit him forward pulling both shirts down his arms.

I thread my fingers into his hair searching for injury and find quite the sizable lump on the back of his head. My hands come away clean, so while I assume that's the strike that knocked him unconscious, at least he's not bleeding from another wound. Setting him down, I'm grateful he's unconscious, because I'm not graceful, and he's heavy as a bolder. The ground is also ice cold as I drop to the ground next to him and yank my stockings off.

His clothes are fairly soiled, streaked with blood and wet earth, but I find the cleanest section of fabric and get to work. I cut his soft undershirt in a zigzag pattern creating a long wrap-like bandage, and a few extra short strips, balling up some of the material to pack his wound. Using the elastic material of my stockings, I secure it around his waist, tying it as tightly as I can.

That should, at least, slow the bleeding.

Now I need to get us somewhere safe so he can rest. As soon as he woke up, we could figure out a plan from there.

But he was huge.

And heavy.

And I needed to move his giant ass in a way that wouldn't worsen his injuries. After walking a few useless circles around him, an idea struck. I tucked the dress shirt under his shoulders and around his arms. Gripping the sleeves allowed me to tug him, granted slowly, to the treeline where we were greeted with a beautiful sound.

The faint gurgle of running water.

Water meant we could float and I didn't have to continue dragging him like this. It also meant no one could track these deep gouges, dragging him was creating, since I couldn't rule out Le or Dain continuing to track us. If we survived a fall from the train window, there was a chance Le did too. And while I had no idea what he had done to Dain's neck, the shifter had stirred as we made our jump as well.

I left him resting just behind the treeline to plot the easiest route to drag the vampire, without hurting him or pulling my arms clear from my body. I needed the shortest, most direct, route. Thankfully, it wasn't far. It took a few times, walking, and rewalking the area, before I settled on a path I was happy with, but as I stood facing the gurgling waters of the river bed, doubts crept in.

Sourly, I hoped this time would be more successful than my last attempt at escaping the trappers using the river.

Maybe this wasn't a good idea.

I didn't want him bleeding too heavily into the water lest we attract yet another predator, and I wanted to keep his wounds clean and dry so... I needed something to float him on if this was going to work.

I dragged him as far as the riverbed, before setting him against a softer patch of mossy earth. With a quick glance over my shoulder, I trudged off into the trees, searching for solutions.

About an hour later, and just as the sun was setting I'd collected a few hollow reed-like branches from nearby trees, and set them side by side on the bank.

I dropped onto the soft mossy patch beside his shoulder and frowned at the vampire.

"You're not a lot of help, you know?"

He had paled and his forehead was clammy as I brushed some hair from his face with a sigh.

"But don't worry," I said, patting his big shoulder, "this will work."

It had to.

I told myself, if I didn't drown us both, I would reward myself by surrendering to my curiosity. Jason was covered in tattoos, starting at his hands and trailing up his arms, across his chest, and down his back. I was nosy by nature, and he was half naked, but I wouldn't allow myself to waste time right now. There would be time later.

We would make it.

So gripping my remaining stocking, I dragged the knife down the center, splitting it into two, and braiding it around the branches. It wasn't much, but as I crouched by the river I hoped that the damn thing would float.

I'd seen Bok Lain villagers float down the river along with baskets of flowers, bread, fish, and fruits at summer markets. The women would barter, laugh, and curse. The colorful beads braided into their hair, casting rainbows across the sparkling surface of the river. It was magic.

This ... was not.

My raft was rickety and not nearly large enough to hold the mammoth vampire, but I found that if I supported his upper half, letting his legs drag in the water, I had more control over the raft as I pulled it. And there was far less chance of me waterboarding him unintentionally.

I was a strong swimmer. My brother and I had spent most summers submerged in any nearby waters we could find pretending we were watershifters.

The sun began to set, but we had made progress. At first it was frustrating trying to balance the raft while I swam, but eventually I'd looped my collar around a branch centered on the raft, and using the clasp, hooked the leash around my waist, so that I could swim with both arms dragging him behind me. After that, I was able to pull us much faster.

As the sun sank lower, and lower, casting the trees into darkness, the water temperature continued to drop. Finally, I reached a point where I was no longer able to be grateful for the cool sting against my aching muscles, and started to struggle to catch my breath. Chills chased me even as I worked harder, pulling him faster to keep my body temperature high.

Night had fully descended. The riverbed was a slip of grey against the dark treeline. The waters darker, even when I waded over to a flat alcove.

I turned, gripping the edge of the raft and tugging him to shore, that leash biting into my back. I knew leaving him floating in the water wasn't an option, but damn was it tempting. If my body felt ledden as I waded out of the water, pulling him to shore was like pulling a house. I was breathing hard and cursing colorfully by the time he was resting against the nearest, and I mean nearest, flat patch of earth I could find.

I collapsed beside him, curling up against his chest, hoping sleep would find me before the cold could seep further into my skin.

Mercifully, it did.

But when morning comes, he still won't wake. His skin feels cool and hard, but after a night on the ground that's not surprising. I'm not entirely certain vampires can develop a fever or infection, but all the same I check his wound, cleaning the fabric of the undershirt I'd cut into wrap-like strips the day prior. I set a few along the branches to dry, while rebandaging his wound with the shorter strips and my stocking. It would hold for the time being.

I wasn't going to move him right away. This morning I needed to go find some food if I had any hope of being able to swim him down river again. That, and I needed to get an idea of where we had landed. Maybe there were resources nearby. Someone, or something, that could help.

I made sure to mark my direction with the sun. I was going to head north. North was safer. The closer I got us to the border, the safer I would be as a human towing her catatonic owner.

The earth became steep and rocky sooner than I would have hoped. The trees thinned the farther I went.

This wasn't good.

There wouldn't be much in terms of food here. Living in the free camps and moving from place to place with my mother and brother, we learned how to forage properly. Coming up empty handed, and growing more frustrated, as my stomach growled for attention, I moved east. I had climbed high enough to see a town in the distance. It was probably a good day... maybe two's, swim from where I'd left Jason... and west of the bank. So with that in mind, I shifted goals for the day. Today, I needed to eat, and get back in the river.

So, east I went. I hoped it would bring me back parallel to the river and into a more fruitful environment for foraging.

I pulled the dryer branches from trees along the rocky incline as I descended east. Firewood would still be useful, and it meant this trek hadn't been a complete waste of time. I ignored the pit that opened up in my stomach at the thought of an open flame.

It was necessary.

Necessary.

I could do this.

Thankfully the trees became denser, the earth damp and rich. Feeling more confident, I took time to scoop up raspberry leaves. It was too cold for the plant to fruit, but it would be a comforting tea if I could start a fire tonight.

A little positive to lighting a fire I knew would reopen fresh wounds.

I ignored the way the skin of my arm heated, the blisters had healed, the harsher burns had already scabbed and were beginning to scar.

After another hour, I had come up frustratingly empty. The sky was darkening and as I stood from my crouch, I had to leave another mushroom where I found it. Not edible. My stomach growled and I groaned a wave of lightheadedness washing over me.

"Fuck this," I groused.

I was better off going back to Jason, and continuing down the river. Hopefully, that would put us somewhere more promising. I could go another day without food.

The sky thundered overhead and I thundered back cursing and grumbling as I went. It eased my frustration and anxiety as I hiked back to Jason. Maybe it was my concern, realizing that he may have woken up while I was gone, or the dizziness that buzzed around my head, but I tripped on a root sprawling onto the ground with a cry.

The branches I'd been carrying scattered across the wet ground.

"No." I set my head against the ground fighting tears.

"No." Pushing myself onto hands and knees, I crawled a few paces, recollecting the scattered branches that hadn't become too saturated. It took me a few moments- a few deep breaths, to get my bearings, but thankfully, my hands had taken the brunt of my fall.

I wiped my skinned palms on my little dress and seeing the blood streak the material drew my attention to my dirtied palms.

The blood budding along my skin gave me pause. And an idea.

Maybe he needed to feed to gain strength. If I fed him, and he grew stronger, his consciousness would return ... I hoped.

With that thought, the need to return to him, heightened. I decided on a direction that felt correct and pushed myself to continue. It was harder now, with the cloud cover, to use the sun. The river felt farther than it should have been, but maybe it was just my sore foot that made it feel that way.

The damn storm rolling in made it harder to find my way back, and I'd be lying if I said I hadn't panicked when I thought I'd lost him amongst the trees. The storm made it harder to hear the river. It soaked my branches and tested my willpower to keep from continuing to scream at the sky lest I draw attention from unwanted sources. But I made it back to my vampire.

I watched him as I crouched by the riverbed, blade in hand.

Not wanting to risk infection, I clean the blade and clean it again. Ok, maybe I'm stalling. And with a deep breath, not allowing myself another thought, I pressed the tip into the skin of my palm right where the outer edge met my wrist. It was an easy spot to bandage with little material. Plus, I could pull it away quickly if he woke up.

I let the blood run over his lips. Cupping the back of his head, I held him upright hoping he wouldn't choke.

Nothing.

"C'mon Jason. Drink!" I drug the knife a little deeper allowing more blood to fill his mouth and finally he swallowed. "At least one of us gets dinner tonight," I quipped, beaming at the handsome vampire.

He swallowed in response and he may as well have wrapped his arms around me, peppering me with praise.

I was soaring.

Finally something had worked out just the way I'd hoped. After allowing him a few good swallows, I swept a thumb under his lip and combed his hair back from his face.

"We've got this big guy."

I bandaged my wrist and got him situated on his raft. The rain had ensured it would be nearly impossible to light a fire tonight, so instead, we would focus on getting closer to the town I had spotted this afternoon.

This evening was like the last.

I swam until my muscles burned. Until it became too dark to navigate safely. Now that he had been fed, the darkness held another worry as I pulled us through the cold currents.

I didn't want him to startle awake and flip himself into the water. Especially, when it became so dark, that I feared I may be unable to find him, if that happened. Tugging him to shore proved just as exhausting as the night prior, so when I tucked myself under his arm, I told myself tomorrow I would find food.

Tomorrow we would both have breakfast.

When the next morning came, I realized that the river we had been travelling in, let out into a large lake. Once I situated Jason, washed his bandages, and rewrapped his wound, I walked the perimeter of the lake hoping to pluck a few freshwater crustaceans from the shallow pools. I was about half way around the lake when the sound of a radio caught my attention. It seemed someone else had similar intentions.

A withered shifter sat in a folding chair. A pipe rested between his teeth, and a wide brimmed hat sat low across his brow. He hummed along to the music playing from the little radio set at his feet, and there, not far from the radio, sat a tackle box. Surely there'd be something there I could use to score a larger meal.

So I waited. I watched him for what felt like hours until he eventually sat back, his hands folded across his belly, his hat pulled over his face. The fishing pole was set into a spike and latched to the tree beside him. I crept forward as I watched his rounded belly rise and fall. Adrenaline coursed through my veins at the prospect of food, but I steadied myself with slow silent breaths as I snuck up behind him to rifle through that tackle box.

Crouching low, I lifted the latch on the small container, and nearly sobbed when I was greeted by a small wrapped package. I didn't waste time with greedy fingers. I took only what I needed. The package, a single hook, and some line. I crept back, knees shaking, eyes glued to the shifter, until I was well behind the treeline again. Only then, did I crouch down unwrapping the package with shaking fingers.

Tears wet my eyes when the wrapping gave way to a sandwich, packed neatly. I wasted no time eating the first half there in my crouch as I watched the shifter sleep. This way, if he caught me I'd at least have eaten half before having to forfeit the other. I let myself relax as I walked back to Jason blissfully happy with each bite of the rest of my sandwich.

With a fuller belly than I could have hoped for, I took time washing my hands and some fresh dressings into the river as I prepared myself. I'd stitched wounds before, but only ever on humans. I wouldn't think about how easily he could startle awake and simply flick the head from my shoulders, without another thought.

"Sorry, sorry, sorry," I breathe as I push the hook through his skin.

He doesn't move, and I don't know if that disappoints, or relieves, me. Leaning towards the former, and feeling good about my little hunt this morning, I decided to feed him once more, before slipping into the chilly waters again.

Putting that leash over my chaffed waist is an effort, but the cool water soothes the sting. I take the long way around the lake, slipping back into our routine of swimming until dark, dragging his giant, heavy, ass up the shore, before settling him against a wide trunk. The food sat blessedly well in my stomach, but it still grumbled as I sat against the cool wood. Jason's head rested in my lap as I ran my fingers through his hair. Hair that somehow still felt soft. I told myself he felt warmer as I reopened my wound, letting blood run into his mouth. I stroke his hair, his chest. Tracing the dark swirls of ink along his shoulders with my fingers. I can feel sleep lurking in the darkened corners of my vision, in the weight of my eyelids, but as I pull my wrist away from his lips I sit resting his head back against the earth.

"Please wake up Jason," I groan, as I stand, stretching my sore legs.

Cleaning and bandaging my wrist, I decided tomorrow I'd make a new cut. While Jason seemed immune to infection, I was not. The wound was hot and had bruised from the constant reopenings. If I was being honest it was just so sore that I couldn't stand the thought of touching it again.

As I trudge back to Jason, I knock him lightly with my toe in his muscled thigh.

"You awake?" I laugh as I debate sleeping sprawled across the vampire. His body, though still cold, is warmer than the ground. But with my luck, that's how he would wake. So instead, I tuck myself against his chest wrapped in his button down.

Chapter Four

I feel warmer than I have in days when the morning comes. Awareness reaches me slowly, confusion granting me a few blissful moments of comfort, before I remember where I am.

Jason's warm body is wrapped around mine, his arm tossed over my side, pinning me to him. I startle, rolling over, and scooting out from under his arm.

He'd moved! He'd moved in his sleep and - I set my hand to his cheek cautiously- he's definitely warmed.

"You awake?" I shake him and he rolls onto his back with a groan, but doesnt stir further.

I chew on the inside of my lip before standing and kicking him, hard, once in the thigh.

"Oooow. Shit!" I hop away holding my foot. "What the fuck are you made of?" I gripe, setting it down tentatively. Shit. That hurt worse than the root I'd tripped over.

Spurred on by his progress, I grab the blade from where I'd been holding it in my sleep. At first, I figured it wise to have it nearby, should we be attacked in the night, but now, I was grateful I hadn't stabbed him when he'd tucked himself against me. Clearly I would have been no help should someone have snuck up on us.

I shook my head digging the tip of the blade into the opposite wrist. Right on the outside under my palm.

I croutch beside him, lifting his head, and letting the blood run over his lips, fighting off the pounding in my head. The racing of my heart.

"Please." I swipe cold fingers through his hair. "Please, Jason."

His only response is a swallow.

Another.

"C'mon you giant-

His hand materializes around my own. His eyes snapping open, that red ring more pronounced around umber irises.

"Finally." The sigh slips from my lips as he shifts to a sit, my wrist still held suspended between us. Blood weeps between his fingers.

His eyes flicker to my wrist, before returning to study my face, the lack of recognition concerning.

"Good morning." I smile and pause. I'd been talking to him. Well... unconscious him, for days without realizing I'd spoken to him so few times when we'd met.

"You remember me?"

His eyes scan the surroundings and I know what he sees. I also realize just how confusing it must be in this moment.

"What are you doing?" he asks, voice cracking with disuse.

"Breakfast," I breathe and try for a smile.

The corner of his lips twitched, and I breathe a full breath for the first time since he opened his eyes.

"I didn't know what you needed..." I tried to pull free, but he held firm. "You'd been out a few days, and I was trying to help. Was I wrong?"

"No," he huffs, shaking his head, looking like he's trying to clear it. He eyes my wrist once more before running his tongue along the cut and releasing me.

I fight the urge to wipe my arm on his shirt, and instead, move to crouch by the river bed, intending to rinse him off of me, and cool the sting.

"Don't," he stops me. "My saliva will do more to heal your wound, then anything else. Leave it."

I eye him skeptically.

So he wasn't just licking the plate clean then. I stand, watching him as the tension between us eases.

"Where are we?" He braces himself on the tree to stand and I pace towards him arms out to steady him before I think twice.

His eyes flicker to me, brow raised, but when he winces on that left leg I kicked, I turn on my heel letting the smirk die amongst the trees.

"I'm not exactly sure. Still southern. But there's a hotel about a quarter mile that way," I turn and point. "But I can't get near it without you."

When I turn back to him, he has lifted his bandage and I freeze as he scowls. Those dark eyes catch mine, the scowl deepening further.

"You'll barely have a scar," I say, aiming for lighthearted, but it sounds a bit breathless. A bit too scared. I let his shirt fall down my arms and hand it to him.

"Keep it," he shakes his head.

"I shouldn't. It will be better if I look like this," I waved to myself, my dress far too short, dirtied with earth and blood. "And that you look like you could survive another brawl if needed."

I incline my head towards his bandages, and he rolls his eyes as I smile, happy to avoid ever dragging his body across another surface, *ever* again.

To my surprise, he relents with a, "Fair enough. C'mon then."

I fetch the collar and leash from where they are tethering the raft to a tree near the river, and clasp it back around my neck. He buttons up his shirt as he watches me, taking in the little space once more before ushering me to lead the way.

"You're going to have to catch me up," he says, voice stronger as we pad through the trees together.

I do as I'm told.

Just this once.

The walk into town had been a silent one, the air thickening with tension as we approached the outskirts of the main street. The inn was situated on a small street alongside a bakery and a few local shops.

I ran my hands down what was left of my outfit, smoothing the garment and taking a deep breath. One I'd hoped would calm my nerves, but did no such thing. Stepping back into a building full of shifters, this far south of the border, was the last thing I wanted to do.

Jason seemed to be doing the same as he stood, posture too tense, where we had paused tucked into a little alcove along the side of the inn. He scowled at the leash in his hand, his gaze darkening, as he followed the silver chain back to my throat. I stilled watching his eyes linger there, fervently hoping that feeding him my blood these last few days hadn't given him a taste for it.

Thankfully with a flicker, that bored mask slid back into place, calming his gaze, before he allowed it to coast over the rest of me. I knew what he was seeing, a stained, tattered dress that had seen far too many plunges into the river, too many nights spent sleeping on the ground, feet dirtied, and decorated with little scrapes.

Nothing remotely like the prize he'd spent all that coin on.

A humorless laugh crept up my throat as I wondered whether my new appearance would be more, or less appealing then the polished version Jason had purchased. Southerners had a reputation for their treatment of humans, pets, or otherwise.

Stepping through the doors of the inn was a shock. The cool air of the lobby caressed my still-damp skin as Jason led me across the pristine space. His confidence was in place as he strode to the black lacquered desk, that preternatural sense of power rolling off of him. The shifter behind the desk, a beautiful woman with colored feathers encircling her neck in a plume, smiled up at him. Her eyes flickered to me and I prepared myself for the way the others had let their greedy eyes move over me, but she surprised me when her eyes flickered back to Jason, her only reaction the slight uptick in her black tipped nose, and a pretty scowl.

Her distaste for me, barely registering, as my attention was snared on the tray of freshly baked cookies on the desk before her.

Jason took a card from between her extended forefingers, and watched her indicate towards the small elevator, before scooping up two cookies.

And suddenly he was my favorite being in existence.

We crammed ourselves into the elevator, and for a moment, I breathed a sigh of relief happily chewing my cookie. The chill of the air in the elevator, and Jason's nearness, had me shifting closer to his side, soaking in some of that warmth his large frame offered. Absent-mindedly, I had begun picking at the scabs on my wrist, surprised indeed at just how quickly it had begun healing. But the moment I realized my error, was the same moment I found myself pinned to the wall, Jason's body humming as his next exhale coasted across my neck.

His exploration of my skin paused at my shoulder, where he dragged his nose up neck. My immediate response was fear, followed briefly by a physical reaction to his touch that I chose to bury *very* deeply. However, when he laid his fangs to the sensitive skin under my ear, anger bloomed chasing away any fear that may have lingered. I hissed, the muscles in my back coiling in preparation for the pain I knew would follow.

"Please."

My legs shook with exhaustion. Exhaustion born from dragging his stupid body in and out of the river for three days. He had had his fair share of my blood. My hands curled into fists at my sides.

"Don't beg," he snapped, voice sharp. But speaking brought those fangs away from my skin and that relief sparked retaliation.

Without hesitating, I jammed my thumb into the knife wound in his gut. My muscles shook with adrenaline that I barely had the energy to maintain, and tears pricked at my eyes as betrayal trickled through my veins, steeling my resolve.

How dare he.

"I fed you for days," I seethed. "I am not giving you a thing now, and you will not take it." His head dipped to my shoulder and he took a breath. Taking that as a good sign, I continued. The elevator had stopped, and all I wanted was a shower, a warm bed, and not to be consumed here in this fucking elevator.

"I dragged your body down that river. Protected you and sacrificed myself." I grit out digging my thumb deeper into his wound. His abs spasmed under my fist. "You're here because of me. You *owe* me." I dipped my chin, protecting my neck, and holding his gaze.

"Now. Back. Off," I bit out harshly, twisting my thumb in his wound, and shoving at his chest with the other.

I swallow down the sigh of relief as he shakes his head, those eyes I'd waited days to see open, swirling with barely leased emotion. His hands, which were still planted against the wall on either side of me, caging me against his chest, shifted.

But, when someone tsks from over Jason's shoulder, we both startle. Or at least, I do. Jason just stiffens a fraction, his gaze darkening as he sends the interloper a look that has me cowering against the wall.

And I wasn't even on the receiving end.

This version of Jason, the one that seemed to be toeing the line of his self control, was terrifying.

"Now that's no way to speak to your owner," the new voice scolds.

Jason snarls at the shifter as he steps in close, crowding us, and my stomach plummets. "If you can't handle that little human of yours, we'd be happy to teach you a thing or two about more effective punishment."

"Mine used to be a mouthy thing too," a second shifter chuckled, stepping into view of the little elevator shaft and snapping something loose from his belt.

Fear pounded behind my ears as Jason's fangs extended, his arm wrapping possessively around me. Violence lingering just behind his mask.

"You're in the South. If you can't keep your pet, I'm inclined to take her from you. I like 'em with some fight." His gaze flickered to mine. "Like watching the light go out behind your eyes the moment you submit" he said, eyes landing on mine.

My breath was audible.

We were right back where this started and I was desperate. Desperate to make it out of another altercation alive, desperate to make it out of the south with a living, breathing, owner, because humans didn't make it out without one. And I was desperate for a solution, so when an opportunity presented itself, I took a chance.

Slowly I shifted towards Jason catching both of their attentions in the process. "Did I say the lines wrong?" I reached up to run a hand down his chest. "I practiced what you asked me to, just the way you like it," I murmured, keeping my voice sweet, submissive, unsure.

C'mon, I begged silently. *Play along*.

"I can do better next time," I allowed, nodding.

His eyes widened a fraction before narrowing dramatically.

The shifter's gaze jumped between the two of us, confusion settling into realization. Jason pet my hair, straightening his posture to something more casual. Frustrated, but good humored.

"You did so well, Pet" he purred, and I closed my eyes, settling into his praise. Admittedly, only partly for show. "It's not your fault we were interrupted."

"We can start over," I said, lacing my fingers through his as I pulled him past the shifters. "I can do better. Be meaner." I smiled sweetly with a wink over my shoulder to the two men.

The shifter's eyes widened, a smile blooming on his face.

"Our apologies," the latter chuckled. Acid churned in my stomach as he re-clasped a short whip to his belt.

I felt the blood drain from my face as I wheezed out a final breath, just as Jason shouldered his way through the door to our room.

"You owe me," he groused as I all but collapsed against the closed door dropping his hand immediately.

My eyes flew open.

"Why? Because a handful of shifters think you have mommy issues." I laughed harshly just once feeling at the edge of my own self control. "Not a chance. I wouldn't have had to lie had you just been able to control yourself."

He turned snarling harshly. The sound rippled over my skin and I straightened glaring right back.

"I just ensured we didn't have to fight our way out. Again. I was saving myself. If your ego can't take the blow, then that's on you."

He took two angry steps towards me and I refused to back down, something in me finally snapping. I took two equal steps towards him and met him with a heaving chest.

"I refuse to live the rest of my life controlled by fear like that." I pointed to the hall behind me. "If that's what this is- If that's who you are, then show me right here. Right now. I'd rather you kill me, then live waiting for the moment you snap." I took another step towards him. "Do it! Let's see it! Show me how fucking scary you are."

He blinked, then blinked again, and I watched, feeling crazed, as his eyes calmed before traveling down my body, and hungrily right back up.

"What are you?" He hisses, the space between us buzzing with tension.

I steady myself before lifting my eyes to his. Like this, my nose brushes the very edge of his, and that contact makes my stomach tumble.

"Angry." My voice is only a breath, but I know he hears me. "I'm angry." I plant my hands on his chest, but before I can shove him away, he steps back, his gaze falling over me.

"You're lucky you've been wearing my shirt long enough to smell like you're already mine."

I had no idea what the fuck that meant. "Glad to know it wasn't your self control, or respect for me, that won out. Just your scent," I spat venomously.

He looked genuinely angry.

"What are you gonna do?" I chuckled humorlessly, my adrenaline tanking.

"You do realize I could kill you with half a thought."

"I'm not afraid of you." I lie over my shoulder. I'm hurt and angry and hungry and exhausted. I don't know what I'm doing, but I can't seem to stop.

He grumbles something under his breath, but I swear the corner of his lips twitch as he turns away from me. Ignoring him completely, I push my way towards what I hope is the bathroom door.

"You're severely lacking any sense of self preservation."

Yeah, that's not news.

"And you, any self control." I step into the beautiful bathroom and nearly sob. "Go compare kinks with the monsters downstairs. I'm taking a shower."

Jason paused and the door cracked open.

"Thank you for what you did for me." He says in a voice that raises the hair on the back of my neck. "But I owe you nothing."

I only slam the door in response. The tears spilling over my cheeks as I sobbed into my hands hoping to smother the sound.

Chapter Five

I stood under the warm water letting it run over me until it ran cold. It had been a relief to find the room still empty when I stepped out of the steamy bathroom. Not wanting to put the little scrap of a dress back on, and not having had another option, I dove under the sheets of the bed, nesting myself in the surprisingly plush pillows.

I was nearly asleep when I heard the door open again.

I stilled, listening.

"It's me," he said softly, moving across the room to the chair tucked into the corner by the window.

It was then that I noticed he had changed. Setting down a new book onto the table, he tucked his hands into fresh black trousers. A simple black cotton t-shirt stretched over his arms and broad chest. Rolling over, I pulled the sheet up my chest so that I could sit against the pillows. With our luck, black was a smart choice. At least it hid the blood stains.

He turned, then paused.

I knew that he ... owned me. I grimaced. I know I'd accused him of having no self control, but I also reminded myself how lucky I was to have been purchased by someone who hadn't immediately torn into my throat.

Immediate death was apparently the bare minimum. The reality of pet ownership was bleak. The bar was in hell. Or so I thought. He dropped a few bags onto the foot of the bed and began unloading them before me.

First, was a large container of fried potatoes, along with a bottle of steamy broth that smelled of rosemary and garlic as he poured it into a mug from the bedside table. I watched him cork the bottle of broth, the steam from the mug swirling beside him as he turned back to me.

I popped a potato wedge into my mouth and chewed greedily while wondering if I could hurt him with garlic breath. Kissing him would allow me to skip my tongue into his-

"What are you thinking so hard about over there?"

My eyes flashed to his as I coughed around another potato wedge.

"Spitting in your mouth" I lied. Then cringed.

That was somehow ... so much worse.

He cocked a brow, his lips pressing into a line as he looked like he thought better of his rebuttal.

Embarrassed, I threw the half-eaten potato wedge at his chest, which, of course, he caught.

"Myth" he said, tossing the wedge into his mouth and chewing thoroughly as he placed another bag at my feet.

"What?"

"Garlic. It's a myth. Why would a vegetable keep me from killing you?"

I shrugged, my response dying on my tongue, as he pulled out a soft grey sweater and a matching pair of sweatpants, followed by a simple white t-shirt. "They may have come from the men's department, but I think they'll fit for the time being." He ran his hand roughly through his hair, shoving it back from his face. "These were the only things I could find in the women's department that looked even remotely capable of keeping you warm," he groused, setting down a pair of fur lined slippers.

My stomach did another stupid tumble as I leaned forward, still carefully holding the bed sheet to my chest, as I ran my finger along the soft fur lining of those beautiful slippers.

He stilled.

I, in fact, had everything to lose here. But he had clearly taken steps- many, many steps- to clear the air between us. So I'd let him.

“Pets are normally barefoot,” I allowed.

It was a symbol of our low status.

His brows dropped. “It's too cold for that bullshit. Besides, I didn't think you'd care about upholding traditional pet policies.” he paused. “Unless I was wrong,” he finished snarkily.

That didn't deserve an answer. So instead, I matched his reaction and just dropped my brow in a glare. I hoped it conveyed my message, but I was worried I'd been too softened by his gesture. He'd bought me clothes. Warm clothes. And he didn't want to dress me like a pet.

“Where did you stash those papers? We will need them to cross the border.”

I tense, carefully returning my eyes to him. “You knew I had them?”

“I saw what you did. So did he.” He shrugged. “He just didn't get the chance to act on it," he smiled but it was harsh.

“Explains why you just hauled his ass out the window then.”

I opened the drawer next to the bed, where I’d hidden the damp folded little square. And with a careful exhale, I tossed it to him at the foot of the bed.

He watched me a moment longer than I was comfortable with. An expression I couldn't quite read, flashing across his features, before he tucked it away again.

“When we get home, I'll need his details. There's no guarantee a fall like that kills a vampire, so we will need to make sure he can't show up in your life again.”

I just watched him.

“It was my intention, in purchasing you, to give you the best life I can.” He turned and placed my ownership document on the table. “Come here.”

I freeze, tightening my grip on the blanket against my chest.

He pulls a little canister from the bag before him, and I take advantage of his momentary distraction to pull the sheet from the bed. I keep it pinned to my chest, but wrap the rest around my back as I take ginger steps in his direction.

My body aches from the soles of my feet to my temples.

I arrive before him, and he holds out the little tub.

"This will help that cut along your midsection. As well as this one," he says, gripping my arm and turning it to get a better look. Being constantly submerged in water hadn't given it the opportunity to scab, but the skin had still begun to knit together. However, that wasn't what caught my attention.

One, it struck me that he had gone out of his way to bring this back for me, especially for a superficial cut along my arm, and two-

"How did you know about that?" I asked, almost certain that I had kept it covered since he'd woken up this morning.

"Broken skin has a very distinct scent," he said simply. "The blood is closer to the surface of your skin."

Warm umber greeted me as I studied him wondering if that was what had set him off in the elevator. The broken skin around my waist, along my feet and across my arm must have been why he looked like he was trying to grip a fraying rope.

And then I'd picked that scab.

Though he looked firmly in control now.

He spun his fingers in the air, a clear instruction to turn, so I did.

"What's this from?" He runs a salve covered finger across my back where the leash had rubbed the skin raw in a wide arc. I hiss at the contact, his other hand catching my hip. Whether to steady me or hold me still, I wasn't sure, but I didn't move. And I didn't need him.

"I used the leash to pull you along the river. It was easier swimming with both arms, then to drag you behind me with one."

"Does it go all the way around?"

It was worse on the front, but I wasn't about to tell him that, so I just nodded. In the same instant, I flick my gaze over my shoulder.

"I'm not turning around," I snap, and his lips turn up in the corner as he nods in return. Instead, he simply scoops up some more salve and reaches around my stomach under the sheet and runs cool fingers around the length of the rope burn.

His fingers dip back into the tub of salve as he reaches for my wrist. I allow him one at a time to ensure the sheet covering me stays in place. He eyes my wrist a moment, his thumb sweeping over my palm studying that bruised, broken, skin, before he coats each cut in salve.

He swipes what's left across the cut on my arm, before sending me back to bed.

Dipping into the bathroom to wash his hands, he gives me a moment to rearrange myself back under the blankets.

He sets his knuckle against the steaming mug before handing it over. "Small sips this time, yes?"

I roll my eyes, but do as I'm told. If only because it's not worth burning my tongue gulping down hot broth to spite the stupidly handsome vampire.

The broth is delicious. It's rich, and spiced generously, and I enjoy every drop over the next few minutes in between finishing my potatoes. We watch each other as I do. He looks no worse for wear. It looked as though he had washed up. Though, I had no idea where. His new shirt a more relaxed replacement for the finer clothes we bloodied up. The dark cotton accentuating the exposed whirls of dark ink crawling down his arm and up around his neck.

"We have a ride arriving in a few hours."

I jolted, caught daydreaming about his pecs and popped the final potato wedge into my mouth. Now that I've finished eating he settles into his new book.

"You should try to sleep." He doesn't look up, but I see the way his lips quirk up at the corners, before he smothered the reaction. The asshole could probably hear the near heart attack he just caused.

"Can you turn around?"

"Why?" he asked, looking up from his book instead. Of course.

"So I can go to the bathroom and wash my hands."

"You can wipe them on the curtains for all I care," he griped. "Fuck this place."

Fuck this place indeed. However, the curtains still required me getting out of bed, so instead, I wiped them on the sheet. On his side of the bed, obviously, because crumbs, and snuggled back under the comforter.

His low chuckle coasted across my skin like warm fingertips down my spine. The appreciative tone raising gooseflesh along my arms. A reaction I stubbornly ignored, as I tried to forget about the vampire lounging in the chair across the room, and why his presence had begun to feel like more of a comfort than a threat.

A while later - which Jason insisted had in fact been a few hours, and not the handful of moments I was sure I'd been asleep - he woke me to change, so we could meet the car downstairs.

"I trust your trip went smoothly" A kind older man held the door to a sleek town car that I climbed into without a speck of grace.

Jason snarled, and I smirked.

"He wouldn't know. He slept most of the way here."

I grin, feeling delirious as I sink into the sweater I'm wearing, letting the leather cushions absorb me into their delicious warmth. The cab of the car was cozy and dark. I didn't stand a chance.

Jason turns to me with a spark of something in his eyes, but I can see him fighting a smile in the twitch of his lips, or maybe I dream it.

The grey haired man slips into the driver's seat a smile reflected in the rearview mirror. A warm chuckle filling the cab.

I set my cheek to the door and close my eyes. For the first time, in a long time, feeling almost safe.

Chapter Six

Something moved, and I startled from my sleep, but I could barely open my eyes. My body hurt and the utter lack of light reassured me I still had time to rest. The woods felt quiet tonight. I must have been closer to the fire before settling against my tree. The trappers long settled in with their bottles. I couldn't remember the last time I'd been able to get this comfortable, so I wrapped myself tighter around the trunk and slipped back into a dreamless sleep.

Arms shifted as they wrapped around my legs and back holding me tightly as I fought. I worried I'd let them carry me away as I'd slept. And in my panic I wrap myself back around my tree, only to discover this is, in fact, not my tree I'm attempting to coil myself around. But as the memory returns, I'm simply too exhausted to feel embarrassed. Instead, I just relax into his grip. He's a vampire. He wont drop me.

Accidentally, anyways.

Chapter Seven

I wake in what can only be described as the world's most comfortable bed. If curiosity hadn't begun eating at me as it did, I'm certain I could have stayed curled up under the heavy duvet all morning. But, all those unknowns prickled my scalp, forbidding me from going back to sleep.

Instead, I swung my legs over the edge of the bed. It was tall, built I'm sure, for bigger statures like those of my vampire owner. Though I was certain this was not his bed. The room was warm toned and sunny. The duvet and pillows the color of warm cinnamon and soft cream. The rest of the room was quite simple. A large woven rug cushioned my sore feet as I paced to the wood stained armoire in the corner. A long mirror, and a wide window with gauzy curtains, framed the room. I had two bedside tables. One with a little mushroom shaped lamp that made me smile, and the other with a fresh glass of water.

I took sips of the cool water as I opened the armoire, finding it empty. The drawers were the same. So, nothing to change into then. I peeked out the door closest to the armoire and was met with a hallway. The house beyond was quiet. So with glass in hand, I crept into the long hallway. One end had three doors, all closed, while the other looked like a stairwell. Staving off my more nosy inclinations, I made my way down the stairs, and was greeted by a sun soaked living room, adjoining dining area, and an arched doorway I hoped led to a kitchen.

Success.

Holding my glass under the tap, I scanned the room hoping I'd find the refrigerator better stocked than the armoire in my bedroom. But as I turned off the faucet taking a few more sips, I heard a door snick shut, and footfalls moving from the back of the house. They weren't heavy like I'd expect a male of Jason's size to produce, but they were audible; an uncommon practice amongst vampires.

But it wasn't Jason who greeted me with two arms full of shopping bags, and a smile bright enough to rival the golden light filtering in from the window above the sink.

"Good morning," beamed the old man. I recognized him as the man who drove us home last night, but as he got closer, I also recognized my error. The slim ring of red around his silver-blue eyes surprised me.

Male, not man.

He was aged. Deep smile lines framed those kind eyes, grey hair combed, and styled just so.

Shifters and vampires both lived much longer lives than humans, but vampire's aged much slower than even shifters.

Lived much longer.

I myself, had heard of vampires well into their three and four hundredth year still looking very much young and able bodied.

The vampire before me must be ancient.

Jason didn't seem like one to put much consideration into tradition, but having a vampire running his estate was ... confusing.

"I heard you coming down the hall," I said in way of greeting, trying to discern the roles and rules here.

"Well," he turned, setting the bags onto the counter beside me. "No one likes to be startled." His smile was kind as he dusted his hands on his trousers. "Especially before breakfast."

I returned his smile, quite unable to resist the quiet kindness the male seemed to be made of.

"I'm Hartley."

"I'm-" I paused, my brow falling as I faltered, not finding a solution other than the obvious, so I ground out the response trying, and failing, to not cringe.

"Pet."

He chuckled, patting my arm. "Well, you're not my pet, so maybe we find something more appropriate. I'm sure we'll sort it out." He began unpacking the bags, and I followed suit, happy to move on.

We slipped into a companionable silence as we put away the groceries, which mostly consisted of me handing him items from the bag, and trying to memorize where he placed them. However, when he pulled open that refrigerator door, I balked. It was shelf, after shelf, filled with more food then I could have eaten in a month. Not to mention, the counters Hartley had just filled with colorful fruits and vegetables.

He opened a few more cabinets, before turning to find me processing the sheer excess of food. Maybe I shouldn't think of it as excess, but it was hard coming from free camps where we would have never had access to foods, even ingredients, like this.

"You will never go without here," Hartley said softly, pulling me from my thoughts. "I'm sure this feels overwhelming, but you will be taken care of in this household."

I nodded, tucking away my feelings before thanking Hartley.

With that settled, he tried to shew me out of the kitchen.

"Shouldn't I be helping?" I argued, not wanting to be caught sitting down while Hartley cooked. What if Jason had different expectations then the strange gem of a vampire before me?

He turned drying his hands on a lemon printed towel. His eyes were kind as they met mine.

"In a few days, when you've built up your strength, you'll be a great help to me around the house, but I've run this estate for many years before it was owned by Jason, the success of which is not dependent on you."

"I didn't mean to imply -

"And you didn't," he smiled. "I simply meant, that I've seen bananas with fewer bruises. When you're healthy, your help is welcomed. But let's do that first, hm?"

I swallowed the lump in my throat. The ache to tuck my wrists behind my back pressed at me, but I knew hiding them would only draw more attention, and I also knew, thanks to Jason, that the vampire before me could scent the rest. There was no hiding.

Hartley was an enigma.

He knew *I* was human right?

He deemed me fit enough to help him prepare breakfast. "If only to get some food in you faster," he'd crowed as he turned towards the stove.

We cut up melon, fresh berries, and citrus fruits that looked decadent just piled high in a bowl. Hartley had a way of making food an art. Watching him work proved to be enough of a distraction, that by the time I'd finished cracking and whisking the eggs, he had sliced a fresh loaf of bread, buttered both sides setting them on the griddle next to some spiced meats and finished it all off by stacking them high on a plate, dolloped a scoop of that sweet whipped cream, and added a drizzle of something bright over top.

It was magic. It had to be. The soft sweetness of the fresh cream, and warm spices of the toast, brightened by that citrusy berry glaze. I groaned shamelessly around my next bite.

I wanted to cry. I also wanted two more stomachs so that I could keep shoveling this masterpiece into my mouth without consequence. But the ghost of the meal served on the train, and its consequences, haunted me, so I made myself sit back. Only then, realizing how I'd been hovering over my plate like a starved animal.

Harley didn't comment as he sat across from me with two mugs. "Coffee or tea?"

"I've never tried coffee." It had been far beyond our means in camp, but thanks to mom's resourcefulness, and foraging skills, we'd had plenty of tea.

"You're welcome to try it," he said, sliding the cup across the table. The scent was undeniably tempting; warm and earthy, but bright. I took a sip, excitement bubbling at the back of my throat. That excitement died a miserable death as I forced myself to swallow the bitter drink.

He laughed as I forced a smile, committing to finishing the ridiculously expensive bog water.

Another, deeper chuckle, joined in as Jason padded his way across the living room, relieving me of the cup before he dropped into a chair to my right, and took a long sip.

The drink pulled an appreciative groan from his throat that sent a ripple of awareness down my spine.

"You two just lack the refined pallet to appreciate it," Jason rasped, taking another long sip.

Hartley chuckled, sliding the other mug across the table to me as he tipped his own to his lips. Tea as well, I noted.

"It smells better than it tastes," I proffered, taking in the table as I grazed on the fruit Hartley had piled high on my plate. Hartley and I had found our own sense of companionable quiet, but Hartley and I felt much on the same level. Yet, he had set the table for three. Here we sat together, enjoying breakfast as equals. As a household. It was a foreign feeling, compared to anything I could have expected when I'd taken those few steps across the stage and into the pool of awaiting owners at Acropolis.

Jason turned to me. "When you're finished eating, I'll show you around the house, and then we need to make a trip into town."

The house was not at all what I expected. The living room was drenched in early morning light, casting golden rays across the caramel-colored couch. Behind it, was the kitchen entryway and dining room where we had shared breakfast. The couch sat facing a large hearth with framed art. Bold splashes of color in the shapes of mountains, desert sands, a full moon, and a swirl of wildflowers that, despite its bolder counterparts, felt delicate.

Shelves of books lined the far wall. The beautiful wood shelves drawing my eye up, and up, and up, following row after row of beautifully bound books. It was a stark difference from the cold male aesthetic I would have expected from Jason. I couldn't help the smile that budded as I walked along the wall of shelves, curiosity pushing me to stop and read each spine. Building a house filled with this much color and warmth, required a special kind of care. Care that the male behind me dressed in black from head to toe, silver rings bright against the dark ink across his hands and peeking from the relaxed collar of his shirt, must've perfected in his long life. He was a sin incarnate, and yet, he had created so much peace here.

I could feel Jason hovering behind me as I tipped my chin, stretching to read a few titles from the higher shelves. The expression I wore as, what I had intended to be an appreciative glance, must have been too marred by my confusion, because it seemed to give him pause. Instead of continuing towards me, he changed course finding an immediate need to straighten the books and bobbles on the side table. I grinned. The task felt awkward, and the way his brow crumpled, made me think he felt it too.

His eyes cut to mine, "Do you read?"

I nodded and dropped my fingers from the trail they were running along the shelf.

Jason pushed open the set of french doors adjacent to the shelves, the cool morning exhaling her chilly breath across the space. I closed my eyes as the gentle breeze coasted across my face.

"Well, you're welcome to read anything that interests you," he allowed, and my gaze snapped back to his. I'd been ready to appreciate his beautiful home at a distance.

As the help.

As his pet.

Not as a member of the household who would have access to ... Jason's belongings.

We studied each other for a moment.

"Will I have time to?"

Outside of chores, or responsibilities, I was still unsure of what was expected of me, and it was because of that, I'd assumed nothing.

"I imagine you'll have plenty" he said easily. "I told you, Pet, I brought you here to give you a good life."

He stood in the open doorway, his warm eyes leveled on me, hands in his pockets.

"I expect you to help Harltey when asked, but I thought you may enjoy spending some of your time here," he said, stepping out into the cool morning air.

Low-settling mist swirled around a sprawling garden. The center of which was an expansive patch of dewy grass. A tall brick wall rounded either side crawling with flowering vines that scented the air. To the left, were rows of garden boxes, and to the right, near the farthest point of the garden space, was an outer building. At the apex of the two rounding walls, was an opening, and between it, a small paved pathway leading to what appeared to be a small wooded area beyond the wall.

A large tree with strong arms shaded the garden boxes and anchored a hammock. While along the right, nearing that outer building, was a set of cushioned lounge chairs, glimmering with dew.

Jason moved back inside and I followed with a heightened excitement over seeing the rest of the house. Though I doubted much would compete with the living room and garden.

I could have spent all morning out here, but he'd mentioned errands in town, and I wouldn't be the cause of our delay. I found him leaning against the door frame watching me. The breeze stirred his hair, dark strands falling into his face. The golden light filtering over him highlighted the deep chocolate browns and lighter auburn tones in his hair I hadn't noticed. It softened his eyes, dark like the coffee he loved, that thin red ring glimmering as he combed those loose strands back into place with a rough swipe of his fingers.

My feet had taken several steps towards the vampire I hadn't allowed when I stumbled over a paver. And thankfully, he let me. It gave me a moment to right myself, both physically, and mentally. I needed to be more aware of the danger these males could be. They fed me delicious food, and pretty words, but they would have to keep those promises before I let my guard down.

I followed him through the house and up the front stairwell.

My body ached with each step up those stairs. It would be a few days before I felt less like the banana Hartley had compared me to, but Jason didn't comment on it, and for that I was grateful. He simply slowed his pace and let me pretend to appreciate the art along the walls as we climbed.

Upstairs we passed the door to the room I'd woken up in, and moved to the end of the hallway.

The door at its apex sat ajar.

"Now," he paused, the corner of his lips twitching. "You live in a house full of vampires," he needlessly reminded me. "So if you need something, all you have to do is call and one of us will hear you. But should you need to find me, chances are, I'll be behind one of these three doors." First, he opened the door to the left, ushering me inside when I hesitated.

His study was like stepping into a dream. The room was stuffed with more books than I could collect in a lifetime. Though for a vampire, I suppose he'd had few. I pulled my teeth between my lips as I ran my eyes along the endless shelves. This space smelled like him, or maybe he smelled like this space. The earthiness of the wood and subtle sweetness that accompanied aging ink and paper.

I took a deep breath filling my lungs with it as I took it all in. A chocolate leather chair sat behind a large desk, placed in the center of the room. Papers and books were sprawled across its surface haphazardly. For such a particular male, this was a surprising discovery.

Behind the desk was a large fireplace with a broadsword and shield displayed along the mantle. Candles and glass decanters sat on a small bar adjacent to the only window in the space. Its little alcove would make a perfect reading nook, I thought as I circled the room. Brushing my fingers up a few spines, I took note of their titles, building a mental list of books I'd like to stack on the bare bedside table in my room.

I paused at that big window framed by the only patch of bare wall. It was painted a rich dark green that accented the space it overlooked; the garden we'd visited and wooded area beyond the wall. I ran my eyes along the pretty black and tan rug. Its repeating patterns mirrored in each corner, framed by subtle florals, and bold swirls. The design softened towards the worn edges. It reminded me of his tattoos, but it also pulled at a memory.

"Is this from the continent?" We, the humans, shifters, and vampires, lived on the mainland which was divided by the northern and southern territories. The southern colonies were ruled by a self proclaimed royal family of shifters, while the northern colonies had been controlled by a long line of vampires- or a long reign by an elite vampire family whose lifespans far surpassed both shifters and humans. They had ruled for long enough that when the shifter population rose up to claim a portion of the mainland for their own, the vampires seemingly relinquished it to them to honor the growing power. Something neither being had ever considered necessary for us humans.

The shifters, in their rise to power, had established the human trade to further separate themselves from us. A population so beneath them that they kept us as pets.

Collecting humans wasn't as popular in the north. The vampires didn't need a status symbol to establish their dominance, but it didn't mean we were free here either.

However, there had been whispers of a free community of humans on the continent. A place where humans lived by their own rules, and shifters or vampires, were simply travelers. Rare and uninvolved in the lives of the humans lucky enough to be born free.

But that rug, that design, it reminded me of travelers I had met in the free camps.

He'd already been watching me circle his study when I'd asked the question, but my words seemed to awaken an interest in him. His lips twitched in the way they did when I entertained him, but this felt different. It felt less like a smile he'd tried to hide, and more like a male who'd just realized he had something much more valuable than first assumed.

Those twitches felt like an exertion of control over his stony image, where in this moment, it felt like I'd watched him momentarily lose that control, without ever realizing it had slipped.

"It is," he confirmed, leaning against the desk behind him as he appraised me. "How could you tell?"

I looked at the rug again. This was by far the biggest piece I'd seen.

"The print," I said simply, moving my gaze back to the window admiring the garden space from above.

"Very observant," he allowed, and I cast him a withering look over my shoulder. With that, he smiled bright and brief before turning for the door.

Back in the hallway, we stopped before the door at the apex of the hall. That sliver of dark space between the door and it's frame calling out to my nosier inclinations. The inclinations died an instantaneous death when he said, "and this is my room," inclining his head as if I should continue. As curious as I was what his bedroom space would look like, the clawing of nerves in my stomach had me pointing towards the only other door left.

"And what about this one?" I asked, my voice a pitch too high. Nerves too evident.

He hesitated for the briefest of instances before turning the handle and swinging the door open. Another small hesitation before stepping back and ushering me ahead of himself. I stood frozen in the entryway. The answer to the question that had been swirling in the back of my mind finally clicked into place.

Paint.

That bright familiar tone to his scent the night I had found myself pressed up against him had lingered, plaguing me with the root of its familiarity.

Paint.

It was an art studio. Stacks of canvas sat against the far wall. A large canvas rug was draped across the floor under a wooden easel, clearly the focal point of the room. There was little other furniture that wasn't purely for function. Again, the room was drenched in natural light. Little globes of glass hung along the window dressings throwing rainbows haphazardly across the space. Stained glass trim framed the large window casting reds and deep blues, yellows and bright orange across the space in wide swaths. I stepped into a patch of red light watching the color dance over my hands. Little rainbows fluttered here and there as the orbs in the windows twisted and turned.

Unwillingly, I peeled my eyes from the colors racing across my skin, to scan the rest of the space. I followed the ray of blue as it cast it's long fingers over a small counter and inlaid sink, hosting an array of freshly cleaned brushes, towels, sponges and just about every kind of tool I could fathom that it took to create art like the one that rested against the sturdy frame of the easel.

Recognition again tugged at me.

"The artwork downstairs... their yours?"

After a few beats of silence, I searched him out, though I knew just where I'd find him. He remained in the doorway leaving me ample space as I'd been drawn right into the center point of the room. My skin needed to absorb those beautiful colors, just to know if I could feel the magic that I could sense floating around this space. It was the antithesis of ordinary, and I worried that the same could be said of the vampire before me.

He nodded his expression more open, more vulnerable, then I'd ever expected this male capable of before he shuddered it completely.

My initial reaction was to roll my eyes, but that glimpse of vulnerability clung to me. As did the little pause he'd taken before opening the door.

A feeling slotted into place as I made sense of this small clue to just who Jason may be.

"They're beautiful." I held his eyes; still cold. His mask firmly in place. "Thank you for sharing this with me."

Chapter Eight

We went from store to store picking out more things then I'd ever expected to own. It started with items for my room. I hadn't felt anything really necessary past the bathing items we chose, and even then, picking something from the shelves packed full of products, felt overwhelming. I'd followed Jason down the long aisle intending to pick the largest jug of product I could find, simply to avoid having to come back, but my hands paused before the bottle.

Maybe it was too expensive... I shouldn't pick the bottle for it's size, if it meant I'd spend too much.

My gaze flickered to a smaller bottle boasting stronger hair, then another promising shinier locks.

Nerves had my fingers shaking as they danced across the different labels.

"Why don't you start by smelling them."

His suggestion pulled me from my spiral, my eyes flickering to his.

Calm swirling umber greeted me. That thin red ring, more vibrant in the bright lights of the store.

"There's no wrong answer," he cast his arm down the aisle. "Just pick the one that smells best." He glanced along the shelf, his grin faltering for a moment before he returned his focus to mine.

It wasn't a bad strategy. His scent was something I was admittedly too aware of. Casting that thought far from my mind, I turned my attention back to the tidal wave of products before me. There was no way I was going to smell all of these. It was still too overwhelming of a task.

I think he saw the panic and frustration in my eyes.

"We're in no rush, Pet." He inclined his head towards the shelf and I sighed. Part relieved, part resigned to my task.

Jason had encouraged me to smell each and every option before choosing one I liked. Instead, I chose five of the prettier bottles, and smelled those. The winner was dumped into the basket Jason carried with a proud nod that sent happy tingles down my spine.

However, as we moved through the aisles of pillows and bedding it felt wrong to ask for more than I had already. The bed I'd slept in had a warm duvet and a pile of pillows. It needed no improvement.

It wasn't until I paused in front of a knitted blanket, the color warm turmeric tea, that I stumbled in my stubborn advance down the aisle. Mom had worn an apron that very color.

It was her favorite.

It was also mine.

The hurt in my chest unfurled suddenly, my fingers aching to run across the fabric before I remembered myself, and scurried down the aisle and into the next, without a backwards glance.

We'd shopped so long that we'd taken a break to eat sugared buns and smoked meats. Jason still sipped on a hot cup of coffee where he leaned against the changing booth door, those stern brows descending on his darkening gaze.

He was dressed casually in a pair of dark jeans and a cream cable knit paired, of course, with what had to have been a clone of the dark coat he'd worn when I met him.

Shopping with Jason today had not been what I had expected. He seemed relaxed.I thought I may be catching a glimpse of the real male behind the mask.

What had also come as a surprise was just how comfortable I had become moving down aisle after aisle, store after store, side by side with this male who seemed content to sit back while I made my decisions. Only stepping in when the overwhelm became obvious to us both. The shifters and vampires who assisted us along the way seemed happy enough to speak to me. No one sneered or gawked.

The north was a funny place.

It settled something in me as the day progressed.

Maybe it was the fact that I wasn't dressed like a shiny toy, but it felt like more than that. It was the lack of attention we drew as we moved about. And if we drew eyes, they were solidly glued to Jason. I, for the first time since being taken from my home, felt comfortably invisible. I still wore the warm sweats he had purchased for me before traveling back to his estate. Though, that was currently changing.

Jason leaned against the doorframe of the changing stall, his coffee in one hand and a pile of beautiful warm clothes in the other.

"You need at least enough clothes to last you a few weeks, unless you plan on making Hartley do the wash more often than necessary."

I balked at that, but couldn't fathom more. I picked only the things I absolutely loved and nothing more. Nothing, just because. The feeling of excess was so potent, it made me uncomfortable as I gazed up at Jason, exhausted from a day full of decisions.

More so, I downright refused to shove my battered body into, and out of, any more clothing.

"Unless you want me to choose," he teased, setting the cup to his lips. Letting his words sink in while he politely ignored the horrendous groan I unleashed.

While the thought of what Jason would choose for me did threaten to distract me, I was equally repulsed by the idea of being the pet my owner would dress for his amusement.

"No," I bit out. "I'll choose."

I stepped around him and up to the rack. The volume of clothing still available to choose from, muddying my brain. But with a flicker of stubborn genius, I dug out the pieces I'd been avoiding. The items I'd thought indulgent.

Unnecessary.

Purposeless.

Something a pet wasn't supposed to wear...

Fuck.

Realizing that I'd been tailoring my choices based on what I felt was suitable for my position as a pet, strengthened my resolve as I dug through the rack pulling the items I had left behind earlier.

The sundress that tied at the shoulder and made me feel pretty, even if I didn't know when I'd wear it. A sleep set so buttery soft I was confident I could sleep on the floor in, and two pairs of pants that I knew would have pissed off another pet owner, but made me feel shielded and strong. If I could drag Jason's half dead body across the lower city in that wraith of a dress, imagine what I could have done with pockets!

I beamed with pride as Jason nodded, that twitch to his lips, as he handed them off to the drop dead gorgeous shifter who had been assisting us, without so much as a glance.

"Well done, Pet."

Exhaustion beat at my mind in time with my pulse, but I glowed under his praise. Even that name sounding affectionate.

Indulgent.

As we traveled back to his estate I examined those words, turning them over again, and again, in my mind. They were words meant to disarm and they felt genuine, but they were dangerous.

He was dangerous.

This wasn't what I expected of life as a pet. But the confusion that accompanied it, was unnerving in its own way. It left too much open ended. There was no model for me to follow in this new life. I still wasn't certain of my place in Jason's estate, but I knew I needed to figure it out quickly if I had any hopes of surviving here.

It wasn't until we arrived, Jason and Hartley helping carry the bags of all of my new belongings up to my room, that I realized tucked alongside the bathing items I had chosen, was that yellow blanket.

The following morning, I put painstaking effort into organizing all of my new belongings and picking an outfit for the day. Then I took a ridiculously long shower, before floating down the front stairs and into the kitchen to help Hartley craft a new masterpiece he called breakfast.

While I discovered that I did, in fact, have time to squirrel away a book or two from Jason's shelves, and explore the garden, I resisted. Hartley had tried a few times to shew me away from the kitchen, but I refused until I had helped him scrub the counters and the dishes, returning the space to its typical pristine state. Just as I found it each morning. The need to earn my place here was potent, especially after returning to my room now so full of belongings that still felt wholly unnecessary.

So instead, I set to organizing his shelves. Hartley provided me with the necessities to clean the covers and the shelves as I went. His reassurance that my self-assigned task wouldn't cost me my head, only inspired me further. It was also the perfect excuse to move some of the more interesting books to the left most shelf where I could easily return for them. Like my very own TBR shelf.

Jason had been working in his study for the better part of the afternoon, when I poked my head through the doorway. I didn't know what to expect when Hartley had sent me upstairs to deliver Jason the mail and his lunch, which thankfully consisted of real food, and not just a silver tray with a blade to poke holes in the pet carrying it.

While I shouldered through the doorway, I kept my focus on the brilliant silver tray I balanced between my hands, careful not to topple the lunch Hartley had prepared. I already knew the sandwich, stacked high with braised meat and pickled vegetables, was delicious, since he had insisted I eat mine while he finished preparing Jason's. As I arrived at his desk, I picked my eyes up to his success and pride shining brightly at not having spilled his scalding hot coffee across the mail, his meal... or his ridiculously expensive rug.

I was going to need to talk to Hartley about another delivery method.

However, the version of Jason I found was one I hadn't yet met. He sat with his elbows braced on the desk before him, fingers tangled in his hair, thumbs massaging his temples. A frustrated sigh escaped him in a rush as I pushed the tray towards him. Those dark eyes were clouded as they met mine. I think his gaze softened as he took in the lilac sundress I had changed into after my chores. His gaze followed the hem of my skirt, up to the wispy ties at my shoulders, and back down my arms to the tray of food in front of him.

He flipped through the handful of unremarkable envelopes before his fingers paused over the one with the small silver floral trim. Setting the edge of the envelope between his teeth, I nearly toppled the cup I was setting before him as he tore open the envelope. Thankfully his eyes were greedily scanning the lines of the letter in his hand, and not an ounce of awareness spared for the momentary paralysis that struck me with that simple act.

I had just regained my composure when his eyes flickered back up to mine, where they remained, as he watched me set out his food. Though, he only reached for the damned coffee, before reclining into that soft leather chair with a groan.

Maybe it was the urge to remove myself from his line of sight should his mood sour further, but I found myself circling his chair so that I could knead the stiff muscles of his shoulders before I thought to stop myself. I frowned, not knowing where the sudden impulse to take care of him was coming from, but was quickly consumed by the way he melted under my hands, rewarding me by a deep satisfied growl, or a sharp exhale when my knuckles dug into a tender point.

After a moment he took another sip from his mug before setting it down. The action pulled him from my grasp, so I took the opportunity to return to his side and end this sudden impulse to fulfill anything that even remotely resembled my duty as his pet.

"You should eat," I insisted before picking up the tray I'd discarded on his desk.

But he stopped me as I turned, taking my wrist and raising my hand to his lips before setting them gently to my knuckles.

"Thank you, Pet." His eyes were warmer when I met them again.

That.

The utter lack of acknowledgement of just how much higher he was on the food chain then I was. The disregard for my status as a pet. The absolute lack of expectations this male had when it came to our relationship, was how I found myself here, unwilling to leave him alone in this moment. The untouched sandwich and heaviness behind his eyes, taunted me, like a challenge left unfinished.

But how was I supposed to help?

My eyes coasted across his face looking for the answer and finding nothing. I didn't know him well enough to discern the correct path here, so I leaned on what I knew best.

Being as pigheaded as possible.

I set the tray down on the edge of the desk just outside his elbow, and hoisted myself onto the corner. Setting myself down right onto the tray.

His eyes heated, and I swallowed, nerves prickling down my back.

"If you're going to waste Hartley's food, then you may as well have a secondary option."

I arched a brow at him, challenge thickening the air between us.

C'mon.

Play with me.

I leveled my gaze on his, smothering the little voice in the back of my head that warned, should he choose to, he could take what I was offering- serious or not.

"Do you want me to taste you, Pet?" Those dark eyes swirled with molten excitement, but he didn't move towards me. In fact, the opposite. He reclined deeper into this chair, his hands still relaxed where they rested on his thighs; spread wide. Dominance perfumed the space between us.

There he was.

My lips parted, though there was no sound.

He leaned forward holding my gaze the way only a predator could capture its prey. I didn't think I could move away. I didn't think I wanted to. His hand cupped the back of my calf, a smirk finally pulling at the corner of his lips, followed by a slow blink that freed me from his snare.

My heart was galloping in my chest, adrenaline pumping hard, warming my neck and cheeks, but I blinked finding my voice. I had a goal to reach here.

"I hear stubbornness really taints the flavor of pets," I said as casually as possible. "But if you're that comfortable insulting Hartley's hard work then..." I shrugged, motioning with my chin to the untouched sandwich I could still taste on my lips.

When he spoke next, the smile was evident in his voice, even though that calm mask had returned.

"Noted," his deep voice rumbled across the space between us as he released me. Warm fingers slid to my ankle before falling away.

It was rejection... but it was what I wanted. Right?

I smiled and tried to tuck away the relief and disappointment that battled for dominance as they rattled down my spine.

"Can I read in here?" I don't know why, in this moment, I wanted to remain close to him. Surely it was to ensure I could prod him with little annoyances, should he slip back into whatever rut I'd found him in, and not because his acceptance of me in his space would ease the sting of the little rejection I'd only moments before been banking on when I offered myself up as his lunch.

Surely.

"Of course," he said around his next bite.

I already knew the book I wanted. Had set it right at the end of the bookshelf downstairs, so with the invitation open, I scurried downstairs to collect my treasure. Passing my room on the way back to Jason's office, I dipped in to grab my blanket.

We spent the rest of the evening in comfortable silence.

After a little readjusting to stretch my neck, I situated myself back against the little alcove by the window and peeked over the pages of my book to find him watching me. Maybe he was just looking out the window like I'd been tempted to, watching the oranges and pinks play across the sky as the sun sunk low.

He pushed from his chair and stalked out without a word. Before I could decide whether I'd shrug off his hasty exit, or allow some concern to disturb the chapter I was in the middle of, he reappeared wearing an easy grin. And to my surprise, both arms were full of pillows.

He dropped them in my lap unceremoniously letting them spill around my legs. He wasn't one to fuss over me, or make a show, but I wasn't one to graciously accept anyway.

Instead, I got to work building myself a pillow nest as Jason returned to his desk, pulling something from his front pocket. Once I was settled, he turned to me with a satisfied gleam in those umber eyes, his hand outstretched.

"What are these?"

"Chocolate," he said, popping a few into his mouth.

Chocolate wasn't something we often had access to in the free camps, but it hadn't been the first time I'd had it. The colorful candy coating crunched, giving way to creamy chocolate underneath.

"You like it?" he asked, and I snorted.

"How could you not?" Genuinely, could anyone *not* like chocolate. "Where did these come from?"

His answering grin cost me my next breath. "Hartley has a secret stash," he chuckled, dumping a whole handful into his mouth, before leaving the little satchel in my hand.

We both returned to our tasks, and I was happy to snack on Hartley's pilfered chocolate as the sun slipped below the trees. But as the room grew too dark to read in my little corner, I in turn grew bored. So, every now and again, when I found him looking too serious, I'd toss one at him.

You know? To share.

I was shocked when the first one pelted him right in the chest, clattering across his desk.

I sucked my lips between my teeth when his eyes flickered to mine. That mask, gone. Surprise sparkling in his dark eyes.

After that, he proved a bit more aware. Snapping a hand out to catch it mid air. But the last one I threw, he surprised me again by catching it in his open mouth.

I laughed, and he chuckled, chewing as he set aside the notebook he'd been working in.

He reclined in his chair, navy sweater loose around his neck as he shoved up the sleeves to his elbows. He crooked two fingers.

"C'mon, throw me a good one."

I tossed this one high, arching it in the air between us. His teeth clicked together as he grinned revealing the bright green chocolate between his teeth.

"Show off." I shook the smile loose from my lips.

"Should we go see if Harley needs some help?" He asked as he stretched. I only allowed myself a second to appreciate the view, before refocusing my attention on digging myself out of the pillow nest I had created. I left it there, my blanket folded on top, hoping that I would be able to join him again in his study tomorrow. And now I would have a place of my own, here in his room.

He took the chocolate, stashing it in the top drawer of his desk with a conspiratorial wink, before leading me back downstairs.

Chapter Nine

That morning I made my way down the main staircase and through the kitchen on silent feet. Knowing just how sensitive the ears in the house were, I doubted I had very long to pull this off before I was discovered.

And no, I wasn't running away.

Worse. I found myself giddy over the idea of surprising Jason and Hartley with breakfast. One of my favorites. One that reminded me of home. And the prospect of sharing this with them-with him, made my stomach tumble with excited energy.

These males had made my time here as a pet significantly better than I ever could have imagined. I felt almost unprepared for just how different my experience had been. Hartley never expected my help. Half the time I think he made allowances for just how much I impeded his routine at mealtime. Yet, he thanked me for each little task I completed. If it wasn't for the red ring around the old male's eyes, I think I'd forget just what he was. And yet he was kind, and soft spoken, and made sure to stomp his way into the kitchen and down the halls so not to startle me as I was settling in.

I felt comfortable here, cared for, when I'd expected a lifetime of feeling used. And I found myself, as days passed, wanting them to know me. Really know me.

So here I was, in the kitchen as the sun peeked over the treeline, cracking eggs and whisking cream as quietly as I could. I washed berries leaning into those memories of mom as she flitted around the kitchen humming as she went. That pang of hurt rippled through my chest, but I tucked it away before it could linger. Hartley wandered into the kitchen, his footfalls announcing his arrival, as they always did, and I smiled at the kind old vampire.

"Good morning," I beamed.

"Good morning," he smiled, inhaling deeply, before falling into step with me frying some bacon and candying some walnuts. Harley was a talent in the kitchen.

We set everything onto the table. My breakfast cakes topped with fresh berries and candied walnuts alongside a plate stacked high with that crispy bacon, hot coffee, and a carafe of fresh orange juice.

The three of us ate breakfast together, Jason filling his plate twice over as Hartley recounted a time in his youth when cooking looked very different. He told us about the evening he had made his family's meal. A charred disaster, he called it, and how he watched his father eat every last bite. That evening had been what had inspired him to hone the talent we now got to enjoy.

Helping Harley clean proved to be less of a battle the healthier I became. Each day I was less sore, most of my bruising from our ordeal had faded to a milky yellow. All but the bruises around my waist, which still pinched here and there, but were easy enough to ignore.

He left me wiping down the counters and headed up the back stairs. Stairs, I learned, led to a door in Jason's study. I also learned Harley stayed in a suite down a short corridor off the back of the house. The male was a mystery and I found myself distracted by the question of what his private quarters may look like.

Chunking the bar towel into the dirty laundry bin, I caught sight of a small shelf of books above the clean towels. I couldn't quite make out the titles as they appeared handwritten, and very worn, but I tipped one off the shelf with fingertips. Excitement bubbled in my stomach at the realization that the book in my hands was a recipe book. I couldn't be sure who the original author was, but I knew how I wanted to spend the afternoon. I tied up my apron, tucked the book under my arm, and scurried out the door to the back garden.

Stepping out into the crisp early afternoon air, I had to stop to appreciate the magic of this place. The cool air caressed my skin in chilly breaths that pinked my cheeks and the tip of my nose. Catching my reflection in the paned door, confirmed as much. The plush lawn chairs had their obvious appeal, but instead I found myself drawn to the woven swing next to the garden boxes. It was easy enough to settle into the seat. The ropes were soft despite the environment, and they wrapped around my back and legs like an embrace.

This would be my spot.

Smiling, I cracked open the dusty book and though my fingers itched to flip through the pages consuming every bit of the beautiful penmanship and hand drawn illustrations, I drew in a restraining breath, and started from the very first page.

I wanted to see all of it. Take in each detail as had been intended.

The book had a simple dedication: "To the Seeker".

Well here I was. Seeking a way to impress Hartley and hide the fact that the majority of my abilities were learned in shabby kitchens, or wild camps, over an open flame.

My afternoon blinked by, engrossed as I was in the pages.

I cataloged recipe after recipe, making a mental note of my favorites, too afraid to dog ear the pages. But I found myself drawn to the garden boxes as I reached the section focusing on teas and flavored oils. It was as if someone had crafted the garden to follow the pages. A box for teas. A box of fragrant herbs for flavored oils. Two boxes of seasonal vegetables and robust round planters with colorful flowers to cap off the area and sweeten the cool air.

With a few cautious looks tossed over my shoulder, I used the illustrations in the book to work my way around the garden identifying each herb, plant, and flower. A petal plucked here, a bit of herb or leaf there, rubbing them between my fingers releasing their oils and enjoying the mix of new scents. Then I tasted the ones that were promised to be edible, and noted my favorites.

As the sun began to stretch across the sky, I returned the book to its shelf, and my pilfered herbs to the pocket of my apron hanging on its hook, before taking the mail up to the study as I did everyday. However, the room was empty; which I didn't mind since it gave me an opportunity to fan the stack and snoop. My thumb ran over the pretty embossed edge of the envelope towards the bottom, its silver floral design reminding me of the rings Jason wore.

So, after piling the mail in a neat stack, and taking a brief glance at the papers scattered across the desks surface, I headed downstairs to brew a fresh pot of coffee before hunting down an over-caffeinated vampire. Jason wasn't one to rise early, so with ample sleep under his belt, the male rarely made use of his private quarters after breakfast. By process of elimination I knew he was in his studio, and I, being terminally nosy, made my way back up the stairs, a hot cup of coffee in hand, to bribe my way in.

"Knock knock," I opened the door slowly. Taking in the art, the kaleidoscope of colors ricocheting around the room, and that bright earthy scent of paint and coffee.

"I brought you a fresh cup," I said, taking in the room with greedy appreciation, not yet having set my eyes on the male himself. But when I did, regret surged over the time I'd wasted appreciating the art this vampire had created, and not the male himself. He stood barefoot on the canvas rug, brush in hand, jeans hung low on his hips. Muscled thighs tested the seams of the worn denim. He was bare chested, paint flecks here and there, a few brushes tucked into his front pocket drew my eyes down his body.

"Hello Pet," he purred, voice gravelly, eyes bright. That little tug to the corner of his lips tugged at my core. A flutter of nerves left my mouth dry.

"Hi" I swallowed. "Coffee?"

"Please."

He dried one hand on his jeans and held it out to me, paint streaking his knuckles.

He took a long pull before setting it on the little table beside him. The steam billowed from the mug joining a jar with water and brushes, a few rags, and other painting utensils.

He caught me staring. Again.

"Would you like to paint?"

My eyes snapped back to his. No mask to be seen, just warm umber eyes. That delicate red ring, luminescent in the colorful lighting of the room.

"I don't think my contribution to your work could be considered anything other than a mistake."

"You can have your own then." He inclined his head towards the cabinet against the far wall. Even the cabinet, its arching doors, and smooth stained wood, was art itself. Windowed doors displayed neatly stored art supplies and various wood carvings. But on the bottom shelf sat a long row of stretched canvas.

Of which, I chose the smallest size.

Need not waste anything larger.

I sat cross-legged on the edge of the canvas rug and he handed me two brushes from his pocket. One fat and wide, the other long and thin. He followed that with a glass of foggy water, sporting a woodworking guild logo, and opened the box at his feet between us. It was full of paint, some in tubes, others in jars and canisters of various sizes. All with a dab of paint on top to display the color inside.

I wasted time digging through the paint, hoping inspiration could be found at the bottom. Jason went back to painting a river rushing around a large stone leaving me to my task. It was an effort not to just sit and watch him work. My gaze followed the tip of his brush across those paint-stained knuckles and up his arm. Following corded muscle, tracing along the lines of his tattoos, up and over strong shoulders and down his chest to rove over the planes of his stomach as they bunched and tensed with each move. He stepped away from the canvas, then back, adding a detail in a way that didn't seem necessary until it was there.

I set the paint down with a huff. I couldn't paint like that.

"Art is art." His voice startled me after the stretch of silence we had settled into. His presence was quiet. It reminded me of Hartley. There was something about his absence that seemed so loud, but sharing a space with them was a pleasant sort of quiet.

"There is no right or wrong way to do it," he assured.

"Don't be so sure," I warned ominously. "You haven't seen my art."

"That's true," he chuckled. "But you're surprisingly capable."

"Of producing horrors, you mean."

"My eyesight will never be the same," he grinned, returning his attention to his canvas.

"You sleep too soundly for a vampire anyway," I groused playfully, sweeping some nonexistent dust from my canvas.

His gaze landed on mine and I was sucked right into his orbit. Jason was magnetic. And it wasn't his large frame, or the aloof confidence he seemed to exude. I was starting to think it was just him.

I blinked, and blinked again, a ragged sigh parting my lips as I dropped my gaze to the blank canvas.

"Nightmare fuel," I clarified.

"Nightmare fuel," he echoed, shaking his head with another chuckle. My eyes jumped to his face at the sound and I watched the corner of his eyes crinkle with the smile he so often fought.

If I'd had even a fraction of his talent, I would have painted him. His eyes. That smile.

But I couldn't... so I painted a blob. A blob that, after a while, transformed and took shape into something I was excited about.

A set of wishing flowers.

I'd seen them growing at the far edge of the garden, but I'd left them where they were. It seemed greedy to waste a wish with all that I'd been given.

It reminded me of my brother and how we had sat in the field behind camp on the very cusp of fall, taking turns making wishes. He had been excited to share his wishes, things only children could wish for growing up in a world like ours. Wishes unimpeded by the impossibility of their fruition. I loved hearing his wishes, what he wanted for the future... or for dinner that evening. But it became harder to lie to him. To come up with fun wishes I could share. Little lies I could sell my baby brother. So, selfishly, I had told him that only the wishes we didn't share, came true.

It didn't phase him one bit. He'd screw his eyes shut real tight, and blow the petals from his wishing flower and laugh as they sailed along the breeze carrying away his wishes.

My wishes. All those selfish things I couldn't give voice to... sometimes I wondered if Jason had been the reckoning of those wishes.

The male in question, a brush in one hand, a cup of coffee in the other, pulled his gaze from the canvas in front of him. The impact of him. Maskless...shirtless, and dusted in swaths of color, slammed into me. And as I blinked away the breathlessness, he smiled, and I worried I'd never again draw a full breath.

"You alright down there, Pet?"

I nodded. Then scrambling to rebuild any semblance of sanity, flicked a finger towards his cup.

"Can I use that on the canvas?"

He stilled, brows drawing up as he reached behind him. He poured some of his coffee into a small canister, and placed it into my waiting hand with that crooked smile. I found I liked this version of Jason the most.

"Why not?" he shrugged.

Why not.

Chapter Ten

Hartley whipped around, eyes dancing across the wall leading to the front of the house. It was the fastest I'd seen him move- always seeming content to move at a human's pace. I was about to ask if everything was ok, when his gaze snapped to mine.

"Wake Jason. Immediately."

His tone left no room for argument, so I set down the knife I'd been using and nodded. Wiping my hands on my apron, I turned to head towards the front stairwell, when he grabbed me. His grip was gentle, but shocked me nonetheless. I couldn't recall another time Hartley and I had even touched.

"Use the back stairwell," he turned me away from the front of the house. "Stay away from the windows."

My heart beat unevenly at the implication.

We were in danger.

"Go."

He gave me a reassuring nod, and a shove up those first few steps. I hesitated only a moment to watch him vanish down the hall.

Shit.

I took the stairs two at a time, my heart hammering in my chest. I didn't even pause as I pushed through the bedroom door. And Jason didn't move as I took several steps into the room. He was far too heavy of a sleeper for a vampire.

"Jason," I whispered.

He groaned, but didn't wake as I took the final few steps to the edge of the side table. Certainly within killing distance should he strike before realizing who I was. He was sprawled across the bed, deep blue sheets tangled around tattooed skin glowing tan under the low light of the morning.

I shook my head. I didn't have time to waste. Especially time spent ogling the vampire sleeping before me.

With clenched fists, and a muttered prayer, consisting mainly of me muttering "Don't kill me," a few times, I reached out to shake his shoulder.

Finally, he stirred.

A low growl rumbled from his chest as he propped himself up on elbows.

I flinched away, begging one more time for him to not kill me, when he scoffed.

"What are you doing in here?" I ignored the way my body responded to his voice, deeper, rougher in the morning.

"Somethings wrong. Hartley said to wake you." His eyes snapped to mine from around his muscled arm. "I don't know what's happening, but he warned me away from the windows. I think someone's here."

He was up and moving before I could finish. Though as he threw off his sheet, and disappeared behind the bathroom door, I don't think I could have. I caught only a glimpse of his naked body, but it was enough to stun my mind into total disrepair.

He emerged from the bathroom, seconds later, fully dressed and finger-combing his hair into submission.

"Stay here until I come back for you."

He paused at the door. Dark eyes, stormy.

"Understood?"

I nodded, then remembered my voice.

"Yes," I stammered. "I'll be here." I said to the empty room. The door already closed without a sound.

Breath blew loudly from my lips as I surveyed the space.

The temptation to collapse onto his bed was immediate, but I couldn't bring myself to sit on it, let alone collapse face first like my reeling mind was begging me to, knowing that his naked body had just been tangled up in those sheets.

It was only a glance. No need to dwell on what I may, or may not, have truly seen.

Though, he absolutely should have been able to move fast enough to ensure I'd seen nothing...but he'd been sleeping. Maybe he was slower in the morning.

I shook the thoughts straight from my head.

I was his pet. He was kind to me and that was all it was. Why would he want me to see him... I'd had an opportunity to see him when we traveled together, but that was before I had known him as anything other than the vampire who had purchased me. Before I knew *him*.

The impulse to peek out the window chewed at me.

So instead, I appeased my nosier tendencies and rummaged through his things. I started at the far end of the room. Opening each drawer, I ran my fingers along the neatly folded piles of clothes, including shirts that I absolutely did *not* lean in and smell. Then, I moved to the bedside tables. The side farthest from the door had a range of socks. Most of what I recognized as Jason's normal greys, blacks, and a few with small print, but then there were others. They were soft blues and bright oranges, yellows with funny prints like bats and foxes. I couldn't image Jason sporting these under his perfectly tailored suits, buttery soft sweaters, and slacks. It was almost comical to picture.

With a snort, I moved on to the drawer that I quickly snapped shut with a gasp. Boxers.

That seemed a step too far. So, with a bit too much enthusiasm, I yanked open the top drawer, rattling around its contents before I could comprehend what I was seeing.

Toys.

A drawer full.

My eyes roved over the expanse of toys and restraints and ...the blade tucked into the corner.

I didn't think I'd ever blink again. My skin prickled with awareness, and as I whipped around, I was shocked to find the room empty. Certainly there was someone who would be standing over my shoulder in this very moment to bear witness to the roiling embarrassment, and muscle coiling want, that ripped down my spine.

I fought the urge to finger through the items and closed the drawer, turning for the bathroom.

It was the perfect excuse to rinse my face and neck with cool water. Taking in the scarlet blotches across my cheeks and nose, I also caught something else. I dried my face with the deep blue hand towel that matched his bedding and eyed the little cup beside the sink.

Two sinks. Both set up in a way that spoke to frequent use.

My heart raced.

Another woman.

Another?

No.

The only other woman in his life. I didn't count. I was his pet. I was only his pet.

There hadn't been any sign of someone else. Nothing overtly feminine had stood out in the bedroom. Yet, there the evidence sat.

You didn't just use both sinks... Right?

I pulled open the adjoining door to the closet and took a turn around the room. Nothing but men's clothing.

Suits in all his typical neutrals, deep blues, blacks, browns, gunmetal grey, even a few tweeds broken up by more casual sweaters, jeans, plaids. The shelf below lined with men's shoes and the rack above-

Commotion from the window above the closet bench drew my attention from the little mystery I was working through. I was drawing the curtain back an inch and peering through, before I could remember why it was a bad idea.

Two stories below Jason stood facing a woman who tipped her head back on a laugh that rang through the air. Her dark hair, cut bluntly at her chin, shimmered as she did. She wore a fitted green dress despite the temperature. The bronzed skin of her legs and sleek arms glowing in the low morning light. She was beautiful in a dangerous sort of way.

Recovering herself, she pulled a large envelope from the bag slung over her shoulder in a flourish.

I watched Jason shake his head as he spoke, his gaze cast down, focused on the documents in his hands. She moves to brush past him towards the doorway when Jason's hand snaps out, snaring her by the wrist and halting her progress. They exchange what appear to be curt words, hers growing nearly loud enough for me to hear, when she throws her arms up, exasperated, her eyes roving over the vampire. Jason doesn't so much as shift his weight under her scrutiny. There is a familiarity between them in the comfortable way she looks her fill.

It has my skin heating. My eyes narrow as I itch to shove myself between them. But I exhale the sourness in my stomach that feels too much like jealousy, and as I do, I pause.

Because it's in the same instant, that her eyes flicker up along the front of the house, they tumble back down to Jason who has abruptly torn the documents in half.

He turns to leave, a few final words tossed over his shoulder, and I begin to tuck myself back behind the curtain when in a flash of movement, she's in front of him, her arm extended. Jason's head snaps to the side, three lines opened up across his cheek. I gasp and the female makes a show of licking her fingernails clean before they both freeze.

Her gaze is the first to flicker up to the window.

Then Jason's lands on mine. The look he delivers is like a physical touch.

One that wraps its fingers around my throat, and wrenches me from the window.

Shit.

I throw myself back, tugging the curtain closed, and holding it there as I draw a breath. Then another. I'm moving into the bedroom debating if I can make it to my room before he finishes up this little altercation when I find him, arms crossed, waiting beside the bed. Three thin lines of red drying across his cheek.

"Did Hartley not ask you to stay away from the windows?" he purred. His unnervingly pleasant tone contradicted the barely leashed irritation whirling behind those dark eyes.

"Sorry," I whisper.

He barks an aporetic laugh. "Now she's quiet."

My jaw worked as my own irritation inflated. "She hit you!"

"And?" he challenged.

"What do you mean, 'and'?" I shouted, outraged. "Look at your face," I fumed.

"And she would have walked away happy with her little tantrum, but instead she has *seen you.*" His voice drops to a timber that rumbles across the space between us.

"And?" It was my turn to flip the question on the male before me, and if his scowl was any indication, he didn't like it.

Good.

"Am I a secret?" Was he hiding me? Why? Did it have something to do with whoever else had lived here?

"It's - it's a long story." He quieted.

"Why?" I scoffed. "Embarrassed?" I goad him, smothering the hurt burning in my chest, and take a step back, needing some space from him, from this conversation, from the realization crashing down over my head.

"Only of who I have to become to appease her." He shakes his head, those dark curls flopping to the side to curl around his ear as he sighs. "But of you, never."

I step into him slowly, my arms crossing over my chest. His eyes are guarded as they look down his strong nose at me. "Who is she, that she can do that?" My eyes trace the jagged lines her nails had drawn across his face. "Without consequence?"

His eyes harden. "I won't ask you to do anything that isn't in your best interest."

Another non answer. Anger flared and I closed my eyes to keep from shouting, or worse, from this feeling of betrayal from wetting my eyes. He was evading my questions and I was allowing him to placate me. But he was lying. He was hiding something.

"But you still get to make that decision."

"Yes," he bit out and my eyes sprung open. "In these circumstances, yes, I do."

I rolled my eyes, turning to leave, just for him to appear before me. A grin tainted with disbelief painted across his face.

"Did you just roll your eyes at me?"

I throw my hands in the air.

"So you can spot me from the crack in your curtain two stories up, but aren't certain if I rolled my eyes, while standing right in front of you?"

"Don't be a brat," he growled.

A brat! A brat?

"I'm leaving," I ground out.

"I am trying to protect you," he groaned as I marched past him.

"From what?" I shouted as I whirled back to face him "From what!"

"From the male who sold you to me. From anyone else who'd take you from me!" He paused, drawing a settling breath, but mine was sawing between my teeth.

"It is important to me that you live well." He exhales roughly. "I will grant you as many freedoms as I can, but when I ask something of you, I need you to listen."

My next breath was ragged. My fingers tingle as anxiety barrelled down on my spine. All that heat evaporated in an instant leaving cold dread in its wake.

"Le?" I choked out his name, my knees wobbling "He's-

"He will not reach you here." Jason assured, catching my upper arms as if to steady me. The squeeze he offered drew my attention to our contact. His skin on my skin. His hands coasted up my neck pausing to cradle my cheeks. I had no choice but to meet his gaze.

Strong. Steady. Sure.

"You will not be hurt in my home."

He nodded and I blinked, exhaling some of the panic. His hands slid down my neck and over my shoulders.

Finally, I nodded.

"You have my word."

His grip loosened, his fingers gliding down my arm before releasing me completely as he turned at the waist, his eyes sweeping the room.

I watched him quietly as I tucked away the remaining anxiety. Understanding now why that image of Jason hadn't fit. Because it wasn't him. This was him.

An irritating asshole. But a protective, kind, irritating asshole.

His head cocked to the side, dark curls flopping free of their neat coils as he looked over me, something new budding in his expression.

His look caught me off guard. Had I said that out loud?

"Did you enjoy your snooping, Pet?"

I stiffened, unsure what had given me away... maybe the fact that he'd spotted me from the window in his closet.

"Your scent is all over my room," he clarified, looking too pleased.

I preferred pissed.

His gaze dropped to the bedside table. *That* bedside table. The look he wore as he dragged his eyes back to mine was sin incarnate.

"Find anything you liked?" he asked, voice low.

I heard my next breath, but couldn't find it. His resulting grin was devastatingly handsome. And real. He tipped his head to the side, a predator clocking its prey. He was toying with me, and I knew he was, but it didn't keep my heart from pounding out an uneven rhythm, or my skin from feeling hot, and too tight.

I was melting under his scrutiny, playful or not.

"Are you offering to lend me one?" I snipped, crossing my arms so he wouldn't see my fingers shake.

He smiled, his eyes melting into something warmer.

"Consider it an open ended offer, Pet".

I stepped up to him ready to test just how far he would allow me to push him, but his smile wavered. Had I not been so intently studying his face, I may not have seen the way his eyes cooled. The way he stepped back from me without moving an inch.

Fine.

"Great," I chirped, yanking open the drawer and blindly grabbing for the first thing my fingers touched. "Thanks." I waved the thing in his face. Just then realizing what I'd grabbed. I swear both of our eyes widened, just before they clashed together, but I was committed. So I turned for the door, bright blue vibrator in hand.

His low chuckle followed me out into the hallway grating across my overheated skin.

I didn't see Jason the rest of the day, and I didn't go looking for him either. I had no idea what to do with all the information swirling around after my discovery this morning... and after our conversation.

It was also the first night that Jason didn't join us for dinner. So after Hartley and I had eaten, I decided to make myself a cup of tea from the recipe book I had been studying. Clipping a few ingredients from the garden, I settled into bed early with my cup to keep me company, studiously ignoring the toy that now lay hidden in *my* bedside drawer.

I dreamt of Le that night, accented by the sounds of fire crackling and mom's screams.

I screamed back.

The heat of the flames eating away at my skin as I tried to beat my way through the burning walls. I screamed until my throat felt raw, but I couldn't reach her. I couldn't reach either of them, and as that wall fell, I wished it had crushed me. I sobbed into the thick smoke coughing and choking as they hauled me away.

Their arms too tight, as the dark trees swallowed up the last of the burning camp. The cool night air stinging my overheated skin.

Pet.

I was going to be sold as a pet.

Pet.

I could feel the bite of the collar against my throat.

"Pet."

Arms sat me up and I fought. Wishing I'd fought harder screaming and thrashing, the dark air too cold.

"Pet." His voice rang through my mind and I gripped his arms, blinking away tears.

"Look at me." The command shivered up my spine as my body lurched to obey.

"Jason," I croaked. My hands moved to his face tracing the familiar lines in the dark. The raised lines on his cheek. Familiarity returned in pieces, as the images of the dream fragmented.

My vision cleared further as he wiped my eyes dry with warm thumbs.

"It's me. You're safe. You're home."

Home.

And it was like a dam breaking. I sobbed as my body lost its fight all at once. He folded me gently into his arms, brushing hands down my back, and through my hair.

He didn't push.

Didn't speak as I put myself back together. He held me long after my tears had dried, settling me against his chest and pulling the blankets around us both. His shirt was soft, his chest warm, and I fell into a mercifully dreamless sleep.

Chapter Eleven

"Pet, will you come here for a moment?" He met my eyes over a stack of books I'd piled next to my reading nest in his office. It hadn't been my intention to build a wall of pillows and words between us… or maybe it had.

I'd woken before the sun rose that morning alone in my bed, as if nothing had happened. It was both a relief and a disappointment. But no matter which it was, it gave me time to shower. Washing away the residual embarrassment and sticky cheeks, I emerged having tucked the awful memories of my capture safely back in the little box in the back of my mind.

I had crept down the stairs intending to try a new tea recipe, when to my surprise, I discovered I hadn't been the only one who'd risen early. Jason sat at the table, cup in hand and a candle flickering to his left. The light by which, he read the letters in front of him.

It had been Jason's routine to groggily pad into the kitchen near noon, so seeing him dressed and functioning before the sun had even risen, was jarring.

"Good morning," I breathed, keeping my voice low. I knew that if we woke Hartley, he'd be raring to start breakfast and begin the morning tasks regardless of the horrendous hour. Most of which I was happy to put off until the sun had risen.

"Morning," he nodded, casting a quick glance over my face, my pajamas… straight under my skin.

I couldn't quite find the scowl I would have normally served him for so blatantly poking for points of weakness. Embarrassment simmered under my skin, but so did appreciation.

"How are you feeling?"

I steeled my spine as the box in the back of my mind rattled, but remained sealed.

"Fine," I breathed, my voice barely a whisper.

"Do you want to talk about it?" His eyes swept over me again before he lifted his brows, a grin dying in the corner of his lips.

As usual.

"Put the daggers down," he raised hands before him, palms out in surrender. And I legitimately took a peek at my own to ensure a dagger had not materialized there. "It is practically a rule. The question has to be at least asked. Does it not?"

I shook my head and he nodded, pursing his lips.

"Would you like to join me in my study this morning?"

Relief batted back my irritation.

"Yes please," I paused. How long had he been up? "Are you hungry?" I asked, feeling inclined, since our first interactions of the day typically took place over breakfast.

Smirking, he flashed some fang eyeing my neck like a prize.

"Are you offering?" he teased, folding his mail and leaning forward, bracing himself on forearms against the table top. My next breath stalled in my lungs. His features were sharper by candle light, but his eyes ...significantly softer.

Molten.

Playful.

I used the little breath I could catch to shut that down.

"No such luck."

He pursed his lips extinguishing the candle.

There had been additional pillows added to my little nest when I arrived in the study. Not only was my reading nook significantly more plush, but there, stacked against the wall was a small stack of books and a satchel of candy. Jason had also procured some reading recommendations of his own.

I smiled. I couldn't help it. It broke across my face as I dragged the pile closer to inspect their spines. My eyes flitted to Jason who I found wearing that crooked grin he so often hid, his fist tucked under his chin. The self satisfied nod that followed was a curtain falling closed over that beautiful smile, before he tucked back into the documents scattered across his desk.

It was only a moment that passed between us, but it was enough to unleash a fluttering in my chest as I settled into the plush pillows. And that was how we spent those early darkened hours of the morning.

This question, had been the first time he had so much as looked up from the map sprawled across his desk, since. Dog-earring the page and leaving behind a star crossed romance between a witch and her king, I climbed from my nest and crossed the room to him. His hair was tousled. Evidence of just how many times he had dragged his fingers through it as the sun climbed the sky. The morning light, just beginning to warm the brown of his eyes as they held mine.

He held out an arm welcoming me into his space. I was surprised when he tucked me between his legs, positioning me before his desk, so that he could reach around me to smooth the map, highlighting his notations.

I'll admit his closeness was distracting, but the opportunity to drink in the material before me, was something I wouldn't waste. This was something he had paid painstaking attention to since we'd arrived here. It had to be important.

"How familiar are you with this area?" he asks, dragging me from the task at hand.

Intimately. I knew this area like I knew the spacing of the three little gold flecks in his right eye.

I shook the thought free, remembering just how inappropriate it was. How impossible.

"I'm familiar," I allowed.

We had moved from the city to small towns as my mom collected and raised my adopted siblings. Then, from settlements here and there, until we landed in the free camps. I ran my fingers along the raised illustration of mountain peaks. There, tucked along the Blue Ridge mountains, was the free camp we called home for the past two years. I could track the general path the trappers took me when they-

It didn't matter.

I shook my head drawing a sharp breath.

"Why?"

And there was the river I traveled in my attempt to escape them when I first met the vampire behind me. He shifted, my attention recentering, as I cast a look over my shoulder.

"This," he said, pulling a torn page from between the already overstuffed pages of a journal, "is what I'm looking for."

The page, while quite withered and frail, depicted a scene that couldn't be diminished by the passing of time. Witches burned, hands outstretched, mouths agape on silent screams. Some stood at sword point bound in rope, hair, a cloud of smoke, expressions stern, stubborn. While others burned on their knees, wailing at the sky. There in the corner was one unbound witch, her face serene as she kneeled along the others.

I swallowed.

"You're looking for a place to commit unspeakable crimes?"

His chuckle was low, but warmed the places that had grown cold in my chest.

"No," he admonished playfully. "I'm looking for these," he said, his index finger tapping against the little flowers scattered along the far corner of the page.

Flowers?

Flowers ... that in fact, after a moment of inspection, were ones I recognized.

In the free camp there was a woman who I would visit. Her eyesight was going, though she still produced the most beautiful linens. Blankets, rugs, curtains. Mom would send me over with leftover stews and biscuits, and I would sweep up the loose threads and clean the dust that collected around her home, while she told me stories of the free continent. Stories of her younger years, and the man who enthralled her, but who vanished one day, never to return.

Or, that's how she told it.

So she spent her days creating beautiful treasures for those who could afford them, and for those who couldn't.

Where this adorable little crone procured the fabrics and threads she used to create the pieces she sold, she never told me, but I was certain it was him. Their love prevailing even though the continents divided them. And in her window box just below her kitchen window, had grown these flowers.

They always looked withered, weak, though the woman fussed over them every chance she had. Having me drag in the window boxes in the winter, so she could care for them from their perch on her kitchen table. No matter how much love she poured into the damn plant, it always looked forgotten. She'd chuckled, a raspy dry sound, telling me they grew sick the day he left, and had never quite recovered.

Just like her.

"I've seen these," I nod, and had I not turned to him as I did, I may have missed the way his eyes flickered with that same winning glint that had flashed through them when I had recognized the rug under our feet now.

"Where have you seen them?"

"May I?" I asked, indicating towards the pen in his hand.

Though he handed it over without hesitation, his touch lingered as he studied me. Confusion blooming.

"You're certain? These flowers," his fingers tapped the photo for emphasis.

"They were a bit wilted..." I allowed "but, I'm fairly certain, yes."

The impulse to help, to be valuable, panged through me. I liked the way he looked at me like he had truly scored a prize worthy of the title. But realizing that the impulse was there, so incessantly needling me to be something he saw value in, made my skin itch.

I paused, pen in hand. "Can I ask you something first?"

He nodded. "Of course."

"Who else lives in this house?"

For a moment confusion is the only emotion I can read on his face. Then it changes. Understanding dawns and to my surprise is followed by a smile. He nods.

"I was hoping to make the introduction in person, but I suppose, your snooping unearthed less answers then I'd assumed."

"Don't insult my snooping capabilities."

"Oh, of course not."

"If I hadn't been interrupted - nevermind." The image of that drawer flashed in my mind. The direction that conversation had taken last time. "Don't change the topic."

He pulled open the top drawer of his desk, revealing a small framed photo, a dagger, and a little wooden carving. A bird of some sort.

He set the photo on the desk before me. "This is Henry. He is expected home in the next few days."

Henry.

Moss green eyes hid under heavy brows. A little crease between them. Facial hair lines his jaw and a mustache outlines grinning lips. His thick chocolate curls are pushed back from his face little streaks of silver dusting his temples.

Henry was ridiculously good looking.

I swallow, nerves erupting.

"Where is he now?"

"The Royal City?" Just the mention had my stomach churning.

"Is he a royal?" I asked. Henry did have the look of someone who would wear a crown well.

"No. Some time ago he worked as a royal guard. He still travels back every now and again, when needed."

A royal guard? I would be sharing a space with a royal guard. I hoped he didn't share the same sentiments as the royal family. If so, I feared I would get away with far less than I had to date.

"And... you're together?" I leveled my gaze on him intent on catching everything.

"Yes," he nodded. "He's looking forward to meeting you." His expression held.

He knew I was here and he was returning home looking forward to meeting me.

Confusion, disbelief, and a little hurt swirled in an uncomfortable cocktail, souring my stomach.

Anxiety pricked my fingers as I turned back towards the desk not sure if my expression would give me away, but certain the closeness now felt wrong. This confirmation that I had been encroaching on someone else's partner... or maybe I hadn't.

Maybe it hadn't meant anything.

Thoughts swirled angrily around my mind as I pasted on my best 'everything-is-fine' expression.

"Thank you for answering my questions." I stepped away from him bumping into the desk and fluttered my hands at his chest. "Now shew," I say, uncapping the pen and perching in the warm leather chair he evacuated.

"I'll get us some breakfast," he says easily. Like his confirmation hasn't shattered this completely unrealistic dream I'd be harboring. One I hadn't realized had grown so strong, until now. Until I had to face how much it hurt to watch it break.

I pause, my mouth open, about to volunteer, but he's out the door before I can voice any amount of concern for my duties as a pet.

Chapter Twelve

I was unleashing my frustration on some potatoes when Jason joined Hartley and I in the kitchen that evening. Channeling my irritation into chopping the vegetables helped soothe some of the churning guilt and hurt that I knew I needed to tuck away.

And quickly.

This was my new home.

My eyes flashed to Jason for a moment while I scraped the potato pieces into the boiling water. He was speaking with Hartley on the other side of the kitchen, while he flipped some leaks in the pan before him. The movement was casual. Easy. A flick of his wrist. Like he was as comfortable at the stove as he was in front of a canvas.

His competence in the kitchen surprised me. Though, I was begrudgingly realizing nothing about this male should.

I swallowed an annoyed huff, knowing he would hear me, and settled on an eye roll as I returned to my task. As hard as I tried to block out his voice as he discussed details of an upcoming dinner we'd be hosting, it proved impossible.

And then he laughed, and my grip nearly failed as I drained the potatoes.

Across the kitchen, Jason sobered, his hand still flattened against his stomach, rings glinting, tattoos dark against his crisp white sleeves.

Oh I was in so much trouble...

Mashing the potatoes proved even more cathartic. By the time I was finished, my arm was sore, and my irritation had abated. Thankfully, I was using a less murderous approach to dinner preparation, mixing in the butter and cream like one would be expected to, when Hartley made his way over to me from across the kitchen. His pace was leisurely, his smile kind, as he peered over my shoulder.

"Those potatoes look delicious," he complemented. Though, I had the feeling he would have passed along the same sentiment no matter what I produced. It was fairly clear my help wasn't needed in the kitchen, but I think he appreciated the company.

And Hartley's company was top notch.

I thanked him and handed over the bowl of potatoes.

"I'm setting up to make dessert," he said, waving a hand towards the island. "Would you like to lend me a hand?"

"Of course," I replied, dusting my hands on the towel tucked into my apron string. "What can I do?"

He set me up a station where I painted melted butter across sheets of thinly rolled pastry dough. Hartley wasn't one to hover, so he settled across from me expertly chopping pistachios and walnuts.

"So tell me, have you any experience with dinner parties?"

I couldn't tell whether he was joking, but I chuckled nonetheless.

"Not in the real sense." I smiled at the old vampire. "I was lucky enough, long enough, to not have any prior experience as a pet." It wasn't unheard of for pets to be traded from owner to owner, so they may have experience in more than one household, but even that wasn't commonplace. "No offense."

"None taken," he nodded.

"And while my mom used to throw 'dinner parties'" I used my fingers to quote the term in the air between us. "They... they were just for fun."

"I can guarantee you, I would have preferred her's, over the one we are about to host."

He grinned as he scraped the chopped nuts into a pan, and I returned it easily.

"She would have enjoyed you Hartley." I swallowed the truth of those words and the ache that came with the realization that, in another world, one where they may have had a chance to meet on equal footing, they would have truly enjoyed each other.

"Tell me about these parties," he said, beginning to braid the layered pastry dough.

And so I did.

I told him about how she had wanted her children to have a background in little luxuries. She wanted us to be able to blend into a world of higher beings. Should we ever find ourselves in a free world, we would know how to belong. We would be able to climb higher.

So we would sit around the table with our pilfered sweets, or smoked meats, a new seasoning or- anything we could purchase, trade, or steal that she felt we should try. And then we would practice. Eating, drinking, proper manners. All of it.

She'd always toasted, 'To a life worth living'.

Wrestling the sticky dough into submission was a battle I was happy to lend my attention to, as I tucked the memories back into their little box. I had no idea how Hartley was creating braid after perfect braid. My fingers refused to produce anything but a sticky, messy, knot. Frustrated, I pulled the dough free of my fingers just for them to stick together in a web of pastry residue, taunting me and my inability to master it.

"You've probably done this differently back home," Hartley intervened, circling the island and arriving beside me. "But let me show you how Jason likes it."

I barely bit back the sigh of relief as the sweet old vampire stepped in to teach me how to braid the sticky pastry pieces into the proper shapes. His patience was quiet, but so was his pride. After a few successful braids, he nodded satisfied, and moved on to his next task. But I swore I caught him glancing across the kitchen with a smile that mirrored my own.

We continued braiding sugared nuts into buttered pastry a few moments longer, when Jason stalked into the kitchen to pour a cup of coffee.

"Has the post come?" He asked, setting his lips to the rim of his mug.

Hartley indicates towards the far table and I realize, in my attempt to avoid him, I had forgotten to deliver it to his office. Luckily it now provided me the perfect excuse to maintain the space I was working to keep between us. I jog over and hastily grab the stack. Arranging them, I note the same silver lined envelope he seemed to receive on a regular basis, just as something slips from the stack.

I stumble to a halt, the air rushing from my lungs, as my knees weaken.

"Jason."

His name slips from my lips before I can remember why it shouldn't be the first thing I call out in this moment.

Because, there on the floor, sits two photos of me.

One from months prior, of my mother and I washing dishes in the kitchen window of our home in the free camp. Floral printed curtains fluttering in the breeze. The other, here. Again, washing dishes taken through the window in the kitchen facing the wooded area beyond the wall.

I never minded helping Hartley clean up in the evenings, because it reminded me of her.

There I was, in a photo from what had to be only a handful of days ago, gazing unseeing into the darkened trees. But I knew what I had been seeing. I remember watching the lightning bugs dance, and wishing I'd been able to dance around with them. Just knowing they would spin around me in the cool night air, the way she used to twirl me around the kitchen as we sang.

It was what I hadn't seen that night, that had my hands shaking as I wiped them on my apron over and over. I hadn't seen the predator lurking in the darkness. I had lost that sense of awareness of just what I was. And the dangers that still existed. Even here.

I hadn't escaped his reach.

He had been right there.

Scrawled at the bottom of the photo were the words: **I see you girl**.

Jason's there in an instant. He kneels before me scooping up the photos. After a quick glance at them, his expression darkens, before he slips them into his pocket. Slowly, he reaches for me, taking hold of my arms. I think he's trying not to spook me, because he regards me like a cornered animal, his eyes studying my face carefully. I cannot hide the fear there. I cannot fight the way my body shivers. He's found me.

I've drawn him here.

Here to my new home.

To Jason's home.

To Hartleys home.

The sound of Jason's breath punching from his lungs as he stumbled back, blade buried in his gut, sounds in my ears.

I shake my head at him, eyes watering, as I try to step back.

He turns at the waist and I know what he's looking at. That damn window. The one the picture was taken through. I pick up my eyes to follow his line of sight and meet Harley instead. Who's standing in the doorway of the kitchen looking as angry as I've ever seen him before he disappears into the kitchen pulling the window covers closed. He moves around the space pulling curtains closed as my vision blurs.

Jason catches my chin with his knuckle.

"You're safe."

I hear the words. I watch them leave his lips, but I cannot accept them.

I don't deserve them.

I can hear my breath as it rattles from my lungs.

"Pet." His fingers are warm as they brush curls out of my face.

"They watched me." I blinked. "Before that night." The memory of smoke and screams had the tears finally running over my cheeks. "Was it my fault?"

I need someone to tell me that it's not. I need someone to absolve me of this terrible guilt that has locked my chest up so tight

"No." His grip tightened. "There's often no rhyme or reason why a village will be targeted. You could not have drawn trappers like this on your own. They would have already been watching your camp when they found you. Decided who would draw a price." He flinches, closing his eyes for a moment. When he returned them to me they were calm. Certain. "You couldn't have stopped what happened, and you did not cause it."

"But I brought them *here*." My voice wobbled.

He stands, his hand catching my chin taking my gaze with him as he rises.

"I wanted you," he growled. My stomach flutters as his thumb strokes my jaw. "And in my greed, I paid a large sum to ensure you'd be mine." He shook his head, the memories of that night, I'm sure, playing back for both of us. "I worry that I drew his attention, and inspired this mess, because I wasn't willing to risk having someone else walk away with you."

His eyes blaze as they hold mine.

"This is my fault, and I will fix it."

He releases me and turns to Hartley.

"Change of plans," I hear Jason speaking to Harley, but the sounds are so far away that they may as well be in the other room.

I allow myself a glance around the living space. The sun is setting, warm golds and oranges peeking through the curtains Hartley had drawn. Soon the garden will grow dark again. My hands shake as I straighten my clothes. It's a reaction that I can't make sense of, but the feeling of being exposed, seeps under my skin.

Jason takes my hands folding his around the both of mine. And I realize that he's warming them. Stilling them, as he speaks with Hartley.

It's only a moment before he returns his attention to me. And I know that I should take a step back, maintain the distance I'd been working all afternoon to keep, but I can't. Instead, I step into him, setting my forehead to his chest, and wrapping my arms tightly around his waist. It's a relief and comfort when he holds me tightly against him. One hand cupping the back of my head, the other around my back.

He holds me like this a few moments longer, seemingly happy to hold me as long as I need him to, but that realization reminds me why I need to step back. Disentangle myself. Especially now, as I find myself too aware of his body against mine.

I step back, wiping at my cheeks, and with a deep breath, force myself to regain control.

Jason watches me piece myself back together, but surprises me when he scoops me up into his arms, and in a few long strides makes his way to the couch.

He sets me down, tucking me into my favorite spot in the corner, and in this moment, I feel safe and hidden, tucked into the little nook.

"Stay there."

If I had blinked, I wouldn't have thought he'd moved. A second later, he reappears before me, my yellow blanket in one hand and a book in the other, as he drops onto the couch beside me.

"You don't have to cuddle," he teases. "But humor me? I want you close tonight."

I don't waste time pretending his nearness doesn't soothe the panic, but it's the guilt that keeps me from relenting. Henry the *royal guard* will be home soon and I'd like to keep my head.

Instead, I settle my cheek in his lap and close my eyes as he threads his fingers through my hair in soothing strokes. After a few quiet moments he begins reading out loud. His voice is low and calm.

He reads as the house grows dark, Harley adjusting the lighting before retiring for the evening. Jason pays no mind to the passing of time. He seems content acting as my pillow, reading for the both of us as I lose my battle with sleep.

Every time my eyes snap open, he's there, his fingers gently combing my hair, his calm voice pitched low, as he reassures me, "I'm here", and "You're home".

He simply shifts his book, tucking the blanket around me with the other, and settles back in as I drift off to sleep. This time, without the face of that monster lurking in the dark. And after some time, knowing Jason is keeping watch, I fall into a mercifully dreamless sleep.

Chapter Thirteen

Jason left just after breakfast. That mask I'd come to hate, sliding firmly into place as he stood from the table. He straightened the collar of his gun metal grey coat. A whisper of ink on top of his hand made an appearance as he raked ringed fingers through his hair.

The air was tense.

"I want you out of sight tonight."

His words paused the spoon midway to my mouth.

My eyes flickered to his.

"No one will be able to hear you upstairs, so if you'd like to spend the evening in my office you will have full reign."

My snooping senses tingled, and I worked to keep my expression neutral. Though I mustn't have been too convincing... or by this point, he may simply have known better, because his lips twitched. That mask cracked for only a moment, before he turned for the door.

"You will be safe upstairs," he nodded. I think he was aiming to be reassuring, but there was too much tension there, stiffening his shoulders.

"Promise me," he cast a stern look over his shoulder. "That you will stay hidden."

I set my spoon down, oatmeal abandoned in my bowl, and nodded. I could do that. And I could dig through his drawers... maybe without unearthing something like -

In a flash, he was before me, his hands laid flat against the table, as he leaned into my space. "I want your words, Pet," he growled.

My next inhale was sharp.

"I-I promise." I swore, fighting a losing battle with my own spit.

With a satisfied nod, he headed out the door, a promise to return shortly cast over his shoulder.

Hartley and I spent the rest of the morning and afternoon preparing food and decorating the dining space for Jason's dinner guests. By mid afternoon the food was baking and Hartley, satisfied with all we had accomplished, dismissed me from my task of wiping down the counters.

He was still scrubbing dishes.

Something he'd resolutely refused to let me do. I hadn't loved the idea of standing in front of that window, but I wouldn't let Le insert himself into my new life. He wouldn't taint the spaces I was growing comfortable in.

Hartley, however, didn't buy it.

And he didn't budge.

"Go ahead and collect some books to entertain yourself with. Maybe get some fresh air before we lock you up in your ivory tower for the evening," he chuckled.

Admittedly, it was a brilliant idea, and I did just that. I headed upstairs to change and prepare my space for an evening of entertaining myself as silently as possible. I worked as quickly as I could to allow some time in the garden before we put the final touches on dinner and I slipped up the back staircase to hide away for the evening.

"Well hello there," a voice called from the dining room as I bounced down the stairs, my pilfered cook book tucked into the crook of my elbow.

I'd intended to spend some time in the garden, studying the herbs we had growing in the far garden boxes, and just how to use them. I had been filtering through the tea recipes, cataloging my favorites, but I wanted to try out some of the more advanced recipes.

I fumbled on the last step catching myself, somewhat smoothly, on the railing as I pinned Hartley with a curious look.

His eyes widened a fraction, the look severe, as he inclined his head towards the shifter. He bent at the waist extending the decanter towards the male. "Can I refill your-

"Do. Not." He flicked a webbed hand in the air in front of Hartley's face as he barked. "Interrupt me."

I grit my teeth hating him immediately.

"Can you not see I'm speaking to..." he paused, his unabashed perusal of my bare legs made my skin craw. "And who might you be?"

The warning was clear in Hartley's eyes as he rose to his full height and stepped back. What were the rolls we were supposed to play? Jason had only mentioned dinner guests.

My chest rose and fell with irritated breaths as I stepped onto the landing. I got the feeling there was no fleeing back up the stairs now.

"Pet."

"Yes," he cooed as if speaking to a child. "I assumed so, but what is your name?"

I was careful to keep my eyes pinned to the stranger, lest I raise them to Hartley, and include him in whatever the hell this was. I could navigate this myself.

"He calls me Pet," I explained, setting the book down on the little landing table near the banister.

He seemed to pout, a heavy brow with deeply dimpled skin falling over wide set eyes. "What about your given name?" He pushed, tucking webbed fingers under his chin.

"Dahlia," I clipped. It wasn't necessarily a lie. Technically, the market had *given* me that name before auction. Hartley's hands clenched at his sides, before they relaxed a moment later.

"Ahh," he grinned, flashing sharp needle-like teeth. "Now that's a fitting name for such a beautiful prize."

It was an effort to keep my face neutral as he leered. To keep the scowl from getting Hartley and I into trouble. Speaking of- Hartley had dipped silently into the kitchen where I hoped he was summoning Jason.

But now I was truly alone with the shifter.

A cold sweat crept across my back as I stood as still as I could.

"Dahlia," he tested the name again, smiling as if he liked the way it tasted.

"Come here." His voice was sharp, the command clear.

"I think-

"*I* think," he interjected, "you should leave the *thinking* to those more capable, and do what you're told." He smiled, cocking his head at me in challenge. Like he'd enjoy doling out the consequences if I disobeyed.

It only confirmed my assumption about exactly the type of monster that sat before me, when as I complied, some of that savage excitement in his eyes calmed. He had, indeed, been waiting. Whether it was the chase, if I fled, or the punishment that followed, which he truly enjoyed, I was sure I didn't want to find out.

I did as he demanded, and crossed the room towards him. But I didn't lower my gaze. I held his evenly as he watched me move. He sipped from his glass as if enjoying even this little victory over my will. With a small breath, I paused, setting a hand on the chair at the head of the table.

Jason's chair.

He grinned, displaying thin fang-like teeth in clusters of two or three spaced along his black gums. Controlling the shiver that threatened to rake down my spine was a feat, but I kept still.

Unfazed.

"You may call me Geo."

"Geo." I nodded, smiling plainly. Glad he couldn't hear the beating of my heart.

He didn't like that. In the next moment, he'd leaped from his chair, wrapped an arm around my chest, and dragged me down into his lap. I gasped, the change in position, so abrupt, it had my heart pounding out an uneven rhythm that stole my breath away.

"Let go." The words rushed out reflexively and I cursed myself. Clutching the armrests, I tried to right myself, but he held firm the skin of his hands tacky with a residue that enhanced his grip.

"Excuse me?" he sneered, the words barely a whisper as he leaned in over my shoulder.

I knew that I needed to be still, but it was a battle to lock down the urge to wrestle from his grip.

He was an amphibian shifter of some kind. It was evident in his wide set eyes, webbed fingers, and the frill-like gills lining his neck just above his jacket collar. With each agitated breath he drew, they closed with a wet slap. His exhale blew them open again casting salty air against the back of my neck. I knew nothing about who this male was, but he had to be more dangerous then he looked if Hartley's reaction was any indication.

"Such a tasty little thing. But not too much fight in you," he teased drawing his tongue up the length of my neck. If he was trying to draw out a reaction, he wouldn't get one. But allowing him to torment me without repercussion, soured my stomach. Rage painted my vision as his hand curled around my throat, that tacky residue coating my skin.

"We can fix that," he chuckled darkly. "Just need to find the right buttons to press." His grip tightened. "Is it fear?"

His nails bit into my skin.

"Pain?"

My grip tightened on the armrests.

Hartley came around the corner then a decanter in one hand a glass in the other. His eyes were a stormy silver. I knew then, he must have caught at least the tail end of Geo's speech. Embarrassment burned, as he paused, his eyes raking over the vulnerable position the shifter now held me in.

Seeming to forget himself, the decanter shattered in his hand. The thing just evaporated into glass dust as it rained over his neatly polished shoes.

To my surprise, Geo startled under me.

Hartley set the tumbler on the table roughly, sending it toppling over. It rolled along the length of the table, and I caught it, debating on whether or not I could move fast enough to smash it over the shifter's head, when Hartley barked.

"Clean this up."

It was my out, and I moved to stand, but Geo's grip held firm against my throat. His other arm, a band across my midsection.

"You clean up your mess Hartley." He shoved his chair back angling us so that we sat facing Hartley and the kitchen doorway. "We'll watch."

He laughed, his head tipping back as he did. "Or... would you like to watch, Hartley?"

He used the opportunity to slap that fat sticky hand of his down on my thigh, pining it on the other side of his, using his knees to spread mine and making a show of it.

My next few breaths were choppy. The embarrassment, the anger, the lack of control, became a miserable adrenaline-laced cocktail that I knew was going to get me into trouble. Though I wagered his punishment would be worth knowing what it felt like to smash this glass over his head.

"Dahlia and I are just getting to know each other. Isn't that right, Doll?" the edges of my vision began to blacken. With a burst of movement, I tried once more to throw myself out of his grasp. His nails scraped across my throat and I shrieked, but I didn't stop. I kicked at his shin, hoping to buy myself precious seconds to rear back and decorate his skull with crystal shards, but he caught me, that residue coating my skin, impossible to fight. It was like his skin was melded to mine. And it burned as it tore at my throat.

Resisting him meant forfeiting my flesh.

"There's that fight!" he boomed, hardening below me. Fury tipped over the edge and I debated if I could withstand the pain of having my skin torn from my body in order to free myself.

"Just wanted a little taste before our prince has sullied you."

Prince?

The confusion was enough to cool my rage for a moment.

"I know you must have considered it Hartley. Even an old wretch like you can appreciate just how tender human flesh -

"Pet!" His command drew everyone's attention immediately. Geo released me then, and I stumbled to my feet, bolting across the room leaving the glass discarded on the table, and that nightmare in his seat.

He was here.

His large frame filled the entryway, anger rolling off of him in waves. The sight, a relief so potent, it wet my eyes.

I stopped in front of him, nearly running straight into his arms, but instead I swallowed my hurt, and reached to take his bag. He shocked me, however, by pulling me to him without hesitation.

Tipping my chin up.

His gaze studied mine ... then my neck.

I carefully blinked away the moisture that would give me away. With warm fingers, he swept a curl behind my ear, before tucking his hand behind my neck and easing me to him as he inhaled deeply against the top of my head.

"Good girl," he purred, before he swept me behind him. Breath fell from my lips. He was proud I had fought back. His praise and presence dulled the sting behind my eyes and across my skin.

His attention snapped to the shifter lounging at the table as he released a harsh snarl. The sound rolled over my sensitive skin. "Do. Not. *Touch* what's mine."

Geo only shrugged, his smile unapologetic.

"How could I resist?" he taunted.

"I'd encourage you to *try,*" Jason growled. He shucked his coat aside and prowled towards the frog shifter, rolling his sleeves to his elbows. He stood behind the chair at the head of the table.

"Why are you here?" The question was laced with barely leashed fury. His mask gone.

"Is it not the job of the prince to entertain his constituents' concerns?"

There it was again.

"You're early."

"Just in time for a little appetizer." He had the gall to peer around Jason and sneer at me as he spoke. I knew he was taunting Jason. Stirring up a reaction.

And a reaction he got.

Jason's fist met the table with an awful splintering noise. The thing held strong when it sounded like it should have shattered. A table built for vampires, perhaps?

The tips of Jason's fingers blackened, nails sharpening to talons, as he tapped his forefinger against the smooth wood.

That shut Geo up. The frog shifter seemed to swallow his response. Those gills stilling as he held his breath.

Tension coated the room.

"Pet."

His voice was calm, low, but I startled nonetheless before I drew my back straight. "Kitchen."

I didn't need to be told twice. Not when this was my excuse to leave.

I slipped into the kitchen to help Hartley, leaving the males to their measuring sticks in the dining room. We worked in silence each taking up our usual tasks, which I was grateful for. Because it was in those quiet moments, that I was able to wipe away the few tears that fell loose as I tried to regain my composure.

After the meal was nearly prepared, I hung my apron and turned to find Hartley holding a plate he'd prepared for me.

"Never forfeit your name," he said, setting the plate gently into my hands. "Not until they earn it."

I smiled, though it was watery. "I didn't."

Names were special to humans who were lucky enough to be born free. Even those who weren't were often given names by the humans who raised them. Our way to protect a small piece of ourselves. To keep something, when so much was forced from our control.

"Good." The poor vampire looked his age for a moment before his mood recovered. "Good."

He looked as if he was going to pat my hand but thought better of it. So instead, I tucked myself into his side for a hug.

"The same goes for Jason. I love that boy like a son, but you make him earn it. Yes?"

I pulled away with a nod.

With that, he seemed satisfied, and I slipped up the back staircase to Jason's office. But as I passed my door moving towards the end of the hall, I decided to detour. I dipped into my room to shower, scrubbing myself clean, twice over, before I felt like myself again. I changed into night shorts and a sweater, before stepping into the fur lined slippers Jason had purchased for me that first night, and making my way down the hall to the study.

I tucked myself into the plush pillows piled by the window, snuggling up under my warm blanket intending to work on a little project. And I did. I spent some time sketching out a rough map of the free camp for Jason. I had zero experience in what a good map should look like, let alone drawing one to scale. So after studying the big map stretched across Jason's desk, I got to work sketching a few drafts in a notebook I stole off his shelf. That is, until the door creaked open about an hour later, just as the sky had grown dark. At first, I sat up thinking Jason had come to check on me, but quickly recognized the figure stuffing its way through the door.

Geo.

In that moment, as I tucked myself deeper into the pillows, not daring to move further, I was eternally grateful I had fought my nosier tendencies and aired on the side of laziness, deciding to draft a map from my little nest before I got to snooping. He would have undoubtedly caught me. And worse, I would have been alone with him.

I suppose I still was. But only one of us knew that, and I intended to keep it that way.

I shivered as I watched him beeline for the large desk in the center of the room. He opened drawer after drawer before pausing to examine something in the low light. It was small and I couldn't make out what it was until he slipped it onto his fat finger and lit the wax candle. He chuckled to himself as he dripped the red wax onto the envelope he pulled from his breast pocket and sealed it with the ring. I hoped he was too distracted by his traitorous little task, to hear my heart beating free from my ribs as I hid amongst the pillows. It felt so loud, I swore a human could have heard it from across the room.

He extinguished the candle casting the room back into darkness and I fought back the pounding in my ears as I drew in a small breath through my teeth.

Silent.

I had to be silent.

He placed the ring back where it belonged, before slipping the envelope and its contents, into his breast pocket and waddling from the room.

I'd seen first hand how quickly he moved. That stride was a mask of his own.

I counted slowly in my head, waiting to ensure he wouldn't return, before I leapt from my hiding spot and pulled open the very same drawer. His hands had been covered in residue. I knew that ring would be too. It wasn't as tacky as I had expected, but it smelled like him.

Salt and algae.

So I grabbed the ring, and took off for the back stairwell. It wasn't until I reached the kitchen that I realized the house was now filled with guests. But I needed to reach Jason. I had no idea what the implications of what I'd witnessed would be, or if Geo would stick around long enough for me to tattle. So without putting too much thought into how much trouble I'd be in, I slung on my apron, slipped the ring inside its pocket, and grabbed a decanter from the counter, before tucking around the entryway into the dining room.

Jason's eyes were on me immediately, and they were furious. I almost thought better of my plan, until I saw Geo chuckling with a thin woman who smiled at him the way one smiles at the gallows.

His fat, sticky, hand sat too low on her waist.

The residue clung to her skirt, as he turned to watch me pass with a smirk.

Jason braced his forearms on the table before him as he glared at me. The look was enough to clear his end of the table. The two shifters abandon their conversation, sensing the rage rolling off their prince in waves. Rage he aimed directly at me.

I swallowed, but continued across the room until I was leaning over his place setting.

I had a monster to kill.

Or... at least, make his night significantly more shitty.

"I have to talk to you right away," I whispered as I leaned in to fill his glass.

His eyes cooled as they moved around the room before he nodded moving to stand.

"No." I breathed, setting the decanter down and shifting a few pieces of silverware. "You cannot let Geo leave."

He stilled.

I was beginning to realize this was as close to watching the vampire startle as I'd ever get. His eyes flitted to mine. Then he sat back in his chair calling over another male.

"Yanik."

The man nodded in greeting. Then surprised me, when he offered me the same gesture. Though his eyes tightened as they dipped to examine the skin of my neck. I'd done my best to clean the four angry lines that coiled around my throat, but not expecting to find myself amongst company, had done nothing to hide them. I couldn't blame the male. I knew it would have caught my eye if roles were reversed. But that knowledge didn't keep the wound from heating under his scrutiny. He sat in the chair to Jason's left, his gaze returning to the vampire behind me.

"We're going to have a conversation that I'm not going to hear for a few moments."

"Understood," the man grinned before launching into a colorful retelling of what I assumed was shifter lore... or gruesome gossip.

Either way, it made for good cover.

"What is it?" he looked as if he wanted me to sit to his right, but this wasn't a conversation I could have at such a volume. And leaning in to whisper in his ear felt a bit too obvious, so I stunned us both, when on an impulse, I dropped into his lap. He tucked me under his arm, where I found that if I tipped my chin just so, I could set my cheek to his throat and whisper against his skin. To onlookers, of which we had a few, I hoped it appeared casual. As if this was how we settled together at night to read and enjoy each other's closeness. I knew that if Jason could hear my heartbeat then he could hear my words, but I hoped the other shifters in this room didn't have the kind of talents the male under me did.

After I've told Jason everything I saw, I slip the ring from the apron pocket and set it in his hand under the table.

"You did very well, Pet." It wasn't until I felt him relax below me, that I realized how tense he had grown as I spoke. "Play along a while longer, and I will get you out of here."

The muscles of his thighs roll underneath me as he shifts. He sets my back against his chest, his arm maintaining its gentle weight across my waist, while the other hand settled on my knee. Like this, we both faced the plate Hartley set before us, his gaze locking onto Jason's for a loaded moment. He returned his attention to Yanik thanking him and the male rose to leave, but Jason put out a hand and the vampire sat.

"Tell me, how is your sire? I heard he's traveling the continent."

He keeps me seated against him as he listens politely to Yanik. My thoughts however, are anything but polite. As he eats, his fingers play with the hem of my shorts. Knuckles brushing up my thigh, and back down to my knee.

He feeds me bites off of his plate and I let him... because here in front of a crowd, I recognize my lack of options and selfishly I enjoy his closeness.

The easy affection.

His rumbling laugh echoes through my body, his hold on me tightening, as he tips his head back. And again, when he leans forward resting his chin on my shoulder.

He is so animated, yet it doesn't feel quite honest. Another version of that bored mask. One designed for a different intent. He emanates this energy of ease and comfort. A prince amongst his people. And still his hand tracks my thigh. Simple. Like he's touched me this way a thousand times.

I barely hear the males as they speak, my entire consciousness focused on the track of his hand up and down my thigh. The gentle scrape of his skin.

What it would feel like if he drew his knuckles just higher. The heady mix of his warm hands and the cold bite of his silver rings.

Suddenly the opportunity to return to my room alone seemed appealing for a whole different reason.

"Well, doesn't this look comfortable." Geo appears at my side and I startle, truly feeling caught. Jason's arm tightens around me as he openly bares his teeth at the male. Geo has the good sense to step back a fraction as he pales a sickly green shade, not expecting the reaction from Jason who seemed to maintain his mask in most social settings, but I knew what got under the skin of a male like this.

"Very," I hummed donning a mask of my own. I felt untouchable here in the safety of Jason's arms.

Geo shifted as did Jason.

"I'm surprised to see you," he blustered, eyes narrowing cruelly. "I figured this time of night you'd be leashed to his bed. You've heard the rumors I'm sure." He grinned at the male below me.

I had not, in fact, heard the rumors, but I knew Jason had no interest, past appearances.

I smiled and made sure it was a sharp thing, but didn't respond. It was Jason who said, "Jealousy doesn't suit you Geo."

The shifter fumbled on a cruel laugh.

Jason's back straightened.

"Have a seat. In fact-" he raised his voice inviting the attention of the others in the room. "Everyone join us. I have some news."

Three shifters and a vampire take their seats around the long table.

"Leave us, Pet." His breath coasts across the shell of my ear and I shiver. But as I untangle myself, climbing off of his lap, his fingers finally brush just high enough to feel the evidence of the path my mind had taken. I scurry out of his reach as his hands tighten. It's only an instant. An instant, where I think he may pull me back against him, before he releases me.

I adjust my apron and round the table behind his chair unable to meet his eyes. Eyes I can feel tracking me as I move to duck into the kitchen.

"Dahlia," Geo's voice scrapes against my nerves as I root in place. "Fill my cup won't you Doll?" he sneers, his voice syrupy.

The last thing I want is to be any closer to that male than necessary, but I school my expression, pick up the decanter, and do as I am told, one last time.

One last time.

I know it's a power play, but I also know I still have appearances to keep. I fill his cup carefully.

His hand twitches and I gasp, catching the attention of the vampire beside him. He will not touch me again. I will spear his fat froggy hand with that fork if he does. Appearances be damned. My hands shake, but his glass is full, so I pick my eyes up meeting his with a quiet glare. If only looks alone could poison a glass.

Feeling like in a small way I had held my own against the male, I turned intending to make my escape, when I caught Jason watching me. His dark eyes burning like coals, gaze heavy, and those fingers resting against his lips. I watch him inhale and I'm sure I've been set on fire. Drawn to him like a moth to flame, I move back to his side of the table reaching to fill his glass as well. The physical need to be near him, to bask in the glow of that look a few more seconds, truly undeniable.

He watches me fill his glass and I watch those fingers fall from where he rested them. He's speaking to his guests. I know he does because I can see his lips moving, but the blood rushing in my ears drowns out the words.

But out of the corner of my eye I see Geo extend his hand. It's too quick a movement to comprehend. Too little time to make a conscious decision, but instinct has me hurling myself across Jason's chest and into his lap.

And it's just in time to catch the little iron blade right in the back.

Chapter Fourteen

All hell breaks loose.

Jason roars, swinging us both out of the chair and flipping the table onto its side. Dishes and food go clattering to the floor.

Hartley is there in an instant swiping at the shifter with surprising strength. I hadn't given the old vampire enough credit.

Pain lances down my back as Jason deposits me on the ground behind the toppled table.

"Don't move."

Rage consumes the softer edges of those umber eyes as they rake over me. He then wretches the leg from the table and disappears in a blur.

Apparently, the table is, in fact, *not* vampire proof.

I wait all of three seconds before disregarding his instructions completely. I'm in a room full of vampires and shifters and I'm bleeding heavily down my arm and back. I was either a target, or a distraction. At worst, I was both. And I'd never forgive myself if that frog fuck hurt Jason or Hartley because of me. Because of their nature.

So, I used the cover of the table to crawl into the kitchen and then bolted for the back door. Once in the garden, I made my way around the stone wall and tucked myself into the bushes.

The space was dark. In my rush to escape, I had put myself directly in the path of whoever had taken that photo. Over my left shoulder sat the kitchen window and before me a night-soaked tree line.

I curled into myself. Right now, the threat was inside. The shattering dishes and shouts emanating from the house, was evidence enough. I could hide here in the darkened bushes.

Hiding from chaos inside was one thing, but hiding from the pain was another story.

I closed my eyes tightly against the burning under my skin. The warm trail of blood I could feel down my back. The unnerving numbness in my hands. I wrapped my good arm around my knees, and curled tighter into myself, trying to control the tremors that flitted down my body, and failing miserably.

Sweat beaded on my brow as I set my forehead against my knee, but as my pants turned to keening, I cupped a hand over my mouth in an effort to remain hidden. The movement sent a bright stab of pain down my back, and in turn, a fresh wave of tremors.

"Pet!" It was Jason's voice that broke through the haze.

And it was in that moment that I realized, I wished he'd been able to call out to me by name. I wanted to hear him say my name. I wanted him to know it.

He appeared before me then, collecting me gently into his arms as he stood.

"I've got you."

The realization that I trusted him... that my feelings went deeper than trust, if I cared to acknowledge them, dulled some of the pain as I sunk into his arms with a sob.

He carried me though the garden and back into the house, but ducked his head low, shifting me away from the far wall of the dining room.

"Don't look," he said, voice gentle against my skin.

I did and a gasp fell from my lips without my permission. There, pinned to the wall, was Geo. That table leg speared through his chest, his head lolled to the side.

Jason groaned. "Do you do anything you're told?"

"Not usually. No." I would have smiled, but I was too focused on the way he hung from the wall ... just within reach. "Put me down."

He did no such thing, but he did pause his track through the room.

"What?

"Put me down." I met his gaze trying my best to keep mine steady. "Please."

I knew he could hear the way my heart beat against my ribs, but the pain made me irrational, and the more I thought about the way he had touched me - the way he had looked at me, the more emboldened I became.

I wriggled in his arms, hissing at the way my shoulder protested and he caved, setting me down cautiously. His gaze clung to my neck as I bent to pick up a fork that lay on the ground. I weighed it in my palm as I took the few steps to where he dangled limply against the plaster, and slammed the fork into his eye.

Hartley coughed behind me as I pulled it free. The gooey eye coming with it, before jamming it into the other.

It was worth the pain that now splintered through my back and arm.

Jason's lips quirked. "Feel better?"

"A little."

Chapter Fifteen

He sat me on the counter and I caught sight of the knife in my back for the first time. The handle jutted out from the space between my spine and right shoulder. Seeing it made me sway, the world tipping.

My vision blackened at the edges.

"I've got you," he assured. The first time those words left his lips, I knew they were meant for me, but when they echoed a bit breathlessly again, I worried he was also reassuring himself. Setting the medical kit on the counter, he wrapped a hand around my arm, stilling me. The other he used to turn my gaze from the mirror and back to his.

"It burns," I exhale roughly, breaking under the pain. Finally acknowledging it allowed me to release the breath I'd been holding, but it also opened the floodgates holding back the pain.

"I know. The adrenaline is wearing off. I'm going to do my best to work quickly."

The last time we'd found ourselves in a shitty situation, he had asked me if I trusted him, and I had told him no. This time, I did. And it felt important that he knew it.

"Jason."

The stubborn vampire continues to dig through the kit on the counter with one hand. The other still wrapped around my arm, his thumb drawing long soothing strokes across my skin.

"I know. I'm sorry," he breathes a frustrated sigh, his eyes narrowing on the contents he is shuffling around.

I took a shallow breath that splintered my shoulder. It had to have. The pain flared as I reached out, placing my hand on his forearm.

"Jason."

His eyes flickered to me, his hands stilling.

"I trust you."

I watched shock physically roll through his body.

His face.

His eyes.

Suddenly, his hands had abandoned the kit and found their way back to me. One cupping my neck while the other settled on my thigh as I winced, the pain biting sharply.

He was quiet, but I didn't need his words. For once his face hid nothing. Those eyes were raw as they flickered down my body.

His thumb tracked my jaw.

"I've got you." His words a vow, his grip tightening as I nodded. It had to be now.

"My name-" I took another shallow breath battling back the waves of pain and let myself fall into those churning umber eyes. Just this once. Just this once. I'd let myself feel what I did for the male before me, without guilt, as I offered him this piece of me. There was no one left in this world living who knew my name. I carried it alone. Held it heavy in my heart. The most significant piece of me I could offer. The only thing I had left, given to me by my family.

And now he would have it.

He would know me.

His eyes widened as they held mine.

"My name is Amelia."

He blinked his eyes flitting across my face like he was meeting me for the first time. When they returned to me, the look he wore was so intense, it nailed me in place... but why did it look so much like devastation?

"Amelia," he echoed.

His breath shuddered, his head bowing over mine as if he'd set his forehead against my own. But his eyes snapped open determination burning brightly, before he pulled back, his gaze settling on my shoulder in the mirror.

Those points of contact-his hands on my skin, that had tethered me to him, rooted me in place, and kept the pain at bay, vanished, and I found myself back on his counter, my body shivering as a fresh stream of blood leaked from the wound.

His fingers collected the material of my sweater tearing it away from where the blade sat. It hung heavy, the blood soaked material flopping down my shoulders as it fell away.

Determination swirled in those eyes as they met mine one last time before he shifted and dumped the contents of the medical kit on the counter.

"Jason!" A voice boomed from downstairs.

The male appeared in the doorway, hand gripping the frame, his chest heaving as he took in the two of us. His eyes roved over Jason, calming a fraction when he found him unharmed. I should've been insulted by the relief on his face, when he realized the trail of blood he'd been following was leaking from me.

"Look who you found." He smiled, but it was short lived. He let it fall as he dropped his hold on the doorframe, and stepped into the ensuite bathroom.

Henry.

He stood a few inches taller than Jason. The vampire was a mountain made male. His broad shoulders were capped in leather armor that fell to his elbow. A long strap of the same leather material was wrapped from his forearms down to his knuckles. One he quickly unraveled as he eyed the blade in my back with a steady gaze that came with experience.

Discarding them on the floor, he reached behind himself to pull free a sheath of daggers, the silver dotting his broad chest. The weapons landed in a heap on the ground followed by the long sword that hung from his hip which he set against the wall.

Jason groans, "I need an extra set of hands".

"You need more than an extra set of hands. I don't know what you're expecting to do with that." He motioned at the kit on the counter.

Jason growls sharply. The sound so animal, it started me, but Henry simply shoulders his way around him without so much as acknowledging the snarl that had just ripped out of his partner.

Now unarmed, he quickly washes his hands before stepping up before me.

"May I?" he asks indicating towards my back I think.

I sway in response.

Pain and what, at this point, must be significant blood loss, has my thoughts twisting. I watch Henry, taking his face in, piece by handsome piece, as he moves in slow motion gripping my knees and shifting me so that he can fit himself just behind me. His green eyes were warm that dusting of silver at his temples complementing the warmer chestnut hair he wears knotted on the back of his head.

Prodding gently around the blade lodged in my back, Henry makes conversation. "You didn't tell me you'd be redecorating while I was gone. The new art in the dining room is sure to raise some eyebrows."

I snort appreciating his twisted humor, but the resulting flash of pain is brutal punishment for my misstep.

Jason, who had shifted to stand in front of me, remains silent as I take a choppy breath trying to recover myself. I clutch at his shirt letting my forehead fall to his chest.

"Please" I groan. "Just get it out."

Jason's hand strokes the back of my head, but Henry's response isn't aimed at me.

"This isn't soft tissue." He speaks over my shoulder to Jason. "There could be bone shards, and muscle damage... internal wounds. We can't just stitch this up. And as soon as I pull that blade out-"

My vision was continuing to darken. The pain lanced down my arm and back up in quick whips that seemed to match my slowing pulse. Suddenly, the panic in Jason's expression made sense. It was worse than I thought, but I couldn't bring myself to regret it entirely. That blade would have struck him in the chest. And it was iron. Geo had intended on killing Jason.

With a sinking feeling I realized I may have been the catalyst; the cause of this attempt on Jason's life. Geo died assuming he'd gotten away with his devious little task, so why in that moment had he -

"Ah!" I jolted hissing at the vampire as he shifted the blade in my shoulder. The pain ripped the thought straight from my head. A fresh rush of blood trailed down my back and I shivered.

I was going to be sick.

No.

I was going to pass out.

Tension in the room mounted as Jason held me tighter, his thumbs never ceasing their soothing strokes. Realization settling between us.

"It was my fault," I huffed.

"It wasn't," he snapped harshly. "And it's not your job to protect me."

Slowly, I pick my head up to glare at him.

His eyes sparked with that familiar glint of malice as they held mine.

This time, the hurt that echoed across my chest had nothing to do with the blade in my back.

"He threw a blade at your chest." Disbelief cleared my head, if only a bit.

It was Henry who chimed in over my shoulder with a coughed, "Excuse me?"

"It was iron," I fumed, ignoring him.

Jason's body jumped under my touch. "You only know that now!"

"Yes," My eyes water and I summon all the volume I have left. "Now that it's in my back and not your fucking heart!"

A violent snarl ripped from Henry silencing the both of us. Jason glared at me and I tried- I really tried to hold my own, but my vision swam, and the room spun.

Jason's attention snapped over my shoulder to where Henry set his hand to my back, the other gripping the blade.

"She won't have the option to do it again if we don't stop the bleeding right now. If you weren't arguing so incessantly," he aimed at me, "I'd worry this punctured a lung."

"I'm done arguing," I breathed letting Jason support my weight entirely. "Ungrateful asshole." The little tremors were becoming more evident.

"Jason," Henry growled. "It's now or never."

Seeing my hands shake where I held Jason's shirt made me angry... angry and scared. I couldn't still them. I felt less in control of my body then I could ever remember. The pain was lapping at my mind. Twisting the room, and garbling their voices.

My heart beat in my ears. Heavy and uneven.

"She's not replaceable."

Thud, thud, thud.

"Henry," he bit out his name, a growl simmering.

"You can't."

Thud...Thud, thud.

"I can."

Thud.

"I can do it. Let me."

I woke sometime later curled into a warm chest. A thick thigh was tucked between my own. My mind buzzed happily. Warm tingles traveled up and down my back, as I snuggled into the heavy blankets, kept in place by an even heavier, muscled, arm.

A breath away from letting sleep claim me once again, I paused, taking another deep breath. But this one had my body reacting in a way that was uncomfortably out of my control. My leg, which was slung over his hip, curled at the knee, tucking my body more firmly against his. And as much as I would have jumped at the opportunity to curl myself around Jason like this a few days ago, a cold unease vied for attention at the back of my mind. I'd spent most of my days watching Jason, and I'd have believed I was fairly aware of his body, his scent- and this ... lacked that familiarity.

I pulled away slowly, disentangling myself from the male in my bed and found myself... not in my bed.

I was, in fact, in Jason's bed.

With Henry.

I only got as far as standing on wobbly legs, beside the bed, before his scratchy voice reached me.

"Stop. Sit."

My body responded immediately. Doing exactly as I was told, was not something I was used to, and my mind itched uncomfortably as I tried to rebel. But my body did not move.

I heard Henry rise from the bed at the same moment I caught him circling around the room to face me.

He wore sweats that now hung low on his hips and a soft cotton shirt that clung to his broad shoulders. How it was possible, I had no idea, but he was in fact built wider than Jason. His chestnut hair was a mess, moss green eyes still clouded with sleep.

"You're safe," his gravelly voice reverberated up my spine. "No need to sneak out. What do you remember?"

My response died on my tongue as the memories, I thought missing, pulled to the forefront of my mind. My mouth closed with the click of my teeth as the events of the night slid into place one by one.

I remembered being held by Jason as Henry removed the blade. I remember screaming until my vision went dark, collapsing into him with tired sobs. The pain was so bright it brought me back, when I'd only wanted it to pull me under. Henry had taken me from Jason then, supporting my weight as he bit into his wrist, and held the broken skin under my nose.

A cool cloth pressed to my shoulder. Jason's warm hand settled against my back, steadying me.

"Drink." The command coasted across my skin and I obeyed. Taking pulls that grew stronger with each swallow.

"Good girl." His hand slid down my back, his praise starting a fire in the pit of my stomach. But it was as I fought off my inappropriate reaction, that he dragged his tongue up my shoulder and my eyes fell closed on a shuddering breath. The world tilted on its axis.

"My blood will repair the wound and any internal repercussions," Henry said, voice steady, meaning simple. "Jason's venom will clean the wound as you're healing." His eyes rose over my shoulder, his voice sharp. "As long as he controls his greed."

A snarl ripped through the room sending shivers racing through me. Jason's arm wrapped around my waist, dragging me infinitesimally closer. Removing the space that had barely existed between our bodies. Until Henry's hand flashed over me reaching for Jason in a lightning fast movement. Both males froze something passing between them.

His eyes dropped to mine, his face still severe. "It will go no farther than this," he swore. "Understand?"

I tried to focus.

I did.

But with both sets of warm hands holding me, Henry's blood like a drug pulling me to the edge of unconsciousness, and Jason's tongue lapping at my skin in a torturous rhythm, I could barely breathe.

He dipped his chin to catch my gaze where it had fallen.

"Answer me."

I nodded and so did he, satisfied with my agreeance. But it wasn't until later that I grasped what he really meant. Later, when my body became a living flame. Need burning me alive and every touch of Henry's hands, light as they were, worked me to a crest just out of reach.

My mind could only focus on him. And those delicious tingles that rose under my skin trying to reach through me and touch him back. I'd clung to him, until he surrendered climbing into the bed with me and trapping me under his heavy thigh. He had simply chuckled as I protested and closed his eyes, relaxing into the bed with a familiarity that landed with a pang as sleep claimed me.

My cheeks burnt with embarrassment as I lifted my eyes to his. He leant me a crooked smile, one eyebrow quirking in question.

"I remember." I grumbled, fingers knotting in the soft duvet.

He nodded and had the good sense to bite back that smile he was wearing. "Good."

The mirth in his eyes burned away that pleasant tingly feeling as mortification consumed me where I sat.

I rolled my shoulder, waiting to gauge the pain, and Henry tipped his head to the side, seeming to wait for my reaction.

Nothing.

I repeated the motion. This time with less restraint.

Nothing.

I felt like I'd just had the sleep of my life. My body felt stiff, a bit weak, sure. But uninjured. Even the skin on my neck felt cool and smooth as my hand flashed up to cup it.

No ridges. Not a scrape to be found. I reached back, stretching fingertips up to trace a thin raised line across my skin. No pain. Just a scar. As if the wound was months old, instead of hours.

Reading the confusion on my face, he supplied the answer I was searching for.

"It was healed before your head touched the pillow."

Nothing left of that evening besides this insistent itch to do exactly as I was told, and climb the vampire before me like the giant tree he was.

I shook my head determined to remove that thought immediately.

"How?"

His brow dropped. "You said you remembered."

"I- I do, but... I don't understand."

"Vampire blood." He tapped his wrist. "I apologize for the abnormal introduction, but it was the only way to ensure you'd safely recover from your injuries. And Jason is a royal. By law, he cannot sire, so you're stuck with me."

"Sire?" My heart took off at a gallop. "Like creating new vampires? Is -"

"You're not a vampire. You healed well. Rest assured, I have no intentions of completing the process, and turning you. You'll just be ... very obedient," he smirked. "For the next few hours, until my blood works it's way out of your system."

I hate this.

I scowled deeply and he chuckled.

"Don't worry, I'll be a perfect gentleman," he said. "Blood-drugged women aren't my thing."

And like a gentleman would, he offered me his hand as I moved to stand.

Apparently unable to decline the opportunity to touch him any longer, I slipped my hand in his and we both reacted. Though not nearly to the same degree.

His grin faltered while I choked on the groan climbing my throat as that pleasant tingle erupted under my skin. It raced up my back and down my arm pooling in my fingers as I wrapped them around his calloused palm.

My cheeks flamed as he pulled me to my feet. And as soon as I was standing, I wretched my hand from his.

"Silver lining," he smiled, but it was too controlled to be honest. "Sire bonds may be a bitch, but it keeps the forced proximity entertaining."

My eyes leapt to his. "Why?" I wheezed.

The embarrassment was going to sear me alive.

"It's a physical bond," he explained. "So whatever you feel, I feel. Vampires can't procreate in the natural way since the witch's magic died out, so the sire bond is intended to replace that familial bond. It only heightens existing emotions until the process is complete."

I studied him a moment before forcing my gaze away.

That couldn't be right. "I didn't feel like this before the bond" I groused.

His only response was to lift his brow and smirk.

"I barely know you!"

He shrugged and chuckled.

Cocky asshole.

I felt much steadier on my feet now. The frustration burned away some of the *appreciation* for the male before me. And understanding what was happening in my mind, allowed me to think more clearly. I still felt out of control... but in a way I could wrap my head around.

"Now," Henry said, stuffing his hands firmly into his pockets. "Let's clean you up and go have some fun at Jason's expense."

Chapter Sixteen

I took my time showering and changing into fresh clothes, and was half way down the stairwell, when the pull became unbearable. That damn itch was the reason I had sped through what would have been a wonderfully, roasting-hot, shower. But the need to be near him wasn't something I could wash away, so when I was as clean as I could be, I shut off the water and chucked on clean clothes, worried that if I wasted more time I'd find myself dragged unwittingly down the hallway in nothing but my towel.

With each moment that passed, that itch intensified. I swore I knew exactly where in the house I'd find Henry. This thing was like a homing beacon.

I gripped the banister, pausing to keep from throwing myself down to the landing below, when Henry appeared.

He offered me his hand, then after a quick assessment of my expression, seemed to think better of it, and tucked it back into his pocket.

"The less you fight it the faster it passes," he offered. The male seemed honest, but it didn't stop me from grinding my molars together and narrowing my eyes in warning.

Fat chance.

I released a choppy breath and took the last step delivering me onto the landing without recalling making it down the last half of the staircase.

My eyes drank him in greedily. He must have also showered. Wet hair flopped here and there along the top of his head. I wanted to run my hands through it. It looked so full and soft. And now seeing it hang loose as it dusted the tops of his shoulders. Shoulders wrapped in another worn cotton shirt, this one green like his eyes, and slightly damp in places across his chest... as if, he too, hadn't taken the time to dry off before hunting me down.

The idea of Henry hunting me was far too appealing then was safe to entertain. So with that thought whipping through my body like a live wire, I tightened my grip on the banister, and glared at the gorgeous male who was reaping havoc on my mental state.

"Where's Jason?" The words were edged with panic that I think Henry misunderstood, but I was too scared of what I would allow out of my mouth if I gave my unhinged mind too much freedom.

Henry's eyes bounced to the far wall and back.

"Just taking out the trash. He'll be back." It drew my attention to said wall. A wall that no longer housed the speared frog shifter. Now that I was able to look away from Henry's stupidly attractive face, it became clear that the vampires had been busy. Overnight they'd returned the house to its near perfect state. The only thing missing was the dining room table.

I padded into the kitchen and grabbed what looked to be freshly cooked eggs, spinach, steak, and buttered toast.

Hartley had saved me breakfast. And a hardy one at that. The plate was piled high with steaming food.

I heard Henry drop onto the couch. Or more like, I heard the couch protest under his weight.

"Food also helps," Henry called from his seat.

Food I was willing to accept.

I dug in, taking eager bites as I made my way back to the couch. I piled in bite after bite like I could fill the clawing emptiness with steak and eggs. And while it was undeniably delicious, it didn't entirely quell the itch under my skin.

It also lacked the Hartley flair I'd come to love, and thoroughly appreciate. It was simple, purposely iron rich... suspiciously masculine.

"Did you make this?" I asked around the mouthful of buttered toast I was attempting to swallow whole.

"Don't worry, I can keep you fed until Hartley returns." He called over his shoulder.

I rounded the couch slowly, plate half empty.

"Thank you."

Mistakenly, I thought the food was calming the cloying itch inside my brain, but it was then that I realized the closer I got to Henry, where he lounged on the couch, the more relief I felt. I huffed, annoyed at this discovery, before I found the giant male in my seat.

I grinned and it was a smug, defiant thing.

We were about to find out exactly how tolerant my new owner was. If he wanted me to lean into this bond, then selfishly, I would, but I intended to make it as irritating for him, as it was for me. The faster I recovered, the faster I was freed from this tether.

So be it.

His eyes tracked me around the couch and the urge to be petty battled the common sense rattling the bars of the cage it was currently locked behind. Logic was not in control as I stepped up onto the couch cushion plate in hand and walked my way over the male where he lounged.

He sat back allowing me to step over his hips as he studied me with a grin that wobbled my stomach. I smiled back as sweetly as I could before lowering myself between him and the comfy corner cushion. My lips curl, triumph bleeding into my expression, tainting it, and giving me away just as I plant my feet on the outside of his thigh, my now healthy back tucked against the back of the couch and shoved. His brows rise slowly, disbelief etched across every feature.

"You're in my spot."

For an instant both of us hold our ground. He doesn't move, because, of course he doesn't, as I shove at him wiggling myself into the crook of the couch. His eyes flit to my ankle before returning to my face, and for a moment I hold my breath wondering whether he's going to grip me by said ankle, and launch me into the far wall.

Finally, he breaks, tipping his head back on a howling laugh.

My grip tightens on my plate as that laugh shatters my resolve. It's warm and honest, and I find myself wanting to lay myself across his chest so I can feel it rumbling across my skin.

I'm so fucked.

He shifts down one seat before reaching over to grab my blanket from the back of the couch and lobbing it at my head.

For reasons unclear, he moves at a speed I can easily track, allowing me to snag the blanket before it drapes over my face.

I clear my plate and barely have a chance to eye the table, wondering if I'll be forfeiting my newly won spot on the couch, if I was to move to set it down, when Henry is on his feet. He holds a hand out.

"I can do it."

"I'm aware." He picks up a brow, extending his fingers impatiently. "But I'm offering. You look comfortable."

"Let me guess." I say handing him my plate. "Napping also helps this thing cool off faster?"

I hear him set the plate in the sink with a clatter of silverware.

"You don't want to know what it is that will actually soothe a chafing sire bond." He rounds the couch dropping into it a few seats away. He's not quite at the other end of the couch, but he is clearly giving me my space.

"But now that your hands are fork free, I suppose the danger has lessened, *if* I was to tell you." His eyes flickered to the wall and back to me. My heavy eyelids must be playing tricks on me because I swear they shine with a bit of appreciation. Excitement even.

I mock gasp and he chuckles, crossing his arms and setting his head against the back of the couch.

The space between us that had felt like a relief, now feels like a distraction.

"Tell me what it is that makes this stop."

He turns his head slowly, eyes snapping open. His responding grin is wolfish.

"Nevermind! Forget I asked." My stomach does an uncomfortable little toss as I curl up against the couch pillows, snuggling under my blanket. His sleepy chuckle skates across my skin as I surrender to my eyelids.

The next time I wake I'm thankfully alone. Rubbing sleep from my eyes, I hear Hartley round the corner. His soft foot falls a familiar companion to the quiet tinkling of a spoon and mug. Hartley's smile is warm, as is the cup of tea which he gives one final stir before setting it down on the table before me.

"Good morning."

"Morning?"

Alarm and confusion wriggle their way into my sleep-addled mind as I swing around to check the french doors leading to the garden and find the sky growing dark.

"My apologies." Hartley is wearing a guilty expression when I return my attention to him.

"No need." I say twisting my curls into a knot on the top of my head and scrubbing my hands down my face. "You could have easily convinced me I'd slept the whole week..."

He chuckles, and it's the only sounds permeating an unexpectedly quiet house.

"Where is - everyone?" I ask, catching myself.

"Upstairs in the study." His eyes flicker to the front stairs and I follow them. "Are you feeling alright?"

I nod feeling itchy when, with a flash of embarrassment, I realize just who my body is craving. Hartley watches me tuck my hands under my thighs and I fervently hope he was kept in the dark as to why. Though he's a vampire... I suppose he may have heard...

"We didn't want to wake you." He interrupts my spiraling thoughts to steer us in a new direction. "But I saved you a plate." He rises and returns a moment later, setting down a heaping plate of pasta. My stomach roars her thanks.

As I'm reaching for the plate my hand freezes eyeing the cookbook resting there beside my teacup. When had I last been reading it? I was certain I wouldn't have left it here. My pilfered little treasure out in the open. My eyes jump to Hartley feeling truly caught red handed.

"I found it on the entryway table." He says in way of explanation.

Right where I'd left it yesterday afternoon as I'd been on my way to the garden when Geo caught me.

"I'm sorry Hartley. I should have asked."

He hands me my cup ushering me to drink. "She would've loved that it was being put to good use."

"She? This isn't your handwriting?"

"No," he smiles. "It was Caroline's. My wife."

As I finish my tea and scarf down my pasta, Hartley tells me about Caroline and how they met. She had worked in the Royal city. Not just the Royal City, but the King's estate. And to my utter shock, he reveals he abdicated to marry her.

I choke on my pasta.

"Wait!" I swallow roughly, eyes watering. "Hartey... You... abdicated? As in... you were..."

"The head of the ruling royal family." He finishes with a nod.

My eyes dart around the house before returning to the vampire who waits patiently for me to have my little mental breakdown. I'm sitting here accepting tea from the prior *KING OF THE ROYAL CITY*. This male once sat on the throne and now-

"Then, why..."

"Why am I here running Jason's fine estate?" he supplied. Knowing it needs no confirmation, he continues. "When I abdicated the throne to my brother, he wanted to ensure I knew *exactly* what I was giving up. He did not approve of Caroline, or her family, and wanted to punish me for choosing her. It wasn't easy. I had been raised to put the Royal City and her needs above all else, but then I met Caroline. There was just no comparison. No sacrifice too large. We settled into a simple life with plans that were *enticingly* ordinary."

I smile and his eyes clear. That distant look fading as he returns to me with a sad shake of his head.

"That book," he nods, "was a passion project of hers. She would be thrilled to know it's not just collecting dust in the closet."

I couldn't believe what I'd learned.

"I bet your cooking won her over," I grin around my last bite of pasta.

His responding smile is as mischievous as I could ever imagine Hartley pulling off.

"Her talent far exceeded mine. If she wasn't in the kitchen, she was in the garden." He inclined towards the french doors.

Another bolt of surprise. "This was your home?"

He nodded his eyes touching the french doors over my shoulder. "When I was a much younger male, I built those garden boxes for her. I tell you, she spent so long out there perfecting that space, that for a week, our dinner was speckled with soil."

He chuckled and I couldn't help but follow suit.

Now that I had a moment to think about it, something from last night picked at me. "Why did Geo call Jason a prince?"

Hartley's gaze sharpened at the mention of the frog shifter. "Jason has become like a son to me, so it has been an honor hosting his estate here. But to the king and our Royal City he is the second son. Which is what allows him to settle here and not inside the city proper."

So, Jason was a prince.

And Hartley had been a king.

I was living in a house full of vampire royalty.

Hartley retired to his wing of the house and by that point the itch under my skin had ratcheted up to a nearly unbearable level. That was how I found myself climbing the stairs with a fresh cup of coffee in each hand. I didn't know what Henry preferred to drink, but the idea of nudging my way through the study door with only one cup felt wrong, so when I was pouring the fresh brewed muck into Jason's mug, I hurriedly pulled another from the cabinet for Henry.

Jason sat at his desk, fingers tangled in his dark hair. He didn't move as I approached. Nor when I set down the two mugs.

"Thank you," he clipped, his eyes never leaving the documents he had spread across the desk's surface. I stood there for an instant willing him to look up. To acknowledge me. If he could feel my eyes on him, he didn't show it. The only reaction he allowed was a flicker of his eyes to the mug and a little twinge of something creasing his brow before it smoothed.

I took a shallow breath, nerves tightening my stomach.

"What's wrong?"

Had something happened while I was sleeping? Had something happened with Henry? I glanced around the room. There was no sign of him.

His response was a shake of his head. The sigh that escaped him was barely audible, but I felt it down my neck.

The unease.

The tension.

I straightened.

"If you tell me what's wrong, I'll help you find what you're looking for."

His hand falls from his hair, rings clacking against the polished wood. His eyes finally rise to mine and I am nailed in place by the intensity of his gaze. I suck my lips between my teeth, biting back the reaction my body is having. This is the first time I've seen him since everything unfolded, and all the memories of yesterday evening come barreling back. The feeling of his hands on my bare skin, his tongue lapping at my back. The way his snarls had coasted over me, rumbling along my spine.

That possessive edge hardened his eyes now. The muscle feathering in his jaw as he worked his teeth even tighter.

"That flower you're looking for..." My words were breathless, but I pushed on. "Are you looking for the flower itself, or would the seeds be enough?"

Whenever the little crone would prune her flower box, she would hang the more sickly flowers above her kitchen counter to dry. I found myself, more often than not, sweeping up those seeds along with the dust and threads on her floors. Last spring I had collected a few, slipping them into my pocket as I swept the debris into the dustpan and planted them by the river. I'd hoped they would bloom for her and I'd be able to present her with some healthy flowers to replace her sickly ones. Now, whether or not those seeds had survived, I had no idea, but if there's any hope that her house is still standing I was sure there would be more seeds to be found.

Even if the flowers were long dead.

"Seeds would be valuable nonetheless."

His voice was calm, but I could sense the storm raging just below. I could feel it in the tension radiating off of his too-still form. In the coiled way he held himself, and in the spark that seemed to illuminate those gold flecks drowning in umber.

He wasn't calm.

He was furious, and I was just nosy enough to poke the bear.

Or in my case the probably over caffeinated vampire who, I'm sure, could flick the head from my shoulders.

Fun.

I swallowed, crossing my arms and drawing my spine tall.

"I know where you may be able to find some," I allowed waiting for him to break. Waiting for that little crack of interest that normally lit his gaze when we spoke about the various little treasures he had somehow collected from free folk or the continent.

This time, though, his eyes remained stormy as his brows lowered ever so slightly.

"But I have conditions."

I probably imagined the little twitch to his lips before he cocked his head to the side, challenge flashing like lightening in those stormy eyes.

His attitude triggered mine. Any nerves that may have lingered, now fell silent as I reminded myself where we had left off before that dinner party changed everything. It was the opportunity I needed to catch my breath and reset my mind. Unfortunately for him, my default setting was stubborn.

"You want my help or not?" I asked, crossing my arms.

His eyes danced across my face and down my neck.

He sighed collapsing against his chair, ringed fingers dragging down his face, before he returned his eyes to mine.

"Your conditions?" He asked.

"Tell me what's happened." I watched his lips pop open and heard his draw of breath before I remembered myself. "All of it. The truth."

This time when his lips twitched he allowed himself the briefest of smiles but this one was too clever to be honest.

"You think I lie to you, Pet?"

I had enough wit to keep my mouth shut and not fall into this little trap of his. Instead I just picked up one brow and ground my teeth together while I waited.

Slowly, I watched him peel back that mask allowing me access to the real male behind it.

"I promised you that you wouldn't be hurt in my home."

I watched him carefully, but all I saw was hurt, and then the anger that swiftly followed.

"Jason."

"I let you down," he sighed. "I broke my promise." He shook his head as his gaze traveled over me where I stood. His eyes were soft, but his words were sharp, as he continued. "You were hurt in your own home. I failed you and you gave me your name." His eyes fell closed, and that devastation I had seen painted across his face in that moment, now made sense.

I stepped towards him, and he must have heard, because his eyes snapped open, nailing me to the ground.

"I don't deserve it," he ground out.

My next inhale was sharp. Shock and irritation narrowed my own gaze as I leveled it on his. "You do."

"I put you in danger," he argued, his eyes shifting from my shoulder to my neck. And I knew what he was picturing. The wraith-like wounds; healed but still haunting us.

Gone, but not.

"You asked me to stay upstairs. I... decided otherwise."

His eyes narrowed and I gave him a guilty smile, but pushed on.

"I've lived my life in danger. This is the safest I've felt since I was taken from my home ... and maybe even then."

He shook his head, guilt collapsing his brow.

"Jason, I could've been under the thumb of someone like Geo, but instead I have *you*. You respect me. You see me for *who I am,* not what I am... and you allow me... so much freedom."

His hand fists on the desk. "That is the bare minimum!" His shout breaks the volume of our quiet conversation.

But I step into him instead of away.

Because that is what this feels like. And he doesn't need to do this. He just doesn't understand life as a human.

"I know, but I'm human Jason. We don't ... this-" I waved my hands out around us. "This is as free as I'll ever be, and you've given that to me."

His gaze goes downright livid. His voice falls to a tone so low, so calm, it has my heart racing harder than when he'd raised his voice. "So, you threw yourself in front of a blade for me, because you feel you owe me?" I watched his muscles coil as that cool preternatural predator swallowed up the hurt in his eyes.

"As repayment?"

I sucked in a small breath, hurt blossoming in my chest. He couldn't possibly believe that. He couldn't really think that after what had passed between us that evening... or how we had come to know each other, that I would have protected him out of expectation.

It was as if he didn't know me at all.

Irritation boiled over as I hissed, "Of course not."

"Then why?"

Because I love you.

The thought crashes over me and I panic, swallowing that admission. He wasn't mine to love.

My heart beat sputtered and I knew he would hear it, so I took a deep breath and stepped back. I needed to put some space between myself and this male. Not only for my own sanity, but because it was the right thing to do... and because I wanted to keep my head.

I could feel another sliver crack my heart... but I knew, at least, he couldn't hear *that*.

"I'm here. Were both safe" I tried.

My stomach sank as he cast his eyes out the window, frustration still prevalent, but this time when he spoke it was guarded.

"We have Henry to thank for that. If he hadn't come home..." he shook his head. "I want to know why."

Why had I thrown myself in front of a blade for this male. I thought it had been obvious. Painfully so. So much so that I worried it would get me killed after I realized just how far I had overstepped when it came to this male... and Henry.

But in the moment, knowing he wasn't mine, and probably never would be, hadn't stopped me.

Because he mattered.

It hadn't been a conscious decision to protect him. My body had just acted. Demanded it.

"I didn't even think. It happened so fast... It was instinct." My words are choppy and breathless as I try to battle back my emotions, but he cuts me off with a snarl.

"No you didn't." He growled and pain lanced through me. The rest of my response died on my tongue.

Ungrateful prick.

"I am far more durable, capable of catching blades thrown at me."

"Then why didn't you?" I waited fuming for only an instant before I pushed on knowing I was right. Unlike the vampire before me, I remembered that moment. The way his eyes had been locked on my face in the same way I felt unable to look away from him.

Drawn.

Like gravity itself chose this male as its axis and every ounce of my awareness revolved around him. Held in place only by the tether of those umber eyes and the promise of the sweep of his skin against mine.

"Because you didn't see it."

The look he served me was as close to anger as I'd seen him reach since I told him off in that hotel. I took a deep breath.

You're important to me.

Just say it.

Say it.

"You're an ungrateful prick," I huffed.

So close.

"And you are mine! Mine. And if I tell you that you will not put yourself at risk on my behalf again, you will obey me."

The words knocked me back a step like a physical blow. I didn't want to be back to this place where we bite and snarl at each other, but now I was seething.

"Obey you?"

My pulse filled the silence that stretched between us as it pounded in my ears. I dug my nails into my palms letting the bite temper my anger and stem the tears that welled without my permission.

I nodded, but my lips wobbled.

"I knew you couldn't hide forever."

He flinched, ringed fingers combing through his hair roughly as if he could hide the reaction. But it hurt.

It hurt me to hurt him and that made me furious.

"Fuck. You."

My knees shook as I turned on my heel to leave.

"Amelia."

My name coasted down my back like his finger and I wheeled on him, my voice finally breaking.

"No!" I flung a hand out finger trembling. "You don't get to use my name like an apology."

He looked physically pained as he latched that flint-like gaze onto mine. Emotion sparked bright and fast behind his eyes.

Too fast to catch.

His jaw ticked as he worked out the words I didn't let him voice.

"Fuck you." I ground out the words glad my voice sounded stronger than I felt.

I swear the room darkened several degrees as he set his palms to the desk and rose, unfurling to his full height, eyes never leaving mine.

My back met the bookshelf a moment later. One hand cradled the back of my neck; the other gripped my hip firmly enough to soften my coiled muscles. But the gentle way he coasted his thumb along my jaw as he shifted his hand from the back of my head to my throat, reignited my anger.

Slowly he pressed in, the sharp lines of his body warming mine as the bookshelf dug into my skin. His fingers firmed their grip on my hip as he tucked his lips against the shell of my ear. His exhale had me shivering. Anger and heat quarreling low in my belly.

"Let me hear that word cross your lips one more time."

What word?

Fuck?

My stomach tumbled.

The timber of his voice and the way his scent wrapped around me threatened to disarm me. But I was angry and it was because I was angry that I tipped my chin up, swallowing my nerves and smothering this reaction to him. Breath tumbled from my lips as I bit my tongue against the words sitting on top of it. My initial reaction was to do just what he was warning me against, but this felt different. I couldn't help but think that's exactly what he wanted.

And I adamantly wanted to give him just the opposite. So instead, I said, "You don't get to tell me what to do."

I pulled back wanting to see his face

His eyes closed, a dangerous sort of smile slowly lifting his lips.

"No," Henry's voice was low, but his appearance still startled me. Jason's hand dropped from my skin as I whipped my head around, hungrily taking in the male where he filled the doorway. "But you do have to listen to me."

The hand Jason removed from my jaw now braced against the bookshelf above my head. He didn't move as I stepped underneath his outstretched arm with a glare. I couldn't tell if he was even breathing.

"Give us a moment, won't you?" Henry asked, slowly peeling his eyes from the male behind me to land on my own. The sire bond, I'd been ignoring quite successfully, snapped into place with a vengeance.

That preternatural itch intensified as I locked my legs in place out of pure spite, crossing my arms. It was all I could do to keep from chucking myself into his arms, lust scraping her greedy nails down my back.

He picked up a single brow. My challenge but a fleck of lint on his shoulder, as he turned to hold the door to the study.

"Leave," he purred, sounding alarmingly like the male behind me. His voice was smoke and grit. My legs wavered as need swelled like a punch to the gut. Weak or no, my legs carried me away from Jason and towards the door. Not once did I peel my glare from those cool green eyes, bright with humor.

I was relieved to find that I could still hold up my middle finger as I was dragged out of the room by my own legs.

His deep chuckle followed me out the door, and into the hallway, where my body was returned to my control once again.

Chapter Seventeen

I would not cry here in the hallway like a discarded toy.

No.

My fingers paused on the knob. The door to my bedroom felt too thin in a house full of vampires. I needed somewhere to exist above a whisper. I needed a barrier between myself and their preternatural hearing, so ducked into my room heading straight for the ensuite bathroom.

Not bothering to pause, I strode directly into the shower and cranked the handle.

My gasp echoed through the room as cold water soaked my hair and clothes. The shock helped quell the overwhelming feelings, and by the time the water warmed, it was easier to catch my breath. The tiles had heated under the spray of water, and when I set my back to them, I let myself slide down the shower wall to a sit. As I pulled the wet clothes from my body and worked to even my breathing, I let the water scald the shame and guilt from my skin.

It stopped here.

It had to.

I hadn't intentionally harbored these feelings for Jason, knowing he was in a relationship. He was kind to me, and his stupid handsome face had been a distraction. I fell for him without realizing I was falling. The memories of our last few weeks together haunt me as the steam swirls, dancing along my skin.

I pick apart each interaction, realizing just how differently he may have seen things, without this unfortunate infatuation that had been growing in my mind.

I sit in the shower until the water runs cold once again, not feeling an ounce of guilt for the water I wasted. All that shame and guilt had melted under the hot water, transforming into irritation. Irritation I couldn't assign fully to Jason... though I wanted to.

Each of his touches, so few, so controlled. He had always pulled away. This invisible line in the sand between us that I now realized may have been him respecting his relationship with Henry. He'd been protecting Henry when I thought he'd been protecting me.

Respecting me.

But I was his pet.

His responsibility.

He'd been kind, and I'd been naive.

My head falls back against the tile as I sigh.

He was protecting us both.

None of this had been intentional, and in my hunt to blame someone for the way I was feeling, I'd come up empty handed.

But I *could* fix it.

With that, I shoved myself to my feet, washed away my tears, and shut off the water. While I dried off, I plotted.

Once dressed, I crept down the hall on what I hoped to be nearly silent feet. Setting my ear to the study door, I turned the knob slowly, listening for any sound that would indicate whether or not I was about to be greeted by two very suspicious vampires. The door cracked open on a blessedly silent hinge when their voices reached me. I held my breath, focusing past the pulse in my ears, and realized their muted conversation was actually coming from behind the bedroom door.

The coast was clear.

I knew I was on borrowed time here, and imagined it was only, said conversation, that kept them from catching me in Jason's study. And if I was going to start making things right, then I needed to uphold my end of the bargain. I'd told Jason I would help him find those flowers if he had told me the truth. And he had... no matter how shitty the delivery.

So here I was placing my hand drawn map on his desk and using one of the little candy coated chocolates to mark the spot I hoped they'd still exist. I smiled at the little chocolate, swiping a few and popping one into my mouth, as I tucked the satchel back into his hiding place in the left side drawer.

A girl needed some chocolate after a night like this.

With a handful of candy, I made my way down stairs and out into the garden. I know it's silly, but I felt too exposed sitting on the hammock, or crossing the yard to the chairs situated on the other end... they put me too close to the opening in the wall leading to the treeline beyond.

So instead, I sat next to the garden box running my fingers along the soft leaves. Mom would have loved this garden. I could only imagine the way we would have sat around our rickety kitchen table she loved so much, brewing teas, and baking sweets for all the little ones she collected along our way.

With ingredients like this, we all could have lived so differently. The meals we could have cooked with a kitchen packed so full of food... the way my brother's blonde hair would have been streaked with color after convincing me to hand over my pilfered chocolates.

Because he always found a way to get food in his hair.

And I would have happily handed them over.

It all seemed so senseless, especially now. They were gone... and for what? Because they wouldn't fetch a price. Because they had hidden in the house instead of running. Le had still found me, even here. And in this new home, that I thought had been different, suddenly felt the same. Just as lonely as the free camps had felt. Trying to live under the radar. Live quietly.

And just as naive. I had misread so many situations with Jason. I should have known. I should have seen... I was his pet.

I was a pet.

Nothing more.

A tear ran down my cheek, and I let it. Here in the darkening garden, it felt private. Just me and the plants... at least I hoped.

Every now and again my eyes darted to the opening in the wall scrutinizing the shadows.

How easy it would be to just leave. To just walk into the treeline and disappear. Had I not hoped for a moment just like this while I stood in line at Acropolis?

Where would I go?

Would Jason hunt me down the way Le had?

I stood, my hands shaking, taking a few steps towards the bordering wall before catching myself. But the space beyond the wall only held murky darkness. The sun had set, and with it my ability to discern one shadow from the next.

As I watched the wall and the trees beyond, I could feel something staring back. The sensation of being watched crept up my neck, raising gooseflesh on my arms.

"What are-

I screamed as his gravelly voice reached me. Acting on these instincts that only aimed to get me killed, I spun on him throwing my fist into his ribs as hard as I could.

"Fucking ow!" I wailed.

Hitting Henry was like hitting the damn wall. My hand protested and I swore just as sharply.

I glared at him through teary eyes as he chuckled. "What are you doing out here?"

I swiped at my cold cheeks, "Nothing."

My hand clenched and unclenched at my side. Irrationally, I found myself wanting to hit him again. Knowing all too well, I'd only hurt myself. Logic scraped and clawed her way back to the forefront of my mind. For fucks sake. Seriously, what was he made of?

"Is that right?" He huffed, eyes lifting over my head to eye the treeline.

Could he see something I couldn't? I peeked back over my shoulder following his gaze.

"I just needed some air," I lied.

"Well if you're after a little fresh air, I think I can help." He shoved his hands into his pockets, his eyes crinkling as he teased. "Since you're out here all alone with no one but the shadows to keep you company."

I grind my teeth as I pick up my gaze and level it on his.

The pain smarting my knuckles, and embarrassment of being caught off guard, melding together into a nasty little cocktail that was sure to get me in trouble.

"Let's go for a ride."

"Are you telling me to?"

"I'm asking if you would like to." His smile faltered as he stepped around me. The glow from the house now illuminates his face, his big body blocking the view of the trees. He was like a wall himself ... or a shield. I shifted peeking back at the house wondering if I would find Jason watching from a window.

The second that thought entered my mind, I squashed it. It didn't matter.

Frustrated, I turned back to Henry. Maybe a quick ride wasn't a bad idea. I had wanted a little distance and the car ride here with Hartley had been warm and comfortable curled up in the backseat.

"I get it."

His words sunk under my skin like little pebbles tossed into a pond, disturbing all of those ugly emotions I was trying so hard to keep beneath the surface.

"Do you?" I snapped.

His gaze was even, unfazed, as he nodded.

How could he possibly begin to understand how I felt?

"Why-" I blustered. "How could you?"

His answer was simple. "You're not the first human I've lived with."

Of course I wasn't.

Irritation rippled through me as I was smacked in the face with my own naivety yet again.

"No one wants to live in a house full of vampires who seem to be able to hear your very thoughts, let alone the dinner digesting in your gut".

A pause.

"Or so I was told," he chuckles, his eyes going distant for the briefest of moments.

"It's an open invitation, unless you want to just take a few more swings at me... You could use the practice."

It was a tempting offer, and his little jab had my blood heating. I curled my hands into fists at my side and his grin lit with an edge of excitement. One dark brow lifting in challenge. Or surprise maybe?

For a male who seemed more open with his words and expressions, his emotions were harder to gauge. More convoluted ... more fluid. Maybe it was a vampire thing. I imagined it would take time to get a better read on Henry.

"Fine," I relented.

His smile softened, but the excitement remained as he swept his arm out in front of him, allowing me to lead the way to the front drive.

It was not a car that waited for me out front, but a sleek black bike. The heavy metal body gleaming in just the low light of the moon.

"Safety first," he grinned, brandishing a set of helmets. One he set on the seat, while the other he held between his hands.

I wasn't sure what to do, so I just held still.

He brushed a few wayward curls back from my forehead before slipping the helmet over my head and flipping up the visor.

"Chin up."

His glove-clad fingers brushed the skin of my throat as he buckled the thing in place. Using that same hold, with his fingers hooked under the chin of the helmet, he turned my head back and forth before nodding, satisfied with the fit.

With a flick, he snapped the visor down and gave me a swift pat to the top of my helmet.

He slipped his helmet over his own head swinging a leg over the bike.

His weight settled on the machine with a bounce.

"Climb on." He reached back to lower a metal peg before offering me his hand.

I wasn't going to accept it, until I realized the other means of balance while mounting the bike were pretty slim. So, begrudgingly I accepted. His gloved hand was warm despite the cool temperature. I thought he'd release me once I was settled behind him, but instead he used that grip on my hand to pull my arm around his waist, securing me to him. He held me there for a moment, as he warned, "Don't let go".

As if I'd release my grip on the only thing keeping me on the bike.

With another little pat, he released me, and reached forward starting the bike. It roared to life under us. The feeling, exhilarating... at least I thought so, until we rolled down the drive and turned smoothly onto the main road.

I clung to Henry, now grateful the male seemed to be built like a mountain. His broad shoulders blocked the wind, and his back was warm as I pressed against him watching the trees sail by. The bike tilted taking turn after turn until the road opened up before us. A straight shot.

His helmet tipped down, chin tucking towards his shoulder as he called back, "You ready?"

My stomach tumbled.

"For what?"

"This is the longest patch of straight road, so this is your chance. Howl, scream, curse. Whatever you need to do, just let it out."

"Seriously?"

I got nothing but the sound of whipping air in response.

Ok then.

I sucked in a deep breath and tipped my head back on a scream. Henry tightened his grip on my hand before revving the bike, sending us flying down the road. I could feel the chuckle under my hand, and against my chest, when my next shout was more vulgar.

He reached back curling his right arm around me, pinning me to him. His helmet again tucked low so I could hear him.

"Both arms. C'mon! Let me hear it!"

This time, I didn't hesitate. I flung my head back, arms spread wide as I howled at the night sky. I screamed and cursed until my throat hurt, and my voice cracked. Surprise warmed my chest when he joined me, and before I could catch myself, I was laughing along with him. Sure, he was probably laughing at me and my horrible language, but I didn't care.

I'll admit, it was just what I needed. My body hummed with relief each breath easier than the last. He released me from where I was pinned against him, and I settled more comfortably against his back. He took a much more leisurely pace home, but it still felt like flying as I watched the trees streak by in a bur.

Chapter Eighteen

"Play nice," he said, planting a kiss on the top of Jason's head where he sat reading on the couch. We'd walked in to find him here, seemingly waiting for us. Henry's eyes caught mine as he rose. "Or you'll find out if I can force you to sneeze, just by telling you to."

"You're sick."

"The word you're looking for is creative," he called over his shoulder as he jogged up the stairs.

I glared after him, no real ill feelings to back it up. And then we were alone. Jason closed his book, setting it on the table beside him and pinned me with a look. Those molten eyes churning as he watched me take a step back from where he sat, now, just out of reach.

"Come here."

He sat forward, his thighs widening to make room for me to tuck myself in his space as we had before. I shifted my weight considering for a moment how difficult I wanted to be... but this exact thought, the autonomy I kept in this household, wasn't something I wanted to risk. Especially with the introduction of a new player. Henry seemed kind, but I would be naive to believe his presence wouldn't change the dynamic in the household. Would I still be able to rebel and speak as freely with Jason as I had before? He'd stepped in right away to put it to an end upstairs.

What exactly was his definition of 'play nice'?

The possible loss left a pang in my stomach as I relented and stepped into Jason's space. I didn't want to fight him.

But I also wouldn't be toyed with.

Selfishly, I just didn't want anything to change. Other than maybe his ability to say the words, 'thank you'.

"I'm sorry," he said, his fingers capturing my wrist.

"So close," I teased sourly. "But those are *not* the two words I was looking for."

"Pet," he scolded, no weight to the warning.

I smiled, but it was tainted. That edge of loss creeping in.

"Getting colder."

The corner of his lips twitched teasing me with that smile, but he shook his head with a groan. "You're a brat"

"You mustn't mind it," I breathed. "You should have ditched me in the south if you did."

He shook his head, his eyes softening as they brushed over my face.

"You were right. I had been distracted."

No.

My breath stalled in my lungs. That moment tumbled across his face as it played out again.

No.

I didn't want to relive this moment with him. Not now. Not when I had tucked all of those little touches into their own box and shut it tight. When I'd spent time recategorizing them as misunderstandings.

"My misstep nearly cost you your life." His hands coasted up my arms, his eyes sinking to my neck. I exhaled roughly, recognizing a path in this conversation I could shove us down to avoid any more hurt.

"I promised you safety and-

"Jason," I sighed, aiming for frustrated. "We've already had this argument."

"No." His grip tightened as if he thought I'd pull away. And I wish I'd had the will to do just that. "It's important to me that I fix this. That you hear it."

I nodded, pulling my lips between my teeth. There was no steering us away then. So, I picked my eyes up to his readying myself.

"You deserve a life that feels like your own. Your wants and interests are important. I want you to explore them."

I shook my head out of reflex, having had entirely enough of exploring my wants in this house and just where that led me.

I'll pass on any more of that.

His face grew stern before his brows raised and I remembered the words he had actually spoken. He'd wanted me to, what? Have hobbies?

"How would that even work?" I shook the words out feeling unsteady.

"Just as it had for me-

"Jason I bit out. You're a prince." I nearly choked on the title. "I am a pet."

His grip tightened.

"You are whoever you wish to be in this house."

His words pummeled the still aching part of my heart. The part that wanted him. I wanted to be his... but it was selfish... and frankly outside the realm of possibility all together.

"This is your house," he continued, oblivious to the way he was breaking my heart without meaning to. Without having intended to. "And it is important to me that you feel safe here. Safe enough to explore who you are and ... who you are, who you become, shouldn't revolve around me, or your status as my pet."

I watched him. Watched his eyes filling with determination as I battled each and every word. Fighting for a meaning that didn't feel like dismissal. Like a fissure in a relationship I was hoping, despite my intention to tuck away my misplaced feelings, wouldn't change.

"I will earn back your trust."

I nodded as tears stung my eyes and I'd never hoped to be so misunderstood as I did in this moment. I stepped closer, my legs soaking in the heat of his.

"You never lost it. I am safe here." Here in the house of the man I loved and could never have. But I knew I was safe. I hadn't lied to him when I told him I trusted him. I did. I knew how lucky I was to have found myself here in a household like Jason's, with an owner who cared about me, beyond my blood type, even if it was just as his pet. "In more ways than you can even understand."

For a fraction of a second his eyes darkened with what looked like comprehension, but felt misplaced, until I remembered what Henry had said. I wasn't the first human he had lived with. I'm sure it was the same for Jason. Maybe he understood more than I gave him credit for.

"I apologize for the way I spoke to you earlier. I was angry with myself and I snapped at you." He shook his head. "Seeing you hurt in front of me..." His voice was low as his eyes rose to mine.

I hadn't thought about how that may have felt for him. How I would have felt if rolls had been reversed.

The air shifted.

His eyes smoldered, those gold flecks igniting, spreading to cup his pupil as that warm umber bled wide painting his eye black as the night sky.

His knuckles ran down my arms tucking back black-tipped claws which he curled against his palms. Jason wasn't a threat to me. But this- this power he possessed was unlike anything else I'd seen amongst the vampires or shifters.

I shivered. This thing that he was, was incredible.

Powerful.

Something other.

It was in that moment that I realized the male before me wore many masks.

Some that hid his face; his emotions. The mask he wore when he needed to be someone else. Someone who was cool and calm and in control, or carefree as he tossed his head back with laughter like nothing in the world could touch him.

Unbothered royalty.

Confidence personified.

And the other, that hid his power.

"Staking him to the wall was a generosity he didn't deserve. If you hadn't been hurt. If you hadn't needed me I would've peeled the skin from his bones for touching you the way he did."

Carefully, slowly, I set my hands against his cheeks.

"I trust you, Jason" I vowed, giving him a little shake and then in a moment of weakness, wrapped my arms around his neck, holding tightly. His hands lacked claws a moment later as they spread across my back keeping me in place.

"Thank you, Amelia."

My next inhale was sharp as instinct had me pulling back to study his face. His warm umber eyes, once again familiar.

He smiled a shy crooked smile that had my heart breaking as it galloped against my ribs.

I loved him.

I loved him, and he loved someone else.

This time, when I pulled out of his grasp, he let me go.

Chapter Nineteen

Jason had made it clear when we'd spoken that evening that he didn't expect me to act as a pet, but in this absence of purpose, loneliness crept in. The moments of freetime that he may have intended for me to use on 'being who I wanted to', left me sitting on the sidelines of their new daily routines. Henry was home, and from that morning they spent every free moment consumed with the maps and documents Jason kept sprawled across this desk.

The time that Jason and I had spent reading together, eating together, with Henry home, felt unnecessary now. It felt like an invasion. And I felt like a placeholder.

I told myself it wasn't intentional, the way he had pulled away since that evening.

All that guilt and hurt transformed into irritation. Sure I was more angry at myself for allowing these feelings to take root but, I'd aim them at him first. Because how dare he make me love him.

"Post is here," I said, handing him the stack of envelopes. Even the familiar one rimmed in pretty silver leaves.

I felt him watching me, but I kept my eyes on his rings as I handed over the stack.

I was a blip in this male's life. My whole life, a moment in his.

Impermanent.

Insignificant.

Admittedly, I'd allowed myself to fall for him too quickly. But between falling for the vampire before me, and being forced into an unquenchable physical tether to his partner on day one… I'd interfered in a relationship I had no place in. But I couldn't live in a house I had no place in, so after a few days, I fell back into my role as a pet.

I didn't know how to navigate back towards a normal relationship between owners and pet. I didn't know what that looked like. I didn't know how to be near him in a way that didn't feel like I was doing wrong by Henry.

So I didn't.

I kept my distance. I'd read from my pillow nest in his office, but I kept to myself. I spent time in the kitchen with Harley, or in the garden. It was rare that I caught him so much as looking my way. I convinced myself he hadn't even noticed the difference. Those little ticks of irritation that flared the gold in his eyes every time I performed a task too pet-like, didn't exist. I brought him coffee, the post, whatever he asked for and then I left. Back to my hiding place on the outskirts of their life. I stopped trying to be a menace, a friend, a person. I was their pet.

That's what I wanted to be.

It had been two weeks and my heart was aching, but it was also numbing.

His fingers closed around the envelopes and paused. He held them there long enough that I lifted my eyes to his. It was a battle not to wince under the intensity. He pinned me with those umber eyes and it was like lightning ignited my veins.

Fuck him for having this kind of hold over me. I blinked, letting the anger wash away the hurt, and turned to leave.

"You didn't so much as snoop through these," he called.

I stumbled to a stop and tuned to him, slowly, stealing my spine. Numbing myself.

"Why would I?" I had in fact snooped many times, and apparently he knew that.

"Why wouldn't you?" He shot back.

I narrowed my eyes. This felt like a trap.

"Come here."

I took a steadying breath, but didn't move.

His head cocked to the side appraising me. But there was more.

"Pet," he purred. The name was like a finger dragged up my spine.

"Come here."

He pushed his chair back leaning forward against his knees as I took the few steps back across the room towards him.

"What's going on?"

"Nothing," I breathed, the lie a ghost across my lips.

"Pet," he warned, voice low.

He knew my name. He knew it. Yet it hadn't crossed his lips but once since learning it.

I backed away and in the blink of an eye he was missing from his seat. In the same instant I backed right into him, his hands gripping my arms as I spun around to face him.

"What are you doing?" I barked a bit breathlessly.

His eyes narrowed. "What are *you* doing," he challenged. "Would you like to lie to me again? Maybe more convincingly this time," he prodded.

He was searching for a reaction. The temptation to give him exactly what he wanted was a barely tempered thing, but I held firm, and buried it deeper under my skin.

At this, disappointment bled into his expression.

"I gave you your space. After everything that happened, I didn't want to push you. You were right to be angry with me."

"I'm not angry with you."

It wasn't a lie, but it tasted like one. My anger, though I knew I shouldn't aim it at him, had nothing to do with what happened with Geo. I didn't regret a thing when it meant he had walked away with his life... and so had I.

"You think I haven't noticed the way you swallow each of those comments you would have hurled at me just weeks ago. You think I cannot see the way your light has dimmed."

Genuine surprise flickered along my skin.

"Did you think I wouldn't notice?" His words were low, hurt ringing in the space between us.

I hadn't.

At least, I had hoped he wouldn't.

"You're angry. I understand that" he said, rising to his feet. "You're hurt."

I shook my head, but he pushed on.

"You pulled away after that night." He took a step back, his brow collapsing under the weight of all of that self assigned guilt. "I knew that I let you down... that-

"That's not why," the words bubbled from my lips before I could catch them.

His eyes scoured my face as he paused just outside of arms reach.

His eyes softened. His voice lowered.

"Is it the nightmares?"

Pain lanced across my chest. Hating how much he had seen. How much he cared.

"Tell me what's going on." The words were a plea as much as a command. His fingers tipped my chin up, holding me captive in the swirling warmth of his eyes.

I closed them against him, finding myself quite incapable of pulling out of his grasp. It had been weeks since he had touched me, and I was weak against him. His skin against mine had me at the end of my tether, but I could do this. I could close my eyes and fight the stinging behind them. Protect myself from giving this male everything he asked for at the sake of my own heart.

His thumb lifted to stroke my chin.

"Please" his voice was a breath across my forehead as he stepped into me.

My lips quivered under his touch.

"I can't." I opened my eyes hoping to convey, and yet hide, all the things I couldn't say.

He stilled. His eyes cooled a fraction as he dropped his hold on me.

The loss was immediately painful, and I had to curl my hands tight, letting my nails bite into my palms to keep from latching onto him. My jaw was screwed closed so tightly it ached.

He stepped back, straightening his vest, that mask falling into place hiding his gorgeous features. Dulling them.

And I panicked.

"I had to-"

The words left my mouth before I could stop them. It was only when I heard myself speaking them, that I realized I had lost the battle with my control.

"...distance myself."

My admission had his back straightening. That mask cracking.

"Why?"

His voice was low, vulnerable. I could see him, just there. Just behind the mask that hid him from me.

I took a deep breath shaking my head. Honesty was what he deserved, but it would also cost me everything.

Would cost me him.

"Pet." His voice scraped across my skin, rough and raw. Hurt bubbling just below the surface.

My fists clenched, my eyes screwing shut as I choked on the truth.

"Because Henry came home."

The words felt sour on my tongue. The bitterness of the truth crumpling my brow. And after a silent beat, I opened my eyes searching him out.

"Why would that matter?"

My knees shook. I watched him, my eyes tracing the lines of his face. Because this was where I would ultimately lose him. How could he ever look at me the same way again? I could barely manage to keep my eyes on his as the shame mounted.

But he watched me in that quiet way he studied his maps, and I watched the moment something changed in his expression.

A knock on the door frame startled me, but Jason's eyes didn't move from my face as I turned to cast a glance over my shoulder.

"Time to go," Henry called, his voice even. Calm.

I wanted to sink right into the floor. A gross puddle of shame as Jason slung on his coat, his eyes lifting to Henry over my shoulder with a brief nod.

"We'll talk when I get back," he assured his eyes flickering across my face.

No, we absolutely would not.

My eyes flickered back to Henry tracing the weaponry up his broad chest wondering how creatively he could cut me to pieces. In the end my cowardice won out, and he turned before I could meet his gaze.

Both males left without a word between them and didn't return that evening. Hartley and I ate dinner together and I read in the study before falling asleep behind my locked bedroom door like the coward I was.

The next morning I woke to a quiet house. It was still early, and I was still hoping to avoid any and all humiliating interactions with my owners, so I skirted through the house and out to the garden. I watched the sun color the sky as I snuggled up under my yellow blanket, the gentle breeze swaying the hammock just so. It was enough to lull me back to sleep giving into the false sense of security this little garden granted me.

I woke to the sound of percussive impacts. Dull thuds. Sharp smacks and low grunting. Awareness greeted me like a pail full of cold water as I remembered where I was, who I was supposed to be avoiding, and just who those sounds were coming from.

Slowly, I peeked over the top of the hammock's edge and there he was. Henry. Shirtless. Beating the absolute shit out of the trunk of the large oak. His dark curls pulled back into a low knot at his neck, a few shorter strands sticking to his forehead and neck. I swallowed roughly following sweat slicked skin along his shoulders and up his arms he held raised before him. Strike, after lethal strike, landing against the poor tree. It was only when he threw a kick, his body folding and flexing, that I realized there was padding strapped to the side of the tree. Padding that he had pummeled through.

Oh, I'm so dead.

His gaze cut to mine, a grin lighting those moss green eyes, and I tumbled from my hammock with a gasp as the ground caught me with her cold, unforgiving, hands.

"Fucking ow," I groaned reaching up to untangle my feet from where they hung suspended in a knot of hammock and blanket.

His hands beat me to it, neatly pulling my ankle free with a chuckle.

"Good morning." His eyes glinted with humor as he stood over me. In the span of time it had taken for me to tumble from the hammock and hit the ground, he had shoved those glistening abs into a sky blue shirt and still had enough time to mock me, as he waited, hand extended, to help me up. "Care to join me, or would you like to return to your lurking?"

He set my blanket into the hammock, and held it open as if to help me back in as I shoved to my feet, dusting myself off.

"You want me to train with you?" I huffed eyeing him skeptically.

"Don't worry." He said hands catching his waist. "I won't let you hurt yourself." That was the least of my concerns... though I suppose, the most realistic.

"C'mon don't you wanna learn how to kill the next shifter who so much as looks at you wrong? Or maybe poke 'em full of holes." He grinned and it looked so honest, but I couldn't trust it. I had betrayed him. He had heard the words from my very mouth... but he wanted me to believe... he, what? Cared that I knew how to protect myself.

I suppose he'd seen the aftermath. Maybe if I'd been better equipped, we wouldn't have had such a dramatic end to the evening... and maybe I could have punished Geo for the way he spoke to Hartley.

The way he touched me.

Made him regret ever looking at me... that sounded like something I very much wanted to do.

"Are you only teaching me this so you can maim me without feeling guilty?" I crossed my arms straightening my spine into something less breakable. "Some kind of royal guard bullshit that won't let you kill someone who's unarmed."

He scoffed. "Who taught you to speak like this?"

I tipped my chin.

"Free women." I quipped, grinning at him, wishing I had a set of fangs to show off. His eyes flared regarding me with an expression that looked far too much like fascination to be accurate. I couldn't read this male at all. Nonetheless, I followed him over to the large tree where I'd watched him train moments prior.

I was questioning everything when he pulled three blades from a sheath across his chest. My excitement cooled.

"Hand to hand will be tricky, but not impossible" he allowed. "However, your best bet will be doing as much damage as possible, quickly, and from a distance."

He stepped up beside me, angled his body towards the garden wall, and with a flick of his wrist sent the blades flying one after the other in rapid succession.

The dull thuds of the blades sinking into the rain softened wood sparked three little resulting flinches. Phantom pains radiated from my shoulder and I caught myself absentmindedly rubbing at my arm.

"Do you have experience handling blades at all?"

I swallowed. "Only catching them," I said dryly.

He snorted, his gaze flickering over my face.

He handed me a fourth blade, and my hands shook where they were balled at my sides. All I could hear was the sound of that blade lodging in the wet wood and the resulting spark of pain bright and hot in my shoulder.

Jason's roar echoed in the back of my mind.

The clattering of silverware.

I shook my head, snapping my mouth shut, quieting my breath and turned. I didn't want him to see my fear. The way my hands shook.

"I don't want to do this," I said, aiming for bored, but landed somewhere between breathless and tired as I fled. He didn't let me get far. He was in front of me in three large strides.

"You're alright," he said, blocking my escape. "Just breathe."

"I am breathing," I barked shoving at him when he reached for me. He raised his hands in surrender.

Fear turned to embarrassment, and embarrassment bled into anger.

"Why are you being so nice to me?"

His brows crumple, two lines creasing his smooth skin. "Why wouldn't I?"

I glare at him and to my horror the casual confusion on his face softens. Shame burns in my chest as my anger turns watery.

"You don't need me to be nice to you. Do you, Princess?" A grin spread across his face as he stepped back, his shoulders rolling ever so slightly. "You wanna fight instead?"

Without thinking, I nodded, swinging on him like he'd asked me to all those nights ago when we last stood in the garden. Hesitation gone.

He laughed, dodging both.

His hands came up before him. Big meaty targets.

"Again."

I swung.

"Again."

I swung twice. My heart was pounding in my ears as I walked him back across the garden, swinging on command. He dodged, or redirected my attacks, shoving my arm this way or that. I lost steam by the time we reached the far end of the garden and shook my head in frustration.

"You're not tired." He swatted at my elbows until I picked them up. "You're strong. Again."

I swung twice more with a curse, as I landed one, and missed the second. Then immediately dropped my arms like the useless noodles they felt like.

"C'mon Princess, you're not gonna fight me off like that." He raised his hands between us. "Hit me like you mean it.

He swung at me when I didn't move, and I swung back in retaliation. I growled, throwing everything I had into my swings until breath was sawing between my teeth.

"Good! Harder." He shifted left and I followed, but when I put myself in front of him, he maneuvered again, taking control.

Suddenly, he's stalking me across the yard as I bat at him trying to maintain my footing and the buffer of space between us, and failing at both.

He redirected my shitty swing and I spun using my own momentum to throw a hook right at his head.

I swung and slipped.

He was quick to snag my wrist, yanking me to my left. He spun me as if we were dancing and released me to block a small strike he threw to my ribs. It was slow. So slow and I didn't think he'd make contact even if I let him, but my brain was going hazy.

I'd never win against someone like him.

I wasn't sure if I stood much of a chance against a human, let alone a vampire or shifter. He was just toying with me...

I couldn't catch my breath. He was crowding me and my body was screaming.

"Stop." The plea was a gasp. I shook my head holding up a hand in surrender and his advance halted immediately. He took a step back and dropped to his heels as he watched me. It was the space I needed to drop my hands to my knees and gulp down air.

I screwed mine shut tightly.

"I apologize." He called from his place crouched on the ground.

I wheezed in response. My thoughts still spiraling as panic worked its way through my heavy limbs. I knew Henry was... well, Henry, but the part of my brain that pumped adrenaline and fueled my fear, was now working on overdrive. I was prey before a predator and, no matter how I tried, I couldn't rationalize my body's response away.

Something shifted, maybe just the damn breeze, but it had my eyes popping open on instinct.

His face was calm as his eyes met mine.

"You're safe," he said in that easy tone that spiked my irritation even higher. My brow dropped as I glared at him.

"Take a deep breath," he suggested oh-so-helpfully, mocking me with his even breathing.

I groaned, flipping him off. Noisy gasps echoed through the garden as I fought for more air, ignoring the way my knees wobbled.

The embarrassment had heat crawling up my neck and angry tears wetting my eyes.

Other than men, angry tears were a girl's worst enemy.

I wiped at my cheek with the back of my hand.

"Pet." Jason's voice reached me through the silence of the courtyard. I watched Henry lift his gaze over my shoulder to Jason where he must have been standing behind me, before returning that prodding gaze to mine. I followed his line of sight, turning at the hips to find Jason in the doorway, looking ready to intervene.

I took a settling breath.

"We're fine." I waved him off, swiping at my cheeks.

His gaze bounced to Henry, a warning in the set of his brows, before he blinked, tucking it all away as his eyes coasted over both of us. With a nod, he shut the door behind him. I assume, returning to his study.

"You did well for your first go." He sat back onto the grass and I collapsed onto the ground across from him.

"Fuck off," I choked on a gasping laugh, my pulse thundering through my chest.

I didn't know why, but in this moment it felt easier to be weak in front of Henry. Maybe, because I was fairly certain that we both knew he could rip me to pieces, before I had time to realize I was dead. But he didn't seem to mind, and I was too tired to care.

I shook my head. "I - I don't think there's a point in me learning how to fight."

The grass was cool against my cheek as I turned my head and found him watching me.

"You could kill me before I asked you not to. I don't stand a chance against any of you."

He draws his gaze over my face before he exhales. "We're not quite as far up the food chain as you've been led to believe."

My responding laugh is harsher. My eyes narrow as I catch his. "You know I'd believe you if... no I wouldn't."

He snorts, shaking his head, his gaze flickering around the garden. "You are not alone anymore." His eyes travel the row of windows along the back of the house. "You live in a household made up of the strongest of our kind," he winks. "And we're happy to back up any bad decisions you'd like to make."

"Like killing one of your kind?"

"Oh especially that," he chuckles. "You're buying into what you've been told. Lies, crafted to keep you compliant. To keep you scared, but that's all it is."

"And you're telling me this, why?"

"Because," moss green eyes recapture mine. "You are ours." He nods, the words landing like little stones in my stomach. I narrow my eyes at him, disbelief coloring my vision as he continues. "I see that fight in you. It'd be a shame to see you waste such a sharp tongue, and have no real blade skills to back it up."

I paused his words sinking in. "I'd like that." I closed my eyes, turning back to the sky. "But what's the point of throwing a blade at someone who can catch them?" I repeated Jason's line from so many nights prior.

His chuckle reached me along with the next breeze. "Just because *I* can, doesn't mean *they* will."

I scoff my eyes reopening to watch the puffy white clouds coast across the sky.

"No one should feel entitled to touch you simply because you're human. And you should know just how to cut the fingers from their hands in punishment."

I needed him to stop making me like him. Liking Henry made my chest hurt. He was a good male, and I couldn't help but feel like I'd done wrong by him.

Unknowingly... but it still felt sour where it churned against my tender heart.

"Why?" I groused. "You planning more dinner parties?"

Henry sat forward, his forearms pressed to those strong thighs.

"Just because I'm going to teach you how to exact your own revenge, doesn't mean I'll allow them to touch you in the first place."

My eyes chose that moment to land on his hands, wondering exactly how capable he was. He certainly wore enough steel to warrant a pause from anyone who'd consider moving against him, but could he really catch a blade? Would he? My eyes climbed his chest, his jaw, arriving at his mouth.

He grinned.

"You have my express permission to mouth off however you please." His words jolted me, my eyes bouncing to his, certain I had misheard. It was a very poor choice to give me such hope, because I may just do as he'd suggested. His eyes were steady, honest, as they held mine. His smile was genuine as he continued. "Jason may disagree, but we'd both defend you. No questions asked."

"Now I know you're trying to get me killed. You just want someone else to do the dirty work, huh?"

He shook his head, his eyes studying me for a moment. "Just promise me one thing."

I waited.

"You find yourself in a pinch again, you fight with everything you've got until I can reach you."

I pushed to a sit, shaking my head and dropped his gaze. "I don't think I should be a concern of yours, if-

"I'll do what I want," he retorted.

There was that royal guard stubbornness I'd been expecting. But I didn't doubt the male... I just didn't understand him.

He stood in one smooth motion that made me want to kick at his shins. Lazily, he lifts his shirt to wipe his face and I whip my head straight leveling my gaze on his bare feet. After a moment, they shift as if he's waiting for me to pick up my gaze, but I do no such thing.

"This right here," he said, "was from a blade last summer."

I risk a glance in his direction catching a smooth scar along his ribs. "This one, was a shifter who tried to take a swipe at Jason three years ago." That one is four long jagged lines across his hip.

"This one-" I lose the battle with my eyes and they dip down his abs before I quickly avert them to the treeline behind him.

"I get it," I snap. "You're a glorified pin cushion. What's the point?"

"The point is that I understand. I know what it feels like to have the memories of a moment, haunt you, long after the wound is healed. My hands still shake when I pick up an axe to chop firewood in the fall." His gaze softens as he draws back, no longer looking at me like I'm something to be studied. That crooked smile lifts the side of his lips brightening his expression.

"Do I want to know?" I asked, dusting my hands on my knees.

His responding grin was, in equal parts, brutal and excited.

That was a no.

He reached out again offering me his hand. This time, I took it, and he hauled me to my feet before him.

"We've both put our bodies on the line to protect the male we love."

Electricity ran down my arm stopping my heart.

We. Love?

My breath caught in my throat, my eyes darted to his nervously.

This was it. This was where he killed me.

"And I haven't thanked you for that," he said.

My exhale was audible as my heart pounded against my ribs. And shaking loose the guilt I'd been nursing, I decided to be honest. Even if I sounded like a wretch.

"Don't thank me for that," I ground out quietly knowing it was very possible the entire household behind me could hear us.

He dipped his chin low, the early morning light catching the dusting of silver along his temples. "You were willing to trade your life for his. You love him. I get that."

His voice was low, like he too had thought to temper his volume. There were no accusations there, but it scared me all the same. It was one thing to admit it to myself, and then stuff it violently into a heavy lidded box in the back of my mind, but it was another to say it out loud. To hear it.

"Stop saying love!" I hissed, my heart pounding against my ribs.

I took a stumbling step backwards jerking my hand free from his.

His rough palm caught me gently by the arm as he stepped into my space, his chin ticking down again, this time to notch at my ear. I barely heard him over the thrum of my pulse, but his gravelly voice shattered all the walls I had spent these past weeks building.

"Don't fret, Princess. I'm very good at sharing."

Surprise rattled through me and I froze. Over and over those words replayed in my mind as I turned to study him.

He smiled. It started off small- calm, but it transformed into something genuine. Something sunny and rugged.

"You protected him when I wasn't here. That scar should have been mine," he said, his knuckle stroking down the length of the puckered skin behind my shoulder. "Though you wear it well."

My knees trembled and I couldn't be certain of the cause.

"Let me help you feel safe again."

"I..." I stepped away trying to wrap my head around the turn our conversation had taken.

"You don't have to decide right away," he nodded, taking another step back, granting me my space, as he tucked his hands into his pockets. "Think about it."

And with that he strode across the garden and into the house without a backwards glance.

Chapter Twenty

I was freshly dressed after my shower, my hand pressed to the door frame, lips sucked between my teeth as I closed my door as silently as possible. I made it only three steps down the hallway when I heard footfalls as someone climbed the stairs.

Pausing, I held my breath.

Maybe it was Hartley. Hartley always made sure that I heard him, but these sounded heavier than Hartley's typical stride. The uncertainty had me backtracking. The thought of running into Henry after our conversation… and the feelings that had been plaguing me since, was something I was enthusiastically trying to avoid, So, I turned on my heel retreating faster down the hallway, not wanting to be caught. By the sound of it, he would hit the landing in only a few more steps.

I caught my error a moment too late when I found myself at the end of the hall facing three doors, the study, the art studio, and their bedroom. Only one choice. I dipped into the study, closing the door between us as silently as possible hoping to skirt down the back staircase just as I caught Henry's fucking smirk as he crested the top of the stairs.

"Hello Pet."

Jason's voice greeted me from across the room and I froze. That giant asshole had herded me into sharing space with Jason after all my effort to avoid him.

My hand tightened on the door handle calculating the odds of Henry waiting on the other side of the door, should I just walk right back out. I swallowed a sigh picturing him leaning against it, chuckling in that rumbly way, celebrating his little victory.

I turned slowly.

My eyes landed on his chest as my mind clawed for a solution.

"Can I read in here?"

"Of course you can," he nodded, his gaze quiet, as he watched me watch him.

I caved first, if only to keep from inspiring any further conversation. Dropping my gaze like a coward, I beelined for my pillow nest. And once safely behind a wall of words, I was able to catch my breath taking periodic glances at the vampire where he braced himself against the polished wood of his desk.

He's wearing a crisp white button down under a grey vest that he's left open. I follow the material ticking down each button until I reach his arms. His sleeves are cuffed at the elbows, dark whirls of ink play along his forearm and across the tops of his hands. Those silver rings winking at me as I watch him shove black-tipped fingers through his hair, which has grown. The sides still sit tightly across his temples but the top has grown long enough to part, falling more frequently across his forehead.

As I watch him comb dark locks back into submission, I can feel it running through my fingers as well.

They tighten against the book cover as I snap myself back to the present and return to my hiding place amongst the pages.

It wasn't long before we settled into our old routine. I read from my nest of pillows by the window, and Jason worked quietly, seeming content to enjoy the silence.

As gradually as the sky darkens, my anxiety lessens and I'm able to see the words before me for more than just a shield. As I settle, that dull hum of stress buzzing in my ears quiets, and another sound catches my attention.

My eyes flicker to the lower level of the house where Henry is making his way across the garden. Stacked high across his shoulder, are large planks of fresh cut wood. He strides back and forth across the darkening yard piling these long planks against the wall on the far end of the garden. I watch as he sets a hand on his hip, the other fisting his shirt which he drags up his body to wipe his brow.

Jason's chair protests as he shifts and I startle. My cheeks and neck heat with embarrassment as I sink a little deeper into my pillows. Had he seen me? Had he realized what had distracted me from the book in my hands? My eyes flit to his tall frame as he stands reaching for something on the mantle behind his desk.

The strike of a match has fear igniting in my veins.

The fire Jason has lit crackles to life. It pops and spits as he drops into his chair once more. The heat stroked my skin, raising gooseflesh in its wake. Burnt wood and smoke carrying with it the grievous scent of old memories.

My eyes lock on the flames.

"Pet?"

Panic blossoms in my stomach as my eyes jump to his.

"What's wrong?"

"Nothing." I swallow struggling to hold his gaze as it sharpens. "Nothing."

I stand fumbling over a few pillows that catch my ankles. My hand catches the wall as I steady myself, but my eyes flash back to the flames, her screams ringing through my mind. I shouldn't be able to feel the heat this far from the flames, but I can.

I can feel it against my skin.

Under it.

"I can hear your heartbeat." His words cut through her screams as they ring in my ears.

It's an effort to pull my gaze from the hungry fire as it dances, but I do. Just barely. The fire pops and I flinch tears wetting my eyes, weighing them down as they land on the floor.

Wood splits, succumbing to the heat of the flames, and I don't know if the sound comes from the fire across the room, or the one scorching my mind. Her hand straining as it reaches for me, the wooden beam giving way between us.

My hands clench and unclench at my sides as I steady myself and fight for air. Fight for control over my own mind.

I clear my throat trying desperately to keep my eyes on this male who is so, so, easy to look at. Yet, I'm consumed by the tongues of fire licking up the brick, popping and spitting.

"I should help Hartley with dinner." I relent, needing to escape.

"Amelia," he barks. "Please." It's only my name on his lips that allows me to halt my retreat. He stands from the desk. "You've barely spent any time here. Please stay."

His fingers press to the desktop as he leans against it's map laden surface.

"What's happening? Did I-

"No," I shake my head, taking a step back.

"You can tell me. Let me help." He circled the desk slowly. His eyes snaring mine and allowing me a moment to focus, to sink into the warm umber that melds me to the ground.

He swallows, the motion rolling down his throat as he studies me.

"The fire," I rasp.

Understanding dawns across those umber eyes and he blinks away an emotion too brief to grasp. With that, my eyes latch onto those flames as they stroke the memories, the sounds of her screams reaching an unbearable pitch.

"Look at me." His voice cracked through the space like a whip, the command freeing in this moment. I didn't need to regain control, I just needed to surrender it ...to him.

His chin ticked higher, his jaw sharp, eyes molten.

"I'm going to put it out."

And he did. A flick of his wrist sends shadows descending on the flames smothering them with a hiss. Smoke outlines his frame as he appears before me, the room darkening as it dissipates. His hands settle against my arms and I hate that I flinch as they do. But the contact burned where he touched me. My skin was left feeling raw from the memory of that night.

I pulled away sharply and his eyes softened. Smoke and shadow playing across the planes of his face.

His voice rumbled through me. "I'm sorry."

"It's not your fault."

None of it was. Not me falling for him, not me being hurt, not this moment, none of it.

"I-" He shakes his head, regret scenting the air. "What can I do?" The pain in his voice had me stepping into him on reflex before I backtracked.

"I just...need air." I whispered tears slipping down my cheeks. Smoke burnt my eyes and my heart still hammered in my chest. His fingers twitched as if they would have liked to reach out and touch me, and in that moment, I wished he would. Wished I could tumble into his arms and let him hold me.

Hold this weight that felt like it would crush me.

But Jason never pushed.

Never crossed the line into my space, and I had just asked for more.

I watched him tighten his fist and take a step back with a nod, but why did it ratchet up the pain in my chest? Without my permission a sob burst from my lips as I turned, retreating into the hall. I shoved past Henry without a backwards glance bolting down the stairs.

I knew I was doing a disservice to the both of them, but it was the right thing to do. Right? Henry's words swirled around my mind as I began to question what exactly the right thing was now... Who was I protecting by pushing him away?

I skipped dinner that evening, and they allowed me my space. A plate was left on my bedside table when I woke long after the sun had set. I ate alone. The darkness of my quiet room was like a balm against the wounds that had long healed and the embarrassment that still lingered. I didn't sleep much that night, but when the sun rose, so did I, plan in mind.

The house had been quiet all morning and it was a surprise to find the door to Jason's study locked when I had tried the handle intending on breaking the silence that had been gnawing at my frayed nerves by mid afternoon.

But Hartley, as always, was a reprieve.

"Are you sure there's nothing else I can help with?" I asked the kind old vampire as he dried the last dish, placing it back into the high cabinet.

Hartley smiled, shooing me out of the kitchen before he paused. "As a matter of fact," he said, wagging a finger in the air as he spun for the cabinet once more.

"Can you bring this out to the shop?"

"The shop?"

He pivoted pointing through the back doors. "The outer building... just across the garden," he clarified.

"Oh." It was a good excuse to do some snooping in a brand new building. "Yea, sure thing."

Taking the large pot with both hands, I shouldered my way through the back door and crossed the yard on bare feet.

It wasn't until I shoved my way into the little building, using my elbow to pull open the door that had been propped open on a large stone, that I realized what this was.

It was a set up.

That little traitor.

"Uh..." I rebalanced the pot in my hands. "Hartley asked me to store this out here."

The last word sounded more like a question as I took in the space. My eyes bounced from shelf to shelf, cheeks growing red as I realized this was, in fact, a shop. A woodshop of sorts ... and absolutely nowhere in here, did it make sense to store a soup pot.

"Did he now?" Henry's voice scaped pleasantly across my skin as he wiped his hands on his jeans and set them on his hips.

"You know what, maybe I heard him wrong. Lemme go ask-

"No need." He circled the large work table towards me. "Here," he said, taking the pot from me and hoisting it onto a high shelf. "Since you're here, give me a hand."

I watched him measure and then cut long planks into different shapes. The whine and scrape of machinery filling the space.

I stacked each piece where I was told and watched intently as he carved a design into the shorter arching sections he had cut. He peppered me with little words of praise that admittedly, I loved, and soon we'd slipped into a comfortable space across the table from each other carving and sanding.

But I slipped a little too far and found myself admiring the male while he worked. The way his arms moved as he dug his gouge into the wood, stroke after stroke, creating beautiful designs.

Setting my last plank aside, I wasn't quite ready to leave this little bubble we were sharing, so I assigned myself a new task.

I was cleaning the work table, sorting the spare screws back into their containers, when Henry dipped low, blowing loose sawdust from the freshly carved wood. He caught me staring, and with a rush I spat out the only thing swirling around my mind, to fill the silence.

"I have a question about vampires."

His smile was crooked when he aimed it at me. "Ok, shoot."

"The other day you mentioned that vampires used to be able to procreate... before the magic died out. What happened?" The book I'd been reading had spoken about the witches' magic and the early study of tinctures and salves, but nothing of its origin or why it allowed vampires to procreate in the way only humans could.

He removed his gloves dusting off his hands on his pant legs once more.

"Hmm," he said, swiping his forearm along his brow "Curious about the process, are you Princess?" he chuckled, easily catching the screw I chucked at him. "Lifetimes ago, there was a coven of witches who had assisted the royal family in creating their son. A true royal vampire. Born, not made. A daughter followed. The royals made the coven promises of protection and wealth for their assistance. Seeing this, the vampire population, especially the elites, wanted a way to ensure their strength, their succession. But the coven was loyal only to the royals.

So there were those who sought out other covens. And though they tried, it couldn't be replicated properly. Some believe the magic became tainted. Or maybe those who volunteered to carry the vampire's children, had been. There had long been women who had offered themselves to vampires.... for many purposes."

When I scowled, he grinned.

"It wasn't like it is now. Both parties were willing and both left satisfied." He turned stacking the carved wood along the far wall as he spoke.

"But these women, they began making their own arrangements. Carrying a vampire child in order to gain immortality, a place among the vampires. Again. A trade. But what they created weren't vampires...this was how the shifters were born."

I set my hands against the table tracing the smooth wood grain as Henry continued.

"Most were killed. The women carrying the tainted children.. the witches creating them. But others were hidden away, their parents love prevailing. Some believe the witches purposely tainted the magic intending to create a species capable of rivaling the vampires, but the original coven was quick to squash those rumors."

"What happened to them?" I asked.

He brought his eyes back to mine.

"The royals had them killed."

My jaw slackened.

"Why?"

He smiled, but it was cruel. Harsh. "Vampires live very long lives. They had the children they wanted, and they didn't want to share that power with anyone else. Sure, they could buy their loyalty, but eliminating them saved them the coin and the potential for betrayal."

"After all they had done," I muttered. "After what they'd been promised."

"So you see why some think the shifters were a witch's rebellion." Henry nodded. "The population grew rapidly after that."

My brows drew together. "How do you know so much about this?"

"Most do, but at the time I was still a royal guard."

So he had a front row seat. I caught myself wondering for a moment if he had had even more than that. Remembering the armor, the weaponry Henry wore so well, I wondered if he had a part in the deaths of those witches. The thought, however, brought with it enough guilt to shake lose any remaining interest in the subject.

Henry returned to his task of staining the beautifully carved arches before him. I allowed myself only a moment to admire the male. His dark curls secured on top of his head, one loose over his forehead, another on the back of his neck. His jaw sharpened as he grinned, and that knowing smirk was enough to send me back to my task of sorting screws, before eventually retreating back into the house to help Hartley prepare dinner.

Chapter Twenty-One

That evening as Hartley and I finished cleaning the kitchen he turned to me with three mugs in his hands. "Would you mind helping me take these upstairs before you retire for the evening?" I smirked at his description of my evening. It was a very polite way of saying he knew it had become a routine of mine to scurry upstairs and hide away in my bathtub until my skin grew pruney beyond recognition.

"Sure thing," I took a cup from him and followed him up the back staircase. Henry met us at the door to the study taking both mugs from Hartley before he turned welcoming us into the room with a crooked smile. I didn't realize the change in the room as my gaze tracked immediately to Jason who rose from his desk chair with a smile I was so infrequently privy to these days.

He held my gaze, his eyes warm, smile broad, as he made his way across the room to me. Excitement glittered as he plucked the mug from my hands and stepped back. It was only as I followed his gaze did I notice the new addition to the room.

Gone was the pile of pillows tucked against the large windows, and in its place was a beautiful reading nook. Those tall arches stained a warm tone that reminded me of Jason's umber eyes and Henry's chestnut curls. Plush white pillows rested on top of a heavy cream fur lined blanket. Two shelves were mounted in the space behind the pillows, adjacent to the window, and filled with books and dotted with greenery in pretty polka dotted pots.

My head whipped around to Henry.

"You built this?"

He smiled and the proud nod that followed had my stomach tumbling. "Is this what you were working on?" I asked running my hand along the smooth stained wood.

"It is." The grin in his voice was audible as I traced the titles of the books lining the shelves with my fingertips. A little pot of rosemary from our garden scented the space. Below that a pot painted a midnight blue with gold-tipped stars held mint and lemon thyme.

"For your tea," Harltey allowed, setting down the third mug on the little ledge built into the reading nook along the window.

I swallowed the lump in my throat, and whispered my thanks as he excused himself, but not before I could wrap him in a tight hug. He chuckled, the sound gentle like the male himself as it rumbled his chest. He untucked me from his side with a pat on the back and dipped back through the door. He paused to pat Jason on the shoulder as he passed, and my eyes followed, trailing up the line of him to umber eyes.

"Why?" I asked, baffled.

"Because I enjoy having you spend time with me, and you deserve more than that pile of pillows," he said leaning a shoulder against the warm wood frame.

"I liked my little nest," I allowed.

Henry chuckled from behind me, the sound shaking me free of this stupor and I spun wrapping my arms around his ribs, squeezing him hard.

"Thank you." I inhaled his scent as I squashed my cheek against his chest. "It's beautiful." His arms tightened around my waist, one hand coming to rest on the back of my head.

"Glad you like it, Princess." His voice rumbled against my cheek and I smiled relaxing for the first time in what felt like weeks. There was something about Henry that was disarming in the most undeniable of ways.

I turned in time to catch Jason smiling again. Really smiling, as he pulled open draws I hadn't even noticed. Inside it was another fluffy blanket, treats, and a bookmark.

"You don't like me dog earring your pages," I grinned.

He chuckled, returning to his post against the corner of the gorgeous book nook. "I have-"

"Wait!" I pulled the bookmark free, taking a closer look. It was glossy and colorful covered in vibrant green leaves, herbs and sunny golden rays. "This is yours. Your art. You made this?"

He nodded and I stepped to him expecting him to draw himself up the way he had previously. But instead, he nodded and when I stepped into his arms he was quick to wrap his own around my ribs gently as I squeezed him tightly.

"Thank you."

His fingers threaded through my hair in a comforting stroke and I picked my eyes up meeting his. My chin set against his chest as it rose and fell with a quick breath, his scent permeating my senses.

"Thank you both." I pulled away reluctantly this time. "It's more than I could've ever dreamed."

I flopped into my proper reading nook. The cushion that caught me rivaled my mattress. The blankets and pillows pulled me into their delicious warmth. The males were gracious enough to ignore the obnoxious sigh I unleashed as I reluctantly pulled my face from the warm cloud of plush bedding I was melting into.

"I hope you don't expect me to ever use my room again." I rolled over, flopping onto my back, and caught the little lights that had been strung along the inner arches.

With a flick of his fingers the lights warmed, filling the space with a golden glow.

His eyes were soft when they met mine.

"Can't be reading in the dark," he said plainly. Though if I had any doubt why these little lights had made their way into the design, it died as I flickered a glance to the fireplace to find it cleaned out entirely. No logs. No soot. Vacant except for three stacked books and a plant I recognized from the living room.

My cheeks were wet without my permission. My vision blurred as I blinked away the traitorous tears.

"We needed more room books," he said in way of explanation. I watched him brush something from his shoulder before he picked his gaze up to meet mine. Warm umber greeted me, pulling me deeper as they softened.

"It's too much," I whispered, not trusting my voice to remain steady.

"It's not even close." Jason's voice was low, but something lit his eyes as they raised to the male across from him. "Is it Henry?"

"We take care of what's ours, Princess." He stepped into my space and I sat up meeting him. "And you are ours."

He held my eyes, a smile blooming across his handsome face. "Get used to it." He pressed a quick kiss to my cheek before flicking my nose.

Unfurling to his full height, he turned, his hand catching Jason's jaw before planting a kiss to his lips. He pulled away after only a moment, but it was enough to steal the breath from my lungs.

I think I liked watching Henry kiss Jason just as much as I liked watching him train.

Maybe more.

I fell asleep, book in hand, under the soft glow of my string lights. It was perfect. However, I was startled awake by the sound of Henry barging through the study door.

Slightly less perfect.

"We got it!" he crowed.

I roll over, rubbing the sleep from my eyes, in time to catch Jason shooting a sharp look at Henry who has now made his way to the large desk. He tosses the gilded envelope onto the desk, and drops into a chair looking not the least bit remorseful.

"Got what?" I ask, curiosity itching at my barely awake brain. Nosy tendencies need no sleep.

His eyes jump to Jason. "You haven't asked her yet, have you?"

Jason's eyes hardened. "I have not," he grumbles, running ringed fingers down his face before opening the letter.

Henry leaves Jason to his task, turning to me, a smirk sharpening his features. "Jason thinks you won't help him because he's been acting like a prick."

I tucked myself behind a curtain of hair as I pulled my lips between my teeth, fighting a losing battle with my jaw. Jason's gaze narrowed on the male, but his smile didn't waiver.

"What can I do to help?" I asked, once I composed myself.

"See," Henry said motioning to me as he raised a brow at Jason.

"I'm not agreeing," I clarified. "I'm asking. What is it you want me to do?"

Jason's lips twitched as if to throw the sentiment back in Henry's face, but the male seemed unfazed.

"I hadn't asked you because I didn't want you to think your gift was conditional."

"Oh. You're not taking it back," I smiled, pulling the heavy comforter around my shoulders. "Unless you are getting rid of the both of us. I will lay here until I simply meld into it."

"Gross," Henry mutters and I throw him a look.

"You're just jealous."

"Not in the slightest," he fires back.

Jason clears his throat recapturing our attention, though he studies Henry with wide eyes for a fraction of a second. I think a warning delivered, before his eyes cooled and lifted to mine.

"That was something we wanted to do for you, and it in no way means you are obligated to help."

"Yea, yea, spit it out."

His eyes sharpen but his lips twitch in that way that assures me I'm towing the safe side of this line we walk. I missed this. I missed teasing him, testing him. I missed him.

"We've received our invitation to the free lands."

"What does that mean?" My question is breathless. Whether it's fueled by fear or excitement, I'm not certain. Both maybe?

"It means we get to buy you a pretty dress and go schmooze some dickhead lords." Henry props his elbow on the back of the chair he was filling as he turned to me, a dangerous glint to his eyes.

"Sounds fun."

Two days later Jason drives as I sit passenger, our packed bags stowed away in the trunk. Henry rides behind us on his motorcycle. Jason had encouraged me to bring a few books, and I'm glad he did, because we drive all day. As the sun begins to set, Henry pulls ahead, disappearing around the twists and turns of the tree lined road.

"What is he doing?" I asked, tucking my bookmark into the page and setting it closed in my lap.

"We're not far from where we're staying for the evening, so Henry will ride ahead, greet our hosts, and make sure the cabin is secure."

"Hm," I hum in response, as I glance out the windows, trying to gauge where exactly we are in relation to the free lands.

I think Jason mistakes my curiosity for uncertainty as he sets his hand on my knee.

"You'll be safe," he assures. My eyes are slow to reach his, snagged as they are on his hand, where it rests against my skin.

"I'm not worried," I say.

He nods and we ride in silence a beat longer, before he returns that hand to the steering wheel. I temper my sigh cautious of his preternatural hearing, and slide my gaze back to the window where my disappointment can fade, unnoticed.

I follow Jason as he leads the way to the door, cool night air lingering low in the tall grasses as they twist around my ankles. The house is inviting and well lit, even as the sun sinks lower in the sky. Henry strides from the little cottage as we approach, wearing that easy grin that exudes confidence, and the promise of a stupid comment that I'm sure will send my stomach tumbling.

Annoying, really.

Thankfully, Amara, the sweet shifter who lives here, is quick to shove him from the doorway. Her little frame wriggles between him and the entryway he's hogging, before throwing her arms around my neck in a tight hug.

"Welcome to Carex Manor!" She pulls away her face alight with a smile. A smile she then aims at another figure as it emerges from the hallway behind Henry. This time he takes the hint, and steps aside.

"We're happy to host you. All of you." The new female's voice reflects the smile that Amara wears. "I'm Link." The vampire introduces herself with a handshake before tucking Amara into her side, and leading us all into the dining room.

Amara serves us dinner before making herself a plate, and dropping into the chair Link pulls out for her. With a swift kiss to her bright blue curls, she settles next to her partner and the five of us tuck into our meal.

Link and Henry clear the table before returning with small dishes of chocolate custard, fresh berries piled high, alongside a dollop of sweet whipped cream. I smile at the treat, unable to abate this reaction my brain has reserved solely for chocolate, and the two males flanking me at the table.

Returning to his seat, Henry rests his heavy arm across the back of my chair. From behind the curtain of my hair I watch him run his fingers along the back of Jason's neck. The casual touch wriggles something loose in my chest. And as it tumbles into my stomach, I replay Henry's words.

I'm very good at sharing.

Henry didn't wear the same mask the Prince to my left did, and after a few weeks, I was starting to learn just how to read the male. It was funny that I had thought him so confusing when we first met. I found myself second guessing my instincts and stumbling over his reactions when I couldn't make sense of them, but I was beginning to realize the problem.

Me.

I was reading Henry like I would Jason. Jason was nuanced. The roles he played required tact, and those masks he wore meant I had to look for the real male below, if I wanted to know how he really felt. I had to look beyond what he showed everyone else.

But Henry showed me exactly who he was on day one. And that was where I had struggled to read him. I'd been digging. Looking for the real male. Looking for what was just below the surface. But Henry wore no masks. His confidence was a loud thrum of rough padded fingers against the steel at his hip, where Jason was quiet power. A death sentence issued with the tick of his jaw and a snap of his fingers.

The prospect of accepting what Henry had proposed, had my pulse racing each time I thought about it. The vampires must be concerned I was developing an irregular heart beat.

But... would it be so wrong?

How would I even go about bringing it up?

I toyed with my dessert spoon as my stomach tumbled and my pulse followed just imaging those words leaving my lips.

Jason's eyes dropped to my hands before climbing to my face.

I must have been lost in my thoughts longer than I realized. Leaving a dessert untouched wasn't something I had the habit of doing... ever.

I pick my eyes up to his and I can read the question swirling along the umber and gold, but I track his hand distractedly. Dark tattoos, a contrast against his bright silver rings. They wink, catching the light of the candles flickering in the center of the table as he runs his hand down his chest. I watch as it continues down his thigh before landing on mine. His hand is warm, and the contact pulls a shiver up my spine.

My eyes flicker back to his.

Conversation continues across the table, but I'm struck by him. The little tug at the corner of full lips. The promise of that smile that steals my breath each time he gifts it. Even just by the return to this place where we can touch each other so casually... and yet there is nothing casual about how his fingers grip my skin. The way his hand slides to the inside of my knee, his thumb stroking a path that raises gooseflesh in its wake and draws a breath from my lips that I pray is silent.

His fingers still.

His grip loosens.

And I watch as his eyes study mine.

Again, I realize I've sent the wrong signals, and Jason has misread my reaction. My intention. He lifts his hand and I hurriedly try to correct him in the most inconspicuous way possible. In doing so, I commit to the first solution my brain poses, and cross one thigh over the other effectively trapping his hand between them.

His hand pauses and I can feel him scrutinizing my face, but I hold firm. Finally, he relents before tucking strong fingers back around the inside of my knee. Cold silver warms against my overheated skin, and I flush as he captures my gaze once more.

I smile around a bite of decadent chocolate swallowing the appreciative sound climbing my throat and instead strum my teeth across my lip. Slowly his lips lift into a winning smile. The perceived victory there flutters the muscles of my stomach. Accentuated only by the way his gaze softens, before he notches his chin a fraction higher, his shoulders relaxing as his thumb continues stroking my skin under the table.

I know they can hear the way my heart is pattering against my ribs, but no one seems interested enough to call attention to it, so I return to my dessert and sink back into the conversation. Conversation that thankfully hasn't so much as paused. Henry, while an active and boisterous participant in the discussion taking place between Link and Amara, has managed to somehow key into the change, and takes the opportunity to not be outdone. Warm fingers trace a strong line starting at the sensitive skin just under my ear to my shoulder where he collects a lock of my hair, casually twirling an errant curl around his fingers.

And that is how we spend the evening.

Pleasantly trapped between the two, I fight to maintain a neutral expression, my dessert, for once, unfinished on the table before me.

After dinner we move into the sitting room where, feeling brave, I curl into Jason's side on the sofa. It's because we're situated against each other, that I'm not able to hide the little jolt as I catch Link prepping a fire in the hearth.

Jason's arm drapes across my shoulders as he leans in to whisper in my ear. "Would you like to see the garden before the sun sets?" Henry's eyes snap to Jason's, before touching mine, and then landing on Link.

Henry chuckles easily. "You just want to finish that book so you can guilt me into buying you another from that pretty bookstore in town tomorrow."

I know what Henry is doing. Playing seamlessly into the exit strategy Jason has crafted, but the promise of a bookstore peaks my interest. As does the challenge. As if I would allow myself to fall asleep now without finishing my book, if it meant he'd be buying me another in the morning. But it's Jason who frees a dark chuckle, dragging me to my feet, and towing me behind him towards the hallway.

"Don't be sour Henry. I've offered to teach you how to read on many an occasion now."

Henry rolls his eyes, his chest fluttering with laughter he barely cages.

"But who needs to be literate with a body like that," he purrs, dragging his hand across the male's chest as we pass. I swear Henry inflates under his touch.

"Enjoy your book," he growls, lips curling on a devilish grin. "When you're ready to re-enact some of those spicier pages, you call me."

I blush aggressively as Amara's bell-like laughter peals through the room despite her hands being clapped to her mouth.

The sound follows us outside where Jason takes his time walking me around the garden, but as I get the sense he's simply here to gauge my reaction, I pull away from his side.

"Can I actually read for a while out here?"

He smiles his head indicating towards the big oak tree we are approaching. In it hangs a tire swing and from a lower bow, a hammock. I reach a hand out to run my fingers along the little shapes woven into the design when a breeze rushes against my back. I turn on my heel to find Jason, arms full of supplies.

He sets a pillow and blanket into the hammock and hands me my book, I was certain I'd left in the car.

"Sometimes I forget your fast." I say in way of thanks.

I read as the sun sinks below the tree line and along with it, my eyelids draw lower over my eyes.

Thwack. Thwack, thwack.

The sound echoes across the garden pulling me from my near sleep.

Henry emerges from the woods bordering the garden, an axe tossed over one shoulder, a satchel of logs in the other.

I settle back against the hammock, a cool breeze coasting along my cheek, before bolting upright, and tumbling right out of the stupid thing with a curse.

"Fucking *ow!*" I dust my hands on my pants, and jog to catch up with Henry, who's now made his way behind the tree line.

I bolt in his direction, catching myself on the long reed like trunk beside me as Henry turns, swiping an arm across his brow.

His smile lands like a blow to my stomach. No one is built like this man. Well... almost no one.

I shake myself.

"What are you doing?"

"Chopping wood," he answers easily, setting the axe, eye down, on the ground.

I huff aiming for a more relaxed stance. "Are you already finished?"

"On the contrary, Princess. I was only getting started."

I nod, reaching for the axe. "Will you teach me how?"

"To chop wood?" The question lingers between us as he tips his head to the side appraising me with an intensity only a male made-predator could possess. I'm careful not to squirm as he pulls his gaze over me, but my blood sizzles.

I've been chopping wood since I could walk, but I was confident I could throw a few poor swings and sell my lie. My heart is pounding with adrenaline that I hope he mistakes for excitement. On any other day, chopping wood would be the last thing I'd want to be doing, but I knew I wouldn't be able to return to my hammock nap knowing he was out here swinging that axe over and over.

Having to listen to the sound of the splitting wood... or whatever his trigger may be.

I'm a withered prune of anxious, cuticle-picking, energy when he finally relents.

"Sure, Cmon."

I pick up the axe and follow him to a massive pile of branches and trunks.

"So why are we chopping wood?" I ask.

"Amara and Link were gracious enough to host us, so I'll make sure they are prepared for the cold. Link is older than she looks." He paused, his eyes flickering to mine. "Don't tell her I said that," he warns and I swear there's a bit of real fear lingering behind that teasing look.

Goosebumps dot my arms under my sleeves as I set up next to the large pile of uncut branches and small trunks.

"Hold on there, eager beaver." He chuckles to himself as he snatches the axe from my hands. "I can't return you with any missing digits. Let me show you the basics, then you can give it a go."

I nod scraping my hair back into a braid as I watch him swing the damn thing like he was born to wield it. Cutting the log cleanly he pivots, chunking the pieces into a new pile. Knotting my braid, I used my hip to wedge myself into his place.

"Ok, looks easy enough," I tease right back. He snorts, but ultimately loosens his grip allowing me to retake the thing.

I took a few poor swings clipping the edge of the wood, or missing entirely, before I pretended to grasp the motion. Soon I had slipped into a familiar rhythm. We both did.

I chopped while Henry set piece, after piece, of wood before me on the chopping base. My arms burned and sweat beaded on my back and brow, despite the cool temperature. Still, each swing produced a new log.

I glared at the most recent branch. The offending thing just sitting there until I cracked it just off to the right with a grunt of frustration.

Another.

Henry leaned against the tree to the right of the mountainous pile we'd created, watching me quietly. I held his eyes for only a moment. Just a moment, where I debated how worth it it was to protect this *very* capable male. But I couldn't set the damn thing down and walk away, knowing I'd hear it. I'd hear the axe splitting the wood, just like I heard those knives landing in the training block or thudding into my back. I shook my head bringing the axe down harder than I needed to in order to crack the log before me.

But it felt good.

And miserable.

"I'll finish it from here." His voice cut into my concentration.

"No." I loaded up the next log myself. "I've got it."

He watched me, his large hand curled around another log, but didn't set it down. I think he could tell I was ready to grab it myself.

He set the wood down slowly, his eyes locked to mine, but didn't step back.

I was too tired to argue.

He was a vampire. I'm sure he was fast enough to move, and I was confident enough I wouldn't hit him, regardless.

I split the log and he paced back to the pile, loading on another.

Then another.

I could finish this pile. After this pile, I could stop.

I could shower.

I could nap.

Right here on this very block.

He moved too quickly for me to register. Or maybe, I had burrowed myself too deeply into my thoughts, but as I brought the axe down to split the log, his foot appeared on top of it.

I swung wide lodging it into the cold dirt to the left.

"What are you doing!" my eyes shot wide and I spun on him.

"What are you doing?" he asked, those bright eyes glittering with the promise of a fight.

"What does it look like?" I growl reaching for another log.

"It looks like you're lying to me."

I swallow my anger and he raises his brows as I turn to meet him.

"You've chopped enough wood to get them through winter." His head inclines to the ever growing pile.

"That's barely enough for the month," I bluster.

He laughs, dusting his hands off on his pant legs. "Says the girl who needed me to teach her to swing an axe, huh?"

I swallowed my retort, not wanting to continue to lie to him.

His hands curl into firsts as he sets them against his hips. "How long were you going to keep this up?"

I set my lips into a straight line. "Until we were done," I grit out, irritated with the giant dummy.

I coast my gaze across the trees to avoid watching the moment things click into place, but he's waiting for me, a handsome smirk plastered across his face.

"What?" I snap.

"You like me."

Oh for fuck's sake.

I roll my eyes, leaving him standing there wearing that stupid, handsome smirk, and stomp my way back to the garden, dragging the axe behind me.

He catches up immediately- because of course he does- and sweeps the axe from my grip, notching it over his shoulder, a smug grin beaming down at me.

"Give it back!" I dance around his back on my toes, reaching for the handle over his shoulder.

"I can touch the damn axe, Princess" he turns, gripping the handle and hurls it across the yard, the bit lodging deftly in the tree beside the kitchen window.

That was aggravatingly hot.

"Go upstairs and shower. I'll meet you in the living room when you're finished."

I couldn't decide if I was irritated over the implication I should do as I'm told, or relieved to indeed go shower like I'd been dreaming about for what felt like an hour now.

Nevertheless, I did as I was told and sunk into a hot bath soaking my sore muscles until the water grew cold.

I wasn't sure if I should follow through on the instructions to meet him in the living room after I'd showered, but there really wasn't much to lose. So, I padded down the hall on bare feet to find Henry, also freshly showered, reclining on the couch. Jason was sitting in the chair by the fireplace reading.

"Ah, there she is."

The space was fire free and quiet.

He widens his legs as he pats the space between them.

I pause just outside of arm's reach taking him in. Wet and in the low light of the room, his curls are nearly as dark as Jason's. It sharpens the features of his face. Gone is the leather he'd been wearing. Now I watch as he pushes sage green sleeves to his elbows. The soft, brushed cotton, hugs his broad chest and bunches at his waist as he pitches forward, elbows set to his sweatpants-clad thighs.

His eyes glitter as he teases me.

"Sit." The instruction is clear. That wasn't why I hesitated, but he didn't need to know that.

Henry grabs a bottle of oil from the tableside before catching my eye again. He holds a finger up, spinning it as if to tell me to turn around and do as I'm told.

This time his voice is low, gravelly.

"Sit."

The command in his voice shakes my knees and pulls Jason's eyes from the pages before him. He catches my gaze, a grin of his own tugging at the corner of those full lips. His brow raises, eyes dipping to the space between Henry's thighs.

A command of his own.

I cave, turning slowly and settling between his legs, but my back is straight, shoulders achingly stiff as I hold myself still.

Gently, Henry gathers my hair sweeping it over my shoulder. The sound of him warming the oil between his hands shouldn't make the muscles of my stomach tighten, but it does. Jason's eyes remain on mine as I focus on keeping my breathing even.

Henry's hands slip under my shirt, and up my back, until they can grip my shoulder with a firm squeeze. And all that effort I'd expended into controlling my breathing just winks out of existence. My shoulders soften under his demanding hands, as does my jaw, allowing a sigh to slip free.

Jason's eyes sharpen, umber bleeding obsidian, as he reclines in his chair looking every bit the Dark Prince. The book hangs forgotten in one hand where it's draped over the armrest, the other is set to his lips. His jaw. Black stained fingertips trace his lower lip as he watches us.

One at a time, Henry works my muscles into submission, and my eyes fall closed. It had been months since I'd been taken from my home in the free camp, and just as long since someone's touch had felt so caring. Casual touch, so freely given. Jason and I had had moments of touch, moments where we offered comfort to one another, but they all seemed charged by this undercurrent that ran between us. All of them, too short, too controlled. And by the time he had reached for me, looking for more, I had pulled away. Henry's touch now unwound something in me I hadn't realized had grown so tightly bound.

My body melted under his hands.

Into them.

His hands were warm, and his grip was strong. Calloused palms scraped against my skin teasing little shivers out from under my control.

After he's worked my back and shoulders into warm jelly, I yield to him as he tucks me closer against him. I reclined against his chest, letting his body support me as those strong fingers sunk into my hair massaging my scalp. I turn my cheek into him, notching myself against his jaw, and he continues his assault on my neck. I enjoy the tickling of each warm breath across my skin that this position allows. He massages the oil down each arm, kneading my palms, and gently coaxing the soreness from my fingers.

After a beat of stillness, his hands grip my waist and I think he's prompting me to move, so I stand. But his fingers tighten as he coaxes me to turn back around to face him. I ignore the swell of relief that warms my chest when he reclines, before pulling me back into his lap. Moss green eyes are calm, his hands slipping to the backs of my thighs as I bracket his legs with mine. My arms wrap around his neck and I nestle back into his warmth. Each of his slow breaths swell from his chest into mine, and my eyelids grow heavy.

I close my eyes with my cheek pressed to his collarbone, his hands dragging up and down my back. In my half-asleep state, I barely register the quiet conversation he holds with Jason. Especially when he wraps his arms around my back, allowing me to exhale every last bit of tension left in my body as he cradled me against him. If this is how good submitting to these males could be, I don't know if I want to fight it any longer.

Chapter Twenty-Two

Amara braids my hair after breakfast. The curls she leaves loose, she tucks into two little buns at the nape of my neck. After slipping back into my pants and a soft knitted sweater, I'm heading back downstairs when I catch clipped conversation from behind the closed door at the end of the hall.

My inability to mind my own business, has me tiptoeing closer in time to catch Jason's huffed reply.

"-may not be possible, but if there is even a chance..." he hesitates, and I hold my breath, wishing I could quiet my heartbeat.

"Look," the other voice sounds like Link. "If I can help, I will, but this is a risk."

"I know what I'm asking- of you. Of her."

Her?

What the hell are these vampires up to?

Link's voice grows louder as if she's approaching the door and I freeze.

I can't run. That would give me away faster than if I hunker down and hope to hold my breath long enough to remain hidden.

"You have my support, and on the day, you'll have my loyalty, but-"

Hands catch my waist and a shriek rips from my throat.

Something fumbles behind the closed door as I slap Henry's back.

"Henry!" I slap him again to no avail. The giant brute carries me over his shoulder, his arm a bar across the back of my thighs, without so much as a pause in his stride. "What the fuck?"

Was I in trouble for spying?

While I had a spectacular view of his ass, I had no sense of awareness otherwise. He's too damn wide to see around, so I can't see where he's taking me. We step over the landing and into the cool morning air, before he acknowledges that he has a wriggling human woman slung over his shoulder, and not a sack of potatoes.

"I have Jason's permission to borrow you," he announces proudly.

Well that's nice.

"What about my permission?" I challenge, then pause. "Oh right. Pet," I grouse, and set my elbow to his back, catching my cheek with a resigned sigh.

He chuckles, pitching forward to draw me back over his shoulder. He handles me gently, glittering green eyes catching mine, as he sets me on my feet.

"You can stay here if you'd like, but I'm heading into town. I thought you may want to join me." He motions to the bike parked in front of the house.

I cross my arms, and his grin softens. We both know I'll forgive him, and that realization flusters me. So, with a huff and a shove to his chest, I grab the helmet from the bike seat. I fit it over my head, but appease his twitchy fingers and let him buckle it under my chin.

Safety was Henry's thing after all.

He swings a leg over the bike settling his weight, before reaching back to offer me a hand.

"Isn't Jason coming to town with us?" I ask, as I wrap myself, willingly this time, around the male as he shifts the bike, lifting the kickstand with his heel.

"Don't fret, Princess," he chuckles. "He's helping Link dig out an old map of the freelands and will meet us there."

This ride is different from our last. More familiar. More fun. Henry takes turn, after turn, his arm wrapping around my back, pinning me to him as I hold out my arms and close my eyes.

It's like flying.

But better, because the air smells like viburnum and Henry. It's also thawing. It's still cold, but that bitter wind has subsided and has given way to a cool damp breeze that promises a lush spring ahead.

Shamelessly, I enjoy the way he holds me. His arm relaxes when he realizes I'm content to curl up against him, and the risk of me soaring off of the back of the bike, has subsided. Instead, he curls his big hand around my fingers where they're gripping his leather jacket, holding me in place. There was no denying that Henry was easy to warm to. The big brute was secretly gentle, and funny, and in equal measure, took every opportunity to hold me close, and pick a fight.

Falling for Henry was inevitable.

We walk the market, hopping from booth to booth. Some vendors sell smoked meats, the smell of garlic and rosemary scenting the air as we stroll past. Another that catches Henry's eye, has a few leather crafted items on display. He seems content to keep moving, but I indulge in a sudden interest in a leather sheath, running my fingers along the impressive stitching, and hiding the smile that buds as Henry caves and begins browsing in earnest.

I peek over the rack of shoulder bags, and find him holding a scabbard.

"That would look good on you," I offer, dropping my eyes to the leather bound journal etched with foxglove blossoms.

After waiting as long as I could stand without a response, I picked my eyes back up and found him grinning at me in that sunny way that felt so much like the male before me.

Unfettered sunshine; bright and warm.

I relinquish the hold on the grin I was biting back and watch as his eyes dance across my face.

"Oh," he said, those eyes darkening playfully. "You've got it bad, Princess."

My grin dies as I roll my eyes and prepare to stomp away, when he appears before me, wrapping me in his giant arms as I fight him.

"Not so fast," he scolds, handing over the scabbard and a small thigh holster he had set aside. "I'll take these," he smiles at the vendor while wrangling me effortlessly with one arm.

Fucking vampires.

The males barter, and after some struggling, a distracted Henry releases me to wander to the next booth.

The sweet scented air lightens my mood and my eyes dance across the basins of colorful candies.

"Would you like a sample?" the vendor asks with a smile and a flourish of their hand. My eyes coast across the basins before searching over my shoulder for Henry.

Who conveniently materializes, as if summoned.

"Yes she would," he answers for me, and then confidently collects two of every type of sweet from the effervescent vender. I'd feel a bit guilty if it wasn't for the list he pulled from his pocket, which was egregiously long, and began rattling off sweets we were apparently buying.

As the vendor bags up our bounty, I sample enough candy to make me sick, though I love every minute. He hands me a satchel of wispy spun sugar the color of lavender, the rest he tucks into a leather messenger bag he must have procured from the previous booth.

"Anything with a blue tie is fair game. The others are for Hartley," he informs, me eyeing the bag in my hand.

I hold it out to him as we walk.

"You know about Hartley's stash as well?"

He snorts. "Who do you think restocks it so Jason doesn't lose his head?"

I raise a brow. "Hartley didn't strike me as the 'touch my candy, and lose your head, type'."

"You're too new," he laughs. "Hartley is still nice to you."

It was my turn to snort. "Or maybe, he just likes me more than you."

"Oh, without a doubt."

We make our way to the end of the market, and turn the corner, coming to stop before the bookstore. And it's everything I was promised it would be.

The large front windows are framed a light pink that softens the white exterior. Vines, dripping in little white and pink blossoms, climb the storefront, framing the wooden sign that reads, INK & PAPER.

It's beautiful.

And so is the male prowling across the street with a wicked grin, and three cups in his hands.

"Coffee, coffee, tea." His lips twitch at the growl of appreciation that draws up Henry's throat. The male doesn't waste a moment before snatching the cup and taking a greedy gulp. Jason holds out the remaining one to me.

"I'll have you know I just spent an hour watching her consume her body weight in straight sugar, so caffeine should be a nice cherry on top." Henry mocks, wiping his hand down his beard.

Jason smiles, his eyes falling from the sign above us, to Henry, and then landing on me.

"And now we unleash you on the unsuspecting patrons of Ink&Paper." He winks. "Kate is a friend. So we have some leeway."

I smile at the implication, my gaze returning to the beautiful window display, and the lines of shelves that have excitement bubbling already.

"The patrons have nothing to worry about... but," my gaze jumps to Jason. "You're a big strong vampire," I coo. "How many books do you think you can carry?"

His lips quirk before giving way to a full on smile.

"Let's find out, shall we?"

He holds out his elbow, and I slip my arm through his. With a conspiratorial grin, Jason and I hurry through the door leaving a grumbling Henry where he stands as we disappear into the stacks.

Eventually, we split up in hunt of our books. I went from shelf to shelf, stopping here and there, to examine a cover, read a synopsis, or run a finger along beautiful foil-stamped or gilded spines.

Kneeling on the ground, I flipped through the pages... never to the last page, of course, I wasn't a monster. But enough to determine if it was worth adding to my growing collection of books.

I was meandering down the romance aisle, when another cover caught my eye. The pink spine had swooping letters, and pops of tan and blues that promised a pretty cover. Unfortunately, I barely reach to brush fingertips along the smooth spines of the shelf just below.

Damn.

Taking a peek down the rows of books, I set the toe of my boot to the first shelf, and hoist myself up. Careful, of course, not to touch any books with my shoe.

I didn't want to damage the merchandise... but if I did, I suppose we'd have to buy it. 'You break it, you buy it' and all that. I peeked down at my boot, eyeing the covers at risk of 'damage', before chuckling to myself, and returning to the task at hand.

Steadying myself against the shelf, I reached for the book again.

"Come here," I mutter to the stubborn, beautiful book. "We both know you wanna come home with me."

His voice met my ear at the same moment his hands closed around my waist, hoisting me that last inch.

"You are going to get us kicked out."

I grabbed the book holding it to my chest as he set me down.

"All that for some smut." His eyebrow quirked and my cheeks heated.

"I-

"I hope it's good at least. Let me see." He was grinning ear to ear, and it was a thing to behold.

"Absolutely not!" I smiled, unable to fight it, though I didn't try.

My grip tightened on the book in my arms, turning my upper body away from him to shield my book from his prying eyes.

He chuckled, the sound menacing, as it rumbled up my spine.

"If you show me yours, I'll show you mine." His eyes flickered to the tower of books he must have set down next to mine on the little table. I sucked my lips between my teeth fighting a grin of my own, but my control over my face only spanned so far, because I could feel my eyebrows hitting my hairline.

"Now we're talking!" Henry cawed, materializing out of nowhere.

Someone shushed haughtily from deeper in the bookstore.

My lips popped from between my teeth on a breathy laugh as I rolled my eyes. And Jason tracked the motion, his eyes dark in the low light of the stacks. But as they flickered to Henry, I could feel the moment their gazes collided.

Tension sparked.

"I don't think the princess wants to play," Henry's deep voice coasted across my skin like a physical touch.

"Pity." Jason purred, slipping into that mask of his. Though this one was different. It was softer. A robe maybe. A persona he wrapped himself in. But I liked this version of Jason. Every bit the dark prince; confident and sharp... and seemingly less inclined to keep me at arms length.

He stepped into me, his knuckles finding my chin, ensuring there was no escape from that snare-like gaze of his. My back hit the stacks, and he took one last step, angling me between himself and Henry.

This male oozed dominance, and under his heated gaze I melted against Henry. Maybe, just maybe, I wouldn't mind doing as I was told.

Under very specific parameters.

Maybe I did want to play.

Like he saw that puzzle piece click into place, he grinned and it was edged in that bit of victory that sent my stomach tumbling. I lost my breath as he leaned in, his thumb anchored my chin as his fingers swept open cupping my throat. Slowly, like the smile stretching his lips, his thumb grazed my jaw until he could grip my neck, adjusting the angle of my head, just so. The heat from his hand sunk into my skin as I watched him close the distance between us.

When he was only a breath away, he shifted, his other hand snapping to Henry. He gripped the front of his shirt and towed the male's mouth to his. Their kiss was a competition of wills. Every ounce of that dominance poured into the victory over Henry's mouth. He growled, and Henry swallowed the sound, grinning against his lips in response. I panted, unable to look away, both of their bodies touching mine, yet not nearly enough.

I wanted their hands on me.

I wanted more.

I swallowed and his grip tightened on my throat, the contact sending a shiver of want straight to my core.

Using his body, he pressed me tighter into Henry, and in response, Henry wrapped his arm around my waist, keeping me in place.

Protecting me.

Always protecting.

And like a magnet, he turned, angling out bodies into Jason, his other hand knotting in the back of his hair.

Jason groaned, the sound carnal, and I nearly lost my grip on the whimper I was caging between my teeth.

They pulled away breathing hard and grinning. More than the attraction between them, you could see the love. Henry straightened Jason's shirt with a peck on the lips. Affection and care, this male's second nature.

His eyes dipped down to mine and Jason's followed.

"She may not want to play," Jason smiled. "But I think she likes to watch." He ran a thumb under his bottom lip and I wanted to suck that thumb into my mouth and taste them both.

Oh I definitely liked to watch.

And... I think I wanted to play.

We load our books into the car and Jason turns to catch Henry's gaze. Something passed between them before Jason settled his gaze on mine.

"Do you mind riding back with Henry?"

"Course not," I responded honestly.

"I have one last errand to run while we're in town," he explains. "But I'll meet you back at the cabin."

Henry nods, then wrapping an arm around my shoulders, responds. "We have an errand of our own before we head back anyway."

Henry releases me to hold the door for Jason, and I watch as he climbs back into the car. But not before leaning in to place a kiss to his neck just below his ear. This time I'm not distracted enough to miss the blade Jason slips from the sheath Henry wears across his chest. My heart stumbles. What exactly is this last errand he's running, and why does it require a dagger?

Anxiety stirs awake in my chest as he drives away, but Henry just tows me along behind him as we head back into the quieting market.

We purchase an ungodly amount of camping equipment and Henry brushes off each of my attempts to dissuade him. I don't need any of these things to spend a few nights camping in the free lands, but Henry just spouts some nonsense about how I'd have to get used to being spoiled, and continues on.

After scheduling a time for delivery with the vendor, I realize we aren't returning to Amara's house tonight. From the sounds of it, we will cross into the territory lorded over by the shifters. The same swath of land that borders the free lands where Jason and I traveled. We're maybe two day's travel from my home. Or whatever may be left of it.

Henry squeezes my hand bringing me back just as we pass under an arch of lights I hadn't noticed in the bright midday sun. Now as the sun begins to set, and the market is transitioning from day to night, I soak in all the new details. This place was a bubble of sweet scented air and kind smiles, tucked into the hellscape that was the rest of the south.

Instead of ping ponging from booth to booth we walk around a lake dotted with artists and musicians displaying their talents.

The smell of chocolate fills the air as Henry guides me to a very popular booth at the end of our path. He buys two hot chocolates, and with it, my undying loyalty, as I salivate watching the woman pour the most luscious hot chocolate into our mugs. The steam billows around a hearty dollop of whipped cream with a roasted marshmallow skewered on a little pick, set across the rim.

Henry groans as he sips his, promptly stuffing the whole marshmallow in his mouth and chasing it with another swig of molten chocolate.

We sit on a bench just off the main walking path allowing us to look over the lake before us and the market to our left. The flower vender, a young shifter with bright red hair, packs up her things handing out a free flower here and there to those who walk past. She has roses, peonies, and azaleas in whites and pinks, and an idea has excitement tingling at the back of my shoulders.

Maybe it's residual worry, but I didn't think Henry would allow Jason to walk into danger alone. He was here strolling the market seemingly unbothered, so Jason had to be safe.

He had to be.

And maybe it would be nice for him to come home to some flowers.

The ride back to the new location we were staying wasn't long, but the anxiety over not knowing where Jason had gone, or if he was safe, had the ride feeling nearly insufferable. A sharp pang of relief sounded through me as we turned the corner up the drive to the little cabin to see the car parked safely tucked under the glow of a soft porch light.

He was home.

He was here.

I climb off the bike, and Henry follows suit, grabbing the bouquet of flowers from the hidden compartment under the seat.

I follow Henry as he walks the bike around the darkened side of the cabin, through a breezeway, and into a detached outer building. After setting the bike on its kickstand and our helmets onto the seat as I take a slow spin, soaking in the darkened space. It overlooks a small yard that ends on a cliff face, and from the little open window, I can hear waves lapping at rock and smell the salt that scents the breeze.

Henry's attention snaps out the far window and I follow his gaze, my interest piqued as I'd watched the slow grin that had spread across his face as his eyes trained on something just outside.

It takes my eyes a moment to separate the shadows from one another, but as they adjust, I see him.

There, training in the darkening yard, is Jason. He lands striking after strike to a strong pine at the center of the space. His sweat slicked skin and dark tattoos glisten in the low light leaking from the cabin windows. He turns, and I get a look at his bare back, muscles flexing and tattoos shifting, swirling, and arching as he moves.

Snapping out of my lust fueled daze was like being doused by a bucket of cold water. It set my heart racing as I took a sharp step back, grateful Henry's focus was still glued to Jason. Before I allowed myself to dig too deeply into how I felt ogling Jason alongside Henry, a plan formed, and I jumped at it. My eyes flashed over my shoulder. Keeping my movements as minimal as possible was going to be the only way to pull this off.

I was only a step away from the window so with a shallow breath to steady my pounding heart, I reached up and pulled the little chain dangling above me filling the room with light and hopefully stunning the vampire beside me. I dropped to the ground as bright light went pouring over the yard like a beacon, leaving Henry standing in the window, exposed.

Watching Henry's face as he spun out of frame of the window, his back to the wall as he hid, immediately catching on, sent me into a fit of cackles. We had certainly given away our position, but Henry didn't relent. He crouched low, snagging my ankle and tugging me easily across the floor before caging me under him. My laugh dies in my throat as his weight settles over me.

"That wasn't very nice," he chuckles.

My skin heats, and as if we can sense him, our gazes lift to find Jason standing in the doorway.

"See something you like?" he growls. His knuckles are stained black, claws tucking away, but not before Henry and I caught them.

He was worked up over something.

From what I could tell, they only appeared during times of heightened emotion and Henry's reaction only solidified that. His eyes darkened, concern whirling in that probing gaze.

A gaze that he transforms in a second as it coasts appreciatively over his frame.

"I certainly did," he says, his words pitched low. That gravelly tone rumbles through me. "Princess, what about you?"

I squirm, caught off guard and he rises to his feet, taking me with him.

"I think she needs some time to decide what she'd like," he shrugs.

I don't.

I really don't.

But in these moments I find myself unable to voice exactly what it is I do want.

"Then why don't you put her down." He lifted his eyes to Henry, amusement sparking in that whip like gaze. The command in his tone coasts over us and I realize I'm not the only one affected. Henry's spine straightens and I shiver in his arms.

In a stubborn display of doing just as he's told, on his own terms, he shrugs, and deposits me against Jason's sweat slicked chest with a laugh.

My heart flutters at the contact not knowing what to do. I'd spent a weird amount of time touching Henry to the point where it felt comfortable, but not Jason. Jason had always felt just out of reach, his touches controlled. Restrained. Now, his arm was a bar against my back, my arms wrapped around his neck.

"Thanks for letting me borrow this," he calls over his shoulder.

I respect it... but I'm going to stab that vampire.

"Oh," he paused, snagging the flowers from the counter he'd placed them on. "She picked these out for you," he said, placing the flowers in Jason's free hand and dipping out into the cool night air.

That asshole.

Like he heard me, he turned, taking the porch steps backwards as he winked.

The paper around the flowers crinkled drawing me back to the male I was currently plastered against.

"Did you buy me flowers, Pet?" he rasped against my neck and I shivered, my eyes drawing over his shoulder. Just as I was debating dragging my tongue up the column of his throat, and just what he would taste like, he pulled back with a smile. A real one.

The rumble in his chest echoed in mine.

He tightened his grip allowing me to wrap my legs more securely around his waist. I uncoiled my arms from around his neck and set them on his shoulders.

"Maybe," I shrugged noncommittally, smiling at his tattoos. I ran my thumbs along the dark whorls outlining his shoulders.

When I picked my eyes up to meet his, they were controlled, swirling with his usual secrets. But they heated as I held them, and my thighs tightened around him.

Our next breath knocked our chests together. This is where he'd pull away. Allow me my taste of his skin, and then build that wall right back up between us...but it didn't happen.

He leaned in.

Slowly.

Holding my gaze until he ducked under my hair, his nose running the length of my jaw. He traced a line up to the shell of my ear, his breath skating over the sensitive skin.

"Thank you," he breathed, his lips coasting over my neck before placing a kiss to the skin just above my collarbone. My hands tighten on his shoulders arching to give him more access. Wanting him to continue exploring my skin with his, but he dips forward, releasing me. Stubbornly, I stay right where he sets me, refusing to step away. I won't be the one to allow that space between us to return.

"We should shower and change."

My eyes snap wide at his words, and he laughs.

"We have a party to attend."

Chapter Twenty-Three

Jason's hand lands on the small of my back as he guides me through the thrall of guests.

The males had insisted I get ready with them since zipping myself into this dress was damn near impossible. Slipping into the soft silver-blue satin dress in their ensuite bathroom, Henry had been waiting by the door, twitchy fingers ready to help. The graze of his knuckles up my back had my heart pattering about unevenly. The hand he had placed on my hip warmed me through the bodice. Once zipped into my dress, he stepped back to the bed where he donned his armor and weaponry, blade by blade.

I took that moment to admire the dress in the mirror. It was like it had been molded to my body. Dreamy fabric that draped across my chest and waist, shimmered as I turned this way and that. That fabric was heavy enough to feel warm, but light enough to look ethereal as it gathered over my thigh, cascading to the floor. I smoothed my hands down the skirt admiring the high slit that climbed my thigh showing off an expanse of skin with each step.

Jason turned to me for the first time tonight, his movements feeling unhurried as he knelt before me. I watched deft fingers unclasp a buckle, as he draped something across his thigh before curling his fingers around my ankle. His palm coaster up my calf, guiding my bare foot to rest on his knee.

Distracted as I was by his hands on my skin, I didn't recognize the leather piece.

Until I did.

"You got this for me?" I toss the question across the room.

Henry grins at me through the mirror from where he perched on the edge of the bed, his eyes dancing across us both.

"What's a sharp tongue without a blade to back it up?" his words, a conversation we had had in the not so distant past.

He'd meant it.

And here they were, arming me with my own blade. Skillfully, Jason straps the halter in place, his fingers lingering, eyes sharp. Those gold flecks are already bleeding to ring his pupils iridescent.

The beauty of these males would never fail to stun me. I was certain I could live a lifetime and never get enough.

Henry pulled a blade from his sheath.

"We will make you one of your own once we're home, but this will do for now."

Each step I took through the crowd now emphasized the weight of the blade against my thigh. The soft scrape of leather against my satin skirts. Though with Jason at my back, it's only a moment spent snaking around shifters and vampires alike, before the crowd begins to part for him.

Whether it's their connection to the royals, or the awareness of just how different this creature the male at my back truly is, the crowd takes notice.

Jason has seemingly loosened the leash he holds reigning in that thrumming power. All that power slowly rising to the surface, darkening the tattoos that climb his neck and stretch across his hands. While the claws remain hidden, his fingers are stained black up to the knuckle.

He's a work of art.

And behind him prowls Henry. Strong, confident, and armed to the teeth with weaponry he wears so well. The leather armor he wears along his forearms houses a sheathed blade, the silver glinting as he positions one hand on the broad sword at his hip. His shoulders look even wider in the capped leather that I had watched him buckle across his chest before we left.

Sharp green eyes catch me staring and I whip my head back around. Not that I was in any danger of running into anyone with the wide berth they are now granting us.

A server appears beside me a tray of glasses proffered with a neutral expression. He wastes no time popping a drink into my hand before shifting back into the crowd like a wraith. I eye the drink in my hand for a moment before Jason snatches it away.

I watch as he sets it on a nearby table, his eyes flitting to Henry's for an instant. He gives a nearly imperceptible nod in response.

"What was that for?"

"The drinks are spiked with blood." Jason's breath knocks against my neck as he leans in. My eyes land on Henry who winks before continuing his scan of the room. I couldn't imagine having that same reaction to a total stranger here in such a public setting.

I couldn't believe they could do that... but then again, I could.

My response is a breathless "Oh ... thanks" as I grind my molars into toothy dust.

"Henry will find you a drink." Jason issues the assurance as a command.

Henry leans in with a growing smirk. "Say the word Princess and I'll donate a drop or two for you."

My stomach tumbles pleasantly and I hold my breath, steeling my resolve, before dragging my eyes up his chest, tracing those glittering hilts. I want to see him squirm. To break character, though I know I shouldn't. And when he doesn't, I return my eyes to his and purr, "like I would need it."

His pupils consume that sweet mossy green I've come to love, and in its place, something dangerous blossoms, lighting his eyes with a spark that sends a shiver up my back. Standing before him like this is like standing, arms out, on a precipice. I watch him bite back his retort, unfurling to his full height, dwarfing me, and forcing me to tip my chin to maintain eye contact. A devilish grin quirks his lips before he steps away and into the crowd.

"Careful Pet," Jason grins, turning into my space. He's teasing me. I know he is, but I'm glowing under his touch as he runs a blackened knuckle up my throat catching my chin. "You won't look so smug when he calls your bluff."

"Who says I'm bluffing?" I say swallowing my nerves.

His brow quirks, as do his lips, that knuckle tracing the line of my throat back down my chest. His finger hooks in the v of my dress, towing me forward until I'm pressed to him. He catches me with one hand and I trace the fingers of his other as they spread across my back, pinning me in place.

"Is that so?" He hums, dipping his head low so his breath can fan across my neck and chest.

I swallow blinking up at him innocently.

I will pass this little test of his.

Self preservation is there, I recognize it in that deeply rooted urge to tuck myself away, but I fight it back, and instead, tip my chin up, angling my head as I meet his gaze, my lips practically coasting across his as I smile.

"I -

"There he is!" The voice booms from beside me.

I jolt and Jason's grip tightens in response. He holds me protectively as his gaze snaps over my shoulder, a snarl ripping from his throat. But it quickly transforms into a rumbling chuckle as he greets the male.

"I apologize for interrupting," the new male smiles, looking not the least bit contrite. "It's not often we get a true blooded prince in our midst... Although, I suppose we're still lacking."

"There's enough of what matters," Jason chuckles darkly, clapping talon tipped fingers on the male's shoulder. The male who had been holding out a glass, swallows his next words.

Jason's eyes bleed black and gold revealing the face of the prince below.

This creature that he is.

Power incarnate.

His eyes flit to me as the vampire before him pales, and I note the distinct lack of instinct to do the same. I want nothing but to draw myself infinitesimally closer to this male. Even this version of him does nothing but draw me in.

A reaction I hope he notes when my smile only deepens under his brief scrutiny.

He takes the whiskey dropping into the chair the male waves him into at the table. I pause at the same time Jason does. There are no other chairs. No other pets at the table.

"Can you bring me a chair for my pet?" he asks, catching a server as they pass.

"Yes of course." The young server disappears with a shallow bow.

Taking a peek around, there are, in fact, other pets nearby, but they are sitting on the floor next to their owners. Most sitting quietly, invisible, ignored. Some receive small mindless physical affections from their owners. A hand swept through their hair, or fingertips grazing the exposed skin of their shoulders or arms.

Or throats.

It's the young boy in the far corner who catches my attention. He kneels next to his owner's chair, thighs quivering under the strain of having to maintain the position, left with seemingly no other option. I follow the line of his collar to where he is leashed to the armrest of the shifter's chair beside him. His tether was so short I doubted he could do much other than stare straight ahead as he was doing now.

Jason was not one for collars, leashes, or any of the standard pet fare, so I wore nothing of the sort. But now I felt like I may somehow blow our chances by not blending in appropriately. After all, we were here to ask for permission from the dickhead lords, as Henry had dubbed them.

Jason seemed to track my line of sight.

I watched the pets across from me serving their owner, one cutting her food while the other held his wrist above a glass, his hand tightening as rivulets of blood refill her cup.

My eye twitched.

Thankfully Jason looked disinterested, if not mildly perturbed. Our eyes meet as I reach for his glass, wondering if blending in means serving him, to some degree, as a pet may be expected to.

His hand caught mine as he shook his head. Instead, he draws me next to him where he sits sprawled in the large chair like a king on a throne. His hand anchors me in place where it cups the back of my thigh over my dress. The warmth of his touch bleeds through the cool material. The tip of his thumb traces the curve of my dress where it cups my ass. My focus narrows to those gentle sweeps of his thumb leaving little left to quiet ragged breaths I'm drawing in. I fight the urge to cave to his teasing.

This challenge.

I will not be the one who pulls away from his touch. No. I want this. I want him. And more than anything in this moment, I want to win. So, I shift ever so slightly pushing myself more firmly into this hand and adjusting my hips in a way that, if he was to continue those slow sweeps with his thumb, he would run right along my core.

I track his skin against mine as if there isn't a spec of material between us. His grip tightens, fingers dimpling my thigh as he realizes what I've done. I watch him listen to the male before him and see the moment his attention is pulled from the conversation completely. The slight stiffening to his shoulders, the way his chest rises with a growl I can't quite hear, but can feel in my chest as if it has nested there. I watch him drag his tongue along his lower hip as his thumb sweeps towards the apex of my thighs.

It's at that moment that the server returns with a cushion. He drops it unceremoniously onto the floor beside Jason's chair forcing me to step aside before he backs away. His look said 'you're welcome,' while Jason's hardened, promising bodily harm.

With a settling breath and a flustered smile, I moved to arrange myself on the little cushion when Jason halts me with a firm grip around my arm.

"Absolutely not," he growls, rising from his chair like a storm cloud.

He circles his chair, tugging it out, before helping me into it. And he doesn't stop there. Without so much as a pause, he arranges his own plate before me as the other pets had done, before picking up his glass and turning back to his conversation. His arm rests on the back of my chair and I settle into the safety of his nearness. After the shock settles and awareness dawns, the majority of my energy is spent fervently ignoring the searing gaze of those around me, both owned and free.

The male leaves not long after he'd arrived and Jason drapes himself over the back of my chair, his nose running up and down the column of my throat.

I tip my chin as I convince myself it's all for show, and battle down the reaction as I feel him smile against my skin.

"You want to behave like a pet tonight?" His warm breath fans across my skin and I shiver, biting the inside of my lip.

"Hm?" His lips press to my skin once.

Oh, right. He has asked a question.

"Maybe," I breathe, unable to form a full rational thought.

His chuckle is teasing as he ducks his head to my shoulder. On reflex, I thread my fingers through his hair. I wished we were home. Somewhere... anywhere, other than here, where I could enjoy his touch without monitoring my responses and the heavy stares from those around us. But I also had to admit that he may not be as eager to touch me like this at home.

Was he touching me now because he wanted to?

Or was it just these roles that we played?

It was part of his mask, his princely persona, after all.

"You want to do just as you're told?" His lips press to my shoulder cap, and I turn my head just enough to catch his eyes. Molten umber greets me. "Follow my every command." His voice drops low. "Just so I can tell you what a good girl you are."

His lips press to the sensitive skin just below my ear before using his tongue to drag my earlobe between his teeth.

My breath is audible even to my own ears.

"Like what?"

He releases me, but his lips remain against the shell of my ear, the words tickling my overheated skin. "Like you'd eagerly crawl to me on hands and knees if I asked you to".

My heart stumbles over itself, the scene playing out in my mind.

With immense effort, I straighten my spine, pulling away and putting just enough distance between us to be able to turn my face into his. My eyes heated with what I hoped was convincing malice.

"If only to gut you the moment I reached you" I allowed. The threat passed between us on a whisper.

His chuckle was smoke and whiskey, his final kiss landing at the corner of my jaw.

"That's my girl."

"Excuse me," another voice cut in.

Jason rose slowly, like it had indeed been an effort to pull away, before greeting the awaiting server with a scowl. I pulled my lips between my teeth as I watched the male, extend the tray in his hands before pausing. Dessert was being served around us and the poor waiter, a kind looking shifter, froze taking in the scene before him. Me, clearly a human, in a chair reserved for higher beings while Jason's dagger-like glare had sweat beading on the male's brow.

"Set down the plate," he nodded to the empty space before me and the server hesitated. I couldn't blame him. I think if rolls had been reversed, it would have given me pause as well. Jason smiled, but with his control over all that power, well below normal, the smile he served was barely masked violence. It ebbed from him. I could feel it curling against my back and coasting along the zipper of my dress. The way the darkness obeyed him, seeming to play along his tattoos, and stain his fingers. It was a physical thing, and tonight it was chomping at the bit for release.

When the male remained frozen, Jason reached for the dessert, nodding to the server, who scurried away immediately.

"Enjoy your dessert," he said, setting the plate before me himself. "I'll be right back."

"I'll be right here," I smiled, squirming in my chair with barely concealed delight at the chocolate masterpiece before me. And to my surprise he returned it easily.

I savored every bite and it wasn't until my plate was clean, and I was debating dragging my tongue across it, when I caught the eyes of the boy tethered to his owner's chair.

Regret surged through me, chocolate souring in my stomach.

My gaze fell to the empty plate, wishing I'd saved some.

I wished I could have snuck him some.

I was sure I could have.

Henry appeared beside me, his hand landing on my back when I hesitated, my gaze still locked on the boy. The fizzy drink he set before me, a mockery of what I was doing. My eyes flickered to the glass flute, its contents a subtle pink … or maybe it was the blood filled glasses around the table that made my glass flush pink. Shifters didn't even drink blood. They just allowed their cups to be filled and wasted, simply because they could.

Because it didn't matter what was sacrificed to do so.

And here I sat, in a chair reserved for their kind, eating their food in front of other pets who may not have had the opportunity to eat at all. Bile climbed my stomach. Where their collars marked their skin, mine sat untouched… in more ways than one. Jason peppered my throat with his teasing kisses and… I tried to shake that unsettling feeling free as my eyes tracked the scars along the boy's neck where they peeked out from under his wide collar.

"Can I…" I struggled for what exactly I could do for him. What was I asking? Henry didn't rush me, but I watched his eyes flicker to the boy. I saw the moment they landed on him. I watched them harden, that severe set to his mouth saying more than what either of us could in the moment.

"Not tonight." He shakes his head scanning the room casually. "Too much at risk."

"And he's just a human, right?" I regret the words as soon as they leave my lips. My nails bite into my palms both out of anger, but also regret and shame. Henry didn't deserve that. It wasn't his fault.

He'd given me a dagger and told me to use it as I pleased.

"Pet." The word cracked my chest wide open. It was Jason who intervened, dropping into a now vacant chair beside me. "This is not the place to break skin," he warned lowly.

It was the reminder I needed of where we were. What was at stake. Who I still was, despite just how well these males treated me.

I could swallow down these feelings tonight. Tonight, when I had a roll to play. When a misstep meant not being allowed to enter the free lands. But that crack splintered, aching, as I reached to smother the hurt with my hand.

He reached for me in the same instant. Intercepting my wrist, this thumb swept over the pulsepoint, and for the first time tonight, I pulled away from him.

"I need to use the restroom," I frown, fighting back the angry sting behind my eyes.

I had forgotten.

Forgotten, just what it looked like to be a pet.

To be a human.

These males may treat me like an equal, but we weren't. The chain around the boy's neck weighed heavily on mine as I rose from my chair.

His gaze cooled as he nodded and that phantom grip on my throat tightened.

"Henry will take you."

Henry trails behind me as I make my way across the large dining hall. Large floral arrangements scent the air, offset by the cigar smoke billowing from the bar we pass. The music transforms into something slow and sultry, the lights dimming on the outskirts of the room, highlighting the body's on the raised platform. The hall seems built around it as the focal point. And it does just as it's designed to do, as I can't help but draw to a stop before it.

I pause to watch the shifters and vampires alike float across the floor as they dance with one another. Some consume the space around them, twirling each other around and around, coasting across the floor. While others remain in place, only their hands coasting over each other. And then there are those, like the pair before us, whose only intention seems to be consuming each other.

"Do you dance?" Henry asks, pulling my gaze away from the bloody display. A gentle hand to my back encourages me to duck behind a curtain of curls and weave past the little crowd drawing to watch the pair more closely.

I snort in response, the hideously unladylike sound catching the attention of a shifter who turns hard eyes my way. His lips pull back in a brutal smile that I have no intention of returning, as I duck past quickly. Henry's shoulder catches the male as he stalks past behind me and I hear his drink clatter against the lacquered bar.

"Not like they can," I breathe, allowing my smile to wither against the crowd as I smooth my hands down my dress.

"Hm."

He says nothing more as he positions himself in front of the door to the ladies room.

"Take your time."

He waits with his hand resting on the pommel at his hip, his eyes sharp and jaw relaxed. A male who knows just how untouchable he is. How capable he is of dismantling most others who would challenge him. And for that, I am grateful, because as I exit the restroom stall, I catch sight of *her* at the sink. The woman who had showed up at the house that morning Jason had hid me away.

There was no hiding now.

She was before me in an instant, her arm a bar across the door.

Her gaze was a sharp thing.

"Well, hello again." Her voice is wispy. Excitement paints her pretty face as she draws her eyes over my dress and back up to my face.

Her eyes harden as her fangs lengthen against the cushion of her lower lip.

Fear spikes through me, but I blink, taking a moment to steady myself before I respond. I aim for courteous and innocent as I move to step through her arm hoping she lets me pass.

"I think you're mistaking me for someone else."

To my relief, her arm falls to her side, but her gaze cools as does my blood. Slowly this time, she lifts her hand to my chest running the back of a bright purple nail up my throat.

"Oh there's no mistaking you," she smiles. "No one else lets a pet run around without a collar." She closes her thumb and forefinger around my chin, turning my head sharply to the side.

She tsks, releasing me.

"And without so much as a mark to claim you."

Stepping back, she sets a shoulder against the stall as I pass, her hand held before her as she examines her nails. She meets my gaze over the sharp purple peaks.

"Where is he?"

A shiver works its way up my spine at her question.

"Who?" I ask, keeping my tone even and my eyes on my hands where I wash them until they stop shaking.

"Your male," she snaps.

The venom in her voice tips my gaze to hers where she watches me through the mirror. I pull a soft towel from the basket on the counter and dry my hands.

Turning to her, I don some armor of my own and smile at her. The one I've seen Jason wear time and time again. The one that is, in equal parts, disarming and clever.

"Which one?" I ask, watching the words register.

I drop my arm to the skirt of my dress as I watch as those words not only sink in, but sink under her skin. I know I'm laying claim to males I have no right to, but the sentiment works as a nice distraction as I slide my fingers between the slit of my skirt and palm the dagger there.

"You know," she scowls, straightening, and taking the few steps that put her before me at the sink. "I haven't seen a friend of mine in awhile… though I believe *you'd* seen him recently."

I pause, certain I know no friends of hers.

"Geo."

Her head cocks to the side studying me with barely concealed malice.

His name draws the dagger from its sheath, but before I can use it, Henry's arm materializes between us. With fingers placed to her stomach, he walks her back a step, a growl simmering in his throat.

In the same moment, Jason appears beside me and with a sweep of his arm, he tucks me behind him. Though he doesn't miss the dagger now clenched uselessly at my side.

The restroom is suddenly very crowded.

He steps into me, confidently turning his back to the very woman who had struck him only weeks prior. Jason may be one of the harder vampires to kill, but with Henry here, he was practically untouchable, and his disregard for the female behind him, confirmed as much. His hand cups the side of my neck, his thumb sweeping under my jaw as his eyes coast over me. His touch is settling.

A grin tugs at the corner of his lips when they land back on the blade.

"Good girl."

His praise rumbles over my sensitive nerves, soothing them. My males are here. The danger has passed. I settle myself with a small breath.

The female Henry has crowded into the corner, preens as she watches us. "Interesting that you keep your pet uncollared," she says, and I watch Jason draw himself up as he turns his attention back to her. "I wonder what your father would think."

"Ah." Distaste coats his tongue as he kisses his teeth. "You're the only one concerned with the opinions of our fathers."

"You're flaunting an unmarked pet. Not even a collar to keep her safe. *You*, of all people, should understand the risk. The danger you're putting her in."

Jason's skin practically ripples in response.

"She's safe with me." His pointed glare promises a quick death.

"That's not what I heard," her grin sharpens as her head cocks to the side, glossy black hair falling over her shoulder.

"Enough," he snarls, fingers sharpening to deadly points.

She shrugs, looking unfazed as she picks at her nails.

"Just be careful," she warns, sharp eyes gliding to mine. "Or someone may just take her from you."

Jason stepped forward then and Henry shifted to the side.

"I pity anyone who tries."

Chapter Twenty-Four

Henry situates me on the back of the bike. I gave up my seat in the car to allow for all that camping equipment the males had insisted on bringing into the free lands.

They seemed intent on babying me, though I was fairly certain I'd lived more comfortably in the free lands with the bare minimum, then they would have been comfortable simply traveling with, but I wouldn't turn my nose up at the little luxuries the males had brought along.

We ditched our fancy digs in the car at the town bordering the free lands. From there, we had to travel on foot. The camps within the freelands were built in the most densely packed portions of the forest bordering the south. The forest was maintained in a way that made mass transportation as difficult as possible. Yes, it made it harder to dispense goods, but it also ensured it was hard to trap and transport humans. Trapping had become a way of life for shifters and vampires alike, but survival had become the same for us.

Periodically, I'd been placed on a shift of humans from our village that dug trenches outside of the camp filling them with stumps from trees we'd cut down for wood in the winter. There were also those who would line their properties with fishing line and bells. The old crone, whose house we traveled towards now, used to sell hallowed out reeds she strung on wire that would sway creating a clattering noise with each breeze. On a night where the air was still, it was an indicator that predators were moving through our space. Their speed creating enough force to rattle the ingenious alarm.

Every now and again, she and I would trek the woods hanging new reeds and collecting the damaged or discarded ones the trappers had found. She'd taken to repairing what she could, and decorating them with foul words, before returning them to the trees.

We stop to make camp with only a few hours left to hike in the morning, and the males get right to work. They set up the tent, bedrolls, blankets, and food, all of which they carried on their back.

The perks to traveling with beings capable of carrying the literal car we rode here in.

I take the opportunity to watch the males interact with one another as I make up our beds. The tent, while spacious enough for the three of us, only allows for the bedrolls to be laid out side by side. But I tucked away the little twingle of nervousness that realization inspired, and set to somewhat uselessly fluffing each of our pillows as I watched Jason pace across camp to Henry.

Henry's eyes glittered with the challenge reflected in Jason's. They exchange words I cannot hear, before Henry's arm flashes out, snagging the front of Jason's shirt, and towing him forward. He settled between Henry's spread thighs where he was seated on a stump sharpening his blades. But something in the words they share, softens Jason's posture. I watch his hands move from where they were fisted on his hips to threading through Henry's curls. When they emerge the black staining them, has receded.

Further evidence that whatever tension had been perched on his shoulders, was lessening.

Without releasing his grip on Jason's shirt, he pushes to his feet slowly, leaving the male no room to back away from him as he invades his space, claiming it. Henry surprises both Jason and I, as I spy on their little interaction, when he steps around Jason. His grip shifts to his hand as he wraps the male in his arm and spins him out and away from him. Jason snarls lowly, but Henry just chuckles before dragging him back with a flourish and walking him a few paces back the two fall into step perfectly.

Henry places a kiss on Jason's hand before twisting their grip, pinning Jason's back to his front as they continue to dance together. A begrudging smile tugs at Jason's lips. Seeing this, sparks one of my own, and it's just in time to get caught.

"C'mere Princess," Henry holds out his other hand, an invitation to join.

My legs are carrying me to the males before I can think of a reason not to. I set my hand in his and his reaction is everything. The smile that breaks across his face is winning, and I glow under the beam from his proud smile.

"I don't know how to dance," I allow as his thumb sweeps over the top of my hand.

"Would you like to learn?"

I nod, and he sets my hand in Jason's, who shocks me by tugging me into his chest. His warmth envelopes me. His scent wrapped around me, just as his arm does now, pinning me to him with that quiet strength.

My inhale is sharp as I drown in gold flecked umber.

Henry's presence is a tingle - an awareness, against the base of my spine that connects the three of us. I take step after step following his lead in a dance that feels similar to what I had seen in the lord's manor the evening prior.

My next step lands on Jason's foot and I bite my lip, eyes flickering back up to his.

He blinks, leashing the little spark that fires off behind his eyes, and drops a dry, "ouch," that has me rolling my eyes. He takes advantage of the tilt of my neck, his other hand cupping the back of my head as he lifts me. His thigh separates mine, the stance bringing our bodies even closer. Like this, I can feel the way his body moves against mine instead of simply under my hands. He settles my weight back onto my feet, and in doing so allows me to slide down his thigh. I shiver at the contact, my fist gripping the front of his shirt as he smiles sinfully, his hands coasting down my arms. He collects my hands in his before he turns me in a half spin.

He releases one hand, twirling me outward, dried leaves kicking up under my bare feet as he sends me right into Henry's waiting arms.

Henry wastes no time skillfully tucking me into his grip. My feet leave the ground completely as he spins us round and round.

Breathless, he sets me down, my body sliping down his. His hand drops to my thigh cupping the back of my knee he hooks my leg around his hip dipping me low. His breath is a chuckle against my overheated skin.

"I don't know how to tell you this Princess, but it appears you can, in fact, dance."

I laugh as he pulls me back to him, walking me back across the camp in sweeping steps.

"I think I stepped on Jason's feet as frequently as the ground," I allow.

His responding laugh is a low growling rumble that raises gooseflesh up my arms.

"I'm going to let you in on a little secret," he leans in his voice a whisper against the shell of my ear. "He liked it."

The look I wear must be just beyond my control, because when he leans back to study my face, he tips his head back on a laugh that shakes the trees.

Jason steps up behind me then, falling into step in our dance with preternatural ease.

His hand set to my waist, I throw my right arm back around his neck as we move dancing to the music of the freelands. In a haze of sweat, and drunk on the touch of the two males bracketing me, I threw my arms in the air, spinning and spinning, my toes digging into the soil wishing I was still wearing that beautiful dress.

The sun was beginning to set as I stumbled out from between the males, collapsing on the fallen trunk Henry had dragged into camp, with a delirious smile. They abandon their dance soon after, breaking apart with a kiss and we settle into comfortable silence.

Jason props himself against a tree having produced a book from the tent I hadn't spotted prior. And Henry returns to sharpening the blades from the strap he wears across his chest. Every now and again, he sends one sailing across the edge of camp, before retrieving it, satisfied with the edge he has honed.

Watching him, I'm surprised to find that the anxiety I had expected to swell in my chest was quieter. It was still there, that little sting in my shoulder, the sound of dishware shattering against the floor and wall... but it was overshadowed by our conversation. By the realization that had they not intervened in the bathroom, I didn't know exactly how I would have fared.

That was a lie. I knew exactly how I'd fair, and the ghost of that blade's edge dragging across my throat had me shoving to my feet, and crossing the little camp to Henry.

I could feel Jason's watchful eyes following me. Whether he had heard the off-beat pitter patter of my heart or not, it didn't matter.

I shook off the nerves.

Learning how to defend myself, just as Henry had offered all those nights prior, was a necessity. Futile or not. If I was going to live in a world of monsters, I should know how to slay them.

Henry's eyes flickered to mine as I arrived before him.

Quiet and probing, but patient. Cool green bracketed by dark lashes and warm brown brows. My eyes coast along the details of his face, drinking him in and letting the butterflies curling in my stomach consume any reservations I had left. My next swallow was dry as my gaze landed on the blades in his hands.

I clear my throat.

"Can I try?"

"Of course," he nods and smothers a look that's dangerously close to pride, before it can inspire any bad habits to rear their rebellious head.

"Why don't you help me sharpen these last two and then we can throw a few together."

"Okay," I agreed.

He turned the blade in his hand, offering me the handle, before picking up the other. I follow his step-by-step instruction as he teaches me the proper way to hold the blade against the wet stone, and how to use the burr to tell when the blade is sharpened properly. It takes me a few tries to get the balance just right, but when I feel confident enough in my work to hand it over, Henry gifts me a proud nod.

"Now that your blade is sharp enough to kill, let's work on how to kill someone before they even know you're there."

He shoves to his feet with a wicked grin that sets my heart racing.

I think I'd like to watch this male dismantle another. The way his eyes would darken from cool mossy green to something akin to the firethorn behind him. It was a transformation I had witnessed for the first time last night, and the shift had sent heat up my spine, and over the skin of my neck.

Thankfully a sound jars me from my current train of thought before it derails.

Henry shifts his weight uncomfortably and I freeze two thoughts slamming into each other.

One. That sound just came from the male looming over me, and two, if I dont reign in my reaction, there's every possibility that the vampire before me could punt the head from my shoulders.

Because... Henry's knees popped with the volume of a tree cracking in half.

I pull my lips between my teeth, barely biting back the sarcastic retort sitting on my tongue as his head swivels to mine, his eyes lighting with challenge.

"Zip it, Princess," he warns, the rumble in his voice stroking my skin. The glint in his eyes, just as playful as it is dangerous.

I hold my hands up in surrender.

"Yea, yea big scary vampire," I grin playfully.

Jason snorts from across camp and Henry tosses him the finger as he collects the rest of the blades.

"Give me a break. I'm three hundred years old," he grumbles, petulant.

"Wait." I push to a stand, his words clicking into place one at a time. "Wait, what?" My gaze whips from Jason to Henry who is grumbling under his breath as he lays out our blades. "Are you serious?" I scramble after him.

It's Henry's turn to chuckle as he takes me by the shoulder, turning me towards one of the wider trunks bordering camp.

"Focus." He places a blade in my hand and steps up beside me, brandishing his own. The only thing that could pull my attention from that revelation is seeing Henry handling a weapon. Jason's eyes lift from the pages before him, his eyes dragging over the male before me with a heat that stirs something awake in my chest.

Apparently I'm not the only one affected.

Henry teaches me how to properly hold the blade, pinching it at the tip, and holding it parallel to my arm. The adrenaline from successfully landing my strikes, burns away the residual anxiety from handling the blades, and the phantom pains in my shoulder. As does the praise Henry peppers me with, and the little touches as he adjusts my form.

“Ah, ah,” his fingers graze the underside of my arm, lifting my elbow to an angle he’s happy with. “Don’t drop your elbow.”

My next throw goes wide right.

Fuck.

“Try to hit the tree next time,” Jason offers oh-so-helpfully.

Henry coughs on a laugh as he turns snapping in Jason’s direction. “Better idea,” he says, palming a blade that he hands to Jason who swiftly sets aside his book and joins us.

“Alright Princess,” he sets warm hands on my shoulders nailing me in place with a wide smile. His hand drops to cover mine, tightening my grip on the blade. “We're going to make this interesting. I’m going to give you three attempts for every one of Jason’s”

Three to one wasn't bad odds, but against these two, it wasn't good either.

“What do I get if I win?” I asked.

“What do you want?” His grin spreads wide and slow.

I pulled my lips between my teeth, prying my attention from the male before me so that I could think properly.

“I want your share of dessert.” I nodded feeling confident as Henry studied me. His eyes flickered across my face for the briefest of moments before he tipped his head back on a laugh that echoed through the darkening trees.

“And here, I was going to offer to start removing clothing for each throw you landed.”

My mouth falls open.

“I would have taken that bet,” Jason winks.

Wait.

“But chocolate it is,” Henry crows and I frown, gripping the handle in my hand harder than necessary.

The adrenaline must give me an advantage, because I landed two of my first three throws. However, confidence fails me as I miss the next three. Which leaves Jason and I tied.

"When I train, I like to picture someone I'd very much like to kill," Jason allows. "It could be anyone. A whole lineup." His lips twitch upward, his eyes never leaving the target as he speaks and the thud across the clearing is assurance enough his blade landed firmly where he intended it.

Geo's face comes to mind.

"You want to be capable of killing a shifter?"

He turns to me as I ready my stance.

"A vampire?" he asks, raising his brows. "Then put some of those monsters in front of that tree. Were not practicing. You are hunting."

I sink two more blades into Geo and one into *her*, but I miss Le every time. My fear, still finding a way to override my hate.

There's no sense in muttering under my breath when everyone in camp can hear it, so I curse creatively when I miss my last throw. Henry's quiet as he watches me, but Jason snickers. He holds my eyes, his arm snapping forward like a bolt. I didn't need to check the tree. I heard the blade thud into the trunk and so had he. My eyes narrow as his sharpens, a grin pulling those full lips high.

Disappointment stings, but it also starts a fire in my gut. If Henry's right, I can be as good as Jason. I just need to practice. I just need to keep facing my fears.

Jason dusts his hands on his pant legs. "Henry's going to light a fire and heat some stones to keep you warm, so you and I will take a walk."

I was feeling brave and accomplished, so the courteous offer had those old habits rearing their rebellious head.

"No. I'm ok," I argued, spurred on by all those holes I'd poked in the tree, picturing monster after monster. I had done it. I had leashed my fear.

I could do this too.

His brows drew together as he watched me glower at him.

"I can hear your heart ratcheting up already."

His low tone hinted that he was calling me on my bullshit, while allowing me to save face, but it was aimed at the only one in this camp without vampiric hearing.

"Then mind your fucking business," I snaped, before catching myself. Henry caws a laugh and Jason's eyes glitter playfully.

I stomp my way into the tent studiously ignoring the sounds of Henry stacking wood and building a little nest of brush. It would catch quickly. I knew what it would look like... what it would sound like.

I fought back the memories as they tried to pull free of the little box I kept them stuffed in.

Keeping my distance, I tuck myself into the sleeping bag at the far end of the tent and tuck my face into the flap as discreetly as possible. Even from across camp, the fire warms my back, but instead of sinking into that pleasant heat, it has sweat beading on my neck. I can feel the heat of those flames as I reach for her hand. Her screams are sharp. Wails echo into the night blanketing the sound of Jason, who had lowered himself onto the ground behind me.

I startle when he sets a hand to my hip, a tear slipping down my cheek. With a slow breath I stuff that little box farther into the back of my mind. I didn't want to admit that he was right. I didn't want to admit that this was harder. So, I ground my teeth and focused on the soft slip of my fingers as they gripped the sleeping bag.

He settled beside me, pulling me against his chest and using his back to shield me from the fire. But he's warm enough, and his arm was a pleasant weight around my waist.

I couldn't see Henry from around Jason, but I knew he was close because I could hear him as he hummed nearby. Jason joined in, and their song drowned out the popping of the flames behind us. Eventually my heart settled. Though it didn't keep me from twitching each time that fire popped or spat, Jason was there to wrap his arms tighter. To run his fingers gently through my hair as he whispered how proud he was of me.

I roll over attaching myself to him, but not before I take a quick peek at his face. His eyes are quiet. There's no frustration or discomfort. No pity. Just calm reassurance. My eyes fall to his lips as they part, his warm breath fanning against my face. It would be barely a shift to lean in and press my lips to his. But I tucked myself against his chest, pressing a kiss to his throat instead.

"Thank you," I breathe against his skin.

His hand moves to open his shirt. He makes swift work of undoing the buttons letting the soft cotton fall open across his chest.

"But I didn't win," I whisper.

His soft chuckle sends a shiver down my spine.

"You're right. I did."

With a stubborn huff, I roll in his arms, giving him my back. Undeterred, he pulls me securely against him, his chest and stomach warming my back. His arms, a comfortable weight around my waist.

Thankfully I'm tired enough that ruminating on how I'd forfeited the ability to trace his abs with my fingers... or tongue, won't keep me awake for long.

His breath reaches my ear, and I think he may give me the opportunity to turn back around. Maybe he wants me to as badly as I do.

"Go to sleep."

The chuckle in his voice and command in his tone has my jaw clenching.

"Fuck off," I huff, burying my face in the blanket and surrendering to the weight of my eyelids.

Chapter Twenty-Five

A scream pulls me from my sleep, but as I adjust to my surroundings, her voice is only an echo.

She seems closer, here, in the free lands.

Her ghost, relentless, despite my exhaustion.

The smell of burning wood accents the night air. Here in the night soaked tent, I can't separate the scent of our campfire from the pyre our little home became.

Arms tighten around me.

A heavy breath coasts across the top of my head, clearing it. My sweater clings to sweat dampened skin where he's pressed to my back, his muscled thigh resting between my own. He cradles me against him, even as he sleeps, and the way he's wrapped himself around me, makes me feel safe. As does the way his hand raises to brush at my curls. I hold my breath as I count his.

Even.

Slow.

Still asleep.

I relax into his grip once more, and even asleep, it's like he can sense my submission, because he groans. The sound echoing the praise he affords me before he bites back that smile I love so much. His hips shift and I gasp, finding myself making room between my legs for more than just his thigh.

Panic and heat war in my stomach, setting my heart racing, and before I can stop myself, I do the unthinkable.

I disentangle myself from him like the coward I am.

I don't even glance back to ensure I hadn't woken him, before I dip out between the tent flaps. A shiver climbs my spine as the sweat cools in the chilly night air. The fire is just a few small flames now. Embers glowing here and there. They catch my attention, but only momentarily. Instead, I searched for Henry.

He's waiting for me, I think, watching me take him in.

He sits with his back against a wide trunk across camp.

"Good morning."

His voice is rough with disuse, and it has me wondering if I've, in fact, made it to morning.

"Is it?" I glance around but am met with only impermeable darkness outlining our camp

"Not even close."

His smile is small.

Calm.

His eyes however, feel like they can see straight through me. Ideally, he attributes any nervousness to the flames and eerily silent woods surrounding us, and not Jason's not-so-morning wood I had just run from.

He dusts his hand on the knee bent before him as his eyes sweep over me.

"You're doing very well," he allows.

I grimace as I force myself to take another peek at the flames dancing along the logs, if only to prove him right.

Relieved ... and yet not.

"Facing your fears doesn't always look stoic."

I close my eyes, shaking my head as the memories of everything he helped me overcome last night, comes flooding back. He'd been sitting here keeping watch, so he'd probably heard my heart rate spike... heard my reaction, my gasp, and then saw me stumble out of the tent and had drawn his own conclusions.

How was this supposed to work between the three of us, if I can't shake this guilty feeling everytime I tiptoe that line of what I want, and what I know I shouldn't.

I return my eyes to Henry as he continues.

"Take it from someone who has seen lifetime's worth of men and women, males and females, stand before an enemy. Come face to face with the unknown...

He shrugs.

Maybe this is just another fear I need to face. I cross the camp to him holding those forest green eyes; soft and probing.

I owe it to them both to be honest. I owe it to myself to take the plunge.

To stop holding back.

To face this fear.

Even if the result meant rejection.

Henry was teaching me to be brave, so I would be brave.

My heart trips over itself as I arrive before him.

"I don't know," I allow, breathless.

He holds an arm out, and I take it, settling between his legs.

"It still feels impossible sometimes... the idea of being able to think straight around an open flame," I explain, as I lean into him, setting my back to his chest. He brushes some wood shavings from his lap and I follow the direction of his hand, realizing he had been whittling a figure from a hunk of wood.

A little cat.

"There's success in failure as long as you keep fighting. Keep coming back to face those demons."

Wood crackles, the sound catching me off guard and the finger I had been running down the back of the little wooden kitten twitches knocking it on its side.

I release a sharp breath through my nose and tuck my fingers under Henry's warm arms.

"They get quieter... with time," he allows. His fingers brush my ribs, the bar of his forearms tucking me tighter against him and I sink into him. There's a different fear I'd rather face, and it starts with just how right it feels to be tucked into their arms.

I nod against his bicep.

After a quiet moment he continues. "Before I found myself at Jason's side, I was assigned to guard another royal."

I peer up at him from over my shoulder.

His expression is unreadable, but it softens as his eyes dip to mine.

Vulnerable.

Open.

My grip loosens on his arm as I find myself running hands up and down along his muscled arm in what I hoped would be comforting strokes. Encouraging him to continue with a nod.

I wanted to learn as much about him as he was willing to share.

"The prince had died, and I was assigned to Victoria, the royal's daughter. The then future queen. Jason's royal status as second son could no longer be challenged, and he'd been assigned a guard for his protection. I knew the male well."

He paused his jaw working.

"I hated him."

I chuckled.

"He was blase about Jason's safety. I'd caught him on several occasions, ogling Victoria, when he should have been focused on his duties."

Ah.

"We were traveling south from the northern territories. The shifters were rising in power, strength and numbers. And he should have understood the danger we were in, but it didn't keep him from abandoning his post at Jason's side to ensure Vic's glass was never empty." He traced shapes on the back of my hand where it rested on his thigh.

"The shifters and witches had been unaware of Jason at that point and targeted Victoria one evening as she was dining with some dignitaries. The building was raided. It was chaos. I had Vic in one arm and was shoving my way through the crowd, when I saw Jason. He was tearing into a shifter, his guard prone on the floor. If I hadn't been so focused on getting to him, I may have seen the bolt sent across the room. If I'd been more focused, I may have been able to catch it before it landed in her chest."

Surprise flickers down my spine.

He exhales a choppy breath before threading his fingers through mine. I ignore the way they fit perfectly as I flip my palm up and squeeze back encouraging him to continue.

"Afterwards, the idea of turning my back for a moment around him seemed impossible. My mind was so clouded with fear and anxiety I couldn't relax. I drove Jason mad for weeks. I wasn't myself."

He shakes his head, but surprises me with a throaty chuckle. "So... he started chucking knives at me one evening."

My eyes darted to the tent where Jason slept. Picturing him throwing knives at Henry... well... I could see it.

"After some time, I started catching them in my hands and not my body. It was the penance I needed, and eventually the fog cleared. I was confident enough to return to my post and fulfill my duties... and do so, well. I wasn't just a warm body stationed at a post, I was back in control."

"You kept him safe," I turned into him, pressing my lips to his bicep before I could think better of if. "And he kept you whole."

He pulled me closer against his chest, my hand still running back and forth along his arm. Comfortable here in his arms, I take a small breath and steady myself.

"I don't think there is a speck of doubt in his mind that you'd keep us safe". My voice doesn't catch on the word 'us' like I feared it would. We could be an 'us', Jason, Henry, and I.

The picture solidifies in my mind as he presses his lips to the back of my head.

"You're safe Princess. They have to get through me to reach you."

I shiver and he chuckles, that deep laugh rumbling through both of us. As reassuring as that should feel, a pit opens up in my stomach.

"Who protects you?"

As I ask it, I know the answer. We do. Jason and I. We are a unit... if they'll have me. We protect each other.

He leans down glancing at the side of my face and I turn into him again.

"What do I need protecting from?" he grins, ego the size of a mountain. This is the male Jason helped him find again. Confidence incarnate.

I chuckle. "You're right. The apex predator fears no one."

"Damn right."

I feel his chest swell behind me and it sends flutters through my stomach. We settle into a more comfortable silence when another realization strikes.

"No wonder Jason had been so angry with me," I allow. "I'd accused him of being too distracted to catch the blade Geo threw at him..." I cringle, recalling the conversation. "And he'd lost his sister in such a similar way.

Henry snorts. "He wasn't thrilled, but he knew you were right."

Part of me wanted to apologize, not having intended to hurt him with my words, but the other part of me needed those words to exist outside the cage of my ribs. We had both been distracted by each other. And now we both bore wounds we'd won protecting each other. Blades wielded by terrible males, who'd met their own terrible ends.

And the female who had brought the threat of one of those males back to life when she spoke his name.

"Who was that, in the restroom?" I asked, leaning my cheek against his bicep as I peered up at him.

His brow fell, his jaw shifting.

"Claire," he growled.

Claire.

"And she knew Geo?"

"It seems so."

"Why was Geo... What was he even after that evening?"

A dangerous grin lifted the corners of Henry's mouth before he cupped it in his palm, running his hand down his beard with an exasperated sigh.

"Political gain." He shakes his head. "The king has asked very little of Jason since we relocated to our home with Hartley. But King Croft is only patient when it serves him. And Jason had been evading his request for long enough that it appears he may have assigned others to see it completed."

Hm.

"And a less cryptic answer might be..." I hedged.

His responding chuckle was warm as he continued.

"Geo saw an opening to forge documents he was sent to *negotiate* and he took it." He dropped his gaze to mine and we studied each other for a quiet moment. The smile he freed softened his eyes as his grip tightened pleasantly around my skin. "Had it not been for a very pretty little snitch, he may have just gotten away with it."

"All that for some documents?" My brow crumples as I consider Henry's words. "How does that make sense?"

Henry exhales.

"Not just any documents, Princess. Jason inherited some land that bleeds into the freelands we are currently traveling."

I stilled, those puzzle pieces inching closer together in my mind. I could feel it. The answer. Hovering just beyond my reach.

Jason owned this land?

The land we had to ask permission to travel.

Land that humans had used as a safe haven for at least as long as I'd been alive, and probably much longer.

"Many, many, decades ago he made an agreement with a certain shifter's little sister to grant them the use of his territory to claim as their own and build a stronghold. Land that would give them the foothold they needed. You see shifters were just establishing themselves, still vying for-

"Wait."

He paused while my mind spun

"Jason gifted this land to the shifters to rule over."

"Loaned," he corrected. "But yes. Along with the agreement that they would never cross the border they put in place to expand into the free lands."

"So Geo..."

"Used Jason's signet on a contract he had drafted that would have made it look like Jason had agreed to sell the lands back to the crown."

If it was all about the land...

"Then why chuck a blade at him in the middle of dinner if he could have just walked right out?"

"He wasn't a smart male," Henry smiled in that dangerous way as his gaze slid over the darkened trees. "Just a powerful one. And besides, who inherits what a dead prince leaves behind?"

"The king," I breathe.

"The king," he echoes, and it's not until I feel him relax below me, that I realize how tense he had grown.

"The king would have allowed that? For his only son to be killed over territory?"

But it wasn't just any territory. It was a territory that promised control over the shifters and their established royal family... as well as a massive population of humans who were currently living as freely as possible.

I turn in Henry's arms and he lets me. Reclining against his chest, he wraps his arm around me tucking me back into his warmth as I cast my eyes across those darkened trees.

It was quiet tonight.

Usually the woods here in the freelands were alive with the chatter of night birds and toads who made their home along the rivers.

I wonder if they could sense the predators camping quietly in their space.

I also wondered if this agreement between Jason and the shifters was why the trappers had become a necessity of the trade. Because Jason was quietly protecting humans from poachers, who without him, could be captured and sold in droves. He was keeping the free lands, free, at the expense of the relationship with his father... The king. At the risk of dignitaries like Geo who would kill him to gain favor, or coin, for the sale of said land.

My mind was spinning, and my heart was racing, and for once it had nothing to do with the fire crackling before us.

Henry interrupted both with a brush of the back of his fingers he trailed down my arm.

"Thanks to you, we won't know."

I scoff, because that is the only sound I can draw forward as I pull my gaze over my shoulder, catching Henry watching me again.

"Thank you for sharing that with me Henry."

He nods, a smile lifting the corner of his mouth, and this time that heaviness in his expression relaxes.

"Anytime, Princess"

I cast my smile against the trees, admittedly enjoying the term of endearment. Mostly because that was what it felt like.

"Where does that come from?" I ask, curious. I had asked Jason to call me Pet, but Henry had never once used the name. It had always been Princess.

He chuckles, his eyes glittering with embers from the fire.

I focus on the beauty of the way it reflects against his eyes as they drift to the tent where Jason sleeps way too soundly.

I watch them heat as if he can see through the canvas material to the male inside.

"He is my prince." A smile tugs at the corner of his lips as he returns his gaze to me. The reverence lingering in his gaze warms my chest. This male couldn't hide the love he held for Jason if he tried, but this was Henry, and he never seemed interested in being anything other than himself. "And from the moment I laid eyes on you, you were his."

My stomach tumbles, but it's not the nerves I'd expected. It's something else. Henry had never shamed me for my feelings. He was the first to call me on them, force me to face them, and encourage me to hold onto them when I was ready to forfeit.

I watched him a moment longer testing that molten moss green for any sign that he was feeding me pretty words. But all I can see is the way those words seem to complete the smile lifting his lips and softening his sharp features.

I tuck myself deeper into his arms.

"I'm just as much yours."

“That you are," he growled. His big hand tightens on my waist as he curls his body over me playfully nuzzling my neck with his nose.

“You know my name.”

He paused his lips a breath away from my neck.

"I do." The words curled against my skin like smoke.

I nod.

I knew that I hadn't had the opportunity to give him my name, but he had more than earned it, and I wanted him to know that.

“I'm glad you do."

I rumbling echoed in his chest as he brushed the curtain of curls over my shoulder. His grip tightened, the muscles along his stomach bunching as he held me closer.

“It's an honor, Amelia.”

Those words loosened something in my chest as I melted into him, closing my eyes. His lips pressed to my hair and mine to his knuckles in return.

I loved Henry.

I loved Jason.

I loved them both, and I hoped it wasn't as futile as it felt to do so.

Chapter Twenty-Six

We follow the river as it bends towards camp. The males hover quietly behind me as I walk along river rocks that I'd only months ago, skipped with my brother. They shift under my feet. Their wet clacks chipping away at the stoic expression I'd donned this morning as we packed up camp. Pulling my lips between my teeth, I surveyed the bank.

No flowers.

None living anyway. I paced around the space knowing that it wouldn't be unexpected for an animal to have eaten what had sprouted, looking for anything edible in the harsher winter months. New sprouts could have ended up in the area after they passed through the animal. Little did I realize then that stealing those seeds to plant along the riverbed, wouldn't have led to me presenting the old crone with some healthier flowers. But instead, I was holding my breath as I paced along the trees lining the space searching for a sprout to present to Jason.

I shook my head.

It didn't seem that long ago that I had knelt here digging my fingers into the damp earth, but it also felt like another lifetime ago.

Just as I'm about to set my foot down, I pause, because there, nearly buried under the stronger fingers of nearby vines, is a wilted little sprout I recognize.

Jason kneels beside me and I expect him to smile. To unleash that triumphant look I'd caught him wearing those few times we had spoken about the freelands and these flowers, but instead his expression is heavy. Caution, and something like guilt swirling beneath the umber and gold.

Realization dawned, heavy and slow, like the stone it felt was sinking in my stomach now.

It looked like guilt, because it was.

Dread blossomed in my chest.

I open my mouth before closing it again wordlessly.

My eyes follow.

"I know where we can find more," I breathe, resigned, as the sting of grievous memories prick at my eyes.

"Amelia," he hums, his fingers collecting mine.

His touch is comforting, but mentally I'm using both hands to press down on the lid of the box containing the snarling darkness.

With some effort, I seal those memories back into that little box and return my gaze to Jason. Warm umber greets me. Familiar and comforting. It soothes the jagged edges of the wound I'm reopening in my chest just standing here, but it also weakens my armor. And I can't have that, so I straighten my shoulders and serve him a smile that I hope doesn't look as brittle as I feel.

"It's ok," I nod.

His brow pulls together as he stares down at the little sprout, before unfurling to his full height.

His knuckles catch my chin and I swallow before picking my eyes up to meet his like I know he wants. Warm hands trace the column of my neck, his fingers pausing on the little burn scars that dot my shoulder and opposite forearm.

My mouth is too dry.

My eyes are too wet.

And I struggle to swallow down the emotion climbing my throat.

"They didn't die well," I admit, voice low to hide the way it shakes.

We didn't speak about them. I had never really felt ready to bring them back to life, if even by words, when they felt so freshly torn from me. I didn't think, even now, that I knew how, but doing this for him didn't mean I had to speak about them.

"I can't ask you to do this." He shook his head, his eyes dancing across my face. "I won't."

My hands wrapped around his wrists before he could pull away.

Before he could solidify this rash decision.

"We came all this way."

His eyes trained on me and I felt stripped bare before him. That probing gaze seeing too much. And whatever it was that he saw, had emotion sparking behind the gold flecked umber.

"It's not worth it. I ... I" He turned to search out Henry and I caught him.

"Jason." I straightened my spine and blinked my eyes clear. "We're already here," I said, shaking my head. This much hurt left me feeling exhausted, and as much as I wanted to reassure him, I just didn't have the words. So I shrugged.

Whatever purpose these flowers serve, they're important enough to be here. If I can find them... then maybe that fire had not taken everything from me.

I could do this.

I could do this for him.

He looks ready to argue, so I turn on my heel and stalk off into the trees.

Despite feeling like my soul was being flayed, I kept moving. One step after the other. I didn't stop. I didn't turn back when he called my name, or cursed colorfully, the breeze announcing his arrival beside me. But he didn't stop me and I took the opportunity, as we hiked quietly towards my old home, to refortify my armor.

I had a purpose and I had my males with me.

I could do this.

I could also smell camp before I spotted the charms hanging in the trees along its border. They clatter together on a breeze as if to taunt me. Announcing our arrival to a scorched camp.

Jason's hand catches mine, his fingers gently weaving between my own. He seems content to slow his pace, but as I fight to control the surge of emotions that swell having finally returned after the raid, I push myself to move faster. Like the sheer determination to appear fine, will actually result in me handling this visit to my family's unintentional resting place.

He remains quiet beside me, his thumb sweeping reassuring strokes across the back of my hand. And thankfully, he doesn't comment on the way my fingers shake in his. Lost in my mind as I was, I didn't notice Henry was missing until he reappeared before us, sending a brief nod to Jason.

Of course, he had cleared the camp ahead of time.

Knowingly or not, the vampires flank me like emotional support sentinels as we step into camp. I lead the way to the little cabin with laser focus. The only time I let my eyes stray from the path, is to allow for a brief glance to ensure I have arrived at the right spot. The sight still lands like a physical blow. The devastation was widespread. Luckily, the old crone lived on the very edge of the camp and my males had navigated us to the appropriate end, not requiring me to make the walk across the desecrated space I used to consider home.

Scorch marks travel the eastern wall, but the rest of the small building seems untouched. I nod to Henry who reaches around me to open the door. His big hand engulfs the handle, and with a tug, the whole door pulls free from its hinges. Despite my racing heart, I smile as he grumbles something that sounds like, 'give me fucking break'.

"Easy killer, you're in a camp built for *humans,* remember?" I emphasize the word, like just looking at this male wouldn't be enough to distinguish our species.

"Was this one a moth?" He deadpans, having no idea just how fitting that image is.

I step over the threshold as he sets the door against the exterior wall.

"A wraith maybe," I mutter, my eyes traveling over the soot-lined interior. The single-room cabin is coated from top to bottom, each surface covered with a layer of grey, snuffing out all the color this home had once been bursting with.

I run my fingertips along the tabletop as I pace into the little kitchen space. They come away grey.

Not soot.

Ash.

My face heats as my body temperature plummets. I rub my thumb against my fingers, watching it spread. My throat feels thick as I fight to swallow down the impulse to forfeit my breakfast.

I can hear Jason and Henry as they inspect the living space behind me, so with my back to the males, I close my eyes against the sting. Allowing myself only a moment to pull myself together, I wipe away what was left of the community I lived amongst on my pant leg.

We're here for a reason, and this isn't it.

My eyes snap open, willing the picture to change before me. Under this grey-stained kitchen used to be one soaked in color and the harsh cackle of the little moth who lived here.

I start in the obvious locations. The planter by the kitchen window. Its contents are long dead. I pulled at the dry stems the petals grey, weighed down under the oppressive ash, yet they disintegrated like tissue under my fingers. Setting the planter aside, I dug my fingers into the soil hoping that maybe a few seeds may have laid dormant below the surface, to no avail.

I propped my knee on the counter, hoisting myself up to peer around the window frame ensuring that if any seeds had fallen, I wouldn't have missed them.

The glass jars along the kitchen counter were my next targets. One with flour, sugar, another ... I set my knuckle to my tongue.

Salt.

I opened cabinet after cabinet, pulling down a few spice jars she'd tucked along the plates and bowls, as well as a container labeled 'tea', next to a stack of what appeared to be hand painted tea cups. The bright florals so vibrant against the grey backdrop, it was nearly jarring. I left them where they sat in a high stack, afraid to knock them over as I continued rifling. A few knives, some half carved reeds, fabric tossed over the back of one of the two chairs tucked into the little table. My eyes bounce back to the window, the hand stitched curtain fluttering on the breeze. It must have been how the ash had made its way into the space.

I carried the spice jars to the table, dumping each one into a neat pile before inspecting the contents carefully for any hints of where the clever old crone had hidden her flower seeds.

I spun and reassessed the space yet again.

Henry's watchful gaze burned against the side of my face. That suffocating heat climbed my spine, sweat beading under my coat despite the cooler temperature.

The males had, quite thoroughly, turned the living space inside out. Jason's eyes rose to meet mine and I could already read the placating bullshit he was about to serve me.

"They're here," I choked out.

They had to be. I had sat at this very table and helped her plant them. Though I'd never seen where she kept them. They'd just be here, in the center of the table ready for me to work.

"Its okay-

"No," I bit out. "I'll find them."

I spun back to the drawers and cabinets all hanging open, the contents sprawled across the counters before me.

His voice was too soft when he spoke my name next.

"Amelia..."

"I'll find them!"

My eyes stung and I glared at the counter, at the empty shelves, at those fucking teacups teasing me with their beautiful florals.

"We came all this way. We're *here*. It can't be for nothing."

Desperation, maybe denial, has me pulling down the plates shuffling through them, my grip tightening, the scalloped edged digging into my palms. My hands shook as I searched for somewhere to set them down. But as I did, the top plate slid off of the little stack, shattering on the floor with a crash. It was by far the loudest sound I'd heard since we entered camp. Mabe all morning. And it was jarring.

I stared at the shattered glass on the ground, a sob breaking free, before I dropped the stack in my hands. They crashed down around my booted feet.

The boots Jason had bought me.

The boots I was allowed to wear, even as a pet.

Because I was alive when they weren't.

Because I was lucky.

"Amelia."

Jason's near silent voice sounded as broken as I felt. The hurt in his voice cracked something in me that I was desperately trying to hold together. I shattered standing here in the middle of the floor like those pretty scalloped dishes.

Fractured.

Broken.

Each beat of my heart felt like a fist against an open wound.

It hurt.

I hurt.

I shook my head at him, tears running over my cheeks and blurring my vision of this male ready to catch me if I wanted him to.

But I didn't know if I could bear it. I knew that if I let him collect me in his arms he would feel the need to fix it. And fixing it, meant surrendering the search. Surrendering whatever it was that he needed from these little seeds to protect me from myself. From my past.

A cacophony of wood smashing, ceramic and glass shattering, and metal grinding, nearly sends me airborn. My heart slammed against my ribs as I surveyed the damage from where I steadied myself against the kitchen chair. The bookshelf that housed the books and baubles she must have collected, as well as her heavy-as-sin sewing machine, was now lying face down in the center of the main room.

Hefting that thing from the shelf to the table had been a feat, each and every time. But anytime I suggested she leave the damn thing on the table, she'd scrunch up her thin nose and tut, "I'm not willin' to forfeit half my table, girl". So, back and forth I carried it. Now it was laid on the floor in three bulky pieces.

Jason sent Henry a hard glare from across the small space, his thumb and forefinger pinching the bridge of his nose.

A watery laugh erupted without my permission and Henry smiled as he dusted off his hands with a satisfied smirk. Suddenly the pounding of my heart wasn't so painful.

I whirled, launching the stack of teacups into the middle of the floor, followed by the empty spice jars. Anything within reach that could break, I hurled against the floor. Jars, plates, cups, containers. Nothing was safe and each piece was thrown harder than the last.

Finally I turned, swiping my arm across the table top, sending the spices across the small space before I toppled the table itself with one good kick.

Breath sawed from my lungs, but the warm chuckle that felt so much like praise as it fell from Henry's lips, made my chest feel lighter.

It quelled the hurt that had felt too big.

Too painful to hold.

When I ran out of smashable objects within my reach, Jason stepped over the destruction littering the ground, glass and ceramic crunching under his shoe, to swipe at the only remaining piece left. His rings clatter against the ceramic figurine as he backhands the crude rendition of lovers locked in an embrace, right off the side table.

"It was ugly," he shrugs. That twitch to his lips a balm against the wound that had cracked open in my chest.

My eyes still sting, my chest still aches, but I'm not alone. And as I smile at my males I find myself laughing as I dry my eyes.

But when I sober, the room is quiet. Jason wears a satisfied smirk, but Henry looks ... surprised as he lifts his gaze from the floor. I follow his line of sight, and there amongst the broken glass, are seeds.

My knees wobble with relief, and to my surprise neither male moves to collect them immediately. Instead, Jason takes the two steps to cross the small space finally gathering me into his arms. I cling to him as I steady my breathing. I set my forehead to the soft cotton covering his chest, that despite our long trek still smells fresh. And I fill my lungs with him, letting his arms support my weight entirely as I calm myself.

"Do you want to see anything else of camp before we leave?"

I knew what he was asking. Did I want to see what was left? Did I want to see them?

I shake my head, pressing my cheek to his chest, my eyes landing on Henry who has made swift work of collecting the seeds scattered across the ground. He ties the satchel closed, tucking it into his pocket before he rises slowly, his eyes finally catching mine.

The smile he wears is rueful, but doesn't reach his eyes as they flicker from mine to Jason's. Something passes between them in that way that I'm sure comes with living lifetimes with one another, but whatever it is, tightens the lines around Henry's mouth. He shoulders his pack, swiping his hand down his mouth and beard erasing the tension there. But that's all the analyzing I'm allowed before Jason hooks a knuckle under my jaw, returning my gaze to his.

Warm umber swirls, those little gold flecks bright.

"You're sure there is nothing else you need?"

I nod the best I can as he holds me. His thumb drifts over my lower lip, parting them under his soft touch. His eyes coast across my face as if the truth hides somewhere along my sticky cheeks.

"You're words, Amelia."

My name on his lips

This isn't where or how she would want me to remember her. I was here with a goal in mind and we had accomplished that.

"I'm ready to leave."

His warm fingers dry my cheeks before he nods and turns me towards the door.

"Henry will take you back," he says as if in parting.

I whirl on him and he lets me.

"Where are you going?"

I feel Henry step up behind me, the heat from his body soaking into my back.

Jason inclines his head towards his pack and I realize then why Henry's had looked so much lighter as he slung it over his shoulder. Jason's was stuffed to brim with our camping supplies.

"I'm going to deliver our supplies to a nearby camp." His words carried the tone of admission, but his eyes- his eyes burned with an intensity that chilled my blood. There was something hiding there, and it wasn't because he shuttered the emotion behind that mask like he had done so many times before...

This felt like he was bearing a piece of himself... but I couldn't grasp the image.

Why would he deliver supplies to a free camp? And why would he go alone?

As far as I knew the nearest camp was miles west of here.

"Ok..." I said, glancing over my shoulder to Henry who wore an uncharacteristically sour expression. He didn't seem any more thrilled about this than I was, but while I may have missed the way they repacked this morning, they had clearly planned for this.

"We'll go with you."

He's shaking his head before I can finish.

"It will be faster if I go alone," he says easily, eyes calm once more. "Henry has everything you'll need and I'll meet you at the car."

His eyes land on Henry over my shoulder before he hefts his own pack onto his shoulder.

"Besides," he says, raking those eyes over me once more. "You need to eat."

As if on cue, my traitorous stomach growls and I narrow my gaze on him.

"Nice party trick," I comment smarmily.

His responding smile is winning and damn him if it doesn't send my stomach tumbling.

Bet he can hear that too.

I turn on my heel and refuse to look back as I trudge out the door. I'm a good mile past the tree line when I falter realizing I'm heading back towards the direction of our last campground... and there very well be another route we should be taking.

As if he'd been waiting on me to lose steam, Henry steps past me, a hand brushing my back as he leads the way just as silently as he had followed.

Questions plagued me as we hiked back and it was a mountainous effort not to harass Henry in turn.

Jason was a prince, born into royalty and power... and yet he was delivering supplies to humans... on his back. I knew now that he owned this land and maybe a part of him felt responsible for the humans on it. Henry said that he had established the agreement with the shifters to protect the humans, and while that seemed like a feat of its own, trappers still hunted these lands. They still torched free camps.

Was this penance?

A misplaced sense of responsibility?

Did he have a Robinhood kink?

I didn't know much about the royal families, but I imaged this wouldn't be popular with the vampires or shifters. And while he held sway over the shifters for 'lending" them the land they now ruled over, there seemed to be no obvious benefit to the relationship with the humans.

I eyed Henry as he ate, and when he caught me, you would've thought the log he perched on caught on fire for how quickly he rose to his feet, quick to find something that needed tending to.

Convenient.

The vampires were hiding something.

The thought coiled round and round my head while we hiked back to the car where we met Jason. I chose to ride with Henry since I needed a little time to build up an argument as to why I was going to insist the males spill their secrets. Despite knowing I had no right to them.

Maybe it was the mess of questions swirling through my mind, or the way I could feel his dark gaze on us as we rode ahead of him, but I was distracted enough to only notice something was wrong when Henry dropped his speed, tucking the bike around the back of the car. His hand gripped my hip as he peered around me to the car I hadn't heard approaching from behind.

I see Jason throw a glare over his shoulder through the rear window of the car as Henry bites out a curse, muffled by his helmet and the roaring wind.

The bike swerves to the right as a blade flies past us, lodging in the bumper of the car. Jason looks as if he's trying to pull the car around us, but Henry weaves the bike back and forth across the asphalt, dodging blades and blocking Jason's attempts at using the car like a shield.

I swear I can hear Jason's roar from here.

Henry would never allow Jason to put himself in harm's way. If I'd learned anything from our talk last night, then I worried having me here at his back, with Jason at his front, would only be a distraction.

"Can we outrun them?" I called.

He dipped his helmet to his left shoulder.

"Not likely," he called back.

Another blade zipped past our heads just as Henry dipped the bike to the right.

I loosened my hold on his waist, strengthening my resolve.

"Pull me to the front of the bike."

His body tensed under my hand.

"My aim is shit as it is facing forwards," I argue without a hint of embarrassment. "And you can't throw a blade without elbowing me off of this bike, but if you swing me around then we both have a shot."

He growled something unintelligible and I cursed, flinching as a blade crashed through the back window of the car. I wasn't waiting any longer. He was strong enough not to drop me and I didn't think I'd win this argument if we kept going, so with a huff, I committed. I curled my right leg up and hooked it around his thigh. His hand latched onto the front of my coat as I swung my left leg over the back of the bike, balancing my weight on the foot peg.

This time there was no hesitation as he tugged me around his waist. He tucked me against him firmly. His arm was like iron as it braced my back, but he needed that arm. Locking my legs around his waist, I gripped the front of his leather jacket with one hand, and with the other, I palmed a blade I had slipped from the sheath across his chest. He dipped forward using his weight to pin me to the body of the bike, shifted his hold on the handles, and unsheathed a blade of his own.

With a nod, I release my blade and watch it snap forward with impressive speed that I attribute to us hurtling in the opposite direction. Satisfaction curls pleasantly in my stomach as I watch it land in the front tire sending the car careening for the bank.

And I will go to the grave with the admission that I had been aiming at the windshield.

Irritation nearly mars my relief when Henry's blade flies straight through said windshield, landing deftly in the driver's throat.

Showoff.

The car careens into the bank wrapping around a tree.

Henry decelerates, pulling off the road behind Jason.

He lifts his weight from where he keeps me pinned to the bike, his hand gripping the back of my thigh, the other landing on my waist. I can only see my own reflection in the visor of his helmet, but the picture of his hands gripping my body has my pulse hammering.

He removes his helmet in a flash, chestnut brown hair flopping messily into his eyes. Sweat curling the ends. His fingers make quick work of my own, but the gentle way he pulls the helmet free, the way his hand cups the back of my neck, the other brushing the hair from my face, has my pulse slowing ever so slightly.

Moss green eyes bore into my own.

"I'm fine. I'm fine," I pant waving him off.

His eyes glide over my body swiftly before he nods, not trusting my words.

"I'm so fucking proud of you Princess," he growls.

But before I can allow those words to sink in, he swings his leg over the back of the bike, lifting me with him. He lowers me to my feet, but with his ridiculous height it means he slides me down the front of his body until my toes touch the ground.

I can feel his heart hammering in his chest as he does. My fingers grip the front of his jacket. The impulse to tip back onto my toes and press my lips to his, to taste him, breathe him in, to simply pull him even closer is a pressing need I barely avoid acting on when his eyes release me from their snare.

His gaze snaps over my head and I step back following his line of sight. The car door flies open and a very pissed Jason launches from the vehicle.

The sight leaves me breathless. Jason looks absolutely lethal as he prowls towards us, his gaze nailing me in place. A breeze announces Henry's departure as he flies across the space still separating us to catch a shifter by the throat as he hurls himself at Jason from the brush.

That shifter had not come from the car.

I whip my gaze over my shoulder to confirm that the male in the driver's seat is now bowed over the hood of the car, his blood splattered across the shattered windshield he had been thrown through.

It's an ambush.

Trappers, I realize as they pour from the trees.

Two aim for Henry who has snapped the first shifter's neck, the bright blue scales lining his throat and cheeks now broken and bent at an unnatural angle. He draws a blade in each hand and sends the first into the chest of a female who streaks across the road towards Jason. The other, he slips across the throat of a male I hadn't seen before he was lunging for Henry's back, one arm outstretched, ready to curl around his neck. But Henry is lightning fast and brutal in the way he dispatches the trappers with a growl.

Jason doesn't so much as slow his advance towards me as head snaps to the side, and with a twist of his wrist, his eyes bleed black, fingers tipped in inky claws, and the male stumbles. I watch as the male desperately claws at his own throat, ripping and tearing at his skin as dark veins wrap themselves around his throat. I recognized them as the same inky shadows that had strangled Darin in the train car.

My lips part as breathe saws between my teeth. The undercurrent of fear skitters my pulse. An ambush meant someone knew we would be here.

But who?

My eyes scoured the treeline and I caught Henry dragging a blade across a struggling male's throat with brutal efficiency. I swallow roughly trying to calm the thoughts swirling around my mind. Jason slows as he approaches and his stalled progress catches my attention.

He tracks my gaze, halting a few paces away, and I all but watch him draw the wrong conclusion.

The idea that trappers had been lying in wait unsettled me, but I knew I was safe.

I drew in a slow breath my eyes coasting over his form checking for injury and when I found none it helped to settle my pulse. To settle my fear and allow me to think past the cloud of adrenaline to see the male before me.

Jason blinks, returning to himself as Henry grabs the final male by the hair pulling him back into the brush for a reason I'm happy to remain ignorant of.

His eyes dip to his hands before they lift to me, and the hurt that shadows his features heats my skin. I hate that he cannot see, cannot understand, that I know just how safe I am with him.

"I'm sorry." He shakes his head clenching and unclenching clawed fingers at his sides.

My brows collapse as I drink in the male before me. Like Henry, all that power is softened by the careful way he handles me. Always at arm's length. Always protecting me from himself. But I didn't want to be protected. I don't want gentle. I wanted him to grip me so tightly I could trace the shape of his fingers across my skin.

I wanted to watch all of that control snap.

So I tucked away my relief over his safety and evened my expression. Slowly, I dragged my gaze over him making sure to make a show of it before I spoke the words I hoped would poke at the tender spot beneath his mask.

"Ooh scary," I mock

His eyebrows raise, disbelief painting his expression and replacing the guilt. My own mask settles into place and I can only hope he doesn't see the way my knees shake. He fists his hands once more and I cross my arms keeping my expression bored.

Calm.

Unimpressed.

I set my weight against the bike behind me and smirk. "Big bad royal," I snort. "You let Henry have all the fun."

Challenge scents the air between us.

His eyes sharpen and a moment later I'm caged between his arms, back pressing into the side of a nearby tree trunk. He'd never handled me so boldly.

I liked it.

"Is that all you've got?" I thread my fingers through his hair and he chuckles darkly. He uses his hips to pin me tighter to the tree leaving me no space of my own and I punished him because I liked it. My grip in his hair tightens to what I hope would register as a painful level.

His eyes snapped to mine, lust and hunger swirling as his lips quirked in the corner.

"You dont scare me," I tip my chin up ignoring the way my heart flutters in my chest.

"Lie to me again, Pet," he purrs.

With a sinful smile his irises bloom, black swallowing the umber and gold. I breathe in his scent as it envelops me, irritation marring with a deep pang of want. He wanted me to see him as a predator, but my fucked up brain loved every moment of this cat and mouse game we played.

"I didn't lie." The words are a ghost across my lips and nowhere near the truth. Vampires and shifters terrified me. Their power, strength, unpredictable violent tendencies... but Jason, though arguably the most deadly of them all, didn't scare me. Not in the sense he assumed. He had proven time and time again that I was safe with him. And that trust bred an infallible certainty that no matter how dangerous this male was, he would never be a danger to me.

He grins, ducking his head to run his nose along my jaw. My exhale is damn near a moan as I set my head against the tree, tipping my chin, and allowing him access to explore. His hand cups the back of my knee pinning my thigh to his hip. I need no encouragement to curl my leg around his waist, his other hand bracing my back allowing me very little movement. Like this he had full control and I glowed under the closeness of our bodies. A closeness he only extenuates by using his thigh, notched between mine, to press me into the tree behind me when I smiled.

"You lie so prettily I almost don't mind" his throaty chuckle coasts across my skin, his breath caressing the shell of my ear.

"Please," I shiver.

"Please what, Amelia?"

I turn to him wanting to see my name leave his lips.

"Say it again," I breathe.

His eyes are an inferno. Smoldering umber churns as he locks me in his gaze.

"Amelia."

I don't know who moves first but our lips clash together. He angles his mouth over mine, his finger threading into my hair to maintain the control I gladly forfeit. And as a reward he claims my mouth without a spec of restraint. He swallows down the gasp of surprise that climbs my throat as I wrap myself tighter around him.

The warmth of his body bleeds into mine, igniting a fire. His heartbeat echoes in my chest and I revel in the way he rocks against me. Pinned pleasantly between the tree and his body he devours the sounds that climb my throat, mirroring them with his own.

The rest of the world, the danger that had been lying in wait, my anxiety over their safety, all wink out of existence melting into the sole awareness of the places his body melds to mine. The way his fingers brace the back of my head and sprawl across my back. The feeling of his thigh nocked between my legs.

I am consumed by him.

Until Henry lets out a boisterous whoop from the treeline.

Jason smiles against my lips, our kiss softening until he rests his forehead against mine, a breathy laugh coasting across my flushed cheeks.

"Subtle." His voice rumbles, grip shifting to something less urgent. Less demanding. I melt, enjoying the way his lips shift against mine as he smiles, placing a kiss to the corner of my mouth once more before turning to greet Henry who has arrived beside us.

"Not my specialty," Henry grins wolfishly. "Plus I have waited too long for this moment. Subtly would be an insult."

I unravel my arm from around Jason's neck, but he keeps me neatly pinned between his body and the tree. He swipes his thumb under my lip dropping his hand from where he cupped my jaw and I tucked under his arm to send Henry the finger.

Unsurprisingly, he chuckles unfazed.

“Should I be worried that you chose a moment where I was dismembering a male not forty feet from you to make your move?”

I rolled my eyes not realizing that Henry was, in fact, speaking to Jason. Breath stalled in my lungs. It was the confirmation I needed knowing that the three of us had been barreling towards the very same destination

Each other.

Well two of us anyway. Apparently Henry had been plotting this the whole time. I caught the corner of my lip between my teeth to hide a smile. Henry wanted this for the three of us.

I wanted this...

But if Henry had been in his ear... and Henry knew how I felt, then what had kept Jason from acting until now?

Chapter Twenty-Seven

"You bought me a dress?" I ask admiring the material he had laid across the bed while I showered.

The males are dressed and waiting for me when I emerge from the little ensuite bathroom of the inn. We had stopped at the cottage perched at the very edge of town to freshen up after our run in with the trappers. The car, a little worse for wear, had survived Jason driving it headlong into the ditch on the side of the road, though Henry had decided I would be riding with Jason in the car until we made it home.

Thankfully we had only one more stop.

And apparently that stop called for another dress.

"She wouldn't take my coin unless I was purchasing something," Jason said over the rim of a steaming mug.

The scent of coffee, cologne, and leather swirled around the small space taking up far too much space in my brain.

Jason had set a platter of fruit on the bed before ducking into the bathroom shortly after we arrived. It was a mouthwatering array of colors and I was looking forward to trying each one. And then retrying them over and over until the platter was empty. But before I could dive in, Henry had the absolute audacity to wink at me as he popped open the fly of his pants before following his prince into the shower.

That fruit platter still sat untouched beside my dress.

"I don't know that it was *pride*," I say, running my fingers along the hem and shaking the memory free. The delicate flower petals stitched into the violet material was reminiscent of the old moth. I liked the idea that maybe she had escaped and was filling a new camp with her colorful curtains and that rusty laugh.

A smile tugs at my lips as I return my eyes to his. "She was probably worried some handsome vampire had arrived to play her into a trap."

His jaw shifts as he grins, those umber eyes filled with mirth. "So you think I'm handsome?"

For fuck's sake.

I roll my eyes, snatching the dress off the bed without so much as a thank you and realize I cannot in fact storm from the room.

We are standing in the only room

"This," I say, my finger spinning in a circle between us, "is the trap."

Henry's low chuckle coasts across my skin from where he stands windinding leather up his forearms. I can feel his eyes land on my face, my chest, and down my arms but I keep mine pinned to the capable way his fingers move as he dons his armor. My skin heats under my towel and I ignore the flush that must give me away as I lift the dress from the bed.

The males are gracious enough to turn their backs to allow me to drop my towel and slip into the dress. Padding up to the mirror I turn, both hands pulling at the zipper when Henry's rough hands settle on my hips. He gathers the material of my skirt, the grip at the base of my spine awakening an awareness I immediately battle down. He zips my dress in one smooth slow motion careful not to pinch my skin.

The shape of the dress is simple, the material a bit coarse against my skin, but it fits like a glove. It may lack the quality of what's normally worn in the north, but it is beautifully made and reminds me of home, and of the human who probably spent days dyeing, cutting, and crafting this dress.

"It fits perfectly," I breathe, my fingers coasting along the fabric of my skirt. This one is shorter than the dress I wore to the Lord's estate, only falling to my knees, but the slit reaches up my thigh, the material folding over itself to offer plenty of coverage and movement. Designed for not only beauty, but utility. A duality that seemed uniquely human.

"Yes, it'd be a shame had all that ogling gone to waste." Henry smirked, stepping around me.

I snort as I finger comb my wet hair dragging it into a braid

"Like a snake studying its next meal."

"Brave," Jason growls as he knots his tie, rings glinting in the low light. "Taunting me like I wouldn't devour you if you'd ask.

My pulse rockets and I know they can hear it. Henry's only response is to wink at me as he hands me my blade and sheath.

Henry pulls the car into another large estate just north of the border. As he opens the door for me I eye the light blue wisteria crawling across the white-washed brick that frames the front door. The delicate blooms flutter in the evening breeze scenting the air as we cross the threshold. Henry nods to the human girl who answers the door. Whether it's the sheer size of him as he steps past her, or the glint of the metal lining his chest that has her taking a hesitant step back, I can't be certain, but he doesn't seem to notice. Henry leads the way down the ornate hallway, his focus on the throng of people gathering in the main room.

While I have no idea whose estate we are visiting, it seems another party is in full swing.

Wondering idly if the gold plated scones, shaped like human hands were fashioned for another 'dickhead lord' or simply another shifter with far too much time and coin, I watch my males survey the space. Henry posts up at the mouth of the great room, his back pressed to the wall as Jason continues without pause towards a large lacquered bar at the far end of the room.

His hand remains on my low back as I stand beside him. He orders a whiskey and a hot tea before we make our way to the smattering of tables towards the large windows. Dusk is settling, painting the sky in soft violets and navy blues. I'm not sure if it's my feet that carry me towards them, or the hand at my back that leads me, but I pause near an open table set at just the perfect angle to appreciate the view. Jason helps me into my seat before returning with a plate of sweets.

The smile I serve him fades as a group of vampires make a raucous appearance from down the long hallway. I watch Henry bristle as they pass, drinks and slurred words sloshing between them.

Jason's hand catches my chin and I'm surprised when he doesn't drop into the chair beside me like I'd expected. Instead, he sends Henry a nod before turning back.

His thumb slips gently down my lower lip, his own tipping up at the corner ever so slightly.

"We'll be back," he nods and I follow. "And I expect to find you in this chair when we do."

I barely restrain the eye roll at his tone, and judging by the way his mouth flattens into a tight line, I assume the sentiment lands without so much as blinking.

"You left me enough chocolate to buy you some time," I smile.

It dies against my plate as he straightens his tie, running ringed fingers down the silky material. I bite my lip wanting to do the same, but thankfully he misses this reaction as he turns and cuts through the throng of monsters. He tucks around the doorway left of that bar and I watch Henry's broad back fill the space a moment later.

I sink down into my seat and reach out to run my fingertip along the edge of the mug of tea Jason had set before me. I wasn't a patient person by nature, but here in this estate filled with shifters and vampires alike, I was happy to sit here and eavesdrop.

I sigh around a bite of chocolate allowing my attention to flit from table to table listening in until the start of a new conversation has the hair on the back of my neck rising.

"Good evening gentlemen," the server smiled, looking earnestly pleased to be there.

"Men?" The shifter cocked his head, tufts of brown fur that lines his skin, pulling at the collar of his button down. His rounded ears sit high on his head. A short snout lifts, lips curling, to reveal two very pronounced canines. A barely distinguishable brow raises as he appraises the server, his thick paw wrapping around the glass before him. One nail tap, tap, tapping on its fragile rim.

My next inhale was purely for show. Not an ounce of oxygen reached my lungs and they burned their protest. My eyes flickered to the young man.

I'd made that mistake before.

More than once... before catching on to the new rules.

"*We* are not *men*," the other sneered, his thin snake-like tongue darting out as if to taste the fear radiating from the server as he fidgeted with his pen, straightening his apron. The bear shifter reaches out, tucking a ridiculously long claw between the buttons of the server's shirt.

I hold my breath as he tugs the man close.

For an instant I let my eyes dart around the room looking for anyone else who may be watching. Anyone else who may be able to stop what I could only fear was about to happen.

No one.

No one heard, or seemed to care about the rail thin man that was about to become this bear shifter's appetizer.

I return my gaze to the males, gripping my fork so hard it's a competition of wills between the metal and my fingers to see who will break first.

"I own men." He sneered, baring his teeth. "*I*. Am. Male."

With each word the poor server curled in on himself as if he could hide in the back of his own shirt. Wishing, I'm sure, to create as much space as possible between the male's claw and his frail human hide.

The young server looks horrified and embarrassed as he takes a quick glance around apologizing profusely, searching for help.

Help that wasn't coming.

But the shifter was done toying with the man, and with a flick of his clawed fingers, tore the server's shirt. The material hung in ribbons from his shoulders exposing the server's chest which now sported four angry red slashes. He didn't gut the man, but he drew enough blood to make him a target.

My hands grip the arm rests of my seat, the plate of sweets before me, forgotten. To top off his tantrum, he swipes his arm across the table sending the glassware shattering against the floor. In that moment I am glad for the death drip on my seat, because it's the only thing that keeps me in it.

"Clean it up, *boy*." He spat the word like a curse.

I sink deeper into my chair as the shifter's gaze jumps from face to face, searching out the validation that will only encourage him to torment the next human he comes in contact with. And I am determined not to be her.

I swallowed thickly as I watched the man place a hand to his wounds while dropping to his knees as he scooped up shards of crystal with the other. My teeth dug into my cheek so sharply I worried my next attempt at swallowing down the fear lurching up my throat would be iron coated.

But judging by the way several heads tipped back, nostrils flaring, pupils blooming as their attention snapped to the table beside me and the bleeding man on his knees, bleeding here was not wise. I carefully released my cheek, running my tongue over the worried flesh to ensure I hadn't broken it.

That essentially summed up the fragile male ego of these shifters. Don't get me wrong, vampires could be overconfident pricks, but shifters hadn't held power as long. They were still grasping at it. Still desperate to ensure we knew how low we sat on the food chain.

He was right though.

They weren't men.

They were monsters.

A hand settles on my shoulder and I jolt in my seat despite the recognition that settles my frayed nerves.

Henry lowers himself into the chair to my right, his hand gripping the leg of mine and scooting me in close. His scent envelopes me as his fingers run up the chair leg before landing on my own.

Moss green eyes capture mine.

"You're safe." His voice is pitched low, both of us understanding the lack of privacy here.

I nod and his grip on my knee squeezes in two reassuring little pulses as if to echo his words. My hand settles over his as I breathe him in. His scent. His nearness. The air of safety he provides allows me to take my first full breath.

A raucous cackle from a vampire nearby sends my pulse skittering again. My gaze travels the room as I realize I don't even know where Henry came from... or where Jason is now.

"Princess."

I tug my eyes back to Henry where he waits, eyes too gentle for a male so large. So dangerous.

"You are safe because you are capable." He pauses, his fingers stretching to tap the blade strapped to my thigh, his eyes searching mine. The cool steel is a pleasant sting against my overheated skin. "They're not so far up the food chain as they'd like to believe."

Brave thing to say here where most could probably hear my hair growing, let alone the comment Henry just made. But no one seems to be listening.

I'm sure for someone like Henry that is easy to believe. I imagine there are very few above him on said food chain... but being here, surrounded by shifters and vampires, I cannot help but surrender to that instinct that demands I make myself invisible. That insists I keep the target off of my back, because that is what I feel like.

A target.

Prey.

Patient moss green waits for me as I recapture his gaze.

"Henry, I-

My chair lurches forward as someone shoves past our table nearly jostling me out of it as if I was in fact invisible.

Okay so maybe invisibility had its flaws.

Henry's arms shoot out steadying my chair with one hand his other landing on my shoulder, but before I can settle back into my chair recognition crashes over me like a bucket of cold water. My body goes rigid, fear thickening my throat. I swallow down a gasp, as I draw in a careful breath confirming what my body was already reacting to.

I knew that smell. That cologne.

I had watched Le douse himself in it before we arrived in the High City. My stomach flipped, my body breaking out in a cold sweat.

I'm sure he wasn't the only one who wore that garish cologne, but my heart was already tripping over itself at the idea that he could be here. That he had been within touching distance. That he may have, yet again, seen me when I hadn't seen him.

Henry's fingers curl around my upper arm.

"Did they hurt you?" His eyes sharpen as they lift over my head, I'm sure following the direction they had retreated.

I suck in a sharp breath.

"No. No," I hesitate swallowing down the fear and smoothing a hand down my skirt. "It's nothing."

I settle back into my chair, drawing in a small steadying breath, and take a calculated bite of my cake. My fingers shake, and it tastes like ash on my tongue, but I need to keep my head. Jason and Henry are here. I'm safe, and the likelihood that Le is the only vampire in the south who wears that cologne is slim. It's just an unfortunate coincidence.

I set the fork back onto the plate with a frown.

Henry reclines, his legs widening as they bracket mine and I watch him drag a powerful hand down his mouth and beard. My eyes trace the sharp lines of him, all the way up to his eyes. The nearness of him further calming my racing heart.

How could I fear anyone with Henry here?

I convince myself that there's no reason my heart should be beating so hard against my ribs. Nor should the room feel off kilter. I watch Henry's hand spread over his wide thigh and turn my thoughts elsewhere.

That shouldn't be hard right?

And yet, fear coils around my stomach and climbs my throat.

"What aren't you telling me?" Henry's question- the timber of his voice, draws me back to him.

Le.

His name rattles through my mind.

The sound of his harsh laugh and bruising grip. The smell of his breath.

The smell of that fucking cologne.

I shiver, my eyes widening with a fear I'm not certain I'll ever be able to leash, and I know I'm caught... and so does he.

"I can't tell you here." The story of Le wasn't one I wanted to recount. Especially not here, in a room filled with listening ears.

He nods, but if I expected him to pull away, to stand and return to guard-mode, punishing me for not being able to give him what he asked for, I would have been very wrong. Because his response is to pull me into his arms. He tucks me into his chest, my legs draping over his strong thighs, his arm curling around my back, hand gripping my thigh, while the other hand settles against the side of my head holding me to him.

Like this, I feel shielded. Safe against his chest. His fingers weave into the hair at the nape of my neck and I close my eyes. And after a few moments, a few more even breaths, I sink into him. There was nothing about the way he held me that was for show. Nothing about the care he afforded me was for the benefit of anyone around us, except for me.

I didn't know if Henry had a carefully crafted image he maintained in situations like this, but if he did, it didn't seem to matter in this moment when I needed him.

His thumb swept over my brow brushing away the last wisps of tension in my body and replacing it with awareness. The awareness of just how deeply this male had wormed his way into my heart.

I turned my face into his palm, pressing a kiss to his calloused skin. His thumb swept down my cheek, capturing my chin between his fingers, and tipping my face back up to his.

Those green eyes were soft, but backlit with a hunger that had my stomach fluttering with confidence instead of fear. The placement of his thumb against my jaw presented me the opportunity to turn into him again, propping his thumb against my lips and scraping my teeth against the pad.

His eyes closed for the briefest of moments, his thighs shifting underneath mine. And when they opened, it was like a snare snapping around my ankle before it flipped my world upside down. Those eyes burned into mine, and I could taste his hunger on my tongue as I drew his thumb between my lips. My tongue molding to the shape of him. My cheeks hollowing as I sucked.

His pupils bloomed, eyes flashing with something primal as he pressed the pad of his thumb against my tongue. His forefinger curled under my chin and he pinned me there. The smile that followed was full of promise. His grip on my thigh moved up to my ribs. His fingers grazed the underside of my breast, thumb teasing my nipple over the material of my dress as I set my teeth to his skin once more.

My lips tipped up as he growled, the sound low and carnal as it rumbled through me.

He retrieved his thumb, sweeping the moisture across my lower lip, before his grip shifted and he turned me. My back now pressed to his chest, he leaned low into the crook of my neck.

"I'm going to make a mess of you Princess."

My eyes snapped up to the crowd around us, my exhale audible to even my own ears. I had to press my thighs together to ease the ache that blossomed with his words.

"But not here..." his breath tickles the sensitive skin behind my ear. "And not alone."

Not alone.

Both of them.

He straightens and I can sense his gaze sweeping the room over my head as I settle back against him. I aimed for a relaxed posture.

I did.

Or, at least I had tried before something bumped into the back of my thighs. I shifted and his grip tightened like a bar across my ribs, a hiss escaping his teeth as that bulge nocks between my thighs.

"Where is Jason?" I ask not caring for an instant how needy my voice sounds. I was both enjoying the idea of being pressed between them in this moment, and needing some relief from the pressure building to a near painful ache at my core.

As I voice his name, I catch his face in the crowd. Umber and gold nail me in place against Henry's chest and I feel his sharp intake of breath underneath me. This need seemed to have weighted the air between the three of us, even from across the room.

He looked as if he'd been pulled from whatever interaction he had been entertaining, and I found myself wondering how long he'd been watching.

Henry chuckles underneath me and something sparks in Jason's gaze, his ringed fingers sweeping through tousled hair, before that mask falls back into place, a hand landing on his shoulder.

We watch as he turns, falling into what appears to be a friendly conversation with... Link?

Why is she here?

Distracted, I scan the faces amongst the throng of shifters and vampires here in the main room searching for Amara, but come up empty.

"Are you needed...over there?" I ask Henry, not really wanting him to leave, but knowing this wasn't the reason we were here.

And I assumed Link *was*.

"Trying to get rid of me?" He asks, his chuckle brushing over my skin.

"No," I grin, tucking the toe of my shoe against the back of his calf.

"Good, because some would consider it rude for me to sport this," he says, dragging me over his length earning a groan from both of us. "As I cross a crowded room," he says, voice tight.

"Probably rude." I agree, breathless and wishing he would do it again. I think I may be on the verge of losing my mind. I want these males and I've arrived at the very end of my ability to pretend I care whether it's right or wrong to feel this way.

Henry's fingers skim the rim of my plate, the chocolate cake long forgotten.

"Are you hungry?" I think he aims to make casual conversation, but I'm not quite ready to let this moment flutter away.

Instead, I tip my head back against his chest and smile.

"Starving".

"Princess," he warns, the timber of his voice peaking my nipples.

The next sweep of his thumb ensures we are both well aware of the effect he has.

"We'll put a bow on this," he inclined his head towards Jason. "And I'll get you a plate."

That is the absolute last thing I care about right now. But he lifts me from his lap and sets me on my feet before taking his time smoothing my skirt back into place. I wobble where I stand as his heavy hands run over my hips and around the curve of my ass.

I all but collapse back into my chair, my knees as steady as Jello as he straightens himself discreetly and tosses me a wink over his shoulder.

Henry cuts through the crowd towards Jason and I am able to regain my composure in time to see Link lean in and press an envelope into Jason's hand, before slipping through the doorway. I catch just the edge of that silver-grey floral print as he tucks it into his jacket pocket. My eyes widened.

The envelope.

I had delivered letter after letter to his office with the very same embossing.

They had been letters from Link and Amara.

I add the question to the growing list I intend to ask the vampires once were home, but as the males follow Link into an adjoining room, I find myself unable to sit here any longer.

I need some air... and I need to finish my dessert.

The former, expressly breaks the rule Jason set when he told me to stay put until they returned, but as my eyes flit around the room I catch sight of an exit to what appears to be a covered deck. I also realize I'm not the only one studying the crowd tonight.

A human about my age, sits on the deck watching as partygoers eat, and eat, and eat, themselves sick. She sat with a thin arm wrapped around her waist, and an angry set to her brows.

My next exhale is a barely restrained sigh.

This place was going to get me in trouble...

Common sense burns away as I watch her scowl at the plate of picked over bones and a few errant vegetables someone had left on the table adjacent to where she sat. I'd like to blame my anger on the awful display the shifters put on tonight, but knew it was something deeper. Something I wouldn't inspect too closely, because if I wasted time, I would miss my window. I had known what was at stake if I messed up at the Lord's manner, but here, I imagined the stakes were lower.

I gathered my plate and slunk my way to the balcony.

Invisibility and a small frame served me well as I maneuvered through the crowd dodging elbows and crystal flutes, ducking under the manicured nails a flutter in conversation. My skin prickled with awareness. It felt like at any point the phantom gaze I could feel against the back of my neck would result in a hand materializing there. But I shouldered through the patio door, the drone of conversation quieted with the snick of the door falling closed behind me. The quiet twilight air was a relief, but it wasn't what I was after. I drew in a slow breath regathering my wits and told myself that if she was still there, then I would speak to her.

Offer her some food.

Maybe make a friend.

My eyes flitted across the patio finding it blessedly monster free. And there, lounging in that chair, was my new human friend, dark hair fluttering in the cool evening breeze. She sat with her eyes closed as she reclined against the lounge chair and she would have looked relaxed if it wasn't for the little pucker between her brows.

As I circled her chair, a smile budding on my lips, I realized she wasn't alone. A male had joined her and he stood as I approached. He was only a few inches taller than me, his sandy blonde hair and bright blue eyes complemented by a smattering of freckles across his nose. They crinkled as he smiled at me.

"Hello," I said, hoping I didn't sound as breathless as I felt as I shifted my weight nervously.

"Hello," he responded, eyeing my plate unabashedly.

"Hi," I smiled again, nerves trickling down my spine. "I- I have more than I can eat." I lie, then cringe at my poor choice of words. "Would you like some?" I rush out, shoving the plate forward, arms extended.

Finally her eyes open. They were green, ringed by a softer brown. That sharp gaze snapped to my neck. Bare. And then back to my face, her eyes narrowing.

"You're human?"

"Yes," I said, holding out my plate encouragingly.

Please. Please take some...

"Are you not a pet?" She asked in a voice just as confused as I felt.

"I am," I allowed and clearly that was enough for the sandy haired man, because with a shake of his head he reached out to scoop a pastry off of my plate.

She watched him chew a moment before turning cold eyes to me.

"I do not speak to other pets."

The chilled evening air competed with her tone.

"Oh," I breathed, some of my excitement cooling. "Why?"

She shrugged. "What's the point?"

I turned to the blonde who was now reaching for one of the chocolates with greedy fingers and a meek smile.

"He's a pet," I qualified.

"We're from the same household," she explained, throwing a glare in his direction. "And don't let his smile fool you, that dumbass mouth will get him killed and *this,*" she motioned between the two of them, "will be just as much a waste as you'd be".

Ouch.

"Ouch Sierra," he echoed.

"I'm not wrong," she shrugged

"No, but she comes barring food," he grins, reaching for a walnut pastry.

"Food we were told was *not* for us," she seethed, picking at her fingernails, studiously ignoring the plate in my hands.

" *We* didn't take these from a table," he hedged, before unhinging his jaw and stuffing the entire pastry into his mouth.

Was this how Jason and Henry felt watching me eat?

"I'm glad you did though," he smiles. "I'm Jeremy and this is Sierra," he whispers, eyes flickering around the empty space.

He somehow still had room in that mouth for words as he chewed hungrily.

My smile fell flat as Jeremy hummed around a mouth full of raspberry cream and sweet honey glaze.

I'd wanted that one.

"How exactly did you pull that off?" Sierra scoffed. "What household are you from?"

She was cold, but she was still talking to me despite her previous declarations.

"Jason's..."

Was that how pets identified households? I didn't know my address. I hadn't kept track of the direction we'd traveled to use that as a clue either.

"So," Jeremy scratched at his brow "They don't make you wear a collar *and* give you shoes?"

My eyes dropped to his bare feet. He wiggled his toes as if knowing they were now on display.

"Well-

"Wait." She fluttered a hand in front of Jeremy's face, shooing him away as she sat up, swinging her legs over the chair to face me. "Jason? Prince Croft?" Her brows rose as she leaned forward. "The sired son?"

Sired son? I mentally added that to the list as well.

"Ha! No wonder she's so confused," she snarked. "She's barely a real pet."

I started.

"Sierra." Jeremy snapped.

"Where did he even find you?" she bristles.

Barely a real pet? Pet was the only title I had. It was the only thing I *was*. The only thing collected humans got to be. Could I have ended up in a worse household, absolutely. I knew just how lucky I was, but it didn't make me any less a pet. None of us were free.

"What else would I be?" I scowled, pulling my plate to my chest as Jeremy the pastry vacuum reached in.

"Honey, you wouldn't know what it *meant* to be a pet. You're a *prop*."

Jeremy was quiet then and it was clear, on this at least, he didn't disagree.

"What do you mean, a prop?"

Jason seemed wholly uninterested in upholding the image of a typical pet owner... though I suppose that was mostly at home. We both played rolls here in public-

"Does he punish you?" She interrupted my spiraling thoughts as she raised her brows.

She watched me expectantly.

"Do you serve him?" Those wild eyes went calculating, a smile gracing her pretty lips "Does he fuck you?"

My next breath was sharp. My cheeks heated and she laughed.

"That's none of your business," I ground out looking over my shoulder, finding the space blessedly empty.

"From what I heard, he spends his days fucking anything with pulse and once he made his way through the continent and his guards..." Her words faded into an implication that I apparently was supposed to grasp. She chuckled lowly.

My eyes narrowed and I bit the inside of my cheek to keep my retort caged. The way she was speaking about my males made my skin heat. Jason wasn't a monster. Jason was-

"But royalty doesn't stoop to fucking their pets." She cawed, dragging hard eyes over me. Her lips pursed as she waved a hand over me. "So here you are all dressed up and prancing around without a collar, eating food reserved for *their* kind. Not ours."

Her vitriol surprised me, but so did her words. Her opinion of Jason. Of me.

I was shaking my head before she could finish, but Jeremy was silent, his eyes cast down, brows pinched together.

Fine.

I took a small breath battling back the sting behind my eyes.

"You have no idea how wrong you are."

She laughed and it was a loud, harsh thing. But as she did, she reached across to my plate, snagging a chocolate. A smug smile lit her lips as they parted and I almost reached for her, when a hand beat me to it, catching her wrist.

"What did I tell you?" The male snarled.

The rest happened in seconds, but it felt like slow motion. The vampire dragged her out of her chair and to her feet as she erupted with a squeal.

Her eyes wide with fear then shot to me, accusations flying like daggers. Her dress wrinkled under his fist and I realized that she was about to be punished for the food I provided. And though I disliked her and her opinions, I didn't want her hurt because of me.

Dragged into action by my own guilt, I held out a hand on impulse.

"I'm sorry it was mi- "

I didn't even see him rear back to strike me before I was tugged back into a hard chest.

Henry's chest.

Jason materialized in the space between me and the male, standing over the shattered plate that had been knocked from my hand. His hand was wrapped around the male's wrist. Black tipped talons sunk deeply into the flesh of his arm.

Like the predator he is, Jason cocks his head as the male's mouth falls open, agape in a silent scream. Slowly those shadows pour down Jason's arm, slithering over razor sharp talons and worming their way under the male's skin. I watch as the skin of his hand begins to blacken, fingers withering as they curl. With a flick of his wrist, Jason removes the male's hand all together. It crumbles onto the floor like stone.

"That was unwise," he admonishes, voice eerily calm. Breath stalls in my lungs as he leans in loosening the leash on all that power looming just below the surface. "You do not touch what's *mine*," he growls.

He picks up his hand to tap a razor sharp talon just below the male's left eye.

"If you so much as look at her again, I'll take your eyes next." Shadows swirl around my ankles, the cool stroke of their presence, the antithesis of their wielder in this moment.

"Understood?"

Sweat beads on the shifter's face as he nods rapidly. A monster looking to escape the maw of a beast far worse than he.

But still, I couldn't find it in me to fear him.

Instead, my heart pounded out a heavy rhythm that felt possessive.

"Good." He pulls away, dusting off his hands on the male's jacket, before releasing him to collapse onto the ground. Not a second is wasted before he scuttles away mumbling his pained apologies.

Sierra is white as a ghost, her breaths audible, as her eyes flicker between Jason and her owner's ruined hand.

"Thank you," she stammers.

Jason smooths black-stained fingers down his tie before leveling the woman with a look equally bored and stern.

"You may thank me by keeping your input to yourself."

He had heard.

A flush erupts across her pale cheeks. "I...I-

Shifters step forward pushing the girl aside as she mumbled her apologies and I watch Jeremy collect her in his arms before hauling her back inside. Jason simply rolls his shoulders and dons his mask.

"Pity. I suppose he should have kept his hands to himself," he says in way of explanation.

A server arrives to collect the hand, looking disturbingly nonplussed by the task.

Henry's grip loosens and he steadies me on my feet. I'm sure he wants his hands free as things appear to get heated. A few shifters bleat their complaints over the situation.

Jason holds his hands in the air and after a moment they fall silent.

"I may do whatever I wish where it concerns my pet...or is that not a privilege you'd like to maintain?"

No one, shifter or vampire alike, had a leg to stand on here. Any proposed argument would only give Jason room to lord over the way they acted where it concerned their pets. He was their crowned prince after all.

So, as the crowd dispersed, seeming as unwilling to kick their prince out as they were to argue with him, he exhaled roughly. I watch the muscles in his back relax under his jacket before he turns, stepping into me. And for one blissful second I'm pressed between them both. My hands settle against his stomach as music drifts across the patio from the open door.

"I'm sorry." I whisper, breath still uneven. I was sorry to have put him in this position. Sorry that he had to hear Sierra's shitty retelling of his sexual prowess. True or not. I didn't care. I knew this male and I knew that wasn't what was happening between us.

His thumb coasts down my cheek, his fingers curling under my jaw and delving into my hair. I close my eyes as I lean into his touch, feeling forgiven.

"Dance with me" Jason's voice reaches my ear.

I don't hesitate even a moment to place my hand into his. And for that I'm grateful, especially as I register the expression he wears that looks far too much like worry. Like I could even fathom not taking an opportunity to touch this male. Like I wouldn't accept him.

Black stained fingers curl around my own.

I trust him.

And not because I had no other choice, but because he had earned it.

His smile as he kissed my knuckles was so bright, so earnest, so ... uniquely Jason, that it took every ounce of control I had not to throw myself into his arms, onlookers be damned.

He led me by the hand into the main hall, those shadows skimming his fingers and curing around my wrist possessively. Henry's hand rested on my back as we cut through the crowd of guests. The heat of his presence was an awareness at my back. One that dissipated as he watched us continue, remaining at the cusp of the dance floor. Jason twirls me into his arms, my rough exhale drawing a smile as my chest met his.

"Why can't we dance with Henry?"

His eyes hold mine, something dawning in them. "Henry doesn't like to be distracted."

"But you're no stranger to breaking the rules," he smiles teasingly.

"I don't break them," I argue.

He nods solemnly. "Would you prefer, 'disregard'?"

My next step lands on his foot, earning a sharp smile. Jason's arm wraps tighter around my waist as he pulls me flush against him, his hands tracing the shape of my hips.

We follow the same steps he and Henry had taught me while we camped and he spins me to and fro walking me back across the dance floor that predator surfacing in the most thrilling way. But as quickly as that hunger surfaced, he smothered it, his eyes calming his expression cooling.

"I'm sorry."

My eyes land on his hoping to coax him back to me.

"Don't be." I had no idea what he was apologizing for, but nothing about what had happened had been his fault.

"You shouldn't have had to hear-

I slid my hands from the back of his neck to his jaw, setting my thumbs over his lips to silence him.

I smiled at the sight.

The fact that this ridiculously powerful male had let me shush him here in a room full of his constituents, had a thrill running through me. Our steps slowed as the other couples twirled around us.

"I don't care." I shook my head. "About any of it." I nod as I study the flecks in those umber eyes. "True or not, it changes nothing," I vowed, and I meant it.

He was allowed his past.

His eyes fall closed as his grip tightens. "I will be a male worthy of that devotion," he says. His eyes open and my world is consumed by gold and umber.

"You already are," I breathe my answer just for him. I wanted to have this conversation, but not here. Outside of the two of us there was only one other who deserved to see this side of Jason. This piece of himself he was offering, and that person was currently standing guard at the edge of the dancefloor. My eyes flitted across the faces lining the walls searching him out. I could feel him. His presence was like a magnet tugging at my mind.

It's in a tick of a moment, a flicker of my gaze around his arm as I search out Henry, that I catch a face in the crowd that has me missing my next step.

Le.

Jason collects me gracefully, but my grip tightens as does my throat, and he spots my fear immediately.

His gaze whips across the room, a possessive snarl rumbling from his chest. His arms and shadows coil around me like he can sense the male who had once tried to take me from him.

Le was here. Here watching us from the crowd.

Henry steps out from the throng of shifters, and a tip of Jason's head is all Henry needs to stalk off after the male. Nerves stir at the thought of Henry alone with Le.

Jason tows me gently from the dance floor and into a darkened corner near that covered patio.

"Pet." his hands land on my cheeks.

"Will he be ok? Alone?" He grins without a trace of that mask he wears to hide his feelings.

"Don't let him hear you voice concern like that." His eyes grow serious as he dips his head low "Don't worry. Henry is the most capable male you will ever meet." the reverence and certainty in his voice couldn't be argued with.

I wonder if he knew that I had learned of Henry's past.

"Even more than you?" I tucked my hands into the material of his shirt, needing to hide the way they shook.

He steadied them in his own hands, his eyes dipping to recapture mine. "Leagues more," he swears.

With a nod, I smothered my fear. Tucked it into a little box where I could take it out later. Later after the sun went down, I could inspect every sharp edge.

"We've got you." he breathes, tucking me into his arms. I wrap my arms around his neck letting him hold me as the last of the tremors subsided. "No one will take you from me again."

When I feel steadier I lift my cheek from his chest but I can't keep my eyes from searching the room. Both for Henry and Le. The faceless danger in the room was still hanging heavy over my head, and I didn't think I'd be able to settle my pounding heart until we had Henry back.

"Pet."

When I linger on the crowd his knuckle tucks under my chin turning me back to him.

His eyes sharpen as he walks me back into the wall and uses his body to pin me there. His wide shoulders shield me from the room.

"Eyes on me." The easy authority in his voice clears some of the panic muddying my mind.

He waits, holding my gaze and I crack.

"Distract me." I shivered, the anxiety lessening as he blocked out the world, my focus once again narrowing down to the swirl of umber and gold. He leans in his breath coasting across my mouth, and I watch as they heat.

"Pleas-

He doesn't make me beg, angling his mouth over mine. The weight of his lips over mine, the sweep of his tongue, the growl that travels from his chest echoing through me

My fingers thread into his hair, my grip tightening and he smiles against my mouth. It's the briefest of praise before he crushes his lips to mine with an intensity that steals my breath.

His arm at my waist tightens, dragging me flush against his chest, his lips dipping to my ear as I suck in sharp breaths.

"Harder," he growls, his tongue tracing the shell of my ear, drawing a shiver up my spine.

I arch into him; my mind consumed with nothing but how our bodies fit together and the friction I so badly crave.

A moment later, as those words sink in, I oblige, tightening my grip knowing he can take it.

The sound that climbs up his throat dampens my thighs as they brush together.

"Now close your eyes," he purrs, leaning in and my breath catches but this time I do as I'm told without hesitation.

"Good girl." His tongue laps at my neck, lips dragging elongated fangs across my skin before cooling the little sting of venom with his lips and tongue again.

"Wrap your arms around my neck." His voice was a cool breath against my overheated skin and I lost my battle with a moan as it slipped past my control. If we drew attention from the crowd around us I didn't know because in the blink of an eye, and the snick of a door closing, we found ourselves on the balcony swathed in cool night air and quiet shadows.

He spun me, his hand cupping my throat as I let my head fall back against his chest, his other arm bracing my waist.

"Open your eyes, Pet."

I did as I was told fully under the spell this male has woven.

And there was Henry, eyes molten. His hand gripping the pommel of his sword as he leaned against the balcony wall. Completely unscathed.

Relief potent and consuming rushed through me at the sight of him.

But in the next moment, Jason's hand traveled low over my belly and down my thigh to the opening of my skirt.

There, just below the apex of my thighs, is where his hand paused.

"Should we give Henry a little show?"

I nod against his chest, my eyes nailed to Henry. His chest rose in deep controlled pulls that tugged the harness taunt over the leatherlike armor.

"I need your words, Pet."

"Jason," his name was a plea and a curse.

His slow exploration of my sensitive skin was torture, and I got the distinct impression that I wasn't the only one as Henry's grip tightened on the pommel at his hip.

Finally, his fingers slip behind the thin lace, applying exquisite pressure as he swirls strong fingers around my clit. His hand cups my mouth, caging in the moan that escapes my control at that very moment.

He leans in. "Those cries are only for us." His voice is smoke and grit as he drags his teeth down my earlobe.

I whimper into his palm, my knees going weak as he increases the pressure dipping into my folds to sweep moisture across my already sensitive flesh.

"You feel so good, Pet." His fingers test my entrance and I squirm nerves prickling my neck need swimming in my belly.

Henry shifts, eyes glued to Jason's hand hidden beneath my skirt lifting the material just enough.

"Do you want Henry to touch you like this?"

I nod melting under his assessing gaze. His eyes snapping to my face the moment that Jason's fingers push into me. My knees shake and his grip tightens his fingers pushing deeper, deeper, until they curl brushing against something inside of me that has my legs collapsing. I fall into his hold completely

Henry's growl is low as his lips part eyes snapping to Jason over my shoulder

His fingers stretch and plunge over and over as I moan shamelessly

He pulls his fingers from me swirling them against my clit before dipping back inside me and he follows this torturous rhythm until my vision blackens a cry ripping past my lips. I keep my eyes on Henry burning alive under his molten gaze until I lose my battle with my eyelids and let my head fall back against Jason's chest as I come apart around his hand.

He growls appreciatively his grip keeping me firmly pinned to his strong body

Jason's hand slips from my mouth and down my neck to cup my throat.

"Henry wants a turn."

"Should I share you with him, Pet? Do you want to cum for Henry against his strong hands." I groan nodding again "Or maybe that mouth?"

He pressed a kiss to my temple as Henry prowled across the balcony arriving before us. His hand catches Jason's wrist where he was tucking my skirt back into place raising it between them the air buzzing with electricity

Holding Jason's eyes, he sucks his two fingers into his mouth as his eyes darken flickering to mine.

"Home," he growls, voice sin incarnate. "Now."

Jason shifts his grip as he sweeps me into his arms.

He leans in close, and I revel in the way his lips lift in the corners, eyes sparking even in the shadows wrapping around us. He chuckles, the sound rumbling against me as he murmurs, "I think we're in trouble".

Chapter Twenty-Eight

We make it to a long stretch of road leading north. Leading home. The sun has long set and the back of the car is dark, which I am thankful for. The seats below my thighs are cool against my overheated skin, and it's the way Henry's hands grip the steering wheel that keep me from sinking into them completely. Instead, I sit, back straight, pulse hammering in my ears as I watch the males in the front seat and imagine what might await us at home. The car slows as Henry pulls the car over tucking us into the darkened shoulder of the road and it pulls me from the way I am climbing these males like a tree in my mind.

Jason tips his head back on a dark laugh.

"Henry's impatient," Jason clarifies as Henry unfastens his belt and climbs from the car. He is pulling open my door in the same instant his closes.

"My control can only be stretched so far Princess, and I'm starving." He echoes my sentiment from earlier this evening and it sends my stomach tumbling.

The smile he serves me only punctuates his words and he ducks inside the cab. He grips the underside of my knees sliding me across the backseat. The movement bunches my skirt around my hips leaving me nearly bare before him. He strums his lip with his teeth as he straightens to his full height, jerking me against him roughly. I gasp as my core makes contact with his strong thigh, soft green eyes glitter with promise as he rakes those eyes over me.

"Henry," Jason warns. "Gentle with our girl."

His hands glide up the back of my thighs, his finger brushing across the soft lace that I already know is soaked.

He growls his approval and my next breath is uneven.

Henry's eyes catch mine. "You don't want gentle do you, Princess?" he asked like he already knew the answer.

"No," I shook my head. I wanted to be devoured by this male.

That confirmation was all he needed before he's moving again. He slips the lace down my thighs before his control is tested again, and the pretty lace pays the price, disintegrating between his fingers. A tremble of anticipation works its way down my spine.

Watching Henry go to his knees before the open door is a visceral experience. He drapes one of my legs over his shoulder as he spreads me open. His lips press to the inside of my knee hooked over his shoulder, his hands curling around the front of my thighs locking me in place. The lack of possible movement makes me squirm, but Henry's only response is to grin up at me.

It's a savage, hungry thing.

And with that his lips were on me tongue delving through my folds. His mouth is ruthless. Plundering. My back arches on a cry as my fingers grip the leather strap of the sheath he wears across his chest, pulling him even closer.

I make zero effort to quiet the moans that echo through the darkened car.

Henry's arms sweep underneath my back, his hands splaying under my shoulders as he lifts me, pitching me even closer, the pressure from his mouth ratcheting up.

"Amelia." Jason's voice was sharp enough to catch my attention.

My name on his lips has stars bursting behind my eyes. The low light of the car accentuates the sharp angles of his face, as he nails me in place with a look so full of lust it's all I can do not to fall apart right there.

"You do not cum until I tell you."

My eyes go wide.

How was I supposed to do that?

How was I supposed to stop?

I could already feel it building like a wave ready to crest as my back bowed.

"Not yet," he warned.

Henry growled against my core and a cry broke past my lips. The muscles of my stomach fluttered as he ruthlessly pushed me towards orgasm, determined to undermine my fraying control.

"Please..." My fingers move to knot in Henry's hair and his responding growl rumbles my bones.

"No."

"I can't." My moan echoes off the car windows as his heavy hand splays across my stomach pinning me in place. "I have to."

Henry chooses that moment to push two fingers into me. My thighs clamp onto the sides of his head as he works me infinitesimally closer. There was no fighting Henry. There was only submission. Only surrender when it came to the way he worked me higher and higher. Closer and closer.

His fingers delved deeper curling inside me and I could do nothing but cry his name as I clenched around him.

My head falls to the side searching out Jason through watery eyes and Henry slows dragging his tongue slowly over me like he is in fact savoring me.

I can feel myself at the edge of shattering and as he draws his fingers back preparing to plunge back in deep, I know I cannot fight it any longer.

His thumb swirls around my clit just once as he draws his tongue up, up, up once more.

Jason's eyes were luminescent with hunger as he smiled, slow and saccharine.

"Good girl," he purrs with a nod.

By the time those words crossed his lips, it was as if his voice alone detonated something inside me. Henry latches onto my clit with his mouth, those fingers reaching deep and curling right where I need them. The orgasm that rips through me is all consuming.

Henry brings me down gently. The only thing I wanted *gentle* when it came to this male.

My eyelids were leadened as I collapsed against the backseat. Jason shucks coat and I collapse against the seat below me, no longer cool but just as warm as my skin. I breathe tracing the tingles that flit through my body as if the blood in my veins has been filled with that effervescent pink drink, he served me. Henry takes his time straightening my dress before tucking the heavy material of Jason's coat around me. I wasted no time curling up underneath it basking in his scent. Henry leaned across the seat sweeping the hair from my face before standing and adjusting his pants. The car door closed as did my eyes and I slipped into a dreamless sleep accented only by the sounds of their quiet conversation as we made our way home.

When I wake the next morning I find myself tucked underneath a familiar blue comforter and the lingering memory of Henry stripping me out of my dress before tucking me between himself and Jason. The warmth of their bodies beckoning me back to sleep.

My bare skin is cool against the sheets as I roll over searching for Jason's warm arms. I only peel open my eyes when I discover his side of the bed empty.

I scrub at my eyes as awareness greets me in pieces. The sound of water running in the shower and the smell his soap tells fills in the gaps, but the bed isn't empty. As I roll back over, Henry's back is on full display lit by the early morning light seeping through the windows.

He had shown me a few of his scars before, but this...

His back was covered in them. Some puckered and round, others long with striations of skin running this way and that. I couldn't fathom the brutality he had experienced to earn these. And I wondered how many had been won, protecting Jason.

Without thinking I ran my thumb across a particularly long scar under his shoulder. The slow smooth breaths shudder, then stop his whole body locking down. I hold my breath in turn as he rolls over, the movement slow. Gentle. But as his gaze meets mine, I can see the storm he holds at bay behind those eyes.

I curl myself into him, setting my hand on his jaw.

Moss green eyes sparkle in the golden morning light, but for the first time they're guarded.

I think he expected pity or judgement, but I had none of those things for him. Each scar was a mark of pride. A victory. Proof of how strong he was and how many times he may have protected Jason. They were evidence of just how safe we both were with Henry here to defend us.

Suddenly a piece I'd seen in the studio clicked.

"You're his shield," I breathe, running a featherlight touch to a particularly jagged scar just under his collar bone.

I watched his expression open, his eyes soften and then heat as his arm wrapped around my back. The hair along his arm tickled my bare skin as he pressed me closer to him. I wove my arm around his neck and my leg over his hip. What I didn't expect was just how perfectly we fit together despite his size, and what I should have expected was the bulge he notched against my core.

Unfortunately, he was wearing sweats and I cursed him for it as the contact pulled a gasp from my lips.

In the next instant his lips were melded to mine moving hungrily swallowing up my gasp of surprise and the following cry as want swelled inside of me and he stiffened against me.

I was finally kissing Henry.

And Henry kissed like he did everything else; unhurried, strong, confident. His tongue swept into my mouth angling me right where he wanted with sure hands and a rumble that softened my bones.

He pulled away only long enough to allow me a gasp of air. His lips tugging up into a satisfied smirk, his teeth catching my lower lip, before he rolled tucking me under him, his warmth a long line of muscle down my body. His hand grips my knee, notching it back around his hip as he uses the new angle to torment me. With a smooth pump of his hips, he runs himself through my folds providing delicious friction. I moan pulls from my throat as the bathroom door opens. Jason appears stepping out from a swirl of steam and the concentrated scent of male.

"Well isn't this quite the development," he said with a grin. "And on a morning where my attention is required elsewhere." I freeze and Henry chuckles against my mouth pressing one last chaste kiss to my lips before he lifts himself from me and strides towards the bathroom.

I prop myself up against my elbow watching him go. Jason's eyes dip shamelessly to his erection before he drags heated eyes up his body. I swear as his eyes land on me there is a hint of shared disappointment in letting all that male go to waste. But he blinks, and blinks again and that look dissipates tucked behind the warm smile that pulls his lips wide as I flop back against the pillows.

Jason takes Henry's bike into the Royal City and Henry goes to work building a new garden box for the seeds we brought home. I spend the remainder of the day unpacking and helping Hartley as I organize my thoughts. Sort each of these churning emotions into a plan that has my heart racing with anticipation.

Chapter Twenty-Nine

I'd showered, changed, and walked myself into Jason's study before promptly chickening out and making a beeline for my reading nook. Grabbing the book off the shelf, I peek over the pages to spy on Jason, my pulse hammering in my ears.

I could do this.

I wanted to do this.

Steeling my spine and sucking in a settling breath, I closed the book not having read a single word when I spied something just over his shoulder that gave me pause.

"You hung it?"

I watched his brows pull high as he turned his eyes to me.

"Hm?"

"My picture." I pointed to the wall where the little canvas hung amongst the rest. "You hung it.

"Of course I did," he says, eyes probing as they coasted across my face. "It was your first piece."

He sat back in his chair, spinning so that he could see it and grinned, that bit of pride making my heart flutter.

"An artist's first piece is important."

I watched those words leave his lips wishing I could taste them. Instead, I closed the book in my hands with nervous fingers.

"I'm not an artist," I said, trailing a finger down the soft pages. My gaze returned to the vampire still studying the canvas on his wall like it may speak back to him. And maybe to an artist it would. Maybe there was a language spoken in the whisper-like strokes of brush against canvas.

He shrugged, an easy smile lifting his lips as he eyed the painting. "What made you choose dandelions?"

Warm umber filled my vision as he continued.

"When I prep a canvas it's like unearthing the picture beneath. Henry's woodwork is quite similar. Maybe more so," he allowed. "I saw the moment it hit you. The flash in your eyes when you saw the picture underneath." I watch him turn the ring on his index finger as he reclines further in his chair.

"What was it you saw?"

His eyes crinkle ever so slightly in the corners as he smiles, and I bask in the beauty of this male before me.

"You," I murmured.

He stilled, surprise settling over his form before he turned to me. There was something just beyond my grasp swirling in his eyes as he pulled his gaze over me.

"What?" I asked, climbing from the nook and padding towards his desk. I paused leaning my hip against it and picked my eyes up to the little brown flowers. I could feel my skin heat under his gaze.

"It..." I shuffled before stealing my spine. "They're wishing flowers," I explained, returning my gaze to him and he nodded. "Painted with coffee."

He blinked. Then blinked again. His eyes flickering to the painting.

"It's you. You're everything I could have wished -

He was out of his chair and before me in the blink of an eye. His lips were on mine swallowing down the rest of my words, his tongue sweeping into my mouth. My heartbeat in my throat as I arched into him. The groan he unleashed coasted across my skin and he collected me greedily in his arms as I wrapped my legs around his waist just as eager to mold myself to him.

The hand cupping my jaw, skates down my throat, cold silver sending a shiver down my spine. Too soon, he pulls away full lips tugging up into a roguish smile, and I pant unabashedly into the quiet space between us.

I want nothing to do with the air he's allowing me, so I hook my arm around the back of his neck, the other hand gripping his hair as I drag my tongue up the column of his throat. I press a kiss to his jaw and another to the corner of his mouth where his lips quirk up.

I love his lips. I love his smile.

I suck his lower lip between my own reveling in the way those umber eyes darken under heavy lids.

The feeling of him under my hands as I coast a hand down his chest draws a moan from my lips. The muscles of his stomach bunch under my touch in response and I smile. He strains against his zipper, his erection pulsing as I trace the length of him.

He swallows a curse, the timber of his voice pebbling my nipples.

"Amelia," he catches my wrist raising it between us so he can press a kiss to my pulse point.

"Jason." I mean to match his tone, but my voice is a whisper.

Too thin.

I want these males. Crave them to the point of pain, and if they'll have me, I want them. Right or wrong, I want to be theirs. They've been claiming me for a long while, but now it was my turn.

My fingers wove into his hair, my grip punishing as I tugged at his scalp, tipping his head back. The growl that rumbles from his chest only encourages me as I hook my leg high on his hip so that I can run his thick length over the thin lace covering my core.

His eyes fell closed, a shuddering breath pulling at his chest as he loosened a dark chuckle.

"If there is even a hint of doubt in your mind," he growls, eyes flashing open. "You need to leave now, while I can still let you".

My stomach tumbled.

This was it.

The moment where I hoped he would unleash all of that control he had been recollecting since we'd arrived home.

Holding his eyes, I leaned forward slowly until I dipped under his jaw. My grip on his hair loosened in case he wanted to pull away and cling to that control.

Though I hoped he wouldn't.

With my lips a breath away from the sensitive skin under his ear, I smiled. And breathed the words he'd asked for all those weeks prior.

"Please," I cooed, dragging my tongue across the sensitive flesh. He shuddered under my touch as I scraped my teeth along his ear lobe. "Fuck me like I'm yours."

The muscles of his throat work over a swallow, but that moment was the last still moment he granted me.

He captures my mouth in a kiss that steals my breath. He consumes me and I love every second.

Dark eyes snare mine as breath heaves between us.

"You *are* mine."

His hands drop to my thighs, silver rings cool against my overheated skin.

"I am," I vow with a grin.

It's a grin he matches before claiming my mouth thoroughly. He firms his grip to a point that has pain and pleasure sharing space in my mind as he works me against himself drawing another moan from my throat.

The hand bracing my back splays as he lays me across the desk. His weight follows me as he continues to work me against him. His mouth moves to my throat, his tongue lapping, teeth teasing. He plants his hand next to my head on the desk as he smiles down at me, gold and umber glittering. He presses slow kisses to my lips as he lifts himself from me. As he reaches between us to adjust himself, I follow his hand, unable to help myself and we both pause.

I've made a mess of the front of his pants.

Our gazes collide and the chuckle that slips from his lips is rightfully smug.

His smile, sin incarnate.

He takes a slow breath tucking some hair behind my ears as he tips his gaze towards the door. I can read the intent.

Henry.

But as he looked ready to call for him, his eyes widen, before narrowing dramatically. Under my touch, his body goes unnervingly still. I feel the muscles of his back coil and lock as his body tenses. Fangs sharpen as his body pulls over me like a shield before he erupts. A snarl like I'd never heard ripping from his throat.

I've heard Jason snarl at shifters and vampires alike. Shit, I've heard him snarl at Henry, but this sound was something other. It was dark, violent and yet ebbed with a hurt I hoped I was imagining. I dragged my eyes over what I could see of him. No injuries.

Henry?

Hartley?

My eyes flew wide as his grip tightened, securing me to his chest, his face snapping towards the window.

Had someone been here?

Was someone here now?

Fury ebbs, as do the shadows that climb the walls slipping from that preternatural control he held over them. I don't know what he heard, but it had been enough to pull him from the moment and sour his mood exponentially.

My heart pounds unevenly in my chest as his gaze falls to mine...and for the smallest of moments, fear trickles into my blood.

Not for myself, but for whatever was unfolding. Whatever he was hearing that I couldn't.

He blinks once, fighting back the inky blackness that has consumed his eyes. With a ruff shake of his head he snaps his eyes closed. A pained sound pulls from his chest and I find myself flattening my palms against his stomach like I can stop whatever is hurting him.

"Jason?"

Umber and gold greets me once more.

"Stay here."

His pleading tone catches me off guard long enough that I allow him to leave the room without protest. The door snicks shut an instant later and I'm left reeling as I push to a sit on his desk. The last time he'd asked me to stay hidden had been when Claire had shown up unannounced.

I shivered.

Unannounced visitors and I had a reputation for poor outcomes.

But having a distinct dislike for being told what to do and a pension for situations likely to get me killed, I hopped off the desk and ran to the window. On the first floor Jason was flipping through something while Henry's gaze scanned the drive looking murderous. If that didn't shock me into motion then seeing Henry hand Hartley a blade from his sheath would have.

I was flying down the stairs in record time.

The door gave way to a set of males who looked about three seconds from lying to me.

I'd traded speed for stealth, but I doubted there was a world where I could sneak up on these two anyway. So they knew I was coming, but I hoped that hadn't given them enough time to craft a lie.

My eyes danced over the three males before me.

"What happened?"

Jason's gaze flitted over my face, his expression softening.

No mask.

But the anger that had painted his face before it softened was still there in the iridescent gold that ringed his eyes.

My stomach sank.

"Didn't I ask you to stay upstairs?" He sounded exacerbated instead of angry.

"Did you?" I ask innocently, preparing for a fight. "Human hearing" I mumble, losing my steam as he settles his hands on either side of my face.

"I want to know what happened." I breathe, holding his gaze. There is a sadness that I don't understand whirling around behind those gold flecks.

His eyes close and I do my best to harden my voice.

"Jason."

"Amelia." He matches my tone.

I took a shallow breath tucking away my feelings and what hearing my name cross his lips does to me. "That won't work this time." I shiver. "Spill."

He takes a measured breath, but where I expect that calm mask to fall into place, it's noticeably missing. Instead, I can read nothing but vulnerability, anger...and fear.

He steps back, releasing me, and hands me an envelope. Unmarked on the front, yet I recognize it.

My stomach plummets.

My eyes flicker back to his and he nods. I can feel him studying me as my lips part on a shaky breath. I do my best to steel myself as I pull the photos free with trembling fingers.

The first is of Henry and I sitting in camp, his head tucked into the crook of my neck as he folded over me, our faces lit by the flames of the campfire. My heart stumbles over itself at the implication... the repercussions. Scorch marks climb the lower corner. I run my finger along the burnt edge of the photo tracing the indentations along the otherwise straight edges, as if he had held it over a flame.

The second photo is of Jason and I dancing together after Henry had left to hunt down Le. My thumb runs over his smile, hurt blossoming in my chest. Tears sting my eyes as I flip to the third. The car pulled over onto the shoulder of a darkened road. Henry kneeling before an open door, my leg slung over his shoulder.

Fuck.

Concern battled down the vomit-inducing fear that had been strangling me.

Not only had someone been able to take these undetected, but they had been able to deliver them right to our door.

My fingers shook too badly to place the photos back into the envelope, so I didn't even try. Instead I drop them on the entryway and blink my eyes clear. Jason reaches for me as I rounded him in search of Henry. That sadness, so potent now that the pieces were clicking together. With a squeeze of Jason's hand, I reached for Henry.

He doesn't look at me even as I smooth my hands down his chest. He's there just under my hands. His skin warms my palm where it rests on his stomach. But even here, my skin against his, he feels unreachable. The next few rapid beats of my heart ache. This wasn't going to happen.

It couldn't.

I wouldn't allow it.

"Henry."

I had to swallow when his eyes landed on mine.

All royal guard.

This wasn't Henry.

No.

I panicked. One hand taking hold of the sheth across his chest, the other tugging on the end of his beard. It was like tugging on a statue. He gave me nothing.

"Henry?"

Nothing.

My jaw clenched. This wasn't his fault. There was no reason for him to pull away. To punish himself. And he needed to know that. To hear it...

"It's not-

"Take her inside" His voice is cold, cutting, as he speaks over my head to Jason.

Jason remains silent behind me, but I swing my hand back to stop him anyway, swallowing down the hurt.

"No."

His gaze slid down to me, stony, but cracking at the edges, his anger bleeding through. Fine. I'd take anger. I could work with anger. I knew anger.

I set my hands against his chest and shoved.

"No."

Thankfully, he had the good sense to step back, or maybe he did it to spare me from snapping my wrists in half if he hadn't, either way he moved with a huff.

I shoved at him again and he let me.

Using all the strength I can muster, I shove at him over and over again walking him across the front of the house.

And once more before that cold exterior brakes.

"You're going to hurt yourself," he growls, eyes finally seeing me.

Tears sting my eyes.

"*You're* hurting me."

He drew himself up, anger narrowing his eyes and tightening his expression.

"You have no idea how hurt you could have been-

"Of course I do!" I cried, throwing my arms out. "Of course I do... I'm human! We don't get to live lives safe from hurt, but... I *want* this one. I want this life with you and Jason, and I won't let you blow that up because you're going to shoulder all the blame for something that *hasn't happened.*"

His brow dropped, casting his gorgeous eyes into shadow and I latched onto him to keep myself standing. I couldn't let him pull away. I couldn't lose him now just when I had worked up the courage to claim this life I wanted.

Selfish? Absolutely, but my heart was pounding all the sense from my mind as I watched this callous version of the male before me pull away.

All that pain in Jason's expression landed like a blow across my chest as I held Henry's eyes. Those soft moss green eyes hardened like stone.

Impenetrable.

I couldn't lose him.

"Henry," I begged, my voice cracking. "We're right here and we're safe. Nothing has happened."

But as I say those words, I know I'm wrong. Something had happened. Henry had let himself become distracted. He had missed the male hiding in the brush taking these photos of us.

Jason's arm wrapped around my ribs, lifting me off my feet. I hadn't heard him approaching and his touch had startled me, but I didn't struggle against him until he tried to step us away from Henry.

"No!" I sob. Tightening my grip on the leather sheath across his chest. He hadn't given me enough time.

I hadn't had any time.

I try to pry Jason's fingers from my ribs with one hand as I pick my gaze back up to the male before me desperation sinking her claws into me as I tightened my grip on Henry.

"Henry. Please!" I cry begging him from behind wet eyes.

He dropped his gaze to mine and I held my breath, my pulse thrumming in my ears. But I didn't see my male. I only saw the way his hurt and self-loathing consumed him.

Please no.

That was worse than the cold lifeless stare he had worn moments ago. It was like watching him surface from beneath murky water. He pulled forward just enough to show me his hurt. To show me he was still there, but he wasn't in control.

But as swiftly as relief had prickled at my scalp, watching him sink back below the surface of this cold exterior, had pain lancing across my chest.

"You'll be safe" he swore, voice stony.

"No!" I forfeited my grip on Jason's fingers to bang against his chest trying desperately to reach him once more. But my male had sunken back into those murky waters, letting the surface freeze over between us. And for all the yelling I'd done, it wasn't reaching him. He couldn't hear me.

My breath sawed between my teeth.

"I don't want to be safe. I want to be loved." The words sprang free, all desperation and honesty.

Jason froze as did Henry, but he wouldn't look at me. Instead, his eyes flicker to the tree line.

"Please," I sobbed, tightening my grip on his shirt to the point that my knuckles protested. I would do it. I would bare my whole soul to keep him.

"Don't do this." I placed a hand to his cheek, trying to be gentle when all I wanted to do was scream.

I sucked in a broken breath.

"I need you." I tried to swallow, but fear and hurt thickened my throat. "Not this. Henry, I need *you*."

The little tick to his brow, had me hoping he could hear me. That he was listening. I sucked in a sharp breath, my heart racing as I hung there suspended between them.

His eyes landed on me and I could only see the male underneath. My Henry. Our Henry. The male who had pushed me to fight when I wanted to fold. Now, I would fight for him with the only thing I had left to give.

"I love you."

He blinked, his eyes returning to me. I held my breath as they coasted over my face. I waited for the moment where he broke, where that cold exterior cracked and warmed and I could tuck myself against his chest...

But they didn't.

Resolve surged, cold grey green eyes lifting to Jason's just over my shoulder.

A muscle in his jaw feathered as he clenched it.

Silence rang in the space between us.

Breath woodshed from my lungs, his rejection a physical blow.

It was everything I had... everything I could give this male and it wasn't enough.

I shattered right there pinned to Jason's chest desperately clinging to Henry who wouldn't even look at me. Jason's arm tightened and I could feel his heart pounding against my back. He lowered his lips to my ear as I cried.

"He just needs time, Amelia" his voice was quiet, but as broken as I felt.

I shook my head blinking away the tears as he wrapped his hand around my wrist intending to free Henry from my hold.

"Amelia." His voice was low, gentle. "I don't want to hurt you." As he spoke his grip tightened trying to pry me loose as gently as possible. His big hands felt so warm as they curled around mine.

"Please Henry." My voice broke.

He didn't so much as flinch.

Everything hurt.

My chest ached. My throat felt raw. My eyes stung and my knuckles screamed their protest from the way I had clinged to him.

I drew myself up, swallowing down my next words and dropped my hold on Henry, his cold exterior feeling like a brand against my trembling fingers.

It felt like giving up. It felt like failing, and the fissure opening up my chest stole my breath as I turned in Jason's grip clinging to him as I fell apart.

He didn't hesitate as he turned on his heel and carried me over the threshold and back into the house. And I refused to pick up my face from where I buried it in his neck. I couldn't watch Jason walk us away from him.

He carried me upstairs and right into the shower, clothes and all. Once the water warmed he set me down on my feet and I swayed. His hands were achingly gentle as he steadied me. Wet hands coasted up my arms and neck to cup my jaw. I had failed. I hadn't been able to bring him back. To keep him here with us. Jason set his lips to my forehead and I collapsed into him. I didn't deserve his comfort, but I needed it.

He collected me once more, letting me cling to him as I cried. Neither of us spoke. We just stood under the water holding each other together. I don't know how long we stayed like that, but when I felt more steady, he brushed the hair back from my face, his thumbs gently stroking the swollen angry skin under my eyes. He made quick work of stripping us both before letting me trace the lines of his abs, while he washed my hair.

My knees shook as he dried me in a fluffy towel and swept me back into his arms.

Without so much as a second thought, he tucked us into their bed, where I curled back into him as he wrapped me in his arms.

But I couldn't sleep.

I wouldn't.

Instead I waited, drawing long strokes down Jason's arms as I set to work plotting. Hurt slowly transformed to anger and I had to work to control my breathing, keeping it slow. Measured. And as I laid there, I counted Jason's. Knowing he wouldn't sleep until he knew I was safe. Until I didn't need him. After he had been asleep long enough to where I hoped I wouldn't wake him as I climbed out of bed, I made my way downstairs.

I collected every knife I could find in the kitchen. Every last one. And then I sat on the steps with my pile of knives and waited for Henry to come home. I don't know how long I sat there, but eventually my tears dried and the front door opened. The doorway darked as he stepped over the threshold filling it with his wide frame.

I counted.

One.

Two.

Three.

The butcher knife I'd been toying with sailed across the room narrowly missing his fat handsome head. I was panting. Anger, a tangible thing, as I gripped two more.

He jolted, looking as if I had truly caught him off guard, but before he could take me in, I hurled a paring knife that he caught, and a butter knife that he let bounce off of his chest.

"Stop." His gruff response was a balm to the anger I'd spent all evening feeding.

I threw another. This one a bread knife. It was harder to throw because of the shape but I didn't care.

"Stop."

I stood with a knife in each hand and hurled them at him with all the force I could muster.

He caught both.

"Fucking stop!" He barked.

Fucking make me!" I shouted.

He took three angry steps across the living space scooping me up and pinning me to the wall.

Our chests knocked together with each breath. I wrapped my legs around his waist, hooking my ankles and pushing myself up the wall. My hand gripped the collar of his shirt. Like this, I could look him in the eye as my other hand drew the butterknife I had sheathed in the waistband of my sleep shorts.

I held it against his throat, tears stinging my eyes again. I think he expected me to argue some more, but I just pressed the blade tighter against his flesh.

His jaw ticked up as his eyes took note of the utensil I was using to hold him captive.

Humor lightened his eyes and it hurt. Relief was so potent it was like a fist clenched around my broken heart. But I tightened my grip on the metal, the knuckles of my fingers going white as I bit back a sob, holding his eyes...watching the fissures and waiting for the crack.

My hand dropped his collar, reaching around my thigh as I narrowed blurry eyes to buy time.

"Have I taught you nothing?" His voice was rough as it rolled over my skin.

"You tell me." I breathed letting the sharp tip of his own blade, drawn from the sheath across his chest, bite into the seam of his trousers where I held it against his balls.

He stilled below me, surprise widening his eyes just a fraction. That warm light greeted me in fractured pieces as his hand coiled around my wrist. Effortlessly he pinned it against the wall over my head. The blade clattering to the floor.

My breaths were quiet sobs.

Henry and I weren't soft. We weren't gentle. We fought, and I wanted a fight. I was here to fight.

With him.

For him.

For us.

"Beautiful, violent thing," he murmured, dropping his head to my shoulder. I felt him soften around me but I held firm.

He drew in a small breath.

"Henry," I gripped his curls at the root. As he straightened I drew another blade from the sheath across his chest.

"Ah. Ah." He curled his hand around the blade and I froze not wanting to hurt him. Some of the hurt and anger cooling at the risk of his skin.

"Let go." I breathed past the ache in my chest as frustration blossomed.

I forfeited the blade as tears slipped down my cheeks. "I don't know how to help," I admitted breathlessly.

His eyes settled on mine and I could see my male just under the surface. Henry was there in the soft probing way he studied me now. I tugged at my wrist and his grip disappeared. His hand remained on the wall above my head but he allowed me to slip free, trailing my fingers down his jaw.

"Please let me help."

He shook his head and I screwed my eyes closed, setting my forehead to his.

"Henry-

"I need you safe, Princess." Anger bubbled up my throat as did my words as he continued. "Both of you. I can't-

"That's not my name," I growled, my eyes snapping open.

His mouth opened and closed again wordlessly.

"You know my name. You know me, or... at least I want you to. I'm trying... and I'm sorry it's taken me so long."

He swallowed as his eyes bounced around my face. And my pulse skipped in my chest as a shiver raked down my spine in response. Overwhelm and desperation was an exhausting cocktail that was quickly draining my energy.

His arms shifted as concern battled back the chill still lingering in those eyes. In the set of his jaw.

"I don't want to live this life with you half in. I only get a fraction of the life you do, but I will spend it loving you both with everything I have... but I want all of you Henry." I dragged in a ragged breath. "You love me." I softened my grip. "I know you do. I'm not afraid of them" I flickered my eyes to the door. "I'm not afraid of Le," I lied. "... but I am afraid of you."

I physically felt the shock roll through him.

"I'm afraid you'll disappear before I can tell you how much I love you. I'm afraid I wasted too much time getting here, to this point where I can't deny my feelings for you both, and just how badly I want to be a part of your lives... and I've lost you... I'm too late."

His eyes sharpen as he shakes his head, and I can see Henry staring back from under the frozen surface. So I push on.

Honesty, the dagger twisting in my chest with each piece of my broken soul I offer this male.

"I brought danger to your door and caused all this." I shook my head. "I don't know where to go, or how to fix it."

I'd leave.

I'd leave if it would fix this. If I had anywhere to go. Maybe if I was braver, I'd leave anyway.

His hands caught my face and I sobbed once allowing him to hold me. Surrendering. Yielding to the commanding way he gripped me now, after not having been certain he would hold me like this again.

"You're not leaving," he growled as he dipped to catch my gaze. His skin was rough against my own. The feel of him only inspired more tears.

"It's my fault. I put Jason in danger from our first moments together, and that danger followed me home... It's hurt you."

"You have done nothing to hurt me."

"Of course I have! I've hurt you both. Look at what's happening..."

He adjusts me in his grasp, his arm winding around my back while he dried my cheeks with a warm thumb. And I couldn't resist melting into him.

"Amelia." My name on his lips drew another sob from mine.

"I don't know what to do." My hands clung to his chest as the dagger twisted deeper into mine. "Tell me to leave," I begged. "Tell me what to do."

I picked my eyes up to his, afraid of what I'd find. Logically we both knew me leaving made the most sense. And I may not be brave enough to leave on my own, but if he told me to... if he confirmed what I suspected, that that part of him that only existed to protect Jason, would be honest, even if it hurt. He'd stood there unmoved when I told him I loved him, so if he asked me to leave now, I would.

I'd have to.

And that lingering fear of dismissal gripped my heart and squeezed.

His eyes burned as they held mine. All that ice had melted away and in its absence his gaze was searing.

"Forgive me," he ground out, voice ruff and broken.

My lips wobbled as I pulled them between my teeth. Tears still streamed down my cheeks but as I blinked them clear, soft moss green eyes greeted me. A sight like coming home.

"Forgive me Amelia." His voice was as raw as I felt as his thumb swept across my cheek.

I nodded against his rough palm letting my eyes close as relief washed over me. Wrapping my arms around his neck, I held him close until his shoulders relaxed below me. I held him until I could breathe a little easier past the knot in my chest. I held him until the thundering in his chest slowed where I could feel his heartbeat echoing against my own chest where we were pressed together.

I brushed my fingers along the side of his neck as I sat back in his arms to take him in.

He swallowed, the motion looking strained as he tucked a curl behind my ear. His fingers lingered on my collarbone, warm once more.

"I was distracted." His words were a pained confession.

One I'd been waiting for.

I knew this was why he had been tormenting himself. And Jason and I, in turn. But I wasn't going to let him play into this royal guard bullshit.

"I fucking hope so," I said narrowing my eyes. I watched surprise widen those beautiful green eyes in response before I ticked my jaw, leaning back into my previous irritation. "Since your face was buried between my thighs."

He tips his head back to the darkened ceiling, a pained chuckle shaking his chest where it is still firmly pinned to mine. He shakes his head, sobering, as his eyes land back on mine. "I can no longer imagine a life without your smart mouth in it... and I've... I've made you question not only your place in our home, but your place in my heart and for that Amelia, I owe you so much more than an apology."

He ran his thumb along my lips and they part beneath his touch. I watch him as he watches his thumb move across my skin before he returns his gaze to mine.

"The idea of someone taking you from us makes me feral. I- I lay awake at night knowing that there are males, who still breathe air, who have put hands on you. Who have hurt you. Hurt Jason and... it has been far too long since I've been human, Amelia. There are times I cannot even recall what it's like. What *I'm* supposed to be like. But I do know how to be *this*." He waves a hand over himself. "I know how to keep you safe. Keep you alive."

"I don't want that," I press.

A fractured smile breaks across his face in a flash.

"I know." The skin bracketing his eyes crinkles as his brow drops low. Those eyes darkened with a malice I'm very rarely privy to. "But so help me, if you try to leave this house," he warned, tone deadly. "I will chain you to that bed until you're no longer a flight risk."

"That doesn't sound like much of a threat," I say, serving him a watery smile.

He leaned in slowly pressing his lips to my crown.

"Believe me when I say, there is nowhere that you could go, that I wouldn't find you. And there is no territory north or south that would be safe should they stand between us. We would level cities to reach you. No one above punishment, should they so much as lay a finger on you. Death herself would drop to her knees before my blade."

I study him carefully, not doubting a word.

My heart aches with relief and swells with the ridiculous amount of love I hold for this male. I lean in slowly until my lips are a breath away from his.

I pause there, my eyes flickering up to capture his.

"You are the most capable mother fucker on this continent and the next." I kiss the corner of his mouth as I see it flicker. "That's a direct quote from Jason by the way." I was paraphrasing, but it didn't matter, because he smiles broad and true, and it's all Henry.

All Henry as he runs the tip of his nose up mine, his hands firming their grip against my skin. Holding me like he doesn't want to let go. A rumble starts in his chest and I lean back against the wall wanting to take him in.

All of him.

"Its true," Jason confirms from the stairs above us.

He pads his way down to us, shirtless, sweats hanging low on his hips. He came ready with his own arsenal. Pausing on the step just above us he crosses his arms, those tattoos on full display.

"And I agree with Amelia. The next time I have your cock in my mouth and your focus is anywhere but my face, I will remove it from your body."

I pull my lips between my teeth and it's the battle of my life to stay silent. But Jason draws himself up, his brow dropping to cast dark eyes into shadow. Or maybe it's the preternatural control he holds over the shadows themselves.

His tone is deadly as he continues.

"And the next time she tells you she loves you," he growls, the warning in his tone, unmistakable. "And you don't respond, you'll be shitting out your own teeth for a week." Jason hones that chill inspiring gaze on the male before me. "Understood?"

I can feel Henry's chest deflate underneath me.

"Understood" his lips quirk just a fraction and relief has me sagging against him. It feels like we have moved past this. Henry is safe and thoroughly scolded. And that little crack in my heart begins to mend.

When he returns his gaze to me, I check it once more. Soft moss green eyes hold me together as I lean in, pressing my lips to his before unwrapping my legs from around his waist. He growls his disapproval before he claims my mouth more thoroughly, and when he sets me down, my knees shake. Relief and need battering my tired brain.

"I'm sorry," Henry repeats.

"I'm not the only one you need to apologize to." I incline my head to Jason, who quirks a smile at me, before leveling Henry with a glare. But there is too much affection there, too much relief, for it to carry any weight.

He grips the male's beard roughly, claiming his mouth in a plundering kiss. A battle of teeth, and tongue, and dominance. One Henry seems happy to lose.

I'm just glad the wall is here to steady me.

Jason pulls away with a snarl.

"Never again."

Henry nods.

"Never again," he echoes.

Jason blinks, his eyes coasting over the living room.

"Good." He nods, flattening ringed fingers across his abs and smoothing it down his front. I'd seen him perform the motion countless times, always smoothing his hand down his shirt. It seemed to be his way of settling himself. But watching him run his hand down his shirtless body, had my mouth going dry.

"Now clean up my house."

I move to wiggle past them and do just that, when Jason catches the back of my shirt.

"You." He nails Henry with a look. "Knives."

"You." He turns me towards the stairs, a smile briefly kissing his lips "Bed. Now."

I blink, then shrug, tucking my lips between my teeth to fight back the smile that will probably get me in trouble.

"Yes sir," I mutter snarkily under my breath. Clearly not as in control of my mouth as I thought.

I only get a step or two away before he lands a smack to my ass that has me hurrying my pace, my heart in my throat once more.

I flop into their bed letting the soft bedding swallow me whole. It's not long before they join me and I fall asleep tucked back where I belong.

Right in between my males.

Chapter Thirty

I finished my cup of tea and set Caroline's book aside. My eyes drifted across the garden before landing on the rain-sodden wooden target. As I study it, my fingers trace the handle of the blade sheathed at my thigh, the memories of yesterday still echoing in my mind. We may have Henry back, but the root of the problem still persisted.

Le.

Every time I thought of that male... of what would happen if he got past Henry or Jason... or worse, hurt them, it only strengthened my resolve to take back control. I needed to face down the paralyzing fear that male held over me. Because, my fear, my reaction to that male, would get us hurt. I wouldn't let it be the excuse Jason needed to shield me from the truth. Nor could it be the reason Henry was swallowed up by his role as our sentinel.

Neither of my males needed to shoulder this alone and I didn't need protection if it meant remaining in the dark. If I was going to claim this life, these males, then I needed to conquer this.

The sun sails across the sky and my patience wanes.

Swallowing my frustration, I scrape my hair into a braid and throw it over my shoulder, convinced it's the hair in my face that has sent the last few throws left of the dark outline of the target. The majority of the blades I send sailing across the yard, land in the large wooden target. But they aren't as accurate as they would need to be to kill a vampire.

With my luck, these wounds would only piss him off.

They thud into the softened wood outside of the outline I aim for or bounce off the target, the hilt meeting the wood before the blade ricochets, littering the lawn with steel.

I curse as I wipe the moisture from my palm onto the leg of my pants.

My aim had been better last night, but I'd been angry, determined... desperate.

Based on past experiences, it wouldn't be anger or determination driving my interaction with the next vampire or shifter I found myself face to face with. It had always been, undiluted, stomach-churning, terror.

That feeling of being hunted.

Of being stalked.

The reminder that you were prey.

An acknowledgement so bone deep that, even now, it still felt like an impossible task to reign in that kind of fear.

So I needed to sit in that fear.

I needed something as distracting as the presence of another monster.

... I needed a fire.

I made my way into the shop, grabbing a few logs and splitting them just as Henry and I had at Amara and Link's. My hands shook as I built a little stack in the brick pit. It sat under a tall tree, its long arms stretching high into the sky. I followed those long limbs, catching on the little glass globes that hung here and there from branches as they reached for the color-streaked sky. The magic of the garden was perpetually calm and that little bit of magic, the breeze that brushed along my cheeks like the stroke of cool fingers helped calm my pounding heart. I took a deep breath, steadying myself.

I could face this fear.

Use it.

The little box in the back of my mind rattled, reminding me that the last time I'd struck a match, I'd been lighting a fire in the hearth of our kitchen. But if I couldn't face this fear, how was I supposed to face Le. With a breath that felt too shallow, I opened the lid on that box. Letting all the memories of mom slip free. The memories of my life before the night the trappers raided our camp... and the memories of that night.

The fire.

It took two strikes of the match for it to light, but as I dropped it into the pile of shavings I had placed at the base of the logs, it burned hungrily. The wood cracked and smoked, and I swiped away the few tears my pounding heart produced.

But this time I sat in those feelings.

I sat *with* them, listening to the fire crack and pop until the sounds of their screams fell away, and all that was left was the gentle breeze and the flutter of a hungry flame. I stacked the logs higher and continued throwing blades at my target, not allowing myself to picture anything but Le as I hurled blade after blade across the yard. Every now and again the pop of the fire would send a blade clattering against the metal siding of the shed or landing in the wet grass with a thud.

But they were still victories.

I was still functioning.

Swiping a few tears from my cheek with the back of my hand, I blow out the breath I was holding. I could see his face. The sneer that curled the left side of his lip, the scar in his brow that ran to his hairline. The way his hands felt against my wrists... my shoulder.

My throat.

The fear that had strangled me as he had sent me airborne, throwing me into the freezing lake to clean myself before we made it to Acropolis to ensure he got the coin he felt he was owed for his effort. How the skin of my back had heated despite the frigid water as his eyes roved over my still healing wounds like they brought him joy.

My pulse pounds in my ears, but I land the next three strikes. A slow smile stretches across my face as I exhale a shaky breath.

The heat from his body curls around me as does his arm, his fingers splaying across my stomach as he steps into me. His familiar scent chases away the demons I was summoning as I lean into him and shiver. His hand moves from my stomach to my ribs, the other brushing the curls from my face so he could peer at me.

That old instinct to pull away, to hide my weakness, was barely an echo in the back of my mind and recognizing that had pride bubbling up from my stomach. So in this moment, as I was facing my fears, I turned *into* him instead.

"I'm practicing."

His hum tickles my shoulder as he lowers his lips to my neck.

Arching to give him access, I drop my arm keeping the blade pinched between my fingers.

"Ah ah," he scolds "Keep going. That last throw-"

He finishes his sentence with a huff as I jab my elbow into his ribs behind me.

"I was going to compliment you."

"It was off to a terrible start," I critique as I turn in his grasp, lifting my eyes to his.

Warm moss green eyes cradle my own.

He takes the blade from my hand sheathing it against my thigh before he drags his gaze back up my body.

"Amelia," his deep voice strokes my skin. His hands cup my face, thumbs sweeping my cheeks dry. "I am so sorry."

My heart flutters and I shake my head.

"This has nothing to do with you."

It had everything to do with what happened yesterday, but realizing what this looked like, it probably inspired some undue guilt on his end. His eyes traveled over the space, blades littering the lawn, a fire crackling behind me and tears staining my cheeks.

"You were right," I explained. "I need to feel safe."

He winces and I grab his wrists recapturing his attention.

"But in order to do that, I need to feel capable." I shrug. "I'm getting there."

He nods, his eyes glittering with something he doesn't share.

"What can I do to help?"

I draw in a slow breath, my eyes flickering towards the fire I lit.

"Will you sit by the fire with me?"

To my surprise a smile quirks his lips as he nods.

"Give me just a minute."

He places a kiss to my brow and disappears into the house.

I use the time spent waiting for him to return, cleaning up the blades and rehearsing my questions. He doesn't make me wait long. Moments later Henry returns with Jason in tow, both with their arms full.

They easily evade my efforts to relieve them of a few items, and instead, move right past me to set everything up at a pace just faster than natural.

As they set up, I catalog all they've collected. A few blankets and cushions, skewers, marshmallows, chocolate, and graham crackers. Jason pressed a kiss to my cheek and handed me a fresh cup of Hartley's peppermint tea, before continuing after Henry. I warmed my fingers as I sipped from the mug, watching them lay out the blankets and cushions.

Henry drops down, reclining against the cushions before patting his lap. I smile at him as he takes my tea, setting it beside himself on the ground before catching me around the waist and wrestling me into submission in his lap.

"Tired of shivering out in the cold, huh Princess?" he teased.

"You're mistaken," I chuckle. "It was that roasted marshmallow."

"Worth it," Henry agrees.

"Good thing we brought more," Jason supplies, spearing two on a skewer and handing it to me. Thinking roasted marshmallows peaked when skewered over hot chocolate, was a fallacy Henry promptly corrected when he built me a s'more.

I was finishing my third- this one I'd built for myself- when Henry's attention caught on the corner of my mouth. His fingers caught my chin as he grinned leaning in.

"You're distracting me," I smiled as he swiped at the corner of my lips. His thumb came away with a little glob of marshmallow he quickly cleaned with his teeth and tongue.

"My apologies." His eyes crinkled at the corners as he smiled wolfishly, looking not the least bit remorseful. "Was there something else you needed to be focused on?"

"Actually," I said, licking my fingers clean. "I have some questions."

"I don't know. This smells like a trap," Jason teased as he held up another log. The question lingering. Did I want him to feed the fire, or let it die?

I nodded, but he hesitated, his eyes scouring my face searching for the truth, I think. But I'd given it to him. I could do this.

He nodded once more, eyes soft, as he set the log down. His hand dipping into the flames.

A gasp ripped from my lips pulling Henry's attention away.

"What is wrong with you?"

"Is that one of your questions?" he chuckles dusting his palms together like the woodchips were more of a nuisance than the flames he had just dipped his hand into.

"Should it be?"

"Should we keep a tally?" He fires back taunting me.

I chuck a pillow at him that he catches easily, stuffing it under his elbow as he reclines.

"I apologize," he dips his eyes to his hand, that he holds out to me, before returning his gaze to mine. "I wanted to avoid dropping the log and creating an unnecessary scene. I didn't realize you thought I was so breakable."

He was being delicate, I knew that. I understood what he meant and could appreciate he was taking my feelings into consideration having seen my previous reactions to flames and the sounds that accompany them. But putting himself in a position to be hurt was unthinkable. Especially at my expense.

It fanned my frustration. Not with them, but with myself. Unfortunately for Jason, I did in fact, aim it at him.

"I'd rather you spike the damn log into the fire next time." I bluster, eyeing his hand.

"Noted." I think his face softens as he follows my gaze, but he maintains the clever grin that I love.

And hate.

Something about Jason feels noticeably lighter since returning from the free lands, especially so this morning.

"You're a dick." I shake my head, sinking back into Henry's arms.

His only reply was to wink.

"I'm getting used to the flames, I don't know if I could get used to either of you putting yourself in a position to test your durability."

Henry's lips press to the top of my head. "We'll behave," he murmurs into my hair.

Jason nods, his eyes sharpening as he watches Henry's fingers track up and down my arm.

"Ask your questions Amelia."

I watch Jason reach for another marshmallow to spear as I shuffle through my questions.

"Why deliver the gear to a free camp?"

He rotates his marshmallow over the flame, the image of a male at ease, but lines bracket his lips giving him away. That flicker of tension eases as he sets his eyes on me.

"It was the right thing to do," he says simply. But I know there's more. I want more from him. More than the obvious. So I push.

"And you had to go alone?"

"I did," he answered without hesitation, forfeiting his marshmallow to the flames. They burn brightly the flames devouring the wooden skewer.

I shake my head, returning my gaze to the male, watching him as he watches me.

"Why?"

His resulting smile didn't hold an ounce of humor.

"Because at my core, I am a selfish creature."

My eyes narrowed as he swept his over my face. I felt his gaze like a physical touch as it ghosted along my cheek, over my lips, and down my chest. It settled on my shoulder, cupped under Henry's hand. Which a moment later, stilled under his scrutiny.

But his gaze softened and behind that handsome exterior was what looked like admiration, longing.

And shame.

"Because if I walked you into a free camp... I knew asking you to walk back out with us wouldn't be the right thing to do. I also know that I would not have been able to walk away from you. To leave you unguarded, and if it had been your choice to stay... I couldn't have argued your reasoning. It's where you belong."

He shook his head, his brows lowering as a line formed between them. I couldn't help but mirror him, shaking my head. I knew what I would have chosen.

It wouldn't have even been a choice.

"But you see Amelia, I didn't give you that choice, because my selfishness wouldn't allow it." His eyes locked on mine and the next breath I dragged in was thin.

"Because you don't belong there anymore. You belong with us. You are ours." he growled, pupils blooming.

Slowly I crawled the few paces between us.

"Amelia."

My name was a warning as it crossed his lips. He straightened as I reached him. Rising up on my knees, I ran my fingers along his jaw before they met at the back of his neck. A muscle feathered in his jaw as he held my gaze.

"You're right," I climbed into his lap, straddling him as my fingers raked through his full hair. His brow furrows, apprehension scenting the air between us as he tenses beneath my touch. It feels as though he's waiting for me to cast the killing blow and that breaks my heart.

But I had told him before, and I had meant every word.

"I am yours." I vow.

His eyes snap to mine, gold flecks luminescent as a whirlwind of emotions shuffle across his expression.

"That is not my home. Not any longer." I run my fingers along the stubble as I trace his jaw. His expression is raw as his hands bracket my waist; warm and large and powerful. "You and Henry are my home. Wherever you are, is where I belong."

His gaze heats as it drops to my lips and he leans in, but as they coast back up to my eyes, he pauses.

"I lied."

His words are a whisper against my lips.

"There is something you need to know," he says.

"Okay," I nod, taken back by his admission. His hands tighten on my waist as if I'd try to pull myself from him and he was prepared to pin me here. I tighten my grip on his shoulders, molding myself to him. It seems to settle something in him so I fold myself against his chest and he tucks me under his chin.

The rumble of his words echo from his chest to mine as he wraps his arms around me and continues.

"I support the free camps... quietly of course. It's not to spite my father, or out of pity. I've done what I can to keep those lands safe, to supply resources where I can..."

I nod, running my fingertips up and down his back. The soft slip of his shirt against my skin and the slow rise and fall of his breathing calms me. And I hope it calms him as well.

"Henry told me some of what you do to protect the humans." I peek at him where he's sitting very still beside us.

A hum reaches my ear from his chest.

"And did he tell you why?"

I shake my head pulling back for only a moment to study his eyes. As if I may be able to decipher the answers between the flecks of gold and swirls of umber gazing back.

"I take care of the free camps because they were once my home as well."

His admission rocks me and I'm not able to hide my surprise as my brows hit my hairline.

"But..."

My eyes land on Henry.

"You said the royals were born." The words leave my lips like a question as I turn back to Jason. "A royal son born in a free camp? ...by accident?"

I admittedly had no idea what labor looked like for a vampire. I suppose only a few select did with how rare it had been.

"I am a prince in title only," Jason allowed. "There had never been an expectation that I would inherit the throne, because unlike my siblings I was sired... an insurance policy, not an heir."

"What are you saying?"

His next breath is thin.

"I was born a human and lived as a pet. Just like you."

Jason... a pet.

Imagining someone lording over this male in that way was inconceivable. And yet, this detail had some of the puzzle pieces clicking into place. That undercurrent of recognition that had been present in our earlier interactions, now made sense. That little light behind his eyes that had looked so much like understanding as he watched me struggle adjusting from free life to my life is his pet.

His smile was small, sad.

"It was how I met Henry."

He inclines his head to Henry who doesn't so much as breathe beside me. His eyes drop from Jason and I can almost feel them settle on my shoulder.

It explained so much. Why Henry hadn't seemed the least bit surprised to find me falling apart in the garden overwhelmed under the microscope of a house with barely a shred of privacy. The gentle way Jason handled me. The freedoms he granted me here... how it had never seemed hard for him to treat me fairly.

"It was a long time ago. The trade was fairly new," he explained.

I swallowed.

"But how are we here?"

There were so many more questions swirling around my mind now, but that one was the loudest. How had this male, a human pet, become what he was as he sat below me. Lethal in a manner that demanded recognition from all species.

Powerful.

Deadly.

Royal.

He chuckles darkly as he settles me on the blanket between them. I situate myself against Henry who immediately tucks me into his side. Jason collects my legs, laying them across his lap as he settles his gaze on the dancing flames.

"I was purchased by a woman who is long dead now. But back then, she was one of the king's favorite consorts. She introduced me to the royals as her son." His smile was sharp and it wavered as he continued.

"My time amongst the royals as a human was fairly uneventful."

Henry snorted. It wasn't a sound that lent itself to a male who bought what he was hearing.

"The majority of my time was spent in the kitchens or on errands for the king while she entertained him. When she met her end, things changed." His eyes narrowed on the flames. "He took ownership of me."

"Your owner was dead; couldn't he have freed you?"

His lips quirked.

"Planning on off-ing me to win your freedom?"

I shrugged.

"It may have been my plan at auction... before I knew you."

"Beautiful, violent thing." Henry tsked playfully.

I crossed my arms placing my toes to his chest and shoved.

"I dragged your half dead ass across the south, did I not?"

His responding smile was warm as he nodded.

"I suppose I'm safe then," he chuckled.

I rolled my eyes, but smiled despite the shitty story he was telling.

"So, you weren't free then."

"No. Though he placed me in the guard for my protection."

"*From* the Royals. *After* he found you beaten senseless," Henry chimed in, voice gruff.

Jason unleashed a breathy laugh before leaning forward to drag ringed fingers through Henry's hair.

"You're just angry their status kept them out of reach."

Henry growled under his breath and Jason smiled, his eyes coasting affectionately over the male.

"Henry took care of me from there. I climbed about as far as a human could through the ranks over the years, and then the prince died... and a replacement was needed. And that is how I came to be the sired son. Royalty isn't meant to sire, but with his son dead and his daughter under constant threat, he needed a living heir to ensure he kept his head... and his throne."

"Why would turning his human pet, ensure he kept his head?" I asked.

"Before the Crofts took the throne, the system for royal descent looked much different. Anyone could challenge the throne... within reason," he grinned like a male who'd seen his share of failed attempts at challenging said throne. "But in order to win the throne, you had to first kill the male seated on it."

I raised a brow before I rolled my eyes. "A male, huh?"

"I told you," Henry guffawed. "Not the superior species they claim to be."

Jason held up a hand in his defense.

"Historically," he qualified, sporting a smirk that was sweetened by the flush coloring his cheeks. "Hartley was the only king to ever step down from the throne willingly. So when his brother took his place, he set into action multiple fail-safes to ensure he kept it."

I blinked.

"Heirs."

My mouth popped open as Jason's gaze cut back to the flames.

"There are many things that need to change, corruption runs deep within both the Vampire and Shifter lines, but there are many who simply want what they have spent their very long lives without."

"Families," Henry finished.

"And after King Croft had successfully bore children, in order to take the throne, those very creatures would have to kill not only the king, but his children as well."

Diabolical.

"He used his children as a last line of defense." I shifted uncomfortably between them. Anger heated my blood making it hard to sit still. "But you weren't a child."

"No, but I was sired, not born." He lifted his hand in the air before him and I watched the shadows skirt across the garden towards us as if the male himself was a beacon that called them home. They rose to dance around the fire. It hissed fighting the suffocating weight as the shadows pressed themselves closer and closer to the flames eating up the oxygen that fueled it.

"There are not many who can successfully challenge vampire royalty. There is a reason we have had so few kings sit that throne. But the chance of success further diminishes when there are two of us with power like this."

His eyes catch mine as shadows whirl around his wrist settling in his palm.

Jason was powerful, and kind, and capable. I eyed him carefully, my mind placing a crown on those dark locks that had grown long over the past few weeks. I wondered... if his power was drawn from the king himself, how much stronger was King Croft?

"Ask your question, Amelia."

He served me a soft smile but I drew my spine straight.

I drew a small breath.

"Had you thought of challenging him in the past?"

Umber eyes flicker like sharpened steel against the flames. Those gold flecks burn brightly as he studies me. I could see the thoughts stirring around his mind. Could nearly trace their pattern in his eyes.

"I've been loyal to a fault when it came to my father." He spit the word. "It allowed me to slip right into his shadow. Barely there. And when I was, I never showed up appearing capable. Having strolled right into the throne room when summoned straight from whatever bed I'd fallen into the night prior, still smelling of whiskey."

Sadness ringed his eyes as they dulled. I set my hand over the top of his and he turned his palm up. Shadow pooled between our palms and I held very still. The darkness pulsed and I was surprised to find that while it was cool like morning mist against my skin, there was a warmth that seemed to ebb from its core. Like the shadowy ball was a creature itself.

Maybe instead of using whatever control he had to bend these shadows to his will, they instead served him… like little harbingers of death.

"It allowed enough time to pass for him to forget who I was." He stroked his thumb around the ball of night letting it seep between his fingers and back into the space around us. "What I was," he cooed, lifting his eyes to mine. "And what I was capable of."

He had been biding his time. Crafting this mask he wore so well.

"I lost everything when I was taken as a pet, most of us do." His eyes cradled mine, that understanding burning bright. "But what I gained in becoming the sired son, I will now use to level the playing field."

"Level the playing field." Those words felt impossible. "How do you find balance between species when the others are so dominant?"

"It's not as hard as you think it is, Princess," Henry reminded me with a playful flick of his brows. "And it's quite fun."

I snort.

"And I'm the violent one."

He grins running a rough palm up and around my throat. I let him tip my head back against his chest.

"Oh I sure hope so," he grins devilishly before pressing a chaste kiss to the corner of my mouth.

Focus.

Focus.

I drew a settling breath and returned my gaze to Jason who sat waiting with a heated look that sent my stomach fluttering.

But he blinked and it vanished.

"How do you level the field then?"

"You hold something each party wants over their heads?"

"And you have that thing?"

Jason smiled and it was a sharp thing.

"I do."

I draw in a breath as realization settles over me.

"The flowers."

His expression flickers with something as he turns his gaze to the sky.

"It's not the flowers themselves, per say, but what they may be able to offer." I watched him spin the ring on his forefinger where his hands rested in his lap as he eyed the stars. I'm sure, seeing more than I could ever imagine. "I've made an agreement with the shifters." His head turned back to me slowly, gaze loaded. "They will allow for changes to be made in the trade agreements in exchange for the ability to start families of their own."

"The witches tried," Henry interjected. "But the magic was long tainted."

"Link and I have researched for decades," Jason continued. "And we think we've found a way to recreate the original coven's steps to allow for safe pregnancies whether by human, shifter, or vampire."

Henry's hand runs down my arm and I sink into his touch.

"It would mean humans no longer need to be the vessel. They may maintain their own autonomy and we all move forward growing our families the way we *choose* to do so."

This would change everything.

"And you think those flowers are the missing piece. You think it will work?"

He reclined against his elbows as his eyes settled on the garden boxes. "I hope so, because I only have a few weeks until they come to collect on our bargain."

Chapter Thirty-One

"C'mon Princess," Henry called from behind the couch as he latched onto my waist and tossed me over his shoulder.

I fumbled the book I was reading, eventually catching it, but losing my page in the process.

"Hey!" I barked. "I was doing something."

"Yes, and you looked adorable doing it, but I wanna cuddle and you can read upstairs."

Well… I wasn't mad about that, but I was gonna pretend to be. This felt like a bad habit I was letting him get away with. Though I'd never admit that I liked it. I also knew that if I asked, Henry would put me right back in my spot on the couch. The oaf was gentle, and sweet, and handsome… and I was gonna let him carry me upstairs so that we could snuggle.

But not without some fight.

Gripping the book in both hands as he climbed the stairs, I brought it down on his ass with a thwack.

He chuckled. "And to think I was going to be gentle." His words landed like little pebbles sending nervous ripples through my stomach.

"Wait," I try to latch onto his shirt from the back, but it's too late. Before I can get purchase, he launches me onto the bed. I bounce, flailing, before the plush bedding catches me.

I sit up shooting him daggers, and ready for a fight, when I catch sight of him crawling up the bed. The sight stops me in my tracks. I bite my lip as he arrives before me, but find myself battling back a chuckle when he flops down unceremoniously. His big arm lands across my thighs, and he wastes no time cuddling up, using his head against my low belly to lay me back against the pillows.

I thread my fingers through his curls, still a bit damp from his shower. The garden box he had built was already set in the yard, filled with soil, and ready for the seeds Hartley and I planned to plant in the morning. Henry groans as I dig my thumbs into his shoulders, and the sound tests the limits of my threadbare control.

That's also when I realize the bed isn't empty.

Jason who is settled against the headboard grins, a book in his outstretched hand. One he holds out, beckoning me into his side. I scoot settling myself against him, and Henry adjusts to stay in my lap. Jason wraps a heavy arm around me, his fingers toying with the strap of my nightgown as he returns to his book.

I could read between the lines. Henry wanted us both in one place where he could keep tabs, but he could do whatever the hell he wanted as long as he did it like this.

Like Henry.

The male who loved us.

Not Henry, Royal Guard, and stone-cold-douche-canoe.

I loved Henry, and if this made it easier on him, then I had no qualms about it.

The male practically purrs in my lap. His arm is still a pleasant weight across my thighs, his hand rests just above Jason's knee, where he strokes his skin with long sweeps of his thumb. And that is where we stayed the remainder of the evening. And when my eyes went beary from reading, Henry tugged me down the bed keeping me tucked between the two of them where I could sink into their warmth and heavy arms.

Jason marked my page, his thumb running across the bookmark before his eyes flickered to mine. And while I was jealous that his eyes allowed him to read for longer, I was just as happy laying tangled in Henry's arms watching Jason read from under my lashes.

Though as if he could, in fact, read my mind, he combed his fingers through my hair and began to read softly from the page he had just marked so I could continue to enjoy my story without needing my eyes. Thankfully, sleep claims me before the handsome vampire reaches the dirtier scenes in the book I know are coming, and it's not until morning that I realize he has added my book to his collection on the bedside table.

The next morning, after helping Hartley in the garden, I snuck my way upstairs not wanting to be deterred again. With a racing heart, I showered and shaved, zipping myself into the lavender dress with the straps that tied at my shoulders. With a quick glance in the mirror, and one last nervous breath, I padded down the hall and straight into the office.

"Hello Pet," he cooed. A grin quirked his lips as he read over the page before him before raising his gaze to me.

I didn't think I imagined the tension already hanging in the air as I crossed the room, my bare feet pausing on the soft woven rug. The way his gaze heated as his eyes drew up my legs assured me he'd been truthful when he told me this dress was his favorite. He wiped his hand down his mouth, those silver rings winking at me. I could already feel their cold bite against my skin.

Craved it.

As I circled his desk, he reclined, pushing his chair back and allowing me space to stand between his legs. His hands drew up his own thighs as they spread, tattoos whirling across the tops of his hands. Hands that reached for me as I stepped into him.

His fingers traced the hem of my skirt as mine skimmed his strong thighs, the material cool despite the heat I could sense just below. My pulse pounded behind my ears and in a moment of weakness I reached forward combing my fingers through his hair. He closed his eyes, seeming content with this casual affection. A hum rose from the back of his throat and I caught my lip between my teeth, emboldened.

I moved to cup his jaw, appreciating the strong angles, when he caught my thumb between his teeth.

"Amelia," he purred, eyes snapping open. "Are you simply here to distract me?"

My resulting smile freed my lip from its snare as I shrugged.

“There's something I've been thinking about," I said lowering to my knees. "You can keep working if you'd like."

I grinned, setting my hands on his thighs, tracing muscle as I ran them up and back.

He tipped his head back on a throaty laugh. The sound softened my bones and started a fire in the pit of my stomach.

"If you think I'd be able to focus on anything other than your mouth, then you've given me far too much credit."

His fingers tipped my chin so he could control my gaze, eyes suddenly serious.

"You're sure?"

I nodded reaching for his belt and he tutted, his other hand catching my wrist

“Say the words.”

I paused, the words ‘I'm sure’ on the tip of my tongue when I bit back a smirk, deciding on a different direction.

“Please," I whispered, watching his pupils dilate. "Cum in my mouth Jason.”

His chest rose on a heavy inhale, nostrils flaring as his eyes darkened. The growl that followed coasted over my skin drawing forth a shiver that sharpened his smile. He stood, slowly unfurling to his full height before me. Molten umber swirled under dark lashes as he watched me drag my gaze up, up, up his body. That simmering growl transformed into a deep hum as he towered over me where I kneeled on the ground.

The fingers of his right hand scraped into my hair, soft pads dragging down my cheek. I leaned into his touch, closing my eyes for only a moment before they returned to his.

Umber eyes coasted across my face.

His gaze was a brand and a caress all at once.

With his other hand, he undid his belt, pulling it from the loops without releasing me from the snare of his eyes or hand.

I licked my lips, nervous excitement fluttering the muscles of my stomach. He was straining against his zipper by the time he freed me, and I him. Taking him in my hands and running my tongue up his length.

There was no way to take all of him, so I compensated with little strokes and twists of my hands. Exploring him with my tongue... and teeth.

He hissed.

His thighs had begun to twitch, little growls rolling from his throat as his head fell back. Seeing the effect I had on this powerful male was intoxicating, so I pushed him further. I flatten my tongue and hollow my cheeks taking him deep.

"Fuck Amelia," he purred my name, jerking against me.

Watching him strain against the way his hips pulsed aching to push deeper into my mouth, the way his thighs shook with short tremors, and the sounds he made as he came apart had me moaning around him.

His eyes snapped to mine, dark and possessive in time to watch me swallow him down. Electricity zinged up my spine as something charged the air. The shift is palpable. It was like I could sense that thread of control he held so tightly fraying rapidly. Little cords pinging as they snapped.

He lifts me to my feet and before I can so much as straighten my dress, he's claiming my mouth. His hands frame my jaw, brushing down my neck and into my hair. Where our first kiss had felt wild and demanding, the way he sweeps his tongue against mine now feels like adoration.

Powerful hands grip my ribs as he sets me down onto the desk.

"This damned dress will be my undoing," he says, his thumbs coasting up thighs and around my hips, looking to hook under my waistband, but finding none.

He growls appreciatively.

"Where are your underwear?"

"In the wash," I grin and he moves hungrily to my neck. I stretched to give him access and his hand appeared immediately to cup the side of my face. Supporting me and angling me just where he pleases. For the briefest of moments, I wonder what it would be like to be fed from now that I knew I'd survive it.

But his teeth don't so much as graze my skin.

Instead, he inhales deeply, his tongue drawing a line up the column of my throat. I gasp that sensation echoing against my core, before he pulls away.

This thumb tracks my jaw as his eyes fall down the front of my dress.

"Today I'm hungry for something else."

His hands grip the underside of my knees dragging me to the edge of his desk. He lowers himself into his chair before me, his hands folding over the front of my thighs and sweeping my skirt up to pool at my waist. Black stained fingers, soft as satin, spread wide over my stomach, flattening as I arch into him. The smile he dons promises pleasure, and I shiver as he dips in close to breath me in. His eyes trap mine as he lifts his hand, slipping one finger into his mouth. Those sharp teeth clamp down on his ring and slide it free from his finger. He grins around the thing before dropping it onto the desk with a clatter. He continues, moving onto the next finger as I watch, squirming under the weight of his hand.

Everything about this male is intoxicating. As hard as I try to keep my eyes on him, to take in every second, he draws his tongue up my center and I collapse against the desk. His hum of approval draws a moan from my lips as I rock my hips into him.

"More," I plead.

And for a moment he appeases me, his tongue swirling and sweeping through me before he pulls away.

A cry pulls from my lips as dark eyes meet mine from between my thighs.

His mouth clamps down on my clit, the pressure bowing my back.

"Like this?" he asks, voice smoke and sin, before pushing a finger into me and curling. I writhe against him, his name on my lips as he works me ruthlessly.

Shadow bands around my waist pinning me to the desk, and before I can get my elbows under me to protest, they coil around my wrists. His chuckle rumbles across my skin as my hands are pinned to my sides.

"Cheater," I breathe.

The shadowing bindings tighten in response.

He slips another finger inside me and my body bucks. Just as I began to shake, that wave cresting, he clamps his mouth down over me again, tongue swirling around my clit and I implode.

He kisses his way back up my thighs, pressing soft lips to the inside of my knee, before he nails me to the desk with a look. A muscle low in my stomach flutters, want already returning as I watch him rise to his full height over me.

Using that grip on the back on my knees he pulls me flush against him, his hips meeting mine with a barely restrained groan. I lift my hips tracing the length of him where he strains against his zipper. He only allows one pass before his hand sprawls across my stomach pinning me, but he doesn't leave me wanting. Folding over me, his hand lands on the desk beside my head. He hovers there a moment, brushing a curl from my cheek where it has stuck. Fangs greet me as his lips pull back, but if he notes the shock, he doesn't show it. Instead, his eyes flicker up, his grin widening and he speaks before I realize we're no longer alone.

"How pretty is our girl when she cums?"

I tip my head back meeting Henry's heated gaze.

"Very pretty," he muses from where he's leaned against the door frame. He straightens taking his time reaching us. "Though I'd like to see it again ... to be sure."

Henry steps up to Jason and I watch him pull his gaze up over his fram before he grips Jason by the back of the head and tips his mouth up to his own. The move draws a hiss from Jason and I practically watch his fangs sharpen. Henry's only response is to chuckle before claiming his mouth, fangs and all. Unlike the others, which had felt like a battle for dominance, this kiss was slow.

Lazy.

Languid.

Henry swallows each sound that claws up Jasons throat, the hand that isn't secured around his neck, grips the front of his shirt holding him just where he wants him. They separate, dual sets of canines flashing behind easy smiles.

Henry presses a kiss to the corner of Jason's mouth, and then his jaw, before releasing him. Those heated eyes shadowed by heavy lids, coast up my body.

Henry adjusts himself drawing my gaze to where the outline of him is pressed to the front of his pants. I squirm under Jason's hand still planted across my stomach. A hand he shifts underneath me and uses to pull me to a sit. He discards my dress next, dragging it over my head and tossing it into his empty chair.

"Fucking stunning."

Henry's rough palms scrape pleasantly up my sides, thumbs teasing my nipples to hard peaks as he takes Jason's place before me.

"Are you going to be good?" He asks, his deep voice rolling over my skin like a physical touch.

"No," I smile and his resulting chuckle is both praise and promise.

"That's my girl," he growls.

The sound, his words, draw a moan from my lips, a shiver working down my spine as need flames hotter. His hands wrap firmly around my thighs and I reach for him at the same time he hoists me into his arms.

Jason's chest met my back. The soft slip of his dress shirt against my overheated skin was both a relief and an exquisite torture. His tongue traveled the length of my neck hardening my nipples to sensitive peaks that Henry was quick to suck into his mouth. I cursed myself over and over for ever having delayed being pressed between these two males.

Jason's arm wrapped around my hip delving between Henry and I to tease me. He swirls his fingers gently around my sensitive clit as his other hand unleashes Henry and pumps him roughly. Henry's answering grin is painfully handsome and Jason must have agreed because he leaned in over my shoulder taking Henry's mouth.

A needy whine crept up my throat watching them. I was tucked so firmly between them that I felt them everywhere. But it still wasn't enough. I wanted more. His fingers slipped from my clit to push into me.

"Patience pet," Jason cooed against my throat.

"No," I growled, pressing myself harder into his hand grinding us both against Henry.

"Brat," Jason drags his teeth across my throat.

A reward and a punishment.

He smiles against my skin before sinking those fangs into Henry's shoulder, taking deep greedy pulls.

And living up to the title, I do it again, grinding myself and his hand against Henry. My first contact with Henry's cock had me dropping my eyes between our writhing bodies. Seeing Jason's ringed fingers wrapped around Henry as he pumped him slowly below me had a flush blooming across my skin. Using his grip on Henry, Jason ran the head of his cock through my folds before notching him at my entrance. I gasp and Henry groans, the sound rumbling through all three of us.

"So perfect," Henry groans.

His hands wrap around my thighs as he works himself inside me. Even after riding Jason's hand, its a slow process. Henry is big. And the way he eases into me with short pumps tells me he knows. I clamp around him fighting for those last few inches.

Sweat beads on his forehead as he pauses, his expression cautious, eyes probing as he studies me. Henry's concern softens me, but Henry and I aren't gentle. So biting back a smile, I drop my hips taking the last inch or so as he bottoms out with a snarl.

I gasp and his hands tighten. Moss green eyes sharpen as they lock onto mine. The smile I'd leashed, fought free. My breaths grew choppy as I watched Henry's control fray.

Jason's hand materialized around Henry's throat, his head knocking against the wall, lust darkening his gaze as they met over my shoulder.

"Slowly." Jason's deep voice carried the command over my shoulder as his arm wrapped around me. His warm hand enveloped my breast, his thumb brushing over the peak. With a shift of his chest he adjusted my body and the angle Henry was hitting inside me.

"Show me how good it feels.

I moaned and Henry's grip tightened on my thighs still snaked around his waist. His brow dropped as he nodded to Jason whose other hand slid low down my belly using two long fingers to spread me. I watched Henry pump into me sliding back and forth between Jason's spread fingers.

"Look how well she takes you."

"Like she was made for us," he growls appreciatively.

I press back into Jason, my breasts rising and falling as I writhed against the two males. The pressure built inside me. A cry broke through clenched teeth just as Jason dragged those wet fingers up to swirl gently against my clit.

Henry works me to the very edge with a brutal rhythm.

Jason's arm that had been wrapped around me just under my breasts moved to cup my throat as my back bowed. His breath tickles the sensitive skin under my ear as he peppers me with praise and kisses.

"Henry," I cry.

"I've got you," he growls, adjusting his angle.

The next pump of his hips draws a gasp. He must accept the sound as the complement it is, because he stays right there. His rhythm borders on punishing and it's just what I need. Jason's fingers work my clit as both their mouths mark my skin and I can feel the wave cresting.

"Give it to me, Princess," Henry growls lowly.

His hips slow and I feel every inch of him as he pumps into me.

Once more.

Twice more.

I cum loudly between them, panting around near sobs as Henry unleashes himself, pumping choppily and following me over the edge.

Jason pins me between them as Henry recovers himself. After a moment he lifts his gaze to me, that roguish smile fluttering my heart. He shifts his grip from my thighs, wrapping big arms around me as he tucks me against his chest.

I smile as his heart pounds against my cheek.

I listen to his pulse steady as he carries me to the bedroom, each shift of his hard body creating new sensations inside me where we're still connected.

By the time he turned, using his back to shove through the door, I could feel him hardening again. Growing longer and bumping into the back of me internally.

I was full.

I was so full.

Henry lays me onto the midnight blue bedding, leaning down to claim my mouth. One hand lands beside my head while the other settles against my hip. His thumb brushes my skin as he unfurls to his full height and his gaze drifts down my body.

I watch him as he watches himself pull free from me.

The quick pang of emptiness is enough to have me drawing a surprised breath.

"Now Amelia," Jason purrs, drawing my attention to where he stands at the end of the bed.

He strides up behind Henry wrapping his hand around his cock as it bobs once, glistening with our arousal.

"Be a good girl and watch me suck Henry clean of every last drop of you."

The men were a flicker of movement as Henry pressed Jason into the far wall, a hiss escaping curled lips. Jason was quick to flip him again gripping him by his throat. Then he slowed it down, I'm sure for my sake, dragging his hand down Henry's body as he lowered to his knees before him.

Henry's head fell back, knocking against the wall, his eyes meeting mine lazily. I squirm under the attention. He gripped Jason's hair with one hand, the other wrapped around his base. Jason was relentless as he drew Henry to orgasm again. My core ached watching them. And a shiver slipped down my spine as a harsh growl pulled from Henry's lips before he collapsed against the wall drawing in breaths between upturned lips.

He bent at the waist to drag Jason up his body, before kissing him deeply.

"I can taste her on your tongue," he groaned appreciatively.

Both males turned then, making their way to me. Henry crawled up the bed settling against the headboard before dragging me into his lap, my back to his front. His skin was cool with sweat.

But it was Jason who captured my attention. His gaze dark, predatory, as he prowled to the edge of the bed with a grin that had my stomach flipping.

He swept ringed fingers through his hair, his eyes hooded as they shifted to the buttons of his shirt. Slowly he undid each one until his shirt hung open exposing whirls of dark ink. I didn't think another orgasm was healthy. It was bordering on absurd and I worried another would kill me. But as I watched him shuck his shirt and move dark stained fingers to free himself from where he strained against his pants, I found myself panting. Aching. *Needing* him.

He grinned, like reading me was as enrapturing as the books he always kept close. And it felt like, in this, we shared a kindred captivation. He looked at me the way I had spent my days gazing at him.

A shared fascination.

A shared adoration.

A hunger.

He pitched forward at the same time I did, that tether in me snapped, sending me reaching greedily for his skin. We collided all arms, and lips, and teeth, as he wound his arm around my waist and hoisted me towards the headboard. Henry was waiting. His hands stroked my sides as Jason leaned out of my grasp.

"Wait," I gasped breathlessly.

"Ah, ah," Henry chuckled, his lips meeting my neck.

I melted into his hold arching to give him space to work my neck as I watched Jason recline. He wrapped one hand around himself. Both Henry and I paused to watch him take one long stroke.

It set us both in motion again.

Henry shifted to his knees taking me with him as he settled behind me where I hovered over Jason.

I drew my eyes over his length landing on his hand where he gripped himself tightly.

Another orgasm might kill me.

But so might his dick.

"You're in control Amelia."

His hands caught my waist alongside Henry's as he notched himself at my entrance.

His brow fell casting his dark eyes into shadow, those gold flecks luminescent, even in the low light. Sharpened by his lust they glinted as I wound my hips in small circles trying to work my way down his long length. My hands met his chest as I bottomed out, my hips bumping against his, but just barely.

Jason was thick. The fit almost too tight. But a few breaths, and a few swirls of my hips, had a whimper breaking across my lips as I adjusted.

Henry gathered up my hair, collecting the curls in his fist and angling my neck so he could drag his tongue up my overheated skin. It softened the edge of that pinch as I stretched around Jason. I rose up on shaking thighs until just the tip of him remained, and then dropped back down savoring the way his length brushed against that greedy spot inside me. Their overlapping grip on my waist promised to hold me together if his dick did in fact, split me in half.

By the third stroke, pleasure had swallowed up the pain, but It didn't keep me from panting around a cry as I met his hips with a swirl of mine.

Henry's arm banded around my waist slowing my descent.

I growled a complaint over my shoulder and his grip tightened. The hand that had been fisting my hair, curled around my front to pinch my clit between his warm fingers.

Breath stalled in my lungs as the sensation short circuited my brain.

"If you want to play rough, we can, but you will not hurt yourself." The warning in his deep voice rumbled over my overheated skin. The devil waiting to dole out his punishment. But I didn't think my clit could take it, so I nodded, taking the next few inches more slowly. Appeased, he released me, his hand moving to knead my breast in a motion that felt more like praise than punishment.

I moved his hand back to my hair where I wanted him and turned my head to take his mouth as I rode Jason with less and less abandon.

Harder, harder, harder.

Sweat broke out along my back. This orgasm was going to break me. Jason was going to break me. I wanted him to split me right in half. His breaths were sharp as he watched me impale myself on his length over and over again.

Henry claimed my mouth roughly, his tongue delving in with strong sweeps that stole my breath. The fingers he'd wrapped around my hair, dropped to my throat. The other, wrapped around my stomach, reaching to swirl around that tight bundle of nerves. I pulled up on a whimper ready to swallow him back down, when Jason stopped me.

Instead of waiting for me to drop back down, he pumped up into me slowly, meeting me where I was and holding me there. His hands not allowing even an inch of relief as he pulsed inside me.

He sent a heated look over my shoulder to where Henry waited. And it was the only communication these two needed before Henry's arm was banding around me once more. His sweat slicked chest met my back as he pinned me to him. He held me there, suspended against him, fingers mercilessly working my clit as Jason grinned.

"Are you going to come on my cock, Amelia?"

"Yes," I gasped.

"You're so beautiful when you come apart between us, Princess," Henry growled.

"Please," I begged, needing him to move. But they held me still. "Please!" I dropped my gaze to Jason, my words a plea and a demand.

Dark eyes, hooded under heavy lids, pulled me deep into that swirling umber. "I want to watch you lose control," he growled.

I panted breathlessly as he dropped his hips slowly pulling from me, leaving just the head of his cock stuffed at my entrance.

His words had me stilling. Jason lived behind a mask of control. How many times had I watched him? Pushed him? Waiting, wanting to see him let down his walls.

To snap.

He had given me that. He had shown me who he was at his core. No hiding. No holding back.

Free of the control that kept us from each other.

He pistoned his hips slowly pumping up into me once more.

My lips parted on a moan.

And once more.

"Surrender," he purred, and my legs shook.

He emphasized his words with one pump. This one rougher as skin slapped against skin.

Now he wanted me bare...but my mask wasn't control. Not in the same way his was.

He wanted me pliant.

He wanted me to trust him. To surrender my control.

And for these males, I could.

I would.

I nodded, curling one arm up behind me around Henry's neck to anchor myself to him. The other, I set to Jason's chest, nails down, before raking them down his ridged stomach.

His responding smile was slow.

His hips were not.

Chapter Thirty-Two

Instead of waking up between my males in the sweet glowy bliss I would've hoped accompanied the earth-shattering orgasms that had been doled out the evening prior, I woke up curled in a ball and covered in sweat as my stomach screamed in protest.

For an instant, as sleep cleared, I mistake the pain for food poisoning. Shame on me for thinking Hartley capable. As I climbed from bed, I recognized the tell-tale symptoms and beelined for the bathroom in my old room hoping for some privacy.

It may not be food poisoning, but the root of my problem still stemmed from Hartley's cooking. All that good food I'd been eating over the last few weeks, the time I'd spent living like a well cared for pet - I rolled my eyes at that thought - had led to my body finally being healthy enough for my cycle to return.

And return it had.

In a house full of vampires.

"Shit."

I stood a few paces beyond the exterior courtyard frustrated that I hadn't prepared for this. I had no supplies and without having a conversation with Henry or Jason, I didn't know the most courteous way to handle everything that came with my cycle. So here I stood, my bare feet in the dewy grass when Henry appeared in the doorway.

"I hope you're not thinking of running," he called from the door.

I watched him step into the garden, something too tense about the way he moved, his body too alert. But the sight of him, sweats hung low on his hips, grey shirt stretched taut over broad shoulders, had nerves prickling in my stomach.

"Henry..." I held up a hand to stop him, but found myself lacking the words to explain why he should.

That teasing tone fell away completely as his eyes sharpened, big arms falling loose at his sides. My heart sputtered in my chest. I knew- *I knew* I was safe with Henry, but his posture had those nerves heating the skin of my neck. He was too tense. All coiled muscle, ready to pounce.

My brow collapsed as I studied him. I'd only heard horror stories when it came to being fed from, but I had a feeling being fed from by this male would be different.

I shifted on my feet.

"What's wrong?" he asked, eyes coasting quickly across the garden.

"I-I'm bleeding." I said quietly knowing he would hear as I wrapped my arms around myself. I'd been in such a hurry to put distance between myself and the house that I hadn't thought about the temperature this early in the morning. The sun was barely peeking through the tall trees behind me.

He paused, his eyes cutting back to my face, before taking another step towards me. One I mirrored as I stepped back, keeping ample space between us. He didn't like that and was before me in an instant. His warm hands wrapped around my upper arms keeping me in place.

His nostrils flared scenting me I'm sure, and I did my best not to start at his sudden nearness.

His eyes flickered across my face.

"Did we hurt you?" his voice was low, concern softening all those sharp edges.

The casual potency that normally emanated from him, quieted. Worry, and what looked like anger, took its place as he drew his thumbs along my skin, his eyes raking over my frame.

I shook my head, startled by his assumption.

"No. No of course not... It's my cycle." I winced, a flutter of cramps forcing me to shift my weight, and huffed out a breath that fogged the air between us.

His brows twitched relief swelling behind moss green eyes.

"Can I run you a bath?" He asked, his hands softening where they held my arms. Like this piece of information ensured him I wasn't going to flee.

He wasn't going to scare me off. Least of all with what happened last night. But I didn't think being the main ingredient in a tub of pet soup would make anyone in the house more comfortable right now.

I shook my head.

"A hot shower then?" he frowned, glancing back at the house.

I shivered at the thought of stepping under a warm stream of water and his frown deepened.

"Won't that make everyone- won't it be hard to tolerate... while I'm bleeding?" I huffed, cold and uncomfortable, and irritated with my half-baked plan.

"The only thing I'm having trouble tolerating is the fact that you're standing out here cold and in pain."

"But-" I flinched, letting loose a sigh that tempered both my cramps and the need to punch myself in the head to end this conversation. "What about the blood?"

"If your blood was going to set any of us off, don't you think it may have happened the night you sprung a leak like a bad water bed in my living room?" He raised a brow wearing a prize worthy scowl and I grinned.

"I wasn't implying that I'm not safe here. I just... I was trying to avoid making anyone uncomfortable." I knew I wasn't in danger... of anything other than raiding Hartley's stash of sweets. Which I'd learned he hid in the heavy stock pot below the sink.

Clever old vampire.

I trusted all three males implicitly. I'd, in a poorly executed way, been trying to avoid making them uncomfortable after they had done so much to take my needs into consideration ... I was only trying to do the same.

"Fuck that," he growled. "We're vampires. It's just a little blood. We've all seen far worse and we have a millennia of experience between us exercising self control." His voice dropped as he crossed his arms over his chest. "Get back in the house.

Before my period-addled brain could argue any further, he scooped me up, holding me against his chest with a grunt. I opened my mouth to protest, but his eyes snapped down to my own.

"Zip it princess," he growled, tucking me tighter against his body as I shivered. "It's too damn early."

He carried me upstairs and right passed Jason who still slept soundly in bed. He didn't set me down until we stood in the ensuite bathroom.

"I'll be back with fresh clothes. I expect you to be in that shower, getting warm, when I come back."

His tone inspired a bratty retort, but I swallowed it. At this moment, there was nothing I wanted to do more. So I did as I was told, and stripped down, before stepping under the spray of warm water. My eyes close under the deluge of warm water, my knuckles massaging my hips and low back as I thaw. When I open my eyes, I find Henry standing there his arms crossed, hip set against the counter, glaring at me.

"I'm sorry."

"You should be," he growled, stepping out of his clothes and pacing right into the shower. His voice was rough, but his hands were gentle as he turned me around. Batting my hands away, he takes over scrubbing my hair. The feeling of his strong fingers against my scalp draws a quiet moan from my lips.

I melt against him. He's warm and strong behind me, but it's only as I lean into him like this that I realize his heart is thundering in his chest.

I turn pulling soapy locks free of his fingers and place a hand over his heart.

My brows pull together as I study his stern expression.

"Henry?"

He huffs, his eyes falling closed as his hand covers mine.

"I woke up to the scent of your blood and a distinct lack of you in my bed."

Even under the warm water, I shivered. Regret was potent.

I wrap my arms around him, setting my forehead to the divot between his pecs. I press my lips to his skin.

"I'm sorry. I wasn't thinking."

As I pick up my chin to study him, he runs strong fingers gently through my hair, rinsing it, but he doesn't answer me for a long moment.

I think I've hurt him with my half-baked plan. And that was the last thing I was trying to do.

He swallows, nodding shallowly. His eyes softened as I reached up on my toes to press a kiss to his lips. His hand splays across my back, pinning me to him, and I smile.

He's quick to wrap me in a fluffy towel as soon as we step out from under the warm spray of water. He dries me thoroughly and helps me step into a pair of underwear and what looks like Jason's shirt, all before bothering to dry himself. But once he does, he wraps a matching towel low around his hips and sets to work drying my hair.

"I couldn't find those." I tip my chin at the pads Henry set on the counter for me to choose from.

"They were here in our bathroom since it's now yours as well." He serves me a loaded look. One that screams 'you should have known better'.

And I should have, but I'll blame it on the period brain and not dwell.

"You're good at this," I say instead.

He meets my gaze through the mirror and his eyes drift down my chest.

"I'm three hundred years old, Princess. I'm well accustomed to the workings of the human body." His eyes heat as his hands run down my arms.

"I'm sorry again."

His hands catch my jaw as he pulls back to study my expression.

"Amelia." The sound of my name on his lips has my eyes fluttering closed as I sink into his touch. "We love you. There's never a good enough reason to not ask for help."

I nod. Part of me wants to fight, because it hadn't been my intention to hurt him like I had. But more than anything, I don't want to hurt him again, so I don't push.

"I understand what you were trying to do, but don't do it again."

Pulling my lip between my teeth, I nod.

With a nod in response, he sets his hand to my back and leads me back to bed where he tucks me securely between their bodies.

Jason and Henry dote on me over the next few days, and I take full advantage of the copious amounts of cookies Harley is willing to bake.

"Do better," I scolded the little seeds sleeping uselessly under the damp soil. After having spent the morning helping Hartley and willing these seeds to sprout, I was ready to dig my fingers into the soil to see if there was anything happening at all. But one could only watch wet soil for so long, so I went in search of a distraction.

And by distraction, I meant I went in search of a Vampire I could annoy.

I climbed the stairs with a cup of coffee in each hand. However, as I shove through the office door, I find the room empty.

"In here," Jason calls from the studio.

I crossed the hallway, pausing in the doorway, my hip pressed to the door frame as I took him in. Jason shirtless was something to be savored.

Dark ink whirled around his sculpted shoulders, plunging down his back, and around his ribs to adorn his chest and arms. The ink ended on the top of his hands; those black tipped fingers muted with paint. A smear of yellow across his cheekbone. A slash of cerulean across his ribs.

"Are you finished ogling me, pet?" He pads over reaching for the mug in my hand, but I pull it back with a grin.

"No, not quite yet" I say, making a show of dragging my eyes over his body.

"You'll burst a blood vessel in your eye flexing that hard," Henry crows from behind me, scooping up the other mug. He disappears into the bedroom as suddenly as he had appeared behind me, and I smile as I hear the water turn on in the ensuite bathroom.

I'm not distracted enough to miss Jason reaching for the unguarded mug of coffee. So, with a laugh, I pull it away once more.

His brows pitch high for a moment before he drops them, throwing those umber eyes into shadow, a devastating grin crawling across his face. My heart takes off at a gallop as he steps into me, his hands closing around my wrists before scraping up my arms. Canines sharpened behind his smile, black bleeding across the whites of his eyes swallowing the soft browns and golds. I'm caught there. Just aware enough to sense him moving around me, but weak to this hold he has over me as I drown in him.

His eyes, his scent.

Him.

He slips the cup from my fingers and surprises me as he sets it on the counter beside us. Black stained fingers soft as satin curl around my neck, angling me just so before he dips to my throat.

My next exhale was loud enough to bounce off the walls as his chuckle fanned across my shoulder. His lips press to the hollow just below my ear.

"I've wasted too much time not touching you." His words caress my skin as does something else. The shadows, I realize. They curl around my waist, securing me to him and emphasizing his words. "Thank you for my coffee, Love" he purrs.

Love.

Not Pet?

I cock my head, appraising him, but he doesn't give me long to look my fill. He hooks his finger into the front of my shorts and tugs me forward, wrapping me in his arms before he captures my mouth.

I grip the waistband of his jeans where they rest low on his hips, slipping my fingers into the pockets. I smile against his mouth when I come away with a handful of paintbrushes.

He kisses the corner of my mouth with a chuckle before his fingers run across my palm, scooping the brushes back. Plunking them into a cup on the counter, he runs his fingers along the waistband of my shorts. His eyes track my legs down to my bare feet hungrily.

"Stay for a while?"

I nod ignoring the way relief seems to soften the lines bracketing his mouth. Like I was capable of denying this male anything.

I follow his retreating form into the room. Watching him move. Watching him set his mug down next to the new canvas and unload the paintbrushes he had sprouting from his other pockets. A grin tugged at my lips as I circled the room thumbing through the paintings set against the wall. And there, tucked amongst the others, was a painting of me.

Caught off guard, I pulled it free, setting it against the stack so that I could take in the details.

It was like looking in a mirror.

Like looking back in time.

The painting tugged at the memory of this moment. There I stood, barefoot and furious, wearing what was left of my dress from Acropolis in the hotel room the night before we made it home.

I remember being terrified and exhausted, and so very far out of my depth. This moment had been a breaking point. I swallowed, reaching out to run a fingertip down her painted hand where it was curled into a fist at her side. Remembering how I had challenged him and how out of control I felt in that moment. Anyone else would have killed me where I stood, or at least punished me for mouthing off the way that I had, but Jason immortalized this moment here in paint and canvas.

The woman staring back at me looked livid. But the way he'd painted me ... there was more than anger. The woman staring back at me didn't look out of control. She didn't look scared...

"This... I look..." I shook my head, emotion welling in my throat.

"Powerful," he supplied, setting his brush down. "Brave. Vengeful."

Brave...

Vengeful?

Was that what he had seen in this moment?

He'd thought I looked powerful?

Jason steps up behind me, the heat from his body warming my back.

"Why this moment?" I breathed, my eyes landing on him over my shoulder. We'd seen it so differently. He'd seen *me* so differently.

He'd thought me vengeful.

I supposed it may have been a fair description since I had dug my thumb into the knife wound on his stomach after he scared me in the elevator.

A small smile lit my lips as I leaned into him.

"Easy." He grinned, his eyes coasting across the painting before returning to me. "This was the moment that I fell in love with you."

I didn't think I was still breathing as I turned to face him.

He'd loved me then?

There at my lowest, he loved me.

"While I screamed at you?" I asked, blinking away the moisture gathering behind my eyes. My brows crumpled and he smiled, smoothing his thumb along my lower lip.

"Precisely."

"Then?" I asked breathlessly. "You loved me *then*."

He's loved me all this time.

"I did. I do," his voice rang proudly through the room knocking something loose inside me. Something that zipped down my spine, coasting under my skin and along each and every nerve, lighting like a flame.

"There in that shitty hotel room, you let me see you for who you truly were at your core."

My eyes blur.

"Angry?" My laugh is disbelieving.

He smiles, his eyes soft as his thumb stroked my jaw.

"Brave," he corrected. "Strong. Beautif-

I'm in his arms before I can register the decision to launch myself at him. My mouth melds to his as I rake my fingers through his hair, tightening my grip at the nape of his neck. The growl that slips past his lips warms my core.

"Say it again," I breathe against his lips.

"I love you Amelia."

He cups my jaw in his hands, a smile lifting the corner of his lips where they brush against mine. Using his grip, he holds me still as he runs his nose up the bridge of mine.

"You found your way to me and I couldn't let you go. I couldn't allow anyone to break you, that spirit, that smart mouth." He pressed a soft kiss to my lips, his eyes lingering there. "It was going to get you killed."

"Your confidence in me is charming," I deadpan.

He smiles, but it's the breathy laugh that works its way into my lungs as we share air, that had my stomach tumbling.

"I followed your camp for days," he admits. "When I realized where they were taking you, I detoured to the Royal City."

His eyes fall closed, the memory playing between us.

"I told Henry everything and he agreed... trusted that I could take care of us, because I couldn't afford to wait for him. You didn't have the time. I didn't know that I'd ever find you again, but I knew if I did..." He shook his head. "You were mine. You were mine from that very moment, and I didn't care what it cost me, or what it took. You were coming home with me ...and then I woke to you feeding me."

The shadows around his feet darkened.

"You could've left me there. But instead, you built a raft with nothing but your stockings, and leash, and some damn reeds, and had gotten us miles closer to safety... and that fucking mouth." His thumb set against my lips. "The way you played those shifters. The way you spoke to me," he smiled. "I fell for you before we even made it home. That night you wrapped yourself around me the way I used to watch you sleep anchored around a tree." He shook his head, his brows dropping low. "I never wanted you to feel like that again. Unsafe, unguarded."

The gold of his eyes glittered, color from the windows behind me streaking his handsome face as he swept his gaze over me.

"You collected all my favorite books and claimed them for yourself. Cleared a shelf and made yourself at home. You are brave, and kind, and clever, and so very, fucking, stubborn."

I laughed, but it was wet.

"I wanted to be worthy of each piece of you that you gave me, but I am not whole as only myself. I am a part of Henry, just as he is part of me, and when you asked about him that afternoon before he made it home, you pulled away...and that was fair."

It was my turn to shake my head as I drew my fingers along his arm.

"I thought it was all in my head. I figured you were just being courteous. I thought I'd misread... everything."

He smiled, but it was pained. "I cannot be so bad at flirting that it can be mistaken as courtesy."

I beamed a smile at him, even as I blinked wet lashes clear. My fingers grazed his stomach as I stepped into him.

"I just hadn't considered the possibility of you wanting me... and then I didn't think you wanted *anyone* else after I learned about Henry."

"Oh, I've wanted you for far longer than I had any right to, but I wouldn't act on it until Henry was home. It was always going to be the three of us."

The pieces clicked together as his words settled against my chest. My heart. I had certainly misread this male... and by that point I had pulled away.

"I love you both."

"We know," Henry chimed in from behind me, his teeth grazing the side of my throat playfully.

Chapter Thirty-Three

"Nothing yet?" He lowered himself to his knees right next to me.

"Nope." I studied his profile. "Not yet."

His eyes were worried as he searched the soil for a bud just as I did each morning... and evening. But as quickly as it had appeared, the emotion was gone. Replaced with a smile that wasn't quite full. Wasn't quite honest.

He turned to me.

"Soon," he assured with a nod.

"They were fickle things, from what I remember. I'm sure they just need time." I set my teacup down on the ledge of the garden bed and turned into him. Wrapping my arms around his neck, I climbed into his lap and he wound his arm around my back, the other catching my jaw.

"I have some ideas on how we could pass some time."

"Do you now?" He picked up a brow and I bit my lip. His gaze tracked the motion and I only had a seconds warning before his mouth was on mine, freeing my lower lip and sucking it between his teeth.

"Mine," he growled playfully, the possession in his tone warming my belly.

"Yours," I breathed, my lips melding to his.

In one swift motion he stood lifting me into his arms and carrying me back into the house while peppering kisses down my throat. He paused in the living room a wicked grin lighting his face before he tossed me onto the couch cushions.

He called out Henry's name, the invitation ringing through the house before prowling towards me, strong fingers whipping his belt from the loops around his waist.

We waited weeks.

Weeks with no change.

Nothing but a bed of wet soil. Until the end of summer when I knelt by the bed as I did each evening and saw the first sprout reaching towards the sky with its fragile stalk.

"Holy shit," I breathed. "Holy shit!"

Two weeks later there were two rows of six sprouts. They ranged in height as a few had unfurled needle like leaves, stretching higher and wider and looking sturdier than others. Henry and I built a cover for the beds to insulate the soil and keep our plant babies warm as the breeze chilled at the end of the season.

The air was growing tense around the house as we waited day by day, week by week, to see if our venture would be successful. Would they flower? Would they produce enough flowers for us to begin testing?

But tonight was my birthday and the males had made it clear we were celebrating. So since Hartley refused my help, insisting it was sacreligious to prepare your own birthday dinner, I found myself upstairs sitting in a warm bath instead. Something shifted in the adjoining room and I lifted my head from the lip of the tub to peek through the cracked door.

"Henry?" Steam swirled rising from my hand as I brushed away the hair that stuck to my forehead. The humid air was scented with the verbena and jasmine bath salts Henry had poured into the tub when he summoned me in here.

I grabbed the fluffy white towel off the edge of the tub, and wrapped it around myself. I stepped carefully, quietly, onto the cool tiles.

"Henry?" I called again as I pushed through the adjoining bedroom door.

The room was empty, but the bed wasn't.

Resting on the dark blue comforter was a box wrapped in red paper with a big silver ribbon.

I lifted the lid, holding my breath. Peeling away the colored tissue paper I unearthed the waiting blade. Breath whooshed from my lungs as I ran my finger along the whirls and waves of the damascus steel.

It reminded me of Jason's tattoos.

The process of making a damascus blade was something Henry had taught me about, after the dragon rider in a book I'd been reading had gifted one to the assassin he fell in love with... which she eventually ended up stabbing him with. Jason had guffawed as he read that page. It had become a routine of ours to read until my eyes went blurry, at which point, Jason would read to me as I snuggled up between them.

They had made me a damascus blade of my own. And it was just as beautiful as I had imagined.

More.

Its slim length was balanced with a wrapped handle. The binding of which looked just like the leather straps of Henry's armor that he wound around his forearms.

A little card rested just below.

The single line read,

Sharp steel for that sharp tongue.

My heart knocked against my ribs as I balanced it in my palm. It was lighter than I expected, yet the weight of my new dagger imbued a sense of strength I hadn't felt before. Their confidence in me to wield such a pretty blade, their consistency in ensuring I felt capable, and the thought that had so clearly gone into the design of the blade, had emotion welling.

I loved these males.

And they loved me.

With their words.

With their actions.

And ideally with their bodies.

I zipped myself into the dress Jason bought me in the freelands and buckled on the sheath Henry had chosen for me at the market.

The blade slipped smoothly into the leather, beautiful steel winking from just under the hem of my skirt where the slit ran up my thigh. I would have never imagined having what I have now as I stepped across that stage at Acropolis, but here I stood feeling strong and beautiful and so very loved.

So I went in search of my males, needing them to see just how perfect the blade they had crafted for me, the blade that felt like the perfect blend of these males, a blade that felt like home, like freedom, looked sheathed at my thigh.

I craved the way I knew their eyes would coast over my skin, and couldn't wait to watch their reaction to seeing the dagger here under my skirt.

Each step I took down that staircase felt like a sin.

The low light of the living room calmed the pounding heart I knew both males could hear. Jason sat at the head of the table in his dark suit. His tie hung loose down his chest, the buttons of his dark shirt, undone. I could feel the soft sweep of fabric between my fingers as I drank him in. His dark hair, perfectly styled, even now as he swept his fingers through it, catching my eye. The silver rings on his fingers winked at me as he dragged them down his jaw unleashing a smile that had heat pooling in my belly.

He sat back in his chair.

A king on his throne and I knew the way his legs would widen a fraction under the table as he reclined.

Candles lit along the table flickered as I made my way to the landing.

Henry took note of the change of Jason's posture, his gaze whipping to mine. He didn't miss a beat, pushing out his chair and rising to his full height. He did, however, take his time reaching me. Every step he took was laced with power, confidence... Lust. It simmered in my veins now. His olive green shirt unbuttoned to his sternum showing off the definition of the muscle below. He folded the arms of his sleeves as he prowled towards me.

I bit my lip as I shamelessly dragged my eyes up the unit of a male before me. Well-worn jeans draped over powerful thighs I wanted to dig my nails into. One because I knew he could take anything I gave him and two because I think he'd enjoy wearing any marks we gave him. He served me that playful grin that I loved and held out a hand for me to take.

Without hesitation I set my hand in his, enjoying the way his fingers curled around mine, swallowing them up. He placed a kiss to my knuckles, his own eyes roving over me as I reveled in the feeling of his lips against my skin and the way his beard tickled my hand.

He wore his curls loose tonight and I was glad he did. I reached up to push my fingers into his hair, scraping gently along his scalp before tracing his jaw, and coasting thumbs over his lips.

Like Jason had said, we had wasted too much time not touching each other.

He grinned underneath my touch as his big arms banded around my waist. He swept me right off my feet. My arm slipped around his neck as he swung me around and around. The low light of the room twinkled in the background like stars in the night sky as we spun.

"You look fucking stunning, Amelia," he growls.

If I'd expected him to set me down I'd have been pleasantly surprised when he took long strides back to the table peppering kisses to my neck and collar bone. He set me down on the edge of the table, both hands cupping my jaw with strength he kept barely subdued. Calloused fingers scraped lightly against my scalp and neck, thumbs stroking my cheeks as he looked his fill before crushing his lips to mine.

We both drew in ragged breaths, his hands finding my hips and pausing for only a moment. His left hand swept my skirt to the side where it had fallen open, my new dagger sparling in the low light of the room. His eyes heated as they rose, latching onto mine.

"Fucking stunning," he growled before pulling me flush against him. My legs opened to accommodate his hips. The contact drew a shiver up my spine and a groan from his lips. I caved to his weight, when he folded forward, pressing me into the table below me. One strong hand braced beside my fanned hair while the other spread under my shoulder blades, supporting my weight.

On his next breath I took the opportunity to suck his lower lip into my mouth, strumming my teeth down the sensitive skin. He caged me against the table, his cheek pressed to mine as he grazed a much sharper set of teeth across the shell of my ear, snarling playfully.

We fought for dominance, neither of us caring who won, but enjoying the battle. He pulled away just long enough to drag the flat of his tongue up the side of my neck. The feeling bowed my back, his strong hand pinning me there. Like neither of us could allow the space created between our bodies.

He hardened against my stomach. The feeling of which had me tipping my head back in search of Jason.

In the flickering light of the candles I found him watching us, looking every bit the royal he was.

Like the devil himself.

The smile he wore was relaxed.

Indulgent.

"Breathtaking," he purred. With his elbow set to the armrest of his chair he raised his hand in the air, crooking two fingers.

He wants me to come to him but it's my birthday and I'm feeling like a fight.

I shake my head, a teasing smile lifting my lips.

“Come get me.”

In the time it takes me to register that devilish grin as it flashes across his features, and the quirk of his dark brow, I'm shooting up into a sit to lunge away from him. But it takes him no time to pitch forward over the table and latch onto my waist.

With a sharp tug I slide across the polished wood of the table arriving before him with a squeal. Glassware and table settings clatter to the floor as he spins me.

“You want us to chase you Amelia?” His deep voice rolled over my skin like a physical touch. His eyes glitter with the promise of just what that might entail.

But I shake my head.

“Not tonight.”

He nods, his warm hands hooking under my knees. He lifts my legs, opening them as I brace myself on my hands behind me. The skirt of my dress pools around my waist and his thumb traces the long slim line of the blade strapped to my thigh.

"Not tonight," he echoes, eyes darkening.

Leaning forward slowly, like we have all the time in the world here to spend tucked around each other, he presses a kiss to the inside of one knee, and then the other, slowly working down the inside of my left thigh. I try to keep my breathing steady, but fail miserably.

"Soaking wet for us," Jason purrs.

His fingers plunge into me and I set my heels against the armrests of his chair. The way he works me is both languid and brutally efficient. Strong fingers curling, coaxing my muscles tighter and tighter inside of me while the other hand flattened over my stomach. But he pulls away before that wave builds too high.

"Would you like to ride Henry's big cock pet"

I nod bliss still sparkling the edges of my vision as I tip my head back looking down the long table to find Henry watching me, cock in hand.

"Henry." His name is a command on Jason's tongue. "On the table."

Henry swings his legs onto the table with a litheness that shouldn't accompany a male of his size and I watch him recline against his elbows.

I give Jason a taste of what wanted earlier by crawling on hands and knees across the table towards Henry. His growl lights my grin and zings over my nerves, knowing I've hit just the button I was searching for.

Using my grip on Henry's neck, I swing my leg over his lap pressing him into the table and letting my curls fall loose over my shoulder as I notch him at my entrance. Inch by inch I lower myself onto him until I'm seated and squirming.

His hands are immediately at my hips, fingers branding me.

Jason rises, silver rings winking at me as he undoes his pants. I watch him circle the table towards Henry's shoulders. With what looks like very little effort, he uses the grip on Henry's shirt to drag the both of us towards him. Jason's fingers delve into Henry's curls, massaging and scraping in slow circles.

With a smile, Henry relaxes, a deep chuckle shaking him, and therefore me. I clench around him and he hisses sharply.

With his head arched back over the lip of the table Jason grips his curls in one hand and the base of his cock in the other before notching himself between Henry's lips.

I brace a hand on Henry's chest as I lean forward, my mouth dry at the opportunity to watch.

Henry's thumb presses against my clit as he groans allowing Jason entry and I moan.

Jason releases himself, using that hand to gently stroke the length of Henry's throat. The action was all the praise he needed and I felt him twitch inside me. The movement sends him knocking against my inner wall and I arch against him, as I rocket towards my own orgasm.

Chapter Thirty-Four

Link and Amara visited once the flowers began to bloom, their stiff yellow petals following the sun across the sky. I watched them like a sentinel because feeling helpless wasn't something I was versed at handling. So when I wasn't tormenting my males, I was out here pretending to prune the herbs in Caroline's garden beds. They were pristine, not that Harley would allow otherwise, but we were out here so frequently, the weeds barely had time to breach the soil before they were plucked. I'd reached the end of her book and even tucked some notes between my favorite pages to mark them.

On their last visit, Link and Amara had collected half of the flowers. And outside of the small section Jason set aside to experiment with, we would let what was left go to seed to ensure we had more to plant next season.

Jason's nose had wrinkled when I delivered two mugs of tea to the office instead of their normal coffee. But nevertheless, night after night they entertained my restlessness, tasting teas and dolling out orgasms.

However, tonight the air was tense. And the cab of the car only seemed to amplify that. Our drive into the Royal City was quiet and I couldn't help but fuss with the material of my skirt nervously. Smoothing it over and over, the fine silk material stuck to my sweat-slicked palms.

When we passed under the arches of the King's estate my heart rate ratcheted up again. Jason, who's gaze had either been trained at the back of Henry's head or out his own window as he spun the silver ring on his forefinger, turned his attention to me then.

He pinned me with eyes I would have once thought too calm. But I knew him better now. I could see past the mask to the male below and sense the emotion churning just below the surface. Neither of us smiled or spoke. He just curled his hand around mine, lifting my knuckles to his lips allowing me to fall into those umber waves as they crashed against the mask he lowered just for me.

Just for a moment.

Tonight would change everything.

In my lifetime I never thought I'd lay eyes on the king, let alone find myself within his gates, bound to the males intending on taking the throne right out from under him.

Jason hadn't let go of my hand since. The sweeping of his thumb, a comfort and a metronome which I used to slow the anxious beats of my heart.

The resemblance King Croft bore to Hartley brought me pause. But appearance was where their similarities ended. In every other aspect, he seemed to be the antithesis of the kind vampire back home. King Croft wore his long blonde hair loose. It fell to his chest, vibrant blue eyes like the sky at midday sparked like steel against stone as they cut to me.

To an onlooker the twitch to his thin lips could be explained away as just that. A twitch. A result of a comment those preternatural ears had picked up from somewhere in the room surrounding us. But as his cold eyes skate over my form where I stand, hand in hand with Jason, disdain colors his gaze. The clenching of his fists draws my eyes down in time to watch the male as tanned fingers extend into long dark talon-like claws. Claws that he flicks one at a time creating little ticks that I swear I can hear from across the room.

Jason falls quiet beside me and I peel my attention away from King Croft's razor sharp talons long enough to peek at him. His eyes are locked on his father, and I can sense rather than feel the way his muscles coil. His thumb continues its sweep across the back of my hand. One that the king tracks a moment longer before he turns his attention to a male who arrives before him proffering a cup.

The breath I drew was even. Slow. Though the relief that washed over me felt so potent it shook my knees. Like standing before the open maw of a beast before he locked onto a new target. I smoothed my hand down my skirt to hide the tremor of silk that may give me away. We all had roles to play tonight, and my role was no longer prey. So, I kept my hand pliant where it rested in Jason's and straightened my spine as he returned to his conversation beside me.

As the crowd drew towards the main hall, Jason pulled me to a stop, tucking us into a darkened alcove. His hands curled around my body, sending my pulse racing.

He curled his tall frame over me, his hand cupping my neck, his breath at my ear. But this wasn't a loving embrace. It felt panicked. He felt tense under my palms where they were pressed to his stomach.

With his free hand he quickly undoes the button of his suit jacket. The panels fall open enclosing me in the darkened space against his chest. His fingers are inky black, shadow, like mist dances around his wrists as his palm lands on the wall just above my head.

His breath at my ear drew a shiver down my spine.

Because that's all his voice was; a whisper. Minding the supernatural hearing of those who still meandered down the main hall towards the room where King Croft held court.

"The rings on my fingers are worth more than enough to buy your way to the continent."

I paused, my heart immediately in my throat as I pulled back to peer at his face. And to my surprise, he let me.

"If this goes poorly," his eyes landed on my lips. "You take my ring. Any of them. As many as you can." His eyes darken as they climb my face and I'm already shaking my head. "And you run."

"Jason."

His hands glide up my neck to cup my face, silencing my protests.

"Promise me." His eyes are molten umber as I fall into them.

"If something happens to Henry or I, you get yourself to Amara. She is the only person in the south you can trust." He crowds me closer to the wall, his back like a shield as a few stragglers pass by. "She will get you to the continent."

Amara?

My eyes sweep the room searching out the shifter who is waiting by the door.

Standing right next to her is the Southern Lord. His toned arms are bare except for the gold cuffs around his bicep and the alternate forearm. His dark hair is pulled back into a crown of its own, gems and gold flecks catch the light as he turns to Amara with hushed words. Heavy Kohl lined eyes scan the room landing on Jason and I tucked into the little alcove.

It's the subtle nod he affords me that sends my heart tripping over itself. A king in his own right, acknowledging a deal that has clearly already been brokered.

He sets his arm across Amara's shoulders in a possessive gesture that doesn't make sense... until it does.

Not possessive, protective.

She crosses her arms as she rolls her eyes at whatever he had said. But as I watch her tuck herself deeper into his side, the resemblance clicks into place another piece of the puzzle.

Amara.

The little sister of shifter royalty. The family who owed Jason for not only their land, but their power.

My eyes round as I return them to Jason and he nods.

"You can trust her. No one else. Understand?"

I know he needs my response. And I know we don't have much time to waste, especially here in the hall, but my eyes flicker back to the pair.

She's waiting for me when I do, catching my eye from under Jason's arm. In a move so quick, I question whether I saw it, she blinks, that shuttered expression lifting for only an instant, before she dips into the room after her brother.

"I understand," I say, because I know he needs to hear it. I understood, now, who Amara was and why she was a safe choice to turn to if this all went to shit. Whether or not I meant to follow his instructions, was my business.

He nods, his thumb tracing the line of my lower lip.

"Now promise me."

I fight the urge to shake my head, to glare at him, or allow the fear to wet my eyes. So I nod, not trusting my lips with the lie.

He studies me for a moment more and I steel my spine, blinking once, then twice, to keep my eyes dry. Finally he nods, stepping back and smoothing the front of his shirt with his hand.

My eyes flash to Henry who has appeared behind him. I can see the fear hiding behind those moss green eyes. But he needs to focus tonight and I wouldn't be a distraction. I would play my part exactly as promised... but that was as far as my promises extended.

These males were my home. I wouldn't go searching out another should something take them from me tonight.

"Don't worry about me." I assure him with a smile I hope is believable. "I'm a pet in the north, I'm practically invisible."

He shifts, trying to mold his grimace into something softer and failing miserably.

"You couldn't blend in if you tried, Princess." His hand tightens on the pommel of his sword. "Behave," he warns, the timber of his words scraping across my very bones. "There are eyes on you tonight."

I swallow down the nausea that had been my constant companion all morning as my eyes land on the door at the end of the hallway. The idea that the three of us may not walk back out...knowing the likelihood of losing one of my males was so high that Jason had taken the time to set up alternate plans for my escape, had my fingers shaking as I smoothed my skirt.

"Deep breath, Love." Jason sets his hand to my back as he leads me through the door.

I watch him run black stained fingers over the top of Henry's hand where he grips the door holding it open for us. Their eyes meet for one loaded moment and there is not a mask between them. My instinct is to look away, to protect myself from the painful realization that I may be watching these males I love say goodbye to one another. But being a part of their lives meant not shying away from the danger that came along with it. The severe set of Henry's jaw is a balm to the raw wound in my chest.

Armed to the teeth, Henry is potent.

Silver hilts line his chest. Leather armor is strapped tight along his forearms and capping his broad shoulders. He's trimmed his beard tight against his jaw. His dark hair is pulled back into a neat bun on the back of his head. I never would have imagined Henry being someone who could blend in, but the guards positioned on the inside of the doors are dressed similarly. Similar leather armor climbs their arms, weaponry is sheathed along their chests, and their facial hair is kept short and neat.

Another mask.

Another layer of disguise that will allow him to blend in... disappear.

We pass under the ornate archway, Jason's mask slipping back into place with the blink of an eye.

King Croft sits at the head of the table closest to the door. The spires of his crown peaked above the chairs back as we approached the table. Jason settles comfortably into the seat opposite his father. The long table between us may as well be inches for how intensely my skin heats under the king's scrutiny. Especially when Jason pulls out the chair and ushers me into it. Henry, to my surprise, paused at the King's shoulder, positioning himself between the guards at the door and the rest of the table. Jason and I are the last to enter and therefore we catch the attention of quite a few at the table.

I peer around the room, my gaze once again landing on Amara. How had I missed it before? I never would have assumed the effervescent shifter who took the time to braid my hair and open her home had shared royal blood.

But in this room she wears a quiet confidence that speaks to regality. Unlike the parrot shifter beside her, an emissary of sorts with a stiff spine and sweat beaded brow, she reclines comfortably in her chair. The unassuming leader to the resistance operating right under the King's nose.

I knew I liked her.

Henry's voice booms through the room and the table falls silent.

I gasp.

The feeling of being caught off guard has my cheeks burning as my gaze locks on Henry in time to watch his eyes land on Jason. I blink, and blink again, peeling my eyes off my male and setting them on the table. Henry needs to be invisible. Which is why I need to catch as many unwanted eyes as possible.

Exhaling slowly, quietly, I run my finger around the rim of the glass before me.

This is not meant for humans. The wine smells like it costs more than my life... and I'm nearly certain it does, because as I tip it to my lips the vampire across from me glowers impressively.

It's almost as if he's had a millennium to practice.

I take another slow breath and pretend to swallow the wine that hadn't so much as crossed my lips.

I force my expression into a knowing smile, and the tremor that racks his form speaks to the millennium of discipline it probably requires to survive in a King's court. Because he looks like he's debating ripping the glass from my hand, or my arm from my body. The knowledge that he, in fact cannot, brightens my smile further.

When I think I've pushed the vampire to his limit, the king speaks, drawing the table's attention away from me.

Henry had reached around King Croft's shoulder to replace his cup. I watch him step back to his position behind the King's shoulder before handing off the empty cup to a female. She vanished quickly through the doors and back out into the hallway, but not before I recognized her. She had been in our home. I had seen her speaking with Geo at dinner just before he got himself speared to the wall.

"Thank you Henry," the king mutters, flicking his fingers, along with his thanks, over his shoulder.

I'm careful not to allow my gaze to settle on Amara or Henry any longer as I search the table for my next target. However, in my attempt to coast over Henry like he doesn't exist, I instead am caught by King Croft. Those steely gold ringed eyes are locked on my face.

Waiting.

And again I find myself standing before that open maw, the inherent danger of this male spiking my pulse.

There was nothing I could do about my heart, but I steadied my breathing and steeled my spine as I held his gaze. If I didn't want to be treated like a pet, I needed to stop acting like one. And here in this room, my role was no longer, pet.

"Son," he said, his eyes flickering to Jason. "I'd like to get started."

Jason, who had been standing to my right speaking with Yanik, a vampire I also recognized from the dinner he had hosted last year, shifted, seating himself on the arm of my chair. The move also conveniently tucked me behind him.

I swear my skin cooled several degrees hidden here in the shadow of Jason's large frame. The King's glare no longer branding me. It didn't, however, keep the fish shifter beside me from brandishing needle-like teeth. A wet hiss slipped from fluttering gills as silver eyes narrowed.

I level my gaze on their face. Breathing slowly. Evenly. Tucked against Jason I can be as brave as I need to be.

I raise my brow in challenge at the same time I feel Jason's gaze snap around mine. I watch the moment the shifter's spine straightens with awareness.

Jason's hand lands lightly against the side of my neck. A claim that I melt into. Shadow slips quietly from his fingers to dance along my collarbone and skim down my spine. The touch is like a cool breath against the heat bubbling under my skin.

In his own time, Jason returns his attention to his father.

"By all means," he motions to the table.

Others in attendance sit very still as they watch the standoff. Only their eyes shift back and forth from King to Prince, every now and again landing on me.

"Put your pet on the floor where she belongs."

His smile is a cool calculated thing.

"She is right where she belongs."

"Humans do not sit at my table," he snarls.

The room goes eerily still as Jason quirks a brow.

"I do."

The King's heavy fist met the table and I flinched. Jason's hand settles on my thigh with a little squeeze. I relax, if only for his benefit, weaving my fingers between his.

"I corrected that part of you when I claimed you as my son. My heir. Now act like it and do as you're told."

I think every ear in the room could hear the dinner sour in my stomach.

But Jason doesn't shrink from his father or his cutting words. Instead, his lips lift as black stained fingertips trace the rim of his whiskey glass. He takes his time raising his eyes to the King. And when he does, they're perfectly calm. His voice is almost bored, indifferent, as he continues.

"And as your heir am I not expected to do what is best for the Royal City and her people? To correct a system that no longer serves us."

"Oh they serve us," a vampire to my right sneers, interrupting the standoff.

If it wasn't for the thud of his head, I wouldn't have so much as torn my eyes from the two royals facing off. But my eyes, along with many others in the room, fall to the male who is pitched forward, his head flat against the smooth wood.

His neck bent at an impossible angle.

Eyes open, red-ringed, and unseeing.

Smoke and shadow pulse around the male's neck, dark veins climbing his throat and over his jaw.

I still, my eyes jumping to Jason's hands that rests lax over the top of his glass.

He hadn't moved. But...

My eyes jump to King croft who glowers at the dead male. His hand held before him reclaims the shadows that snake from around the male's throat, across the table, and back to him encircling his wrist.

"I am speaking with my son," he seethed, his eyes coasting across the table. "Anyone else care to interrupt?"

A king willing to dole out death without a second thought.

Simply to set an example.

Because no matter who that male had been, whatever purpose he served here at the kings table, his life had been reduced to a warning.

Henry's eyes were cold, bored, as he flickered his gaze over the male. My mind reached for a word to describe how he looked in this moment and came up short.

Disconnected?

I knew he was as alert as the others sitting stalk-still around the table, but my male seemed far away.

This was Henry the royal guard.

All efficient brutality.

However, that gaze faltered when it landed on Jason beside me who had done nothing to shield himself from the King's wrath.

King Croft's gaze landed back on Jason.

"You are expected to do as you're told. *For once,*" he growled baring his teeth.

Do you ever do as you're told?

Jason's question rang in my ears. The way his eyes glittered when I toed that line between disobedience and challenge. My heart tugged as another little piece of the puzzle slotted into place. My thumb swept over his hand. Maybe it was our human nature, or maybe just our unwillingness to cave that we had recognized in each other. Loved. That disobedience mirrored in each other, soul deep.

I pulled my gaze across his profile.

"Inferior beings have no place at my table. This will not happen again. I will not allow it. Witches sat at this table not long ago and look at the mess I was left to clean up."

Jason coughed a laugh.

"Is that what we're calling what you did?"

"I secured our bloodline. One, may I remind you, you now benefit from."

"The death of that coven burned the bridge between shifters and vampires, and condemned the humans to lifetimes of servitude and abuse."

The King leaned forward, that hand wreathed in shadow, pointing one taloned claw at my chest. Jason's body responded in kind, as his muscles coiled, tensing beside me.

"The responsibility of whose demise rests solely in the hands of my brother."

Hartley.

The King's smile was slow. "When he chose them over our kingdom," he jeered.

"He chose *her*." Jason growled.

He chose her.

Caroline.

Hartley had told me he had abdicated to marry Caroline. And that the love he had for her had not only been enough to outshine a kingdom, but it had prevailed for decades, centuries... however old these males were.

Caroline, I realized, not only hung over these males here, but very much held a presence throughout our house. I remember stepping into the garden and being able to feel the magic of the space. And it wasn't just the serenity or the beauty of the garden, but it was her.

Her lasting imprint.

Her magic.

Her books still resting on the top shelf in the kitchen as if waiting for her to sweep in from the garden to prepare a meal speckled with soil.

"And she chose death!" King Croft bellowed.

Jason didn't so much as flinch, but Henry looked like he was trying to swallow a mouth full of thorns.

"Night after night, I swallowed her lies, and that brew... and when the time came to face the consequences of the deal she sullied, she tried to pit my brother against me." Venom was pouring from his lips. "I gave her a choice and she chose to die with her coven."

Carolines coven had been the coven Henry had told me about. The coven who was responsible for the magic that allowed King Croft to create his children.

A shiver raked down my spine. The letters sprawled across his desk... the handwriting had been familiar, but I thought it was simply the frequency with which I studied it... but it matched the handwriting in Caroline's book.

It was her magic that Link and Jason were trying to recreate to solidify the treaty. The flowers we had grown, the maps he studied, they had been hers. It had all been hers.

Jason coiled, slowly sitting forward as he spoke.

"You wanted her to bear you another child after you had decimated her coven. What choice is there in that?"

My heart raced in my chest as I lifted my eyes to the king. She'd chosen death under impossible circumstances.

He waved off the implication like it was a fly circling his cup.

"Her coven promised me heirs and mine were gone." He said pensively, collapsing back against his chair.

This conversation was hurtling towards a destination I feared would drag Henry back into the spotlight. Jason seemed to pick up on the same realization as he smiled. A sharp, slow, toothy grin as he lifted our joined hands from his lap and pressed a kiss to my knuckles.

His breath coasts across my skin.

"And what of my heirs?" His eyes flickered over the peaks of his knuckles to the far end of the table.

My heart sputtered as I fought the urge to whip my face around to his. Instead, my eyes remained glued to the King's.

"You cannot sire," He warned the bronzed skin of his jaw fluttering as he clenched his teeth with no less force than would be needed to crush my bones between them. "I will not allow history to repeat itself. You, son, do not have a choice. She," he flicked a clawed finger in my direction and for the first time I flinched. "Is not an option."

The smile that stretched across his face was as unsettling as it was cold. I stole a glance at Henry for only an instant and he was waiting for me. His eyes wider than what was casual and filled with a rage I could feel ebbing across the table.

I returned my gaze to the King, my heart beating unevenly in my chest. Slowly Jason lowered our joined hands to his lap where I felt him work the first ring from his finger. My hand clasped around his, holding him still.

Our gazes collided for the briefest of moments, but it stole my breath.

Was this it?

Did he think something was wrong?

Would the next twitch of the King's finger, in fact, end my life or his?

King Croft snorts and Jason's head snaps back to meet his.

"I have no problem with you fucking your pet. That's what they're for." His eyes hardened and I reached through the slit of my skirt to palm the blade holstered against my thigh. "But that is *all* they're good for." I counted down slowly in my head as I slipped the blade free from its sheath. "You will not parade this human around my court like a princess and-

King Croft flung taloned fingers open, but where the shadow should have obeyed, it simply pooled below his hand against the table.

His eyes flared, dropping to his cup, but in a flash of steel Henry dragged the blade across the King's throat.

A beat later the two guards manning the doors dropped to the floor, dark veins wringing their necks.

Chapter Thirty-Five

The room erupts, but Jason halts them with a snap of his fingers. In the blink of an eye the room fills with smoke and shadow. And when it clears, the dignitaries are frozen, fear perfuming the room.

That power Jason kept leashed, ebbing from him as he smoothed his tie with black-tipped fingers. All that power that King Croft shared with Jason, now belonged solely to the male beside me.

And he wore it well.

The gold flecks iridescent against his umber iris, were now complemented by a heavy gold ring that glowed as his pupils bloomed. Inky black bled across his eyes, dark veins branched across his cheekbones. That dark magic pulsing just under his skin.

Those eyes traveled the room, so silent, I wondered how many of the other beings were daring to even breathe, before they landed on me.

I just looked my fill, reveling in him.

I lifted our still joined hands to my lips to place a kiss to his knuckles, and as I released him, I tucked that ring tighter into his palm.

His face remained frozen as I smiled at him and resheathed my blade. On shaking knees I rose from my seat, confidence a flimsy cape over my shoulders. I could feel their eyes on me, but focused on the only two pairs that mattered.

The two I crossed between now as I made my way from one end of the table to the other.

Henry stood, blade still in hand, as I arrived before him. It took him only a moment to catch on as I tugged the King's corpse from his seat at the head of the table. Henry then held the chair out for Jason who settled himself into it like he was made for it.

And I suppose he was.

This male who had worked tirelessly to protect the humans, his people. To build alliances and trust between species, and stand toe to toe with a king most others hadn't dared breathe before.

With a breath of his own and a devil-like smile, he casts his gaze across the table.

"Vampires were once men," he begins, the timber of his voice so low it seemed to rumble straight through my bones. "Shifters were born to human women. These are our origins, our mothers. At our core, we are the same." His elbow rested on the table, hand raised before him, as he admired the talon-tipped claws that appeared.

"We are *not* the same," the shifter to my right groused.

Jason's attention snapped to the male, his gaze searing. The rest of his words dying on his lips as he pressed deeper into his chair as if drawn up by fear instead of Jason's shadows.

"We owe our very existence to them." His eyes scanned the table. "Or should we feed upon you instead. A lower species. A lower class."

The male was silent. As was the rest of the room.

"I thought not."

His eyes touched on mine.

"I was human. The woman who will carry your future heir is human. And you will kneel at her feet just as you kneel at mine."

There was a gasp from somewhere in the room, but I couldn't tear my eyes from his face. When they slid to mine, I drew forward and his eyes softened.

He spoke his next words as if only for me.

"The trade will end."

My lips parted as my eyes stung and he took the time to run a night-black thumb under my eye, catching the moisture running down my cheek.

Because he could.

Because he wanted to.

His eyes snapped across the table, and I followed, nerves prickling my skin. The anxiety of attack had still not quite passed.

The pet to the right of the sniveling lord across from me rose slowly to his feet. Henry's eyes tracked him as he crossed the room towards Jason and I.

"If you free me, I will kneel before you alone," he vowed.

If the flush on the pet's cheeks were any indication, his heart was probably hammering, but he stood tall. His chest rose and fell rapidly as the shadow that wreathed Jason's wrist traveled around the tanned skin of the man's neck. I expected him to step away, to shake under the contact, but he didn't. He stood firm, his gaze, while wide, remained locked on Jason.

Pride swelled for this man I didn't even know.

With a snap of metal, the collar and shadows fell away, one clattering to the ground, the other returning to dance along Jason's fingers.

Without missing a beat he dropped to his knee, one fist knocking against his chest as he bowed. The blood of the dead king soaked his pants as he swore his allegiance.

"Thank you." He clapped his fist to his chest again, his voice breaking "My king."

Amara nods as Link and her brother stand.

"Each human in our household will be offered their freedom. If terms can be met, we can agree to allow passage of unowned or freed pets across our territory."

Negotiations run long into the evening. The shifters and vampires barely noting the passing of time as they bicker, and protest, and argue, and reform the future of our kinds.

I, however, am not as impervious. My stomach rumbles its complaints as I do my best to sit with my back straight like a royal would be expected to. But Jason runs his fingers down my back, his gaze flickering to mine as I shift.

Umber and gold soften.

"You're hungry."

His voice is low, chin tucked into my hair.

"I'm ok," I breathe, straightening my skirt and pulling away.

He doesn't skip a beat before catching my chin. As if there isn't a debate happening at the table. His table. He studies me, taking his time before my stomach airs her complaints once more.

I see the spark behind his eyes that speaks to a stubborn male who'd undoubtedly pause negotiations to feed me. Or worse, ask Henry to fetch me food leaving him the choice of disobeying his new king, or leaving him unprotected. Neither was an option I wanted Henry to choose between.

Not when I was very capable of feeding myself.

I lean in, placing a quick kiss to his lips.

"You know where to find me," I smile, standing from my chair.

The room goes silent and I freeze my fingers set against the cool surface of the table, my elbows pause, and every eye in the room lands on me.

Jason reclines in his chair, those thighs spreading ever so slightly as he growls fingers slipping into long black talons that click delicately against each other.

"Bow," Jason snarls, the sound lighting up my core.

I hold my breath as every neck bends. Shifters and vampires alike bow their hands as I stand.

I dip behind the throne Jason fills and reach for Henry. His fingers close around mine as they slip through one another and I cannot help the smile I wear as I dip past the two dead guards and into the hallway in search of chocolate.

The desert table appeared like an oasis in the desert. At first glance, the nausea and nerves settle a degree and I blow out the breath I'd been holding. My eyes fill with tears as I fill my plate with treats and settle on the steps of the sprawling back courtyard.

The evening air was turning a bit chilly as the ocean breathed her salty breath across my face. Nightblooming jasmine perfumed the breeze from where it climbed the trellis bracketing the stairs. The space was dark, the sun long set, but floating globes of witch fire illuminated the stone path I assumed led to the sandy shore I could hear those waves lapping at.

It seemed almost perverse how beautiful these estates were that housed monsters and witnessed the cruelty they doled out.

But that was changing.

I took a fuller breath, the skirts of my dress billowing out around me as I stood.

Maybe it was that sense of gratitude that made me overconfident, but as I collected my plate to refill it with desserts, I stopped as I passed a woman about my age. She was cleaning crystal cups to a shine humming a sweet tune. I hesitated on the other end of the long dessert table.

She froze as I approached.

The stiffening of her back and the quieting of her song at my footfalls strengthened my resolve to speak to her. Her head turned slowly, the gold collar she wore peeking out from under her hair.

Maybe it was my lack of a collar. Or maybe it was just the fact that I had clearly been eating their food.

Food reserved for their kind.

For the now dead king.

I smiled ready to offer to undo her collar and share the news when something hard landed across the back of my head.

Her eyes went wide as my vision went black.

Chapter Thirty-Six

Awareness isn't gentle as it greets me. My wrists are bound tightly in front of me. There is material stuffed into my mouth and secured at the back of my head, which pounds as the dark trees swirl around me.

I heave around the gag.

My mouth and lips are dry, cheeks damp, as I shift to sit against the tree I'm laid against. But moving causes my vision to swim, the night sky like churning midnight waves.

I pitch forward using bound hands to yank the gag from my mouth in time to forfeit my dessert. His boots, soles darkened with what I tell myself is mud, appear in my line of vision. I don't know if it's fear or the scent of him that turns my stomach, but his chuckle grates down my spine as I spit into the muddied forest floor.

Le squats down before me, a crooked grin giving way to tobacco scented breath.

"Hello girl."

His voice carries with it an onslaught of memories I had tucked tightly into that little box in the back of my mind. But the strike to the head must have knocked it open, because every nightmare inducing detail comes spilling out. My heart sputters in my chest and tears prick my eyes as I level them on the male before me. That gut wrenching fear crawls up my spine like a spider.

Despite all the time I'd spent preparing myself for this very instance, coming face to face with Le, leaves me immobile. He's too close and I feel too prone tied before him, with my head pounding and vision still not quite steady,

The realization that I had no idea where we were or how long I'd been unconscious, had dread curling up violently through my stomach. I swallowed thickly and he smiled in that predatory way that had taken so many months to stop seeing when I closed my eyes.

But despite everything I was alive. He'd kept me alive when he so easily could have killed me. Which hopefully meant he had other plans. Plans that revolved around me remaining alive.

At least for now.

He sat back on his heels, his fingers tugging at the long hem of my dress where it laid soiled on the ground.

"Did you miss me?" he asks, his fingers grazing my ankle.

With a shaky breath, I bolt myself to the ground refusing to react to his touch as I huff a non response. Angering him is the last thing I need to do right now. But appeasing this monster makes my chest ache.

But my males had taught me better.

They had taught me to be brave, but patient.

I needed to be calculated in my vengeance.

The thought almost made me smile thinking of Jason. He'd thought me vengeful... now I had an opportunity to show him how right he was.

And they would be looking for me.

Le clearly had his plans. Now I needed my own. I needed a plan. I needed to think.

Henry had once made me promise that should anything ever happen, I'd fight like hell until he could reach me. I think at the time he'd meant reaching me from across a room during a fight, but nonetheless that was what I was going to do.

Henry would find me.

I knew, no matter what my males would reach me.

I just had to buy them time.

And if I didn't draw attention to the halter on my thigh, maybe I'd even have an opportunity to poke a few holes in this monster of mine.

Le grins like he's just heard my thoughts and reaches forward to tuck a curl behind my ear. I bite the inside of my cheek to keep still, but cannot help the way I flinch as his skin grazes mine. His grin sharpens in response. A moment later a blade glints against the skin of my neck just above my clavicle. A blade whose edge he scrapes up the column of my throat, trailing the tip along my cheekbone.

I bite down harder on my cheek to keep my lips from quivering. The little seeds of my plan, and those wisps of confidence I was tugging on to pull myself together, floating away on the breeze as I recognized the blade in his hand.

My blade.

The one Henry slipped into my holster before we left.

He had *my* blade.

My heart races and I blink away the tears stinging my eyes, fear potent and distracting as Le cocks his head to the side. The open socket of his eye, the one Jason had buried a knife in on the train, draws my gaze and he tracks the motion.

That sneer he wears falters before it falls and I wonder for a moment if the male before me actually has feelings to be hurt. He latches onto the bandana hanging limply around my neck and I hold my breath as he pauses. His fingers tighten, that smile budding at the corner of his lips before he gives his head a little shake and unties me.

"Are you going to behave yourself?" he asks, voice smarmy as he secures the bandana over his eye.

I nod, quietly fighting back the revulsion, just in case, and send a fervent prayer that he hadn't been wearing that very bandana to cover his wound before stuffing it into my mouth.

He couldn't have... right?

The smell of the material perfumed my mind as I remembered the taste of it in the back of my throat when I woke.

The gag that followed had the tears I'd been fighting back leaking over my cheeks, but it also had Le taking a measured step back. He scowled and I used bound hands to dry my face.

Thankfully when he steps back into my space grumbling under his breath, it's to undo the rope bound tightly around my wrists. Once freed, I scrub at my sore skin wondering again just how long I'd been tied. How much time had already passed?

What direction had we traveled ... and how far?

He frowns, but it's exaggerated. Playful.

"I like a little fight." He runs the pad of his finger along my cheek. "The cat and mouse game we've been playing. You knew what you were doing."

My eyes rounded with surprise. He thought *I* was toying with *him*?

"You wanted me to see you up there in that scrap of a dress."

No.

I shook my head before I could think better of it.

"Yes," he snarls.

I freeze and his hand grips my chin firmly.

"Yes." He nods as if reassuring himself. "You wanted me to see you. To chase you. And now girl, I've caught you again." He smiles as he claps his hand against my cheek in a rough pat.

"I win."

Tobacco scented breath fans across my cheek as I tuck away from him.

My pulse pounds as I track his movements from the corner of my eye. He waves my blade over my chest before tucking it into his boot. "You'll make me some coin and we'll start again," he says, dusting his hands on the legs of his pants as he stands.

"Again and again and again," he rolls his wrist, finger extended to trace circles in the air.

"You found me a worthy foe. A good challenge they were. They made me work hard to get you back." He tips his head in that predatory way vampires seem to have mastered. "But they weren't good enough," he smiles.

"You'll do better next time."

He paces away and I scan the camp looking for any familiar faces. It's only when I find the camp empty, that I remember Jason had killed the majority of his original party. It seemed Le now operated solo. It was just the two of us tucked into a little clearing. A bedroll and a pack rested on his side of the fire. A bottle of amber liquid glinted against the flames.

My head ached where he had struck me and I reached back gently rubbing the bump under my hair.

My fingers knock loose some leaves and debris, but come away clean. No blood. On one hand that kept me safer from Le and his impulses, but I also knew my scent was stronger if I'd been bleeding.

Easier to track.

But spilling any now, was out of the question.

So I needed a new plan.

Any plan.

My stomach growls and I rub at it absentmindedly.

Step one, find something to eat. Step two, find-

He snags me by the hair, his fingers knotting tightly against my skull as he lifts me onto my knees.

I forgot how fast he was. My males never zipped around me like this, but now I remembered why it had been so hard to peel my eyes off of Jason when we first met. I was too afraid to let him out of my sight. It had become habit to quietly, yet constantly, track Le in and around camp.

"Thinking about running again, girl?"

Pain sparks bright especially against the already sore skin on the back of my head.

"I was only thinking about food," I gasp, reaching up to brace myself against his wrists. It alleviates the pressure on my scalp but the pain still wets my eyes as I grind my teeth against it.

He studies me intently before he huffs, alcohol accenting his breath as it fans across my face.

"If you've moved even an inch from this spot when I return, I'll string you up by all this pretty hair."

I blink my consent since nodding is out of the question and he vanishes dropping me into the dirt. My arms shake as I collapse onto my hands and knees two harsh sobs wracking my body. Tears patter against the soil below me.

I wrap my arms around myself, giving into the fear now that I am finally alone and let my body catch up. Because once he walked back into camp, I needed to have my wits about me. I needed to be back in control. But first I needed to cry.

So I did.

And then with heaving breaths I dried my cheeks and brushed my fingers through my hair, braiding it down my back. Readying myself. Because I was going to lure a vampire into a trap of my own.

When Le returned I was seated where he left me, eyes ringed red and swollen, looking every bit the helpless victim he saw me as, but knowing I had collected myself.

Calmed the panic.

Numbed the fear.

He drops a rabbit before me, its head twisted and bent at an ugly angle. It turned my stomach needlessly. I'd seen countless dead rabbits, hunted many myself, but this one laid in the dirt before me had nausea creeping back up my throat. I think it only bothered me because it was yet another creature mangled by Le's hands.

I eyed it where it laid before casting my gaze into the trees. I tipped my chin up following a particularly tall pine. I swallowed, feeling his gaze follow the motion before I turned back to him.

"What now?" he snapped, his eyes not quite focused on mine.

"I..." I made sure to look nervous, cautious, scared. "I have no way to prep it." My eyes tipped towards the fire and back to the little rabbit before me.

Grumbling something under his breath, he drops a blade before me. Not mine, but it certainly looked sharp enough to get the job done. The hilt is crusted in emeralds that matched the oversized stone in the pommel. My hand extends, but before I can reach for it, he has one hand locked to my wrist the other tight against my throat.

But this time I lean into the pressure against my throat, forcing tears to prick my eyes as adrenaline rockets through me. Breath catches in my lungs with a wheeze. The sound has a smile pulling at his lips as he tips his head appraising me slowly.

I swallow, my throat bobbing under his grip, drawing his attention. His eyes drop to his hand, and I watch his pupils bloom as he shifts, his fingers spasming against my skin.

"This is not part of our game girl," he warns. "You let those males use you just to make me work harder. I heard that clock ticking," he sneered, dragging hungry eyes over me. "But now you're mine again, and I will do with you as I please. So..."

His gaze lands on the blade.

"Do something stupid and we will spend the evening testing just how pretty you still need to be to fetch a price."

Fear and rage paint my face ruddy as he chuckles. But the rage at his insinuations...the rage and hurt at just how he knew the details of our lives, helped bolster my determination. I grip his wrists, my nails biting into his skin. The pressure in my cheeks and behind my eyes continues to build as he strangles me.

"Oh and I assure you girl." His smile turns my stomach. "It's a much lower bar than you'd ever guess. I *know*. I know that line. I found it last time."

Last time.

Last time

He'd done this before.

"But don't you worry. We have a long way to go before we reach it. You're much prettier than the last. You'll last much longer."

No.

I couldn't think about that.

I wouldn't.

I'd been told over and over just how breakable I was, but my males had taught me otherwise. My males had proven otherwise.

I could do this.

Even if it seemed unlikely he'd act on these threats after all this effort to bring me to market again, I was towing a very delicate line. It was too bad I intended to lower my own value with this reckless plan.

He grinned; his eyes pit black as his pupils swallowed up his iris. I watched his lips shifting as canines lengthened below.

"I chose well this time."

Air was becoming a limited resource, so it was now or never. So, I ground my molars hard, forcing the consequences from my mind and committed to my plan.

I pushed the rest of the air from my lungs with a whine, making sure to wriggle and tug against his grasp. At the same time, I scraped my nails across his hand making sure the nail of my forefinger scraped a long line across my own throat. And as my vision darkened at the edges, I watched the moment he scented the blood in the air.

Watched him take me in where I hung from his hands, painted like prey.

His lips pulled back on a simmering snarl, and I knew, this time, I had won. But in the instant before he moved. Fear trickled down my spine. Thankfully he didn't make me wait long before taking the bait. He snapped forward latching onto my throat and digging those canines deep into my skin.

I opened my mouth but had no air for the scream rattling through my mind. No ability to thrash as the urge to fight overcomes me because my body was failing.

I promised Henry I'd fight to stay alive long enough for him to reach me. But right now fighting meant surrendering. Surrendering to the pain that flared bright under my skin and behind my ribs. Remaining still enough to ensure he didn't tear those teeth from my skin in a way I wouldn't survive.

He takes three strong pulls before his grip loosens and air floods my lungs. Two more and he pulls free, dropping me back to the ground as he steps back to wipe at his mouth.

I gulp down air, collapsing back onto shaking arms and clap my hand to the broken skin of my neck.

He smiles, licking his lips as his eyes cool.

"Not as good as I would've expected after all that effort," he gripes.

I don't move until he returns to his bottle collapsing against a wide trunk opposite of the flames, sated. I pull my hand from my neck and it comes away scarlet. I place that hand into the debris below me and cup the other over my neck as I watch him a moment more.

Realizing he is happily settled in with his bottle and my blood, I shuffle the leaves in my hand, coating them as thoroughly as possible before stuffing them into the sheath at my thigh. I repeat this over and over as the bleeding stems, coating as many leaves as I can. And when the sheath wont hold any more, I stuff them under my shirt and between the plates of my braid.

As blood grows sticky against my fingers I rise to collect my rabbit, but not before I scoop a little handful of leaves that I crumple quietly in my palms. As I stand, I brush my hands free of the leaves aiming for what I hoped would look like an innocent dusting of leaves and not the spreading of my scent.

Ideally, the alcohol dimmed his senses enough to allow the uptick in my scent across camp to go unnoticed.

Or at least unpunished.

I watch him drink himself into a fitful sort of rest as I skin and quarter the rabbit.

Nausea sweeps over me as the scent of raw meat fills my nose. It's a scent I've never been quite fond of, but it's always been so mild, so necessary that I never paid it any mind. Now though, I find myself sitting back on my heels, pulling in long settling breaths of fresh air, and swallowing down bile as it threatens to climb my throat. I hadn't eaten anything at the King's court before that should have upset my stomach like this. Food poisoning was something I was familiar with and the stomach pain I knew accompanied the plight was noticeably missing. Growing up with very little to eat, meant we ate much of what we shouldn't, hoping the risk was worth a full belly.

It often wasn't.

But this was different.

I wiped sweat from my brow with the back of my hand as my stomach turned with unease. I had assigned the nausea to nerves these past few days as tension mounted leading up to the evening at King Croft's court. But maybe I was due my cycle.

I tried to think back to my last cycle while ignoring just how terribly poor the timing would be for it to start right now.

My head pounded along with my heart as I counted backwards. My cycles had grown more regular, and though they weren't wholly reliable...I was late.

Nearly a week late.

I stared at the bloodied stone blinking over and over as if my vision would clear and a different answer would appear before me.

Impossible.

It had to be impossible.

I'd spent time around the flowers we'd planted and harvested, but nothing more. I hadn't ingested anything that would, according to Jason and Link, allow me to find myself pregnant.

And alone.

With Le.

My heart sputtered in my chest as panic erupted, shaking my fingers as my eyes flickered to the vampire who was thankfully none the wiser where he sat reclined against a fat truck, bottle limp in his lap.

I clapped my hands over my mouth as I keened curling over myself to hide the sound.

I needed my males.

It should be impossible.

I had to be wrong.

But if I wasn't... if Le could hear the bile climbing my throat, how long would it be before he could hear the little heartbeat in my belly?

I swallowed a sob that would certainly wake the sleeping vampire across camp and wiped at my cheeks with the back of my hand, careful not to smear the rabbit's stench anywhere near my face. Tears stung my eyes as I reached for the rabbit. The familiar motions of skinning and quartering helped settle the shaking in my fingers but did nothing for my nerves.

They would find me.

They would.

I just needed to stay alive until they could reach me... us.

I could do that.

I swallowed, setting the rabbits femur bones aside, an idea taking root as I did. They were just about the right length. I slid the bones against the far side of the stone I was using to prep the rabbit, intending to come back to them this evening once Le drank himself into a stupor. Every now and again the vampire stirred. His head would whip around to glare at me through bleary eyes, before he grinned unnervingly and tipped that bottle back to his lips.

So, as I waited, I cooked the rabbit over the fire, hoping the little pops and snaps of the wood would mask the beating of the new little heart.

I didn't understand how this could have happened. If Jason and Link had been wrong, and it wasn't the flowers that Caroline's coven had used to allow for pregnancy, then what? How could they have been wrong when they had spent decades searching for an answer, narrowing it down to these damn flowers... and just as long searching for a map to lead them to it.

They had spent so long searching.

My stomach tumbles.

Searching.

All those pages scattered across Jason's desk dance before my eyes. All the notations, imagery, maps, lore, gossip. Every little detail he obsessed over and yet, in his pantry laid a book, untouched.

A book dedicated to 'the seeker'.

Filled with recipes and growing techniques, brewing instructions and the like. It had been built based on her very own garden boxes. Caroline herself probably carried to and fro from garden to kitchen testing and perfecting... and disguising.

Was she just continuing the work or her coven, or... had she been planning to start a family of her own?

A family with Hartley. My heart broke at the thought, fresh tears flooding my cheeks. Oh, Hartley.

Which tea had it been?

Why did it work?

How had she done it?

How had I?

I counted the days and then counted again.

I could, very well, be pregnant. I released a shallow breath flickering my gaze across camp relieved to find Le, jaw slack, head lolled to the side as he slept. I watched him as I forced down bites of rabbit that turned my stomach. Going without wasn't an option. Not when I had monsters to kill.

Soon I would allow myself to sleep like Le currently was, but before I could, I had one more task to complete. I glanced over at the stone hiding my little treasure and when I glanced back at Le, he was gone.

He appeared before me that, grin wild, as he swayed on his feet.

Fuck.

I tried to keep my gaze steady, but he must have seen more than I realized, because his eyes trailed to the big stone. A smirk stretching the scar across his brow as they rose. He collected my wrists, binding them tightly.

He nodded once taking in my now bound wrists before he raised his hand in the limited space between us. His finger knocked back and forth as he tsked his tongue.

"If I don't find you right here in the morning, then when I do, I will break your legs over that stone."

I nodded blinking up at him as the shock of his appearance sent my pulse skittering. I hoped its wild beating would hide the presence of the little second one, but now I couldn't be sure. So as he studied me, I tapped my fingers against my thighs hoping the quiet rhythm would mask the sound.

"You're fun, girl." His eyes grew bleary, the liquor on his breath stinging mine. "Maybe I'll just keep you for myself." He dragged his eyes over my face as fear once again trickled into my bloodstream.

He must have thought better of his plan, because with a kiss of his teeth, he shoved me away. I scuttled back against the very stone he'd threatened me with dragging the two femur bones under my skirt as I did.

Unceremoniously, he collapsed against the trunk across camp, bottle in hand. I watched his eyes close and his breaths even out as I tucked all my fear into that little box and sealed it shut. Every time Le tossed in his sleep, that lid rattled in protest, but I kept it closed. I needed a clear head to think. And I needed to think if I was going to survive long enough for my males to find me.

By the time the sky was staining pink with the sunrise, I had sharpened the two femurs into points I hoped were sharp enough to kill.

I took time hiding them in my skirts before curling around the stone and closing my eyes.

Chapter Thirty-Seven

As we traveled through the morning and afternoon, I took every opportunity to slip my fingers into my skirt and crumble the leaves coated in my dried blood. Making sure to step soundly into the patches of dried brush to hide the sounds of the leaves I dropped in my wake. I also made sure to linger here and there using a trunk for balance to step over a root. But not before licking the pads of my finger to stamp against the bark or pulling a hair free, if not from my shoulder, then my scalp itself hoping to leave a trail for my males to follow.

Le tossed a look over his shoulder and I froze, fingers pressed against the bark of the tree I was marking.

I made a show of stepping cautiously over the root before me.

"We're close," he cooed, excitement bubbling in his tone.

His game was beginning again.

I nodded as he dragged his eyes over me before turning around with a flourish and stomping off into the giant ferns.

We were close.

But to what?

I don't know why I expected to be brought back to the High City. I was banking on him presenting me at the doors of Acropolis hoping to find my males in the crowd, but we seemed to be traveling deeper into a heavily wooded area of the south.

I had no idea where we were, but the sounds that started echoing over the darkening trees did nothing to soothe my worries.

I'd taken to drumming my fingers against my folded arms or thighs as I walked to hide the little heartbeat that could give us away, still pausing here or there, catching a tree trunk or dragging nervous fingers through my hair to free a strand or two.

That was how he caught me when I turned the bend. I had been following a few paces behind him, and hadn't been expecting to nearly run right into him where he lounged against the wide trunk, waiting for me.

"You don't need to pretty up for this place girl," he chuckled darkly and my stomach sank.

Wails echoed in the distance marred with the thundering beat of drums. The sound rattled the little box where I had stuffed all that fear.

The wails grow louder as we approach the edge of camp. My heart beats heavily against my ribs as Le grips me by the arm towing me down a dirt lined street. Flame bobbed along woven rope that line the road a foot or two above our heads. And on either side of the path are iron cages. Some empty... some not.

Pets decorate the street allowing the shifters who drift past them to window shop. My breath is hard to find as I stumble along behind him. His grip is bruising and I'm almost grateful for it as it serves as a distraction for the bile climbing my throat.

"Don't," he hisses the warning as if it can hear the vomit threatening to choke me.

I glance up at him and he snarls. "You will fetch me a price worth having or I will keep you for myself until we find another market."

Before the lid on that box can burst open, he tosses me into an iron cage just off the main path and lights the little flame above the cell door.

This is certainly not Acropolis.

Unease churned as I drummed my fingers against the iron bars of the cage. There were no guards, only those looking to shop. Shifters and vampires alike strolled up and down the path, their boots crushing dried debris that swept this way and that in the breeze.

I'd emptied the contents of my pocket about a quarter mile from camp knowing that smelling so strongly of spilled blood would only paint a target on my back. Especially after the warning Le had issued.

And I was grateful I had, when I watched a large vampire pull bored eyes over me before turning to the woman in the cage across the path. He strode to her, extinguishing the flame above her door, before baring his teeth as he yanked it open.

"Run."

She shook her head, her back pressed tightly to the bars behind her.

In the blink of an eye he was behind her, his hand fisting her bright red hair, craning her neck back painfully as he grinned.

"Run, or I'll kill you where you cower."

She took off for the darkening trees and he started counting, his voice carrying ominously.

"Five."

"Four."

"Three."

He stood from where he had crouched behind the bars of her now empty cage, brushing his palms against his pant legs.

"Two." His voice shot straight through my chest.

And with a snarl, he disappeared in the direction she'd fled.

I scooted closer to the center of the cage, my back feeling exposed.

The wails pitched high, and I strained to keep my eyes open as I lowered myself to the ground sitting against the cold damp soil. There wasn't enough safety here to close my eyes, even as the camp grew so dark the tents and trees were only pinpricks of light, but as I watched the human in the cage just two spaces down from me his gaze horror struck as shadows climbed his body, I knew I'd been wrong. This wasn't night settling on camp.

This was his magic hunting for me.

They were close...

Close enough for me to dip my fingers into the inky blackness that swirled around the bars of my cage. The shadows ebbed, their cool tendrils climbing my forearm, and in my mind, I picture his hands wrapping around me instead. He was close and the realization drew a sob from my lips as I turned my hand over. The shadow pooled in my palm. A bead of shadow remained there as the rest retreated slowly, sinking back into the forest like a tide being pulled back out to sea.

I drew my thumb across its misty surface like I had once watched Jason do. It was cool on the surface, but as I closed my fingers around it, it warmed like his touch.

"Good news girl," Le barks, having materialized before the cage door.

I gasp, closing my fingers tightly around the little shadow.

"You've attracted a buyer."

He swings the door open pulling me from the cage with one hard tug.

The little shadow pulses against my palm and hope swells that it's Jason here to claim me, again.

But as Le's smile stretches, my stomach sours and a shifter appears behind him. The shifter is a small male. Goat maybe. His facial hair, white blonde, with tufts poking out from around two spiraling horns atop his head. His lower jaw juts out as he smiles, hooved feet disturbing the brush as he leans in taking a closer look.

Le latches onto the back of my dress as he turns me, his other hand catching my jaw. I grind my teeth as I drum my fingers against my thigh.

The shifter steps back with a frown.

"I don't know..." he shakes his head. "*This* was a prize once sold in Acropolis," he scoffs.

Ouch.

I almost smile, but before this little victory can take root, Le claps him on the back of the shoulder.

"She's worth the price." He peeks over his shoulder like he's checking for onlookers down the fairly quiet path. "Why don't you take her for a spin."

No.

Those words echo through my mind falling like a stone through my stomach. Breath whooshes from my lungs as my heart trips over itself.

"You don't like her, we'll work out another deal. I need to make sure you are in fact the right *buyer.*"

The deranged asshole winks at me like we're in this together, before settling his gaze on the shifter, sizing him up where he stood. Unknowingly stepping into this little game Le has crafted.

I needed more time.

They were close. I knew they were. The shadow pulsed against my palm and I took that as confirmation. I just needed to stall a bit longer. I could do that. I had promised that I would.

"Deal," the goat shifter grins.

"Good," Le releases me. "Find me when you're finished if we need to rework her price, but I think you'll find you're quite happy with your new pet."

They exchange coin and my freshly drafted ownership papers, and I watch as the shifter tucks them into his front pocket.

After a rough tug, I'm following the shifter as he drags me through the flaps of a nearby tent.

I stumble forward into the center of the canvas tent. There isn't much here, just a cot and a woven rug. A little rickety chair sits towards the far end of the tent.

"This won't do." He kisses his teeth, eyes drawing over my dress. "Take this off."

I step back and he laughs before his gaze goes steely. "Take it off," he snarls.

My eyes flit over his face drawing a quick settling breath and I smile as don a new mask.

"I thought you may like a show" I coo, calming my gaze. I unlock my fingers allowing the little shadow to coast along my skin and over my shoulder.

His eyes stilled, and that scowl lifted, as he realized I was going to play along. Using just the tips of my fingers, I walked him backwards until his legs met the seat. He drops into it smiling greedily. Thin lips stretch as he does, coarse white facial hair curling this way and that.

Appeased, he lets me step back a fraction.

Using the little bit of space, I pulled the top of my dress down just enough to tease him. Leaning forward, I shook my curls loose allowing my little shadow to slide down my spine undetected.

"You *are* a strange, strange pet," he shakes his head, eyes glittering with interest.

I use his distraction to cup the little bead of shadow currently clinging to the material of my dress at my waist. Gently, I set fingers to his shoulder intending to walk a teasing little circle around the male. The second my fingers land on his coat clad shoulder, I release the shadow, watching it snake around the collar of his shirt as I dragged my nails lightly along his back hoping he'd track me and not any movement he may discern from my friend.

He growled, tipping his chin as he grinned at me over his shoulder. Slowly, he drew in a long breath, his mouth opening to speak words I didn't care to hear, when the shadow shot behind his teeth.

I watched the moment his eyes widened, that hungry shadow swallowing up all the oxygen in his lungs. It bloomed, filling his throat and seeping between his teeth to coil around his neck.

His body jolted, and without hesitation, I unsheathed the rabbit femurs and slammed that bone dagger into the side of his neck. The other I buried in his eye and using the bones like handles, twisted harshly, breaking his neck.

Breath saws between my teeth as he falls limply to the ground in a heap.

I did it.

I did it.

I'd killed a shifter.

Well ... with a tad bit of help. I croutch beside the shifter searching for my shadow. Nothing moves, and it doesn't come back to me when I rest my hand on the dead shifter's mouth. I'd have to do this part on my own then.

I exhale roughly, collapsing back onto the ground to catch my breath. I mourn that little piece of Jason. That piece that made me brave ... but they were close.

They were coming.

And I had a vampire to kill.

Chapter Thirty-Eight

The tent is barren, but the shifter is a resource all on his own. Using the blade he had sheathed at his waist, I pulled the material of my skirt taut before running the blade across it, shortening the skirt so that it fell just past my knees. Dragging the mud laden skirts behind me wouldn't allow for the level of stealth I would need to pull this off. Shaking fingers buckle his sheath around my waist and tuck the blade back into it. I wrench the hooded cape out from under his shoulders before he can bleed on it and secure it around my shoulders, hoping to blend in as just another monster.

As I'm digging the ownership papers out of his pocket, I pause as cool iron greets my skin.

A key...

Staring down at it, I weighed my two options. I could track Le back to camp and exact my revenge, securing the closure I needed knowing the male who has haunted me is gone, or use this key I had a feeling could be used to access the cages and free the pets lining the road through camp.

The latter was a risk, but letting Le once again skirt off with his winnings only to haunt me, to taunt me, to put my family at risk... how could I not at least try to stop him? They'd told me I could do it. They'd told me that I could kill these monsters and I had...

My eyes drift over the dead shifter before me.

I wanted to believe that I could kill Le as well.

But fear swelled in me at the thought of facing down the male, dagger in hand.

I fisted the key, the metal biting into my palm as I stood. I couldn't allow him to continue living in a world I intended to bring my baby into.

Crumpling my ownership papers in my hand, I step out of the tent flap, pulling my hood as far over my face as it will lay. I hold the papers to the lantern flame hanging on the post outside the tent, letting it light, and watching as the flames swallow the paper and bubbling the ink. I hold it until the flames burn my finger tips, and only then, do I drop it on the brush littering the forest floor. It catches quickly as I duck into the darkened trees.

Stubborn tears clouded my eyes as I slinked along the trees and tents arriving at the shadow soaked road where I straightened and walked with a more casual posture. Sauntering like a monster who fears no one.

Freeing the pets caged along the road was a difference I could make right now. My males would find Le. He wouldn't live long enough to breathe the same air as our baby.

I'd hoped I could kill Le.

I told myself I could... but this, this I *knew* I could do.

I set my finger to my lips as I crept up to the first cage. The boy inside, who looked barely past his teens, froze as he watched me slip the key into the lock and twist. We both held our breath as the latch on the door released. A smile broke across my lips as I pulled the door open. He scrambled to his feet, his eyes flickering up and back down the road behind me. I caught his wrist again lifting my finger to my lips hoping he'd make his escape quickly, but quietly.

He nodded and then wasted no time disappearing into the trees bordering the road.

The next two cages were empty, but if the wails sounding from the end of the road were any indication, there were cages still lining this path that were occupied. I went cage to cage, silently freeing the human pets until I reached the end of the road. By that point, smoke was billowing heavily from the north end of camp.

I hoped that meant shifters and vampires would be abandoning their quest for humans to torment, and retreating into the forest allowing me time to free the remaining humans uninterrupted. I slowed my progress to the last cage as two lizard shifters ran past barking complaints about a spoiled evening.

A violent smile stretched my lips as I brandished the key to the final door.

But even once I opened the door ushering her out she didn't move. She just cowered with her back pressed against the bars, forehead against her knees.

"Camp is burning. You have to go," I whispered, pocketing the key. It was only as I spoke that she peeked up at me through long silver blonde hair. Her age had done nothing to diminish her beauty. Her eyes studied me a moment before they widened and I thought she would rise. Irritation warred with surprise as her eyes seemed to harden, narrowing as she took in the road over my shoulder.

Cries sounded farther up the path and I sunk deeper into the hood of my pilfered cape, hoping to blend in. But breath met my ear from the other side of the hood and I froze.

"Even if you didn't reek of fear," he snarled. "You'd still have been caught."

His hand gripped the material of my cape, notching my head to the side as the hood pulled at my braid. Wrenching me away from the door I stumbled ankles tangling together.

The woman broke her silence then, charging at Le with a shout. He was a flash of motion. In the same second he released me, she gasped as her body tumbled roughly across the dirt street. A terrible pound of my heart later, he dropped something at my feet with a wet plunk. My stomach turned as my vision swam, pulsing, as I scrambled away from it. And to my surprise he allowed it. My hood fell back from my face as I tipped my eyes back up to him.

My mouth opened and closed without sound.

"Two human heart beats," he snarled. "You can't hide that."

Those words had ice running through my veins as my own heart slammed against my ribs. I stood slowly making sure to keep my hands away from my stomach. Every instinct in me was calling for me to curl in on myself, to protect, to hide, to cower, but I needed my hands free if I had any hope of reacting to the male before he could kill me.

I watched him lap the blood dripping down his fingers before my eyes darted to the woman still laying in a heap across the path, a gaping hole in her chest.

Two heart beats.

Mine and hers.

I hadn't been able to hide my humanity, but it seemed for now, my secret was still safe.

It took three heavy steps for him to arrive before me, blood soaked fingers tangling in my hair as he hoisted me up against his chest. I struggled, tears pricking my eyes as strands of hair snapped between his fingers. But it was the distraction I needed to draw the blade from where it was sheathed at my waist under my cape. I held my breath as he leaned in, drawing his tongue up my cheek in a taunt, before I buried the blade in his side.

He exhaled roughly, brow dropping, as confusion filled his remaining eye. I twisted the blade, shoving it deeper and baring my teeth as I watched the realization dawn across his features.

I didn't know how fast he could move with a blade in his gut, but I knew my next move needed to be unexpected. The only thing I wanted to do was create distance between me and the hands I now knew he could use to rip the heart from my chest, but pulling away would be expected. So instead, I dropped the hold on the blade, latched onto his shirt and snapped forward smashing my forehead into his nose.

Stars sparked behind my eyes, but the howl of pain that echoed from Le as he threw me across the road, buffered the ache. I fought to catch as much of my weight on my elbows as I tumbled and slid through the brush, grimacing as the skin of my forearms and shin stung.

I lifted my head, snapping my gaze back to his.

His responding snarl was wet.

Blood leaked from his lips as they turned upwards.

I scrambled to my feet in time to see him tear the blade from his side before launching it at me.

Before I can even flinch, a hand appears before my face, halting the dagger. His large hand is wrapped around the handle, having caught the blade mid air.

Breath whooshes from my lungs as I eye the blade's tip between my eyes glinting in the fire.

The snarl that Henry unleashes over my shoulder could cleave worlds in half.

Le stumbles backwards a few paces while a grin pulls my lips wide, my chin raising as his presence warms my back. But before I can breathe in the relief his presence offers, he's gone. In a blink, he's crossed the clearing and pulled two blades from the sheath across his chest. He flicks one into the ground at Le's feet as if giving him the opportunity to fight back. The other, he slams into Le's ribs as he circles the male.

Le howls. The sound is pure pain and shock. But it's silenced a beat too soon when Henry's big hand takes hold of the back of his neck.

Henry's eyes rise to mine and I can see the effort he places into keeping them calm, but it's a veil, and behind it a storm rages.

"Come here, Princess." The timber of his voice shakes my knees but I steel my spine and pace towards my male.

It's only when I arrive before him that I realize Henry has dug his fingers *into* the male's neck, under his skin, and seems to be gripping him by the spine.

My stomach tumbles as Le's mouth works. The air between us remains silent.

I swallow as I meet Henry's gaze

He blinks and some of that rage cools.

"Kill your monster Amelia."

My exhale is rough as my eyes sting. My shoulders threaten to deflate but I hold them firm. High.

His eyes flicker to the blade he left in the ground at Le's feet.

It had been for me.

But it wasn't *mine*.

Instead, I pull my blade from Le's boot, gripping it tightly. Henry's eyes glint with an appreciation that coasts under my skin and along my bones. My lips quiver as I step up, hovering over the vampire, my eyes flickering over his face once more.

Once more, knowing he'd no longer haunt my dreams. Never again delivering the post to Jason with a pit in my stomach, expecting that blank envelope. No longer fearing the shadows in the garden.

No longer fearing him.

I adjust my grip on the handle to allow space for both hands before I slam the blade into his heart with all the force I can muster.

I make myself pause there with my hands against the cross guard and that guard against his chest. To feel those final beats of his heart against my blade, against my palms. I wait until his chest deflates under me, refusing to loosen my grip until I hear the sound of him exhaling his final breath.

Knowing my monster is dead.

Warm tears slid down my cheeks as a sob brakes free and as I stumbled backwards away from Le's body. Henry's there in an instant to gather me up.

I turned in his arms and he pulled me close, coiling his arms tightly around me as I climbed him. Behind all that steel, all that strength, he shook as he held me and I leaned back cupping his jaw.

Setting my forehead to his, I drew my first full breath in days.

"I knew you'd find me," I breathe, my arm hooking around the back of his neck as his lips claimed mine. All of that fear eddies from my mind as his hands travel my body. I sob against his lips and he swallows them down with growls of his own. Finally, I allow myself to deflate against his warm chest, tucking my face into the crook of his neck. His grip gentled around me as his body went rigidly still.

I sense the change immediately.

"What's wrong?" I ask pulling back to study his face. His brows collapse. Those moss green eyes transform into something unreadable, just as Jason's snarl erupts from the shadows painting the trees.

Much like Henry, the forest stills around us.

Jason prowls out from the darkness. Shadow itself opens up its wispy arms as he steps through, his eyes burning. He pauses only once, his expression deadly as he stares down at Le where he lies mouth still agape on the ground. With a snarl, and the drop of his heel, he crushes Le's skull.

I slide from Henry's grasp and he lets me, his arms going slack at his sides, gaze burning into the side of my face as I turn to Jason.

Silver rings wink at me as he drags them down his jaw, calming himself. I watch him clasping and unclasping his palms, fingers still stained black with power as I move towards him. Slowly at first. Shadow still whips around his feet. But he didn't hesitate to catch me as I launched myself at him.

I shook, my whole body reacting to their nearness. His fingers swept the tears from my face as I combed mine through his hair.

His hands lacked their usual steadiness as he brushed matted curls from my forehead, pushing my braid back over my shoulder.

"Amelia," his thumb ran over my neck. Over the skin Le had broken. But Le's blood coated my skin like a balm, for I was certain I wore more of his then mine. And even if I didn't, the ground was swallowing what was left of his, and that had the ache in my body quieting.

I pull his face back to mine and he collects me just as greedily. The heat from Henry's body curled around my side as he placed his hand to my back. Each exhale had his chest reverberating with a growl.

I peeled myself off of Jason's chest to throw an arm around Henry's neck and tug him back to me. By the time I could breathe I was dizzy with relief.

"Jason." The command in Henry's voice left no room for argument.

I felt him still below me, before he set me gently on my feet, his eyes landing on Henry's before they settled on mine. They tracked down my body settling on Henry's arm where it had circled my waist. His fingers sprawled across my stomach as he braced me against his warm body. I'd thought he was steadying me... but he knew.

Could he hear it?

Jason's eyes softened as he reached for my waist. His hand laid over Henry's as his knees hit the wet earth.

Shadows skittered away fleeing the impact.

But he just stared up at me, his gaze welling with emotion.

"Amelia."

My name.

A question. A plea. A celebration.

I nod.

Epilogue

The smell of baking cookies drew me into the kitchen where I found Hartley teaching Charlotte to crack eggs. Our daughter inherited the same love for chocolate as her mama, and Hartley is always more than willing to appease our chocolate cravings. Today they were crafting two big batches of chocolate chunk cookies. I swipe one off the cooling tray as Charlotte digs her hands into the flour mixture Hartley is sifting and smiles. Hartley is certainly fast enough to keep my daughter from planting her grubby toddler hands into the cookie dough, I just don't think he cares to.

Her tinkling laughter rings out and his eyes glitter with shared mischief as they rise to my own. They dip to my swollen belly, his gaze softening as hands wrap around my waist. I lean into Jason who has materialized behind me and he cradles my belly lovingly, his lips dipping to my shoulder.

If our daughter's warm curls and freckled nose had anyone wondering who her father was, those sweet moss green eyes, the carbon copy of her daddy's, would be the tell. Though, at bedtime it was Jason who she reached for. Secretly I think she knew she had these males wrapped around her fingers. And Jason was never one to turn down a bedtime story. Every night he wrapped her in his arms reading story after story until she fell asleep tracing the whirls of ink on top of his arms.

Our son was due in just a few weeks, and his arrival had been a more planned endeavor. In fact it took some trial and error to narrow down which tea had allowed us to conceive in the first place. Amara and Link volunteered to test out teas as they'd been trying to start a family of their own for decades. It was Link who realized it was the men who needed to consume the teas and when Amara fell pregnant with us following closely behind, we knew we had found it. The answer Jason and Link had been searching for. The missing piece to solidify peace treaties with the shifters and continue to ensure the safety of the freed humans. Not everyone had relinquished their control over their pets, but we would get there.

Henry bounds down the front staircase and Charlotte locks onto the sound like a heat seeking missile. She rockets from the room, flour covered fingers outstretched. I feel Jason lean back around the doorway watching our daughter throw herself at a freshly showered Henry. His chuckle rumbles through me, our son elbowing me in the ribs in response. Jason's warm fingers trace the shape of my belly soothing the little ache.

Charlotte squeals her delight as Henry paces into the kitchen, his hand wrapped around her ankle dangling her like a fish before him. Her peal of laughter gives way to a row of little teeth and ruddy cheeks as Henry rights her, scooping her into his arms and finally allowing her to latch onto his beard with both hands. He sets her down with a kiss on the head and comes away sporting two snowy white flour prints.

I suck my lips between my teeth as he beams at us. His eyes track the movement of Jason's hands along my belly. Those eyes heating as he closes the distance between us. His hand lands over Jason's on my belly

"Soon," he smiles, confirming what I've already begun to sense.

Once our son arrives, we have plans to move into the Royal City proper. There was more space and while Jason snarled that the king could live where he pleased, we all knew it was time. But we had one last task to check off before we did so.

The problem of my pesky mortality. Forever wasn't promised vampire or otherwise, but I wanted as much time as possible with my males and my babies.

Creating a safer world wasn't going to be easy, and it wouldn't happen overnight, but it would certainly be easier with a shiny new set of fangs.

Printed in Dunstable, United Kingdom

75735447R00241